DOWN THE ARCHES
OF THE YEARS

BY LEE ALLRED

DOWN THE ARCHES
OF THE YEARS

LEE ALLRED

HEMELEIN PUBLICATIONS

Cover art: *Syria by the Sea* (1873) by Frederic Edwin Church (1826-1900)
Cover design and interior layout and design: Joe Monson

Editor: Joe Monson
Managing Editor: Joe Monson
Art Director: Joe Monson
Publisher: Heather B. Monson
Published by Hemelein Publications, LLC.
http://hemelein.com/

First Edition
First Hemelein printing, April 2022
10 9 8 7 6 5 4 3 2 1

ISBN:
978-1-64278-014-7 (trade paperback)
978-1-64278-015-4 (ebook)

Library of Congress Control Number: 2021946479

✺ Created with Vellum

CONTENTS

LEGACY OF THE CORRIDOR

Way back in 1994, M. Shayne Bell put together *Washed by a Wave of Wind*, an anthology of short works by authors from "The Corridor", an area that covers Utah, most of Idaho, parts of Wyoming and Nevada, and stretches into Arizona and parts of northern Mexico. Sometimes, the area around Cardston, Alberta, Canada, is included, too. For those unfamiliar with this area, it was settled by Mormon pioneers, members of the Church of Jesus Christ of Latter-day Saints.

Shayne's anthology highlighted science fiction and fantasy works by authors from the area, as The Corridor contained an unusually high number of successful authors—for the population in the area—both genre and non-genre, both members and non-members of the predominant religion. That legacy continues today with an impressive list of authors such as Jennifer Adams, D. J. Butler, Orson Scott Card, Michael R. Collings, Michaelbrent Collings, Ally Condie, Larry Correia, Kristyn Crow, James Dashner, Brian Lee Durfee, Sarah M. Eden, Richard Paul Evans, David Farland, Jessica Day George, Shannon Hale, Mettie Ivie Harrison, Tracy and Laura Hickman, Charlie N. Holmberg, Christopher Husberg, Matthew J. Kirby, Brian McClellan, Stephenie Meyer, L. E. Modesitt, Jr., Brandon Mull, Jennifer A. Nielsen, James A. Owen, Brandon Sanderson, Caitlin Sangster, J. Scott Savage, Jess Smart Smiley, Harriet Stark, Eric James Stone, Howard Tayler, Brad R. Torgersen, Dan Wells, Robison Wells, David J. West, Carol Lynch Williams, and Dan Willis.

That's a big list of names, and it only barely scratches the surface.

I had considered doing a follow-up volume at one point, but I couldn't find any publishers interested in the project. The idea sat simmering in my subconscious for a few years. In late 2020 or early 2021, it again occurred to me just how many local (Intermountain West area) genre writers we have, and what a really amazing writing heritage exists here, especially compared to the population. Whether it's something in the water, in the air, or something else, we have an amazing legacy that needs to be shared.

Many of these authors write short fiction of various lengths in addition to all the novelists, and I decided we could never do them justice if we only did one or two individual anthologies. So instead of those anthologies, I thought it would be fun and interesting to put together individual collections of their works to help highlight them. I can't think of anything more exciting than shining a spotlight on individual creators in this area.

Hemelein Publications created this publication series to highlight as many of these authors from The Corridor as possible, both well-known and lesser-known. We think Shayne did a wonderful job drawing attention to these amazing writers back then, and we want to continue what he started.

You can learn more about the series at:

http://hemelein.com/go/legacy-of-the-corridor/

Joe Monson
Managing Editor
Hemelein Publications

LEE-WARD LEANING

JOE MONSON

I've known Lee for almost 30 years now. I first met him way back in the day at *Life, the Universe, & Everything*, a science fiction and fantasy academic symposium, then held at Brigham Young University in Provo, Utah. At that time, he'd published (or would shortly—I forget the exact time frame) one story in two parts in *The Leading Edge*, the science fiction and fantasy semi-pro magazine published at BYU.

When I first met him, he struck me as a quiet guy, but with a vivid imagination, strong opinions on many subjects, and a keen analytical mind. All of that is still true. One of my favorite early memories of him was his presentation of an academic paper at *LTUE* on the anime series *Chance Pop Session*. It was a very interesting dissection of the show, and made me interested in watching it.

Another good memory is working with him as co-chairs of LTUE from 1995-1996. One of my favorite things he did that year was to put together a short history of the symposium, highlighting guests and notable things that happened in various years. Despite it being short, it went into a fair amount of detail, and it was told in a witty and interesting manner. He provided a lot of insight that helped our year of the symposium run much more smoothly than it would have otherwise. I think we worked well together, and I have no negative memories of working with him. He loves history, has a wicked sense of humor, and it's pretty dry, so I love his work. All of these attributes come through in his writing.

Since I met him three decades ago, he's gone on to publish dozens of short stories, been nominated for the Sidewise Award for Alternate History, scripted many different comic book issues, and served three tours of duty in Iraq.

The stories here are a good cross-section of his works in the last decade. We worked together to come up with a good list of stories we thought would play well together. There are humorous stories, more serious stories, and scary stories, and I enjoyed reading all of them. I hope you enjoy them as well.

Joe Monson
Managing Editor
Hemelein Publications

AUTHOR'S PREFACE—
THE HOUNDS OF HISTORY

I fled Him, down the nights and down the days;
I fled Him, down the arches of the years;
I fled Him, down the labyrinthine ways
Of my own mind;

—Francis Thompson, *The Hound of Heaven* (1890)

The Past—to paraphrase the late John Gardner—continues to exert its effect, though dead as doornails. Its Hounds of History, if you will, follow us relentlessly down the arches of the years, down the twisted paths of modernity's frenzied gyrations, and, if we allow it to, catches hold of us in the end.

You hold in your hand a collected volume of some of the many short stories I've written over my twenty-five years in the science fiction field. All of the stories herein are either set in the past or deal with the past, the arches of the years.

How this volume took this particular shape is how my stories themselves take their particular shape: serendipities, coincidences, and the padding paws of the dead-as-doornail Hounds of History.

The night before Hemelein editor Joe Monson contacted me about the possibility of their publishing a collection of my stories, I'd been watching, of all things, a fifty-year-old Billy Graham movie named *Time To Run*.

Don't worry. This isn't a religious tract. I'm of a different faith tradition, besides. But Graham's movie itself, and the why behind my owning a copy of it, *is* relevant.

A well-meaning relative back in the '70s out of the blue gifted me with the movie's soundtrack record album. I grew to enjoy the album's blend of chamber music and soft rock and even managed to track down a little church showing an 8mm showing of the movie in the pastor's basement.

Time to Run is very much a movie of its time, a movie produced by religious squares trying to reach hippie-era youth by dressing up their message with a soft rock soundtrack and dressing up actors in fringe leather jackets. (My own faith did much the same in the mid-'70s with their *Like Unto Us* Seminary filmstrip. I own that soundtrack album, too.)

What sets *Time to Run* apart is that the movie is a modern reenactment of not only Francis Thompson's famous poem, but Thompson's life itself.

Thompson was a Victorian-era failure, a medical school dropout, an invalid, an opium addict, a destitute derelict. He'd spent years mired in the slums and alleyways and gutters of 19th Century London's darkest depths.

Then, in the year 1887, a London magazine received a bundle of tattered, filth-stained manuscripts: poems of genius about misery and redemption, written by a man who no matter how hard or far he ran was eventually pursued and caught by God, the relentless Hound of Heaven. Thompson was that man and that poet. *Time to Run* even opens with a reading of "Hounds" and later showcases a lengthy college English class discussion of it.

As anyone who's watched James Burke's *Connections* TV series knows, history is a never-ending chain of serendipity, the splicing of unrelated elements. The Hounds of History never cease their chase, the past is always there calling us, beseeching us. An 1890 poem inspires a 1972 film released as a DVD in 2013 which I watch in 2021 on the eve of needing a title and theme for a book anthology—and which you're reading now in 2022 or whatever year you're reading this.

Add to this the very reason I was watching *Time To Run* on that particular night in the first place. *Time to Run*'s down-and-out musically-accompanied destitute hitchhiking montage is cousin to the down-and-out musically-accompanied destitute hitchhiking montage in a movie I'd been watching the day before: Neil Diamond's 1980 remake of Al Jolson's 1927 *The Jazz Singer*. Diamond's *The Jazz Singer* is a movie infused with entirely different religious faith and a religious tradition with its own relentless Hounds of History.

I had popped *Time to Run* in the DVD player to compare the two montages and ended up watching the entire movie. That is why I had Thompson's poem still in my head when Hemelein emailed me.

It is these serendipities, these connections, then, that fire and infuse and inspire my fiction.

History—the past—is Mankind's greatest resource, its greatest depository of knowledge. There are two ways of gaining experience: you can learn from your own mistakes or you can learn from others. History is nothing if not a compendium of past mistakes, but it is also often a blueprint for rectifying them.

A knowledge of the past and the ability to apply lessons learned from it used to be considered the mark of an educated person. Too many in current society, alas, believe themselves to be, *sui generis*, the font of new and original knowledge, indeed the *only* font of knowledge and morality. They believe that whatever came before them is suspect, worthless and evil, even.

They believe their very arrival into this world marks Year Zero for human knowledge and progress.

This disdain for the past ironically prevents such people from knowing that other Year Zero attempts have been made. That such attempts all end in ignominy, pain, and blood; the French Revolution devolves into the Reign of Terror, the Khmer Rouge into the Killing Fields; the poisoned fools of Jonestown.

These history deniers' belief of what history *is* is severely misguided.

History is not just dusty dead men reeling off a list of dates or successions to the throne. History is for gleaning, for engaging with, for having a dialog with. It's tough to have a dialog with toppled statues and deleted books.

The stories in this volume have that dialog with the past, sometimes seeking answers, sometimes seeking entertainment, sometimes merely seeking interesting backdrops and local color.

These stories herein, like the Hounds of History that inspired their writing, wend their way through the arches of the years, pursuing those who would deign be caught.

MURMURATION OF A DARKENING SEA

INTRODUCTION

A friend of mine once ran the night desk at the ritziest hotel on the Oregon coast. He had lots of crazy stories about very rich, very entitled tourists, but the one that's stuck with me was the story of the drunken lady who called the desk complaining that the ocean was too loud and demanding that the hotel turn down the volume.

I can sympathize with that sentiment.

I lived for almost ten years in that same coastal town in a little rented cottage just off the beach. At night at high tide, the ocean roar was loud enough to wake you up. Hours and hours of incessant deafening wave crash until the tide receded, regular as a metronome and unstoppable as a juggernaut.

I had that primeval ocean roar in mind when I wrote "Murmuration of a Darkening Sea", but I also had the local geography in mind as well. Cape Foulweather lives up to its name. Much of the year its hidden in fog and low scudding clouds. My first winter on the coast, coastal gales hit hard enough to snap the brown recreation area highway sign naming Cape Foulweather completely in two, heavy signpost and all, and hurl it to the other side of the road where it lay in the bar ditch for the rest of the winter. Truth in advertising.

"Murmuration" was written on assignment for the horror anthology Fiction River: Feel the Fear. *I've always had a Jekyll-and-Hyde relationship with the horror genre. I don't care for (to put it politely) the Stephen King/Dean Koontz modern type of horror, but I'm a complete sucker for cheesy gothic movie monster sort of horror: Bram Stoker's* Dracula, *and Mary Wollstonecraft Shelley's* Frankenstein.

And H.P. Lovecraft, too, of course.

I've always wanted to write a nice juicy Lovecraft mythos story, but how? Lovecraft could get away with all that Lovecraftian pneumatic prose; nobody else can. Try and you only end up with either a bad pastiche or bad parody. Michael R. Collings says in Writing Horror—*his guide to writing horror—that Lovecraft is his language, that "[h]is language...is his horror."*

I turned to somebody else to use for an example on how to write a Lovecraft story. Jim Turner's Eternal Lovecraft *was quite helpful, but David Drake's Nyarlahotep tale, "Than Curse the Darkness", held the key I sought. (Drake's entire* Night and Demons *horror collection is a graduate-level seminar in writing horror.)*

With "Curse", Drake didn't make the mistake of trying to write Lovecraft. Instead, he took what he was already doing in sci-fi and fantasy, took his usual approach to horrific fiction, and then folded in Lovecraft's Cthulhu mythos. "Curse" isn't a Lovecraft story, it's a Drake story with a Lovecraft setting, just as "Murmuration" is very much an Allred story of Allred characters dealing with a Lovecraftian world.

"Murmuration" was not only quite the learning experience, but quite the gamble as well. One of the stupidest things an author can do is exceed word count limits set by an anthology editor. I was incredibly stupid. (And not only stupid, but stupid on purpose; I believed "Murmuration" had to be the length it was and sent it out that way.)

The Fiction River anthology format caps story length at a strict 6000 words. That's why most of my Fiction River stories are roughly all the same length. "Murmuration" clocks in at 12,000, however. Exactly double. The editor would have to use two story slots to print it. It's therefore more than just the question of being as good as two stories combined; it had be additionally good to be worth the hassle. It had to be a must-have for his volume.

I'd like to think it was. Editor Mark Leslie not only bought "Murmuration", but led off his anthology with it.

I wouldn't recommend trying this at home, though, kids.

T hey pulled down Leroy's Gas Station in 1942 as part of a wartime scrap drive, and with it any outward sign that the community of Cape Foulweather ever existed. Some of the hidden houses on the mountain still stand, of course, but unless you know they are there, you cannot see them from the public roads.

I first learned of Cape Foulweather on the Oregon Coast shortly after I answered an advertisement found in the personal want ads of the *Denver Post* during the first week of January, 1928. The ad read simply:

Research Assistant (Male) wanted. Some typing. Good pay. Disabled veterans preferred. Enquire Box 721.

The "good pay" portion was superfluous. That anyone would be offering any pay to disabled veterans—preferred, even—was what caught my eye. The ten years since the Great War had taught me no one was in the market for hiring men who'd returned from the trenches of France crippled or wounded or disfigured such as I was. A German shell had ripped off half my face and severely burnt what remained. I was otherwise physically able, but utterly unemployable in any meaningful capacity. Even my own family considered me, in their more truthful moments, a walking horror show.

And so, as much in desperation as on a whim, I answered the want ad.

A telephone interview soon ensued—a rather bizarre one that placed more emphasis upon my family genealogy than my job qualifications—and I was then wired a train and bus fare for a remote place called Cape Foulweather on the central Oregon Coast.

I felt no small unease at the strangeness of it all, but the telephone interview had revealed that should I get the job, my weekly salary would be more than a year's worth of the pitiful pension the government saw fit to toss its war-shattered ex-soldiers.

And so, early on the morning of January 19, 1928, I found myself alighting from the steps of a Pickwick Stages bus onto the muddy gravel parking lot of one Leroy's Gas Station along a lonely stretch of Oregon's coastal highway.

I stepped out into rain so needle-fine it seemed more a diamantine spray of mist rather than falling droplets. Leaden, low gray sheet-clouds hung just overhead. Conifers of a pine green so dark they looked black completely frocked the steep hills towering over the highway. In the overcast gloom, the gray and the black-green leeched all color. The harvest oranges and blazing reds of the Pickwick bus livery muted into monochrome shades.

On the other side of the road, the sea, tossed about by mid-winter storms, pounded against a sea wall. Gray-green water, frothed into an angry dirty white, pounded so hard against the black basalt sea wall I could feel the crash of it through the soles of my shoes.

The bus driver pulled my beat-up leather grip out of the underside cargo compartment. Despite the rain and his obvious hurry to get back into the warm, dry bus, he checked the paper luggage tag to ensure that the grip did indeed belong to one Randall Dunwich. Satisfied, he handed it over to me, then began restowing the luggage he'd shifted to get at mine.

I leaned in close and tried to shout over the crash of the waves. "You sure this the right place?" Leroy's was boarded up for the winter; no other sign of human habitation save the asphalt highway existed.

"Sure, I'm sure," the driver yelled, drawing back a bit because nobody wanted to be that close to my face. "You think I don't know my own route?"

He slammed the cargo compartment closed. "'Course," he added, "you're the first one I ever had get off at this stop. Don't know why they even put it on the schedule."

With that, he re-boarded his bus and drove away in a black cloud of diesel, leaving me huddling under the sagging overhang of Leroy's Gas Station, trying to stay out of the rain. The overhang helped little; a brisk winter wind blew the rain sideways underneath it.

I shivered in the cold as I waited for the transportation that had been promised over the phone. My jacket, which had kept me warm for so many snowy winters in Denver, kept me neither warm nor dry in the chill and damp and the sidewise blowing rain of an Oregon winter squall.

As the cold seeped through my sodden jacket, I began to regret ever answering that ad. Regret! Had I known at that moment what I was soon to know, driving rain or no, I would have walked—I would have crawled—to avoid what would befall me.

But I did not know.

And so, foolishly, I stood shivering as I listened to high tide come in. The roar of the waves grew even more deafening.

The hue of the gray-green waves darkened and deepened until they were coal-black. Great gouts of white-flecked spray splashed up from the lip of the sea wall. Great arcs of sea water began to arc, to quest across the asphalt highway toward me, as if the crashing sea were a living thing, seeking, searching, reaching for me to pull me into its maw.

Reaching...reaching...

I backed up, pressing myself as flat as I could against the boarded-up exterior of Leroy's. It did me no good. The crashing, arcing waves reached ever closer, closer...

In the crash and the roar and the murmurations of the waves I began to hear voices. Voices calling, *things* calling. Foul things, forgotten things, cries for help, and cries for warmth, and above them all calls for warm, red blood to give them life beyond mere voices and shapes within the waves.

It was *my* name that the sea called, and it meant to drag me down into it.

I began to sweat despite the cold and the damp. I began to shake and not from the chill. I began to feel myself being pulled toward the water, pulled, pulled—

The spell broke with the simple honking of an automobile horn.

The automobile pulled up to Leroy's, a sleek low-slung roadster painted a shocking canary yellow. The throaty purr of the car's V-8 engine carried easily over the crash of the sea.

The appearance of that auto—a man-built product of science and precision and rational thought, a ready example of man-made cities of concrete and Bessemer steel which paid no heed to crashing waves or wispy clouds or root-bound pines but gleamed as an incandescent beacon for science and truth and progress—cut away the fear that had so engulfed my mind.

Surely it had all been the similarity of the surf's sound to that of a rolling artillery barrage. Surely it had all been only a momentary manifestation of the latent fear of the front that still lurked in my nighttime dreams sometimes.

The automobile's driver rolled down his window. He was a man of my age, large and fit and obviously of Germanic descent. He wore his fine white-blond hair closely cropped. As for his face—where mine was marred by shot and shell, a shattered thing from Hell, his was the chiseled face of Heaven, a mortal Adonis marred only by a Teutonic sneer curled upon his lips.

He looked me over like a butcher looking a fattened hog up and down. When his eyes alighted on my ruined face, he laughed, deep barks of laughter, as if I were most amusing, as if I were the clown show of a circus.

"I see the War Goddess has favored you with Her kiss," he said in a stiff and stilted Germanic accent. "She has left her lipstick on your cheek."

And then, as quickly as it had flared, the amusement left his face. "I am von Brauchitsch. Get in, Mr. Dunwich. I dislike being caught on the highway during high tide. You may not have noticed, but the waves along this coast have a tendency to flood their bounds and we are much too close to the angry sea for my liking."

I tossed my grip in the backseat, and climbed in.

No sooner had I done so than the German powered his vehicle down the road, tires sliding and slipping on the sea-splashed pavement. He sped down the twisting coastal highway faster than I would have thought safe in good weather, let alone in this sodden storm.

"So, ah, do you work for Mrs. Dubois?" I asked, trying to break the heavy silence between beats of the wipers fighting a losing battle against the streaming rain.

"I do not *work*, as you put it, for anyone," von Brauchitsch said, as if the very word offended his Junkers soul. "It was inconvenient for the Widow Dubois to meet you, so I am picking you up."

"You are a neighbor, then?"

He thrust his square jaw upward. "Let us say I am a temporary houseguest. I am here for the hunting."

"Hunting?" Coming from Denver, I knew very little about the wildlife on the Oregon Coast, but I did not recall ever hearing it mentioned as any sort of big game preserve.

Perhaps my face gave away my thoughts for he further explained: "The vermin. The local creatures with the clever little hands—almost as clever as men —who think it is their right to get into what does not belong to them."

"Are you talking about raccoons?"

"If that is what you wish to call them, then yes."

It seemed so very odd, a Prussian nobleman hunting raccoon. I tried to make a joke of it. "And what do with them once you've hunted them?"

"I am making a raccoon coat. The great love of my life is taxidermy and leatherworking."

Too late, I realized he was making a joke of his own, but the butt of the joke was me and my American naïveté and perhaps all Americans in turn.

Then the German's face grew serious and suddenly he was no longer joking. "It seems that the trenches of France left me with a taste for the hunt, for the kill. Unfortunately, since the deplorable Armistice, I can no longer indulge in my secret passion. I must settle for a poor substitute in shooting vermin. And yet, is it so very different from what I was doing in the war?"

No, he was not joking at all any more.

He turned off the highway onto a side road seemingly leading off into a solid curtain of trees.

Shore pines—forty, fifty feet in height—lined both sides of the road, their wind-crabbed branches high above us stretched across to entwine with each other.

The effect was one of driving through a vaulted cathedral, but it was a fell, daemonic cathedral for these malevolent unholy trees hated Man and all his works just as surely as those pounding waves far below.

I could not explain my fear. Sounds similar to the terrors of combat I could understand, but trees? How could mere trees frighten me so? It was as if I had entered a world beyond reason, a land where the primal darkness of the mind held sway.

As if sensing my unease, von Brauchitsch barked that same dark laugh he'd employed when first gazing at my face. "I do not think these trees like strangers in their mountains, Mr. Dunwich."

His words, if meant to assure me—which I do not think they were so meant —served only to further plunge me into a whirling confusion of dread and perturbation.

The narrow road began to switchback up the steep slope. As we climbed higher and higher up the mountain, fog began to thicken. Perhaps it was fog. Or perhaps we were climbing into the low scudding clouds.

Through the fog I occasionally caught glimpses of large expensive dwellings, almost mansions even.

Von Brauchitsch must have caught me looking for he said, "The secludedness of Cape Foulweather invites many film stars and politicians and the like who wish to relax away from the scrutiny of the public."

Again, the bark of his Teutonic laughter. "The cape is a place where the laws of Man and Nature need not be observed, and in the main, *are* not."

He spoke these ominous words just as we reached the summit of the mountain and the end of the road.

We had reached a wrought-iron arch spanning the entrance to what I assumed was the house of the Widow Dubois, an ancient Victorian house of immense size and sinister visage as crow-ugly as Death, as crow-ugly as my own face. Even the very trees, the ones that disquieted me so, seemed to lean away from it, as if fearing its vile touch.

The crowning glory, if that is the right word to use about an edifice so vile, was a towering turret on the seaward side of the house. A widow's walkway hemmed in by wrought iron railings formed the top of the turret, deadly sharp spears of cold iron that looked more like a barrier to keep someone, something *outside* the bounds of the walkway than any sort of safety railing keeping onlookers safely inside.

Von Brauchitsch pulled up to the front entrance and stopped. At the switching off of the motor, again I could hear, though it was so very far below us, the roar of the waves.

Pounding, pounding, *pounding*.

"We have arrived, Mr. Dunwich," Von Brauchitsch said over the roar of the waves. Again the Teutonic sneer. "I hope your stay will be as profitable and...*enjoyable* as my own has been."

Loath as I was to enter, I followed von Brauchitsch inside the mansion. He closed the door and latched it tight behind us. For a door constructed with a full-length pane of thin, frosted glass, it blocked the hideous pounding drone of the ocean waves completely.

The house, for all its ghastly exterior, seemed very cheery inside. The furnishings may have been old and out of style, dating back to the Mauve Decade, but they were tasteful and clean and kept quite spotless. It seemed the Widow kept an excellent staff.

That staff, however, did not seem to extend to a butler. I had expected one, or some sort of servant, to greet us but neither a butler nor the Widow Dubois was in evidence. Instead, it amused von Brauchitsch to play the part of host.

He led me into the grand parlor with a dizzying parqueted marble floor and crystal chandeliers and thence up a sweeping curved staircase to the second floor and then down a long dark hallway.

Stopping at one of the doors, he said, "Your room. The Widow expects that you will wish to freshen up a bit from your long journey before she meets with you."

He extracted an old fashioned skeleton key from a pocket and unlocked the door. He did not, however, give me the key. Instead, he pocketed it again.

I opened the door to find a small, but well-furnished bedroom with its own adjoining bath. A cozy little fire burned in the hearth. I tossed my leather grip on the brass bed.

Von Brauchitsch closed the door behind me and locked it.

"*Auf Wiedersehen,*" he said through the thick wood door.

I HAD JUST FINISHED SHAVING and changing into a clean shirt when I heard a tinny voice coming out of a tiny rubber aperture in the wall. An old-fashioned speaking tube, I realized.

"I will be pleased to see you now," the voice through the tube, that of the Widow Dubois, said.

The lock on my door clacked free and the door opened. Again Von Brauchitsch stood in the hall outside. He gestured for me to follow him. "It is easier to lead an American as one would a donkey than ever to try to give one directions."

He led me through a confusing series of hallways, then up two flights of stairs and then finally into a spacious parlor which I readily took to be the Widow Dubois' sitting room.

The room seemed oddly lit until I realized that unlike the rest of the house which was illuminated by modern electrics, this room was lit by the hissing gas lamps of a generation past.

The knickknacks and curios of the sort a woman whose prime was in the Mauve Decade lay scattered about the room, with furniture and draperies to match.

A daguerreotype, bordered in fluted curtains of black silk, of a dashing mustachioed military officer in a French uniform of the Franco-Prussian war period hung above the fireplace mantle between two lambent jets of gas.

I was staring at the portrait with my back turned to the room when the Widow Dubois softly cleared her throat. I had not heard her enter.

She was an old woman, at least eighty if I were to hazard a guess based on the photograph of the man I presumed was her husband, the late Mr. Dubois. Somehow she seemed younger, as if time had stopped, as if it had bent to her iron will. She looked no more than perhaps fifty.

Perhaps it was the décor of the house, but I had half-expected her dress to be in the antique style of her youth, but she wore clothing in today's fashion. She would not have looked out of place amongst society pages of the Denver newspapers.

But it was not her seeming youth nor her modern clothing that caught my attention.

It was her eyes.

They were white. A nebulous, milky, clouded white. And by that, I mean they had no visible iris, no pupil. She was blind, horribly so. Perhaps the victim of massive twin cataracts, perhaps even—

"Yes, Mr. Dunwich," she said as if she could see my gaze. "German mustard gas. The fickle winds, you see, blow quite indiscriminately on both soldier and civilian alike."

"I—I'm sorry," I muttered and I was.

"It is of no matter," she said. "I can afford to hire eyesight, can I not, Helmut?" She pitched her voice toward von Brauchitsch, standing silently against the far wall.

"I wouldn't know," he replied. From the tone of his voice and from the posture of both their bodies, it suddenly became clear that both despised the other and yet still associated with one another for some reason known only to themselves.

No, "despise" was too weak a word, as was mere hate. The incandescence of their mutual antipathy fairly lit up the room.

She glided gracefully across the room, deftly weaving between the furnishings until she stood quite next to me. Before I could react, she reached out and stroked the ragged scars of my face. Her touch was not the warm touch of a handsome woman such as she appeared but cold and clammy, like a thing long dead and drowned in the sea.

I jerked back in surprise.

Von Brauchitsch laughed uproariously.

"This one bears the scars of war," she said. "This one bears the Price." She nodded in approval. "Good, Mr. Dunwich. You have passed the first of the three requirements for this position."

She stepped back and then seated herself in a velvet-plush chair. Her long delicate fingers toyed with the lid of a small rosewood jewelry box with brass corner plates and guilt edgings down the sides.

"I shall now test you on the second. The position requires, shall we say, a certain suppleness of mind and the ability of memory recall. I shall give you a simple memory test. I shall quote part of a stanza from a poem and expect you to continue on with it."

She paused and smiled a wintry smile. "Do not worry, Mr. Dunwich. I shall endeavor to choose a poem that surely even an American should be familiar with."

She cleared her throat and began: "*We have fed our sea for a thousand years/And she calls us, still unfed.*"

I relaxed. Kipling's *Song of the Dead.* Any Boy Scout, as I had been in my youth, had spent hours around the campfires listening to and reciting Kipling.

I answered back: "*Though there's never a wave of all our waves/But marks our English dead.*"

She nodded, satisfied. "Blood truly *is* the Price of Admiralty, young Dunwich, the Price of Civilization, the Price of Mankind's very existence." She smiled in amusement, a cold hard smile that would not have looked out of place on a grinning tyger. "I suspect you reaffirm that simple Truth each time you look in the mirror."

"You are lucky you cannot see him," von Brauchitsch said. He mock-shuddered. "I shall not sleep for days."

"Quiet, Helmut," she said. "This one is promising."

"So did the six ones before him," the German said, as much to me as to her. "They did not work out, did they?"

"They did after a fashion," she said.

"*My* fashion," von Brauchitsch said as he flexed his hand at the memory. The gesture looked almost as what you would use choking the throat of a chicken.

Or a man.

The Widow turned to face me fully. "Sit," she ordered, gesturing at the chair nearest me.

I sat.

"The final and deciding test of this interview," she said, "is, for want of a better term, a test of character. I cannot more fully explain until after you pass the test."

"*If* he should pass," von Brauchitsch muttered.

"I have hopes for this one. After all, we have no use for a seventh failure now, do we, Helmut?"

She withdrew from the jewelry box a small crystal phial filled with a clear turquoise liquid. She removed the stopper and handed the open phial to the lurking German. He took up station upon my left side.

She nodded. "Helmut will administer the chemical."

Von Brauchitsch suddenly seized my left wrist in a hand with steel cable for sinews. He turned my arm over so the veins along the wrist showed.

"No!" I shouted as Penny Dreadful visions of the opium dens of Europe's jaded elite danced through my mind. I twisted and struggled but could not break the German's grip upon my arm.

Von Brauchitsch shoved me down *hard* into my chair. "Quiet, fool," he snarled, "and do as you're told."

The Widow sighed, seemingly distressed at the necessity of physical force. "You completely misunderstand, Mr. Dunwich. A tiny drop of the tincture is applied externally and will do you no harm, save perhaps a small burning sensation. We merely wish to observe the catalyst's reaction against your skin."

When I did not immediately settle down as she wished, she sighed again. "Helmut," she said with no small irritation, "please show him."

The German released his grip upon me. He wiggled his left wrist free of the cuff of his immaculately tailored shirt sleeve, exposing it to view.

He poured a single drop of the turquoise liquid upon the inside of his left wrist. The liquid foamed like baking soda and there was a slight whiff of burning human flesh in the air.

Von Brauchitsch shook his wrist as if trying to smother out a flame burning upon it.

"This is what *failure* to pass the test looks like," the Widow Dubois said. She smiled a wicked, superior smile at von Brauchitsch. The pair's hatred was as implacable as any crashing ocean wave.

"Poor Helmut," she cooed. "Perhaps his proud Junkers bloodline is not so very pure after all."

Von Brauchitsch visibly stiffened. "There is a vast difference between the pure Aryan blood of a Teuton and the mongrel breed of the slightly Teutonic Anglo-Saxon, no matter what *they* thought."

"Perhaps," she replied, "Perhaps not. *What matters* is that the Book *is* bound by what *they* thought, otherwise I would have had you handle the Book long ago."

I had no inkling of what any of this fantastic exchange meant, other than gleaning that whatever it did, these two people, quite possibly mad, believed in whatever this chemical test was meant to prove. I disliked the thought of having a drop of who-knew-what acidic chemical splashed on my wrist, but if it would secure me the job at the wages promised, I steeled myself to undergo it.

I rolled down my shirt sleeve and stuck out my bare wrist. "Sorry about before," I said. "Let's continue, shall we?"

Von Brauchitsch again gripped my arm, more gently this time.

He doled out a single drop of the turquoise liquid upon my bare skin.

It pooled upon my wrist, inert and harmless. No hissing burning foaming, no pain or smell of burnt flesh.

"Excellent!" the old woman cried. "Mr. Dunwich, you have the job. You begin tomorrow. For now, you're free to retire to your room. We dine at six promptly."

I had the job. I could not tell if von Brauchitsch was pleased or not. I think he was disappointed I had not been placed in the category of the previous six applicants.

He handed me the skeleton key to my room. The look in his eye told me he was looking forward to a vermin hunt in the very near future.

∩

At five-thirty I could endure the strange solitude of my room no more. While I had been upstairs being interviewed, the unseen staff of the manor had unpacked my valise, laundered my travel-soiled clothes, and had placed upon my nightstand a map with helpful directions to the dining room.

For some inexplicable reason, the thought of these unseen staff having access to my room, touching my belongings, sent a chill of dread racing through me. The very room that had seemed so cheery when I arrived now felt tainted, felt vile.

I bolted from the room toward the dining room. Even the surly company of von Brauchitsch would be more welcome that the solitude of my room at the moment.

The manor was huge, larger even than it appeared from the outside. Even with a map I became turned around several times, but finally through dint of persistence I arrived at the double doors of what surely must be—if my map was to be at all believed—the grand dining room.

I heard through the twin closed doors the clatter of plates and the scuffle of chairs being moved across the floor. The staff must be inside preparing the room for our meal.

As I reached out my hand for the ornate rococo brass door handles, I felt my blood freeze cold. The clatter of plates had taken on the same surging pulse of the angry sea below. In my suddenly fevered imaginations strange and terrible entities lurked beyond those doors, entities inimical to me and my Kind; hateful, baleful things that would rend me asunder, tear what remained of my flesh into gobbets to feast upon with hungry, gaping maws.

I jerked back my hand. Indeed, I jerked back my body only to stumble back against the solid bulk of von Brauchitsch.

He grabbed my arm just as he'd done upstairs and pulled it well away from the door.

"You were told six o'clock precisely," he said in his humorless Prussian way. "That does not mean five minutes 'til. That does not mean one minute 'til."

The Widow Dubois stood behind him. "We do not disturb the staff. *Ever.* We let them alone as they will let us alone."

The clatter inside ceased. A dinner gong sounded.

"Now we may enter," von Brauchitsch said and swept open the double doors.

A veritable feast had been laid out before us. Three places at the dining table had been set with the most exquisite of china upon the most delicate of linen cloth.

No servant, however, remained in the room.

And no other door in or out of the room was in evidence.

Neither the Widow nor von Brauchitsch seemed to take notice of any of these peculiarities. They seated themselves at the table as if they'd done so a thousand times before and began to serve themselves from the waiting serving dishes.

Sheepishly, I seated myself as well. The warm glint of the lighted candles on the table, the savory aroma of the hot dishes, the heady bouquet of the opened wines. I had been exhuming sinister intents where none existed.

Surely there must be a logical, prosaic explanation for their reluctance for me to see their servants. My mind whirled back to those lurid tales in the popular adventure magazines of the illegal smuggling of Chinese to our Pacific shores. Perhaps the Widow ran or was otherwise complicit in such an operation, that she had at the very least employed such workers for her manor. They could hardly trust a stranger—for that is what I was to them—to keep their secret.

Whether or not this was indeed the case, having a plausible, mundane solution eased my mind considerably. I was able to take part in the small talk of the meal, and indeed, to fully enjoy the repast.

And what a repast it was! Fowl and game of every variety. Dishes far too exotic and European for a simple American like me to recognize. I had once dined at the home of the richest man in Denver—a Christmas dinner he threw for a select group of crippled veterans, a sop, I think, to his own conscience for keeping his three sons out of the war—but his table was never set so fine as this!

Time slipped away until it was eight o'clock, and again a gong sounded.

Bolting upright in their chairs, the Widow and the German ceased dining instantly. Indeed, they dropped the very dessert spoons in their hands, letting them clatter unheeded to the floor. They both turned and walked swiftly to exit the room, rather than remain for the re-entering of the staff.

Confused, I followed them out.

I almost turned to look back—like Lot's wife—at the sudden clatter of plates being cleared, but again that strange sensation of dread came over me and I closed the door behind me without a single glance back.

In the morning when I awoke, I found another note on my nightstand instructing me to report to a marked elevator on the map at 9 o'clock precisely. The word *precisely* had been underlined three times in red, either by von Brauchitsch or the invisible brownies who'd visited my room in the night and tidied up the clothes I had so carelessly flung about the floor when I'd retired.

A Continental breakfast—a croissant, some fruit, some cheese, and a glass of juice—awaited me on a silver salver placed on a sideboard. No breakfasting in the grand dining room for me it seemed.

I performed my morning ablutions and dressed. The meager breakfast vanished in a trice—I would need to have a word with the Widow about the American notions of a hearty breakfast—and I threw back the *jalousie* upon the window for my first true look out my window in the full light of day.

Had I expected sunny blue skies I should have been very much disappointed. True, the rain had ceased—for the moment—but the skies remained much as they'd been the day before. A gray fog that seemed more a slowly drifting cloud hugging the ground leeched what colors were to be seen outside. All was a dull pantheon of gray and black and the deep dark pine of the evergreens.

The trees looked less imposing than before, but perhaps by winning the job I had become something other than a complete stranger.

When I caught myself thinking such, as if the German's black jest was fact and the trees were sentient creatures, I muttered in consternation with myself. Today was a day for celebration! I checked my appearance in the mirror one last time, straighten my tie, and left my room for the marked elevator and the first day of my well-paying job.

The freak show that was my face no longer barred me from gainful employment, now that I had found a rich, blind employer!

My ebullient mood evaporated the moment the tiny metal grill-gated elevator lurched to its stop a full one hundred feet below the deepest basement of the mansion.

Von Brauchitsch rode the elevator with me to set me to my task. The Widow Dubois was nowhere to be found.

The German and I got into the elevator and he swung the lever that sent it dropping downward. It was just as well the Widow had not accompanied us. The tiny elevator was uncomfortably cramped with the two of us wide-shouldered men inside. She would never have fit in with us.

The electrified motor hummed as the elevator descended. The German operated the leer mechanism jerkily; he was much too impatient to be done and gone with the task of showing me to what he called The Vault, the capitalization implicit in his voice as he spoke of it.

And vault it was.

When the elevator at last reached bottom and von Brauchitsch threw back the accordion-hinged grill, I beheld a tiny cramped room that bore no small resemblance to a veritable bank vault. The walls, the floors, the ceiling were riveted plates of cold hard steel. It only lacked a great time-lock vault door, and the inaccessibility of the deep-shafted elevator—the only ingress or egress of the room—provided, I should think, the same degree of security.

A solitary bare light bulb, a feeble twenty-watt bulb, hung on a braided cloth wire above a utilitarian metal table. The dim glow of the overhead bulb cast grotesque shadows on the walls.

The thick stout table was five feet in length, and would provide me an ample working surface I should think. The accompanying hardwood office chair would suffice to both seat me and keep me awake from its stiff-bottomed discomforts.

Upon the table lay two singular objects.

The first was a typewriter of curious workmanship. Obviously a custom-made item, its rows of keys were easily twice as numerous as a normal typewriter although its roller platen was of standard size. Indeed, upon closer examination the keys were not English letters at all. Nor were they letters of any alphabet I'd ever seen, neither Cyrillic, Greek, Hebrew, Arabic, or even Sanskrit. They were a collection of bizarre glyphs or perhaps pictographs, but again unlike any I'd ever encountered, neither Chinese nor Japanese or even ancient Babylonian cuneiform or Egyptian hieroglyphs.

Still further examination showed that one, just one, of the keys had not been installed or had broken. The missing key looked for all the world like a toothless gap in a mouthful of teeth.

But if the typewriter was curious, the second object was fantastical.

It was a book, a slim leather-bound folio of some obvious antiquity. Large bas-relief bronze plates reinforced the outer corners. The spine itself was a hinge of the same bronze carvings. A thick leather strap with a clasp lock held the volume closed from prying eyes. A singular key, with its bow shaped like a grinning skull sat upright in the clasp lock. The key, unlike the metalwork of the folio itself, was tarnished and corroded with age.

The book was thin, very thin—no more than perhaps two or three-dozen folio-sized pages. Its leather binding was a revolting shade of dead flesh. A multitude of curious symbols and shapes adorned the leather. At first I thought the adornments done in jet-black ink, but on closer examination proved to be a blood red so deep as to almost *be* black, a black the color of long-dried blood.

"Pick up the book," a voice behind me sounded. The voice was that of the Widow Dubois, but this time it was no voice from a speaking tube. I turned and there she stood. The elevator had not moved—I would have heard its noisy motor—and there were no other doors in the Vault. How she had managed to enter I knew not.

"Pick up the book," she ordered again.

I did not want to.

There was a fell quality to the tome. The bas-relief gargoyles and daemons carved across its gold corner plates seemed in the shadows of the caliginous lighting almost to undulate of their own free will.

"Pick it up!" she commanded in a low voice as frightening as the crawling carvings upon the bronzed surfaces.

I reached out my quavering hand and brushed the tips of my fingers to the book. The muculent leather binding—how I prayed I would never discover just what creature's skin it was!—slid greasily under my fingertips. The blackened symbols suddenly glowed red—red as fresh arterial blood.

"Pick it up!"

With both hands atremble, I seized the folio and held it six inches above the desk.

"Good," the old woman breathed, as if she were affected by the book as I was. "Now, set it before you and unlock the catch. Turn the key, *but gently!*"

I turned the crusted, tarnished key. The tumblers of the lock sprang free. Just at the moment of doing so, the key shattered under the torque of my twisting, the brittle crystalline lattice of its ancient unknown metal alloys failing under the strain.

The sealed book, as if it had been somehow hermetically sealed, hissed out a sudden flatus of fetid air—a mephitic rush of corrupted gasses that blew ice cold —far, far colder than the mere clammy damp of an underground vault a hundred feet down in the dank deep ground.

"Open to the first page," the Widow ordered, "but do not turn the pages further."

Again, I reluctantly did as she commanded.

The first page shewed the scrawling of an ancient manuscript. No frontispiece to adorn it, no title page to even indicate what it was.

The open text proved to be a solid block of text of some strange kind. Instantly I intuited that these queer raven-inked scribblings were of the selfsame iconographic characters of the typewriter keys and with that I at last had a glimmering of the task for which I'd been hired.

The Widow meant for me to transpose the handwritten manuscript onto typewritten sheets!

My first thoughts upon this, however, were not of there being only twenty or so pages, of this fantastically well-paying job almost being over before it started.

No, my first thoughts were how to escape this tiny Vault, how to leave this house and the Widow and the German and the guardian trees and the strange pounding ocean—how to leave all of Cape Foulweather behind as if I'd never heard nor seen of it.

For the curious squiggling characters written on the page, though perfectly stationary when looked at straight on, had the horrible curious effect of moving, of crawling about the page like scarabaeid *things* when glimpsed indirectly from the corner of my eye.

Von Brauchitsch, of all people, clapped me on the back and shoved a silvered flask in my hands. "Well done, *Amerikaner!*" he roared with approval. "It appears that mongrel Anglo-Saxon blood of yours is good for something after all, however blotted with Picts and Romans it might be! Not as fine as Teutonic blood, but for opening ancient tomes—"

I gulped down two large swallows of a most excellent whisky from his flask so I ignored his insult.

The Widow added her approbation. "Indeed, Mr. Dunwich. Neither I nor Helmut could have opened the *Summa Cacodaemonica Opuscula* without destroying both the book and ourselves in the process."

Before the sheer unbelievability of her statement registered, she continued. "The friars that codified the *Opuscula* may have been holy men, but they were products of their time, predisposed to think that disparate races not of their precious island Albion were somehow inferior and not to be trusted. Whether this is true or false is of no moment. That they believed it true and so became intertwined within the powers placed within their compendium is."

Had anyone told me this a mere twenty-four hours before, I would have labeled them insane. But after the unslaked hungering waves, the invisible servants, the malevolent trees, and above all the crawling, skittering inkblots that even now skirted off the boundaries of their manuscript page and threatened to climb up my very arms if I looked away? No, I believed her wild story—or enough of it that would treat the *Opuscula* as possessing some eldritch power unknown by modern science.

Sensing perhaps, this sudden acquiescence on my part in this mad occult charade, the Widow proceeded to give me my instructions:

I was each day to dutifully type out upon the typewriter the text of a single page of the accursed folio, no more. One day, one page.

I was to work alone in the Vault. I was not to leave—indeed, I could not leave as the elevator would be draw up by von Brauchitsch each morning—until I had completed each day's task. The button for an electric signal bell had been installed upon one wall of the Vault for the purpose of beckoning von Brauchitsch to bring down the elevator.

I was forbidden to turn the pages of the book, save to the next one at the start of a morning.

And I was given careful instructions about the missing typewriter key.

"You note that there is one symbol missing. The symbol is of such great power that no mere mechanical device could hope to contain it. When you come to a rare occasion of this symbol in the *Opuscula*, you will take a lead pencil and scribble randomly in the blank area upon the typed page. You will not attempt to draw it, you will not attempt to substitute some other symbol like a check mark or an X. You will scribble randomly and you must ascertain that each scribble is manifestly different from each other."

I told her I understood all these conditions.

"Then set to work," she said. She and von Brauchitsch ascended in the elevator, leaving me trapped a hundred feet below ground to copy out a magical tome upon a creaking manual typewriter.

THE WORK, though it seemed simple, proved arduous.

Not only were there one hundred and twenty-seven different glyphs to differentiate and memorize their location on the typewriter, but the sheer effort of typing them out drained me in ways far more extensive than mere physicality.

The scribblings, as I have said, ventured off the page whenever I turned my head to peer at the keyboard or the paper in the machine's platen. The visual sensation was not unlike the *delirium tremens* suffered by alcoholics, the illusionary insects that drunkards keep trying to swat away. Moreover, as the day grew on and so did my exhaustion, even looking directly at the folio page did not keep the scribblings steady.

Secondly, each glyph I typed seemed to somehow drain my vitality as if it drew upon my own life force to bind the slippery thing onto a printed page, into a rational world of science and men. The infrequent occurrence of the unnamable unkeyed glyph was worst of all. A simple wooden pencil felt as heavy as a Scottish caber.

By the nineteenth day, the penultimate page, I was fair to collapse completely. All that saved me was that the nineteenth page was three-quarters blank.

As I staggered out of the elevator into the manor proper, the Widow tried to send me straight to bed.

"I'll be all right," I said, trying to bluff it out. "A few minutes away from that cursed Book and I shall recover nicely. A change might do me good, perhaps a stroll around the grounds outside. I have not left this house since I arrived."

The Widow did not think this a good idea but in the end, acquiesced. She counseled me to stay upon the grounds and not wander off into the forest. "You do not have Helmut's woodcraft, let us say. I would not care to lose you in the trees."

With only a single page remaining remained unsaid but nevertheless hung in the air, tainting completely her solicitude.

She turned to leave, then paused. She did not look back, as there was no need to face me in her blindness. "And stay clear of Helmut's workshop in the back of the grounds. He is quite jealous of his solitude."

Besides, I thought, he likes to shoot things out-of-doors and I might very well find myself in his line of fire, accident or not.

As an enjoyable excursion, my stroll of the grounds left much to be desired. The fog lifted only to drizzle rain, then settle back down again. I was cold and soaked to the skin, but I was outside and free of that infernal bugcrawl.

The trees, those malicious, murderous things, kept a baleful watch upon my every movement. With each step I took, their wind-crabbed branches twisted toward me, tracing my progress around the grounds.

I had somehow managed, I think, to time my stroll for low tide for the continual roar of the ocean seemed more distant, more muted than before. Only a trace of its malevolent thirst could be felt. Or perhaps I was just numb from exhaustion.

My wanderings took me to the work areas behind the house, the carriage house and various tool sheds. Beyond them was a recent addition, a large squat building with stolid practical lines.

I knew in an instant that this was the work shed of von Brauchitsch, the work shed to be avoided. But no lights burned in the windows. It looked deserted, and I thought I heard von Brauchitsch's gun banging away in the far distance in one of his supposed vermin hunts. He would never know I looked. And besides, surely he wouldn't begrudge me a single peek?

I peered into the closest window. A series of stretching racks covered much of the floor, rack upon rack of drying, curing leather from unidentifiable creatures ranging from muskrat size to that of a man. In the center of the workshop I saw a tailor's dummy and what I took to be a partially-completed leather coat upon it. The jacket's torso looked complete but the sleeves were missing.

Perhaps the German's jest about taxidermy and leatherworking had not been a jest at all.

Having had my peek, I hurried away from the building before I was caught.

Suddenly, just before I reached the other outbuildings, a murder of ravens launched itself skyward from the sodden grass although I would have sworn that before they flew up no birds had crouched there. There were hundreds of them, perhaps thousands.

The black mass of them dipped and soared and wheeled and curved as if the flock were a living thing unto itself. It was beautiful and mesmerizing and fell in its sinister black dance.

The cacophonous rasp of a thousand crows at once blanketed the sound of von Brauchitsch approaching behind me.

He tapped my shoulder with something hard and cold. I turned and he stood before me with a clutch of dead raccoons in one blood-soaked hand and his Mauser Gewehr 98 rifle. I knew the shape of that rifle immediately. The rifle the German Army had carried—that von Brauchitsch had carried—into the field to shoot Americans like me.

He smiled in the rictus of a man on a hunt who has cornered his prey.

"Did you enjoy your little *schnoop* into my private affairs, *Amerikaner?*" he asked.

"I was curious, that's all," I mumbled.

"Curious? About what? About what kind of animal I hunt? About what kind of hide I dress for its leather?"

He dropped his clutch of dead animals to the ground and worked the bolt action of his rifle to chamber in a new round. As exhausted as I still was, I could not even run.

I was terrified, as I so often had been since arriving, but at least this time I faced a known terror—how well I knew what the high power spitzer bullet of a Mauser 98 could do to a human body! At least this time I faced a danger from the familiar world of science and physics and cold hard facts.

The German kicked at the blood-soaked carcasses at his feet. "Tell me,

Amerikaner, have you satisfied yourself about the kind of vermin I shoot? Have you satisfied yourself that I don't go around shooting and tanning *men?*"

I mumbled that I was.

The German raised his rifle safely to port and let out a blasphemous laugh that matched the noisome cacophony of the stygian crows.

"Then you are a fool," he said "You attempt logic and reason, extrapolating only by what game I have in my hands at the moment."

His evil smile fell cold. "I told you—the petty laws of Man and Nature are not observed upon this mountain."

As if to underscore his point, the shifting black shape of the flying birds seemed to transmogrify into a grotesque Death Head skull. The trees—those murderous killing trees—dipped their windblown branches in time to the fluttering, shifting simulacrum

Von Brauchitsch's eyes were alight with a depraved inner glow. "During the war, I learned to shoot men without compunction. What makes you think I could ever unlearn that lesson? Or ever want to?"

His free hand swept toward the flying mass of crows. "It is called in your language a *murmuration.* Not only the sound, but the visual spectacle of thousands of these crows—single entities of their own self—combining into a tenebrous mass that exudes and exhibit a life all its own."

He suddenly raised the rifle to his shoulder and fired into the murmuration. A deafening *crack* and a single crow fell from the sky. The mass of birds flew on in its intricate dance as if nothing had happened at all.

"Tell me, is the murmuration somehow lessened because of the loss of a single bird? What about an army from the loss of a single man? Do either of them even notice the loss of one of their number?"

"You are a monster!" I snarled, blood pounding in my temple with rage.

He laughed again. "Yes I am," he said. "The War tore away my conscience, my soul if you will—just as the War tore away your face. We are both monsters, we are both horrors, Mr. Dunwich, are we not?"

Before I could answer, he continued: "Imagine those crows are not crows, Mr. Dunbar. Imagine that instead that murmuration were an entity formed from all the pounding waves below, all the waves that crash about the entire world! Millions of angry waves unslaked in their thirst to destroy all before it, to destroy Man and all his works!"

I shuddered visibly at the very thought of something so horrible.

"Now," von Brauchitsch said, and not in some small triumph, "imagine that even a conscienceless monster vile as myself—a murderer and a sadist— standing in the path of that great Cyclopean abomination doing all he can to stop it while *you*—" he suddenly jabbed the hard cold rifle muzzle into my chest "—a supposedly moral person like yourself flees in helpless terror."

He *knew*, he *knew* the terror that was welling up inside my heart. He *knew* beyond certainty what I would do if faced with such a terror.

"Which of us now is an immoral monster?" he demanded.

He lifted the rifle end from my chest and scooped up his brace of dead raccoons. As he walked toward his work shop, he called back one last taunt over his shoulder: "If we do not stop it here, where shall it be stopped?"

Overhead the murder of ravens danced and wheeled and followed their master, while far below the tide came and the darkening ocean awoke.

⋀

Next day I turned to the final page to see it was but a single line. The missing glyph repeated three times at its very end.

Each time I counterfeited that unutterable sigil the distant roar of the accursed waves grew stronger, louder, closer.

By the third shaky scribble of my pencil upon the page, the very light bulb above me danced upon its tangle twisted cord as if the Vault, the entire mountain, were caught in a undulating shaking maelstrom.

My task complete at last, I rolled the paper from the platen and slipped it to the bottom of the typed pages, tapping them into order.

The roaring of the waves stopped

For now, I thought, for now.

And I knew I had but a little while to escape before they crashed over the shore for their final destructive march.

⋀

The Widow Dubois again met me at the top of the elevator. She took the typed pages from me.

"Helmut," she said, "give him his pay."

Von Brauchitsch reached inside his jacket and extracted a sheaf of bills thicker than any I'd ever seen.

As if the waving about of these green scraps of paper were a red flag of challenge, the quiescent waters far below stirred again. The drum of the crashing waves began to build yet again.

The Widow stared at me with those horrible blank unseeing eyes.

"You are free to take this and leave," she said. "There is still a little time left for you to do so."

My heart leapt at this news.

"Or you can stay and fight along with us against the doom that Helmut told you of."

Stay? Against *that?*

"I expect us to die," she said. "Worse, I expect us to *fail.* But if we fail, no place you can run to will be safe for long. In your heart you know this to be true."

I wanted to run. I knew I would run.

I was afraid.

I had been afraid before, going over the top and crawling through the barbed wire tangles and craters of No Man's Land. I had been afraid before when I heard the falling scream of the German shell and knew that it would not miss. I had been afraid the day they first handed me a mirror in that French hospital. I had been afraid every day since when I saw the recoil of disgust upon the face of everyone I met.

I had been afraid every single solitary moment I had been in this hellish house.

I was so sick and tired of being afraid that the surcease of the grave would at least be a *surcease.*

I shook with the thousand memories of night horrors. I shook with the distant memory of what it was to yet be a *man.*

"Tell me what you want me to do," I found myself whispering.

My words carried—just barely!—over the building crash of the advancing waves.

ᴧ

THEY LED me up the dark winding stairs that led the manor's topmost turret, to the bolted door that opened to the parapet, the widow's walk spinningly high above the trees, high above the ocean so very far below.

Stacked near the door were a brace of rifles and other firearms and boxes and boxes of ammunition. Also on the landing was a mysterious bundle, a canvas-wrapped object or objects the size of a dead man.

"Stack those outside," von Brauchitsch ordered, pointing at the ammo and the guns.

I nodded and set to work before my nerves failed me. I unbolted the door and shouldered it open against the howling wind. Rain trickled into my grim-set mouth. They tasted of ocean salts and long dead creatures of the deep.

I stacked the metal cans of ammunition as I had been taught so long ago in the trenches, giving us open walkways to move about upon the parapet yet within reach at all times.

Behind me, hidden in the adumbrated in the shadows of the stairwell, half-glimpsed forms of von Brauchitsch and the Widow busied themselves with the unwrapping of that canvas bundle.

The wind increased.

Gripping the bladed spears of the iron railing, I peered over the edge at the shoreline below. I could see the dipping curve of the highway where the gas station stood. I could see the low sea wall. And I could see the mighty ocean rise as if it were alive and completely cover the sea wall, the highway, and much of the gas station.

The waves crashed, but they did not seem to recede. Impossibly the waters gathered into a horrible indiscernible *thing*.

"And so it begins," von Brauchitsch shouted over my shoulder.

He handed me a drum-fed Thompson sub-machine gun. He held another one for himself. "I trust you know how to use this."

In answer, I slapped back the action and checked the chamber, although I did not know how he expected to fight off the horror that approached with a mere machine gun. An entire trenchline of artillery could not stop the being I sensed, I *felt* was coming.

Winds buffeted us about. Rain spalled against our faces.

Von Brauchitsch laughed against the raging elements. "This is only for the little ones, the vermin with their clever little hands like men."

He nodded at the darkened gloom of the stairwell. "Our job is only to protect the Widow as she reads what you have typed out."

And with those words, the Widow Dubois emerged into the storm.

She wore about her body and her head a hideous, obscene assemblage of half-cured stinking, fetid leather crudely stitched together from six separate pieces: one for each limb, one for the torso, and one ghastly, blasphemous piece that comprised a hood completely covering her head.

My senses reeled as I realized at last I knew the secret of von Brauchitsch's workshop and its leatherworkings, the secret of what I'd thought was a half-finished coat upon a tailoring dummy.

At last I knew the true fate of the six men, my six failed predecessors, who'd fallen into von Brauchitsch's hands. One each for the limbs, one for the torso, one for that hell-spawned, horrible hood.

And worse—far worse than mere awareness—I found myself understanding their monstrous deed, for my time spent with the *Opuscula* imbued in me somehow the terrible knowledge that though now transcribed and typewritten, its words *still* could not be spoken by a woman unless this sickly, ghastly ruse was used.

For when she read, her outer form would be that of a man—or counterfeited enough to fool whatever Powers that be.

Encumbered inside her hideous armor of half-rotting flesh, she stumbled to the railing edge overlooking the sea.

In her leather-gloved hands she clutched the transcribed pages, kept dry with protective transparent sheets. She held them before as if she could see to read them with her blank white eyes swaddled behind the odious wall of human skin that comprised her leather hood.

She read, and her voice carried above the wind and the rain and the angry sea!

AT HER FIRST UTTERED SYLLABLE in a trilling language not of this world, the *thing* that lurked for uncountable eons beneath the crashing waves, beneath the waters of the firmament, beneath the bounds and the metes of the physical universe—*the thing awoke!*

There is no describing the horror that rose from the sea—*that was the sea!* —and yet the frail human mind gibbers at the thought of something that cannot be described, cannot be named, cannot be assigned a place in the world we knew.

And so, my weak and mortal senses tried to shape that which had no rational shape into something I could see and hear, tried to force the unnamable, the unutterable, the unknowable into something—*anything!*—the feeble human mind could comprehend.

What I saw was not what was. What I saw was not as von Brauchitsch saw it, and what he saw was not as how I saw the thing.

But what I saw was this:

It began with the crashing pounding waves. The green black waves of water and brine and white splashing foam seemed to shift and wriggle into long, writhing, wiggling sinuous creatures of the deepest fathoms. But not mortal creatures of the deep, oh no! These were pisciform beings composed not of flesh and bones and fishy scales but of the sea water itself, translucent iridescent things not bound by laws of nature. They flew, heaven help me, they flew!

They flew and snaked and writhed in the air, each individually, to join, to combine as the crows had done into one huge horrifying mass—one towering, terrible being that strode from out of the sea like a dark and angry Neptune stepping onto the shore.

The composite creature—the great murmuration of unworldly denizens of the deep—the horrible and horrifying thing that we must cast back, was fifty, sixty, no! a hundred feet tall. It was a scabrous, squamous thing of bullous greens and grays and inky, stygian blackness. Its piscioid scales were the writhing individuals I have described.

Its massive disproportionate head—horribly, horribly boneless—comprised at least half its cyclopean mass. It looked to my battered, terrified senses to be that of a body of some octopoid horror. Its gaping, growling mouth fringed with gigantic tentacles and with its maw smaller ones that receded down to the tiniest of wriggling disgusting cilia.

Its Herculean torso was that not of some man but of some foul and fetid beast that walked upright as a man, as no beast should be allowed under heaven to do. Its legs remained obscured in the rising waters that swirled about it.

And its arms! Its great sweeping, slashing arms with their clawed webbed hands. Stunted those arms were, but they quested, they reached, they stretched forth for *us!*

As it strode Brobdingnagianly toward the mountain and the manor perched atop it, the writhing smaller creatures dipped and wheeled into and out of its mass just as the crows and their murmurations. A thin cloud of separate discrete creatures continuously formed around it. As the *thing* approached, this cloud of lesser horrors neared us, flew about us above our parapet.

These, these lesser dangers von Brauchitsch and myself could deal with the puny weapons of Men.

They must not be allowed to interfere with the Widow's words of power which was our only salvation!

We fired again and again, expending ammunition without care. We fired until the barrels heated to a cherry red glow. We jabbed the red-hot barrels into the cold waters of the flying horror's very forms to quench them and fired yet again.

We fired until the molten barrels bent, tossed aside that weapon, and plucked up another stacked beside us.

Hundreds, thousands of the lesser creatures fell to our gunfire, splattering under the kinetic impact of the bullets, devolving into harmless sea water once again. Hundreds, thousands fell about us and still it was not enough. Millions, billions, numbers without end filled the sky and countless uncountable numbers still congealed to form the approaching giant horror.

It all—our lives, indeed the lives of all the universe—depended upon the Widow now.

Though blinded by the hood of flesh, though blinded by eyes that could not see, she read from the typescript pages the weird, skirling words of a forbidden, forgotten tongue. The meaning of those words I could not say.

I only knew that as she read, the words seemed to draw the giant horror closer, seemed to enrage him with each trilling syllable.

The giant horror was all but upon us now. Not only was it gathering all the waters of the sea in its unquenchable thirst, but it had begun to suck all the moisture out of the soil, the trees, and even us. I felt the foul horror begin to exsiccate the waters of life from my very being.

The titanic creature reached out its grasping, questing arms to grab and crush us just as the Widow turned to the nineteenth page.

She spoke the short, staccato paragraph that was all that comprised the page and to my wonder, the unstoppable thing—the implacable enemy of all existence—staggered back as if mortally wounded.

This proved but a false hope, for in the briefest instant the Widow took to turn to the final page, the creature was again upon us.

Its hand closed about the Widow, pinning her, lifting her off her feet.

The creature's tentacled maw gaped wide, its hideous foul cilia wriggled in expectant ecstasy.

Too late, foul *thing!* Too late!

For the Widow had committed to memory the final line of the final page. As the last breath of air was crushed from her lungs, she shouted triumphantly the thrice-repeated Word of Power—the very Name of the Unnamable Thing itself!

"Thotsakanos! Thotsakanos! Thotsakanos!"

Like a soap bubble against a pressing pin, like a nightmare shaken away by the touch of a friendly hand—the creature, if that is what it was, was no more.

Even the howling wind and rain ceased to be.

The angry sea became just that—a sea. Angry, but cowed and beaten, confined again to its mortal metes and bounds.

The thing that had lurked for eons under the firmament of creation again was banished therein.

Still...

Still, however, I could hear its challenging rage, feel its baleful stare.

It was not defeated, merely temporarily stymied.

It would rise again.

The Widow Dubois, however, would not.

She lay where the *thing* had dropped her, her crushed and mangled body sprawled.

Kneeling beside her, I yanked off the foul leather hood that covered her face. She was still alive for perhaps a breath or two.

"You did it," I said.

"*We* did it," she corrected.

She reached out her bare hand—the struggle had torn off her leather sleeve —and lightly stoked the mangled scars on my face. "Oh, Randolph," she said, calling me by my Christian name for the first time. "Your poor, poor face."

"Never mind about that now," I snapped. "We've got to get you to a—"

"Sometimes I think in its endless Wisdom, the Guiding Providence that seems to hover over Man and his affairs has decreed that War must ever be fought," she said. "For creation needs the detritus of War if Mankind, if the Universe is to survive."

She was babbling, delirious. "Get a doctor!" I yelled at von Brauchitsch. "For heaven's sakes above *call a doctor!*"

He only shook his head. He knew as well as I did there was no point.

The Widow lifted her head toward me, wanting me to hear the final words she could barely breathe.

"It is only those who have known the horror of War and crippled by it can care enough, be driven enough to fight against the nameless terrors that lurk behind the cracks in our reality."

She coughed and bright atrial blood trickled from her mouth.

"Only a person as blind as I could have blinded herself to the necessary evils needing to be done. Only a conscienceless monster such as Helmut could have performed those evils."

She coughed again. "And only someone stripped of their membership in the brotherhood of Man—cast out from their fellowship as you had been—who had no place left to go would have stayed in a house occupied by two mad monsters such as we."

"You're not a monster," I whispered. "None of us are." I had seen true monstrosity this day. And true nobility.

"It is not over," she whispered. "It is never over. I bequeath to you, Randolph, this house and the burden that comes with it. You must prepare, Randolph, you must be ready to beat it back again. You must dedicate your life and your soul to—to—"

"I will," I promised, but I promised to myself for she had gone.

THEY PULLED down Leroy's Gas Station in 1942 as part of a wartime scrap drive, something I caused to happen. The other houses on the hill, I purchased one by one and tore them down as well.

The name Cape Foulweather ceased to exist on any map other than as a geological feature. In an ever-more-modernizing world of instant communications and globally accessible records, we needed to disappear lest we be exposed.

Helmet von Brauchitsch passed away a long time ago, but I have found others to take his place over the years. There are always Helmuts in our sad, sorry world. It is the Widow Duboises we seem to be in short supply of.

I have tried my best to become what she was. The minor magicks she used—to extend the span of her life, to fashion unseen servants that leave my days free to carry on her work—those are easily mastered. The more important work of searching the world for the hidden knowledge of forces beyond our ken, that is more difficult. And yet it can be done. In the tens of thousands of years that man has recorded the world—and the unseen world—around him, enough of those records survive to safeguard our existence today.

I do not fight alone. Scattered across the world, in the inhospitable places, the vertices where the known universe collides with the unknown and unknowable, there are other houses like mine where dwell searchers of the hidden eldritch ways, where dwell warriors who beat back the *things* that would emerge to destroy us all.

If blood be the Price to save Man and Civilization, we have paid it, and always, always that price has been paid by the cripple of mind and body and soul who have already balanced the book beforehand. The Widow Dubois believed that only those touched by the calamities of war could serve our cause. And since she believed it, for her it was so—just as those who'd penned the *Summa Cacodaemonica Opuscula* projected their mistaken beliefs into reality. That was her blindness, and theirs.

I believe that anyone who has been blighted by the imperfections of mortality can serve—and since *I* believe, it is so in my magicks.

Like the Widow Dubois, I have my own blindness that allows me, drives me to perform the work. She believed, as all others before her, that the ancient evils that lay hidden can never be defeated, that Mankind's extinction can only be delayed. I reject that. I am blind toward such a conclusion.

Mankind and the natural universe *can* triumph. We are a universe of Light.

And in the end, the dark things cannot stand the light.

But to ultimately triumph we will need warriors.

And that is why, rather than placing some cryptic advertisement, I am contacting you directly. Already the unknowable forces are gathering again. And I cannot fight it alone.

I know you to be a person for whom despair and pain and suffering and loss are no strangers. I know it is within you to rise up anew. Will you fight to save a world that has spurned you? Will you conquer your fear?

Will you join us?

Nice Timestream Youse Got Here

INTRODUCTION

One of my favorite science fiction tropes is the time travel organization protecting the timestreams.

Stories like Asimov's End of Eternity *one-shot novel, Keith Laumer's* Imperium *series, H. Beam Piper's* Paratime *and* Kalvan of Otherwhen *tales, and Poul Anderson's* Time Patrol *series. I've even wrote a couple of time organization stories back in the dawn of my newbie days—the second and third sf stories I ever wrote, in fact.*

Stories of brave, selfless, wise caretakers of the timestreams, these time protection agencies.

Protection agencies, eh?

One of my favorite programs on the Sirius XM Radio Classics golden age radio channel is the old Runyon Damon Theatre show dramatizing Runyon's beloved gangland comedic tales, complete with that trademark Runyonesque speech pattern.

Which got me thinking: what about putting a little "protection" in my time travel protecting? Time hopping wise guys looking for a piece of the action?

"Nice timestream youse got here. Shame if anything were to happen to it."

Fiction River: Time Streams bought the story, giving me a chance to butter the necktie of a stale sf trope.

Really, that's all the origin this tale has (or needs).

"Say, you know what the hardest part of being in the Agency is, Vince?" Maizie asked me as she slid her little square of butter off its waxed paper backing and scraped it across her toast.

Her voice carried easily over the clatter of plates and clatter of voices in the crowded Brooklyn diner. Breakfast rush, the joint was crowded, but not so crowded I couldn't keep watch out the window for our collar.

I didn't answer. The dingy chrome trim in the diner was brighter than Maizie.

"Keepin' track of things," she said like I'd answered back anyways. She wasn't looking for conversation, she was what they call waxin' philosophical about the job again.

In this racket, it don't pay to get philosophical about the job. Get in, get done, get out. There's a reason why I'm the number one troubleshooter for the Agency and it ain't cuz I wax any which way, philosophical nor other type wise.

"Like rememberin' what things is called what where," she went on. She held up another papered square of butter. "Like this here. They call it a 'pat' of butter here. That guy at the counter looked at me like I was some kind of creep asking for a flop of butter like a regular person."

She waved the butter square like it offended her delicate sensibilities, not that she had any. "This ain't no pat of butter. It's a flop. A pat is what comes out of the other end of the cow."

"Sure," I said around a forkful of eggs. "Like youse know about cows. The closest youse ever came to a cow was walking past the milkman's cart at 2 a.m."

I bit into my own slice of toast. "So theyse call it a pat here in this neighborhood," I said, swallowing and chasing it down with a cup of black coffee. "So what? So maybe theyse call the other end a cow flop? Who cares? You see me in an uproars just cause they got 'scrambled eggs' printed on the menu 'stead of 'stirred eggs?' I made myself understood like, didn't I? Got my order the way I like, didn't I? Shaddap and eat. You're givin' me the pepto."

She shadapped and ate. For two whole minutes anyways.

Now, some of my other partners have got to waxin' philosophical about the job, and let me tell ya, brother, nothing good ever comes of it. Givin' themselves the pepto about who just got in the White House, who just won the World Series, who just got their ugly dead political mug plastered all over the face of a coin by an Act of Congress.

Who cares?

Life goes on, don't it?

Mugs in the Agency who worry about that kind of stuff don't last too long, and I'm one of the reasons they don't. I ship 'em back upstream without their paddle, they start waxin' philosophical.

Unless of course their name is Maizie. Her, I don't ship back.

I know what you're thinking, and it ain't like that. And don't start smirking like there's something wrong with *me* neither, or I'll butter your necktie. I'm just as red-blooded as the next regular Joe.

Yeah, so it might not look it from the way I act all calm and collected and disinterested around her, but trust me, I know better than anyone else how Maizie's put together. You've seen those newsreels about Our Boys At Sea and all them mighty battleships and whatnot heaving and rolling and yawing and pitching on the high seas? Well, bub, when Maizie walks down the street, you better believe it's Naval Appreciation Day, and let me tell ya, brother, the fleet's in.

Trust me, I *know*. I gotta work with her all day long. And that's just what I do and that's *all* I do.

See, I got to be the one stuck with her as my partner because the Chief he knows I'm his one guy in the Agency who's smart enough not to sink her battleship if you catch my drift.

He knows I wouldn't touch her with a ten foot canoodle on account of a) she's the Chief's daughter; and b) I gotta listen to her yammer day in, day out, all day long—you think I wanna listen to her all night, too, once I get home? And I wouldn't be able to do nuthin' to shut her up neither on account of c) she's the Chief's daughter.

So me and Maizie, we're strictly business. I'm the Brains and the Muscle of the team, and she's the Distraction. Boy, is she ever. Kewpie doll face. Kewpie doll voice. Kewpie doll brain. And her very own pair of Sink-The-*Bismarks* that no Kewpie doll nowhere has ever had.

So I sat there and just let her yammer on about this, that, and some other fool thing while I finished up my eggs and bacon. The way the Agency keeps us on the road, I don't get many chances to eat a real breakfast in a real New York diner like a civilized person—you should see some of the joints I gotta eat at 'cuz of this job—so I was going to enjoy this breakfast, come Maizie or highwater.

Besides, I knew this chump we was tailing was buying his own Kosher breakfast two delis up the street. No hurry. Mister Regular Routine, he was.

Anyways, I like making a collar after we've both had our breakfast and our morning coffee and our blood sugar is nice and level. *They're* less likely to try something stupid on a full stomach, and *I'm* less likely to blow their fool heads off from them givin' me the pepto.

Little touches like that is why I'm the Chief's Number One and got the New

York beat, not makin' the rounds in, say, Racine, Indiana. Or Wisconsin. Or wherever Racine is.

So therefore on account of my advance planning, a few minutes later I'm sitting there leaning back in my chair and just finishing my fifth cup of coffee when I see our pigeon go walking past the window. I slap a silver dollar down on the table to cover the bill, grab my hat, and yank Maizie ("Hey! I ain't finished yet, Vince!") by the wrist and drag her out the door after him.

Like they say, time and tide don't wait up fer no man, even if youse work for the Temporal Protection Agency an' got all the time—and timestreams—in the world.

∩

WE FOLLOWED our prize chump down two blocks and over another block to the crummy little brownstone he was rooming at.

Now, us guys in the Agency got all kinds of fancy augments embedded and gene-spliced and nano-grown and what have you inside us. Some of dese help make us stronger and faster—Maizie could benchpress Joe Louis wit'out breakin' a sweat—and others just help us get the job done, like the gizmo we got that lets us track a time traveler by them chrono-sumpthin's he gives off, him not being a native of the here-and-now.

That's not even counting all the extra augments I've picked up over the years from here-and-there-and-then that the Agency don't know I got (and I ain't telling 'em I got). If youse gonna be the A-Number One, youse gotta have a hole card, ya know?

But I didn't need all that schmanzy stuff to trail this bird. All I needed was my own eyeballs. He was wearing his fedora like he ain't never worn a hat in his life, and also he couldn't figure out hows to cross the street wit'out there being no streetlight. Even Maizie could spot him just by looking.

Still, we had a nice little stroll anyhows.

As far as 1940 New York Cities go, this was a pretty good one. No giant red Schicklgruber flags deckin' the halls, no surrendering your wallet at Henry Wallace Economic Justice checkpoints, no zeppelins filled with killer bees. Just shiny new DeSotos and Hudsons honking their way down the street, ragamuffin newsboys standing on the corner hawking their papers, and brawny construction guys wolf-whistling at Maizie as she bounced past 'em in her checkered sundress.

It was a bee-you-tee-ful Brooklyn morning that promised to turn into a warm, sunny day. The Dodgers were playing this afternoon. I was ahead on my caseload, so I got thinking me and Maizie might catch the game right after this collar. Being A-Number One does have certain advantages, and mister, that ain't hay!

So anyway, when our chump got a half block from his beige brownstone, me and Maizie sped up our pace and passed him just before he trotted up the stoop. We bustled inside, leaving him in our dust.

Now, there are good ways and bad ways to tail somebody wit'out them noticizing you. One of the best is to not be following in the first place, especially if youse know where they're going. Get there ahead of them.

We knew exactly what apartment he was headed to thanks to the lingering chrono trail he'd left schlepping up and down the stairs the past week. We started up the rickety stairwell, floorboards creaking every step of the way, all the way up to the fifth floor. And him trailing five steps behind us, getting the pepto cause on accounts of us being so slow.

Now we wasn't suspiciously following him, see? We wuz annoyingly blockin' his way ahead of him like some Sunday driver and not worth a second thought five minutes later. See the difference?

Just for certainties, I nudged Maizie in the ribs with my elbow and she went into her Distraction routine. Maizie may have a peabrain the size of a dinky .22 slug, but there ain't no finer Distracter than her when she gets going. A regular *idiot savannah* or whatevers deys call it.

She started yammering on like we was some newlywed couple checking out the sublet on an apartment like, and her complaining all the way up 'bout how she liked the other joint better on accounts it was ground floor and how she wasn't going to climb no five flights of stairs what with her being in the family way and whatnot.

Only she was describing the blessed event in terms that'd make a drunken sailor blush, all the time climbing the stairs with a wiggle in her caboose that'd be right at home on the runway of Minski's. *That's* a Maizie distraction.

Pure genius.

See, a decent guy hearin' and seein' that would be going out of his way not to look at or notice us—pretendin' we don't exist, even—and an indecent guy, why he'd be too busy admirin' Maizie's poop deck swaying on the stormy North Atlantic to wonder if he was being tailed, so to speak.

So we got to the top of the landing, takin' in all the glories of the permeating smell of boiled cabbage. Maizie then pulls out a piece of paper and starts carrying on about there not being an apartment 17-E and that she'd told me we were at the wrong address and that now she was going have to walk down all them stairs in her condition.

Our chump, he just shook his head like he's glad he's not married to her, and he dug out his keys and opened his door.

That's when I made my move.

I boosted my muscle and reflex augments up twenty percent and zoom! I'm in the doorway before he can close the door, hustling him all the way inside and slamming the door behind me. Maizie, her augments just a-humming, nips in right behind me as the door slams shut.

I swiveled my head around, aural and visual augments turned up, checking if anybody else is in the apartment. Nope. Just us and the pigeon. Good.

The apartment was as beige and plain as the rest of the building. Beige walls, beige sofa, beige oval throw rugs made out of what looked like beige horse blankets.

Our pigeon, he was beige, too. The boys down at the precinct, if they hadda write him up woulda called him 'non-descript.' Average height, average weight, average mug that went white as your average sheet when I pulled my Agency gat from under my jacket.

Maizie shoved him one-handedly across the room, sprawling him in an over-stuffed chair, beige naturally. I flipped the selector switch on my gat to blue and pull the trigger, plugging our chump dead center in the chest.

He immediately went limp, so tranked up that the only thing he can move is his bugged-out eyeballs. He manage to croak out a horse whisper "Who—?" like he was a big beige owl or sumptin'.

Like I wasn't gonna tell him why I'm there. What a chump.

I put away my gat and told Maizie, "Frisk him, then case the joint."

She patted his pockets none too delicately, coming up with a wallet and some subway tokens. She tossed me the wallet and disappeared into one of the back rooms.

I glanced through the wallet. The idiot still had his home-time Massachusetts driver license (expiration date 2018) and his ATM card tucked inside the wallet, along with a faculty ID card from M.I.T.

My achin' neck. A college professor. Thems always the hardest collars on accounts of thems being just too egghead-stupid to be sensible like a workin' stiff.

"So, Seymour...Herscher," I said, squinting at the name on the driver license. I snapped the wallet shut and tossed it on a table.

I pulled up a wooden chair in front of him and sat on it backward, resting my arms on the top of the chair back. "Youse and me, Seymour, we need to have a little talk what you're doing strollin' around 1940 New York City like you own the joint. See, I work for a little gatherin' called the Temporal Protection Agency and we make it *our* business to find out *your* business and make it *our* business, see?"

"T-t-t-t-" he stuttered. "T-temporal Protection A-agency? Like one of those secret organizations in sci-fi novels that stop people from changing history—"

"Shaddap!" I roared. "You're giving me the pepto." I pulled out a cigar from my vest pocket and struck a lucifer on the side of the chair. I puffed a couple times to get it going. Seymour coughed on the smoke like he ain't never been in a room where they smoke.

"Look, you dope," I said. "We ain't no Buck Rogers make-believe, and we ain't no good-fer-nuthin' goody-two-shoes outfit what wants to put the kibosh on whatever youse doing. We don't care. You wanna bump off Hitler, no skin off our nose. You wanna sink the *Titanic*, more power to you. We don't care."

I took a big puff and blew a smoke ring in his face. "All we wants is our cut."

"C-cut?" Seymour stammered.

"Cut," I said. "Piece of the action. Percentage."

He looked at me like I wasn't speakin' good English or something.

Professors!

I tapped cigar ashes on the threadbare throw rug. Maybe the crummy joint'd catch fire, liven things up.

"Look, Seymour. Guys what do whats you do, go back in time and change things up, no matter what scheme youse guys got, no matter how much youse guys try to dress it up with justifications like, youse guys are all just losers trying to change things up so youse winners. And youse can't go from loser to winner without what there's some sort of profit involved. Well, we want a cut of that profit, see?"

Seymour just sat there, his mouth working like an air-drowning fish.

"Fifteen percent," I said. "Firm. Just like what one of dem fancy literary agencies charge. Nobody blinks at payin' them fer doing nuthin', do they?"

Maizie came in from the back, dragging an old steamer trunk behind her. "Found this in his bedroom." The trunk had three heavy-duty Yale padlocks on it and a chrono-trail shinier than Seymour's sweating beige forehead.

She plopped the trunk on the middle of the floor and busted off the case-steel padlocks with a casual twist of a wrist. She rummaged around. "Lessee, music headphones, electrical adaptor thingie. One of them eye-plop music things." She held up a glass-screened flat oblong electronic device and dropped it.

She dug around some more. "Oh, here we go. One time travel recall switch." She set aside an electronic gizmo with flashing LED lights. Boys back at the labs would want that and Seymour wouldn't be needing anymore, that was for sure.

She looked up and shrugged. "*Pfft*. And that's it, Vincent. Nuttin' else but a useless pile of crummy books."

"Lemme see 'em," I said. I knew from past experience with them professor types, you can usually figger out what they're up to by lamping what books they lug back in time with 'em.

They was all a collection of song books from music big shots. Burt Bacharach, Jimmy Webb, Euell Gibbons. The greats. And these was all hit songs in these books and they all was from a lot later date than 1940.

I also found a couple dog-eared spiral bound notebooks of that musical writing paper my old piano teacher, she had. The notebooks was filled with hand scribbled songs with "Words and Music by Seymour Herscher" written proudly at the top of each song. I ain't no music lover but even I could see that none of Seymour's notebook songs were gonna be in any hit music book.

I busted out laughing.

"Seymour," I said, turning with a smile. "Youse and me, we're gonna get along just fine on a counts of youse being an even bigger crook than I am."

ꓕ

PROFESSOR SEYMOUR HERSCHER, it turned out—just like I guessed—when he wasn't professoring math he was busy back home at night being a jealous little song scribbler who couldn't get his lousy songs published for nuthin'. After stumbling into inventing time travel, does he go for the Nobel Prize? No, he does not.

Seymour gets the bright idea instead of grabbing all the hit music for the past sixty or so years he could carry and lamming back to 1940 so he could publish all that hit music under his own name. (He wasn't stealing, he indignified to me as he spilled his guts. How could he be stealing when he'd be publishing 'em before they got written?) And then when he was good and famous and filthy rich, he could get all those stinkeroos in them spiral notebooks published just like he always dreamed.

I laughed even harder as he explained all this.

"Relax, Seymour," I said, "I'm not laughing at you, I'm just laughing 'cause I rode this particular merry-go-round before."

I pulled out *The Complete Bottles Songbook* from amongst his little treasure trove. It was a big thick book, bigger and thicker than all the rest. "You don't really think them boneheads Lemon and McCarthy wrote all them songs themselves, do ya? I once had their whole band tranked in a chair the same way youse is sitting in yours, and them with a cardboard box full of other peoples' songs. Beach Bums, the Carpenters & Tennille, what have you."

His eyes goggled. "You don't mean that they—"

"—paid us fifteen percent, just like the deal I'm offering youse. Now, one of 'em, their first drummer, he welched on our deal like a rat. You know what happens to rats!" I drew my finger across my throat like a shiv. "*Gkkkt!*"

"I-I thought it was brain hemorrhage," he said. "The accounts all say—"

I smiled, "We know better, don't we, Maizie?" I tapped ashes off my cigar. "So what's it gonna be, Seymour? *Gkkkt*? Or are youse going to be sensible like and pay us our fifteen percent?"

"I don't know. Fifteen percent seems awfully high..."

"You're lookin' at it all wrong, Seymour. Sure, we're taking fifteen percent off the top, but we're adding so much more than what we're taking."

I held up one finger. "One. We lets you keeps breathing, like. That's always a plus. Or maybe not in your case with a phiz like what youse got."

A second finger. "Two. Now, you have what? Maybe two hundred hit songs in your stack of books? We can get you hit songs from over two hundred alternate timestreams. Big names you ain't never hoird of in your timestream an' they ain't hoird of in dis one, neither. Way we see it, the more songs you pinch, the bigger our fifteen percent is. So, do we got a deal nor not, Seymour?"

We didn't. *Professors!*

I shoulda known better. I shoulda seen it coming.

When Seymour shoulda been talking turkey, he wanted to talk about what I'd just said about 'timestreams' instead. These pigeons always get surprised like to find out they didn't go back in time in their own timestream like they thought they was doing, instead they'd shifted laterally into a parallel timestream. Only they usually don't pipe up about that until after we've sealed the deal and they'd had time to think.

Worse, Seymour didn't just take my word for it and shut up. He wanted to argue. Him in a chair all tranked up and me with a gat under my jacket.

"Look, you chowderhead," I finally said to him. "How's you gonna go back in your own timestream? Youse made up of atoms, ain'cha? Whirling electrons and them molly-whatchmacallits—"

"Molecules," Maizie supplied.

I gave her the fish eye. "I know that, you dope. That was a rhetorical whatchamacallit."

I turned back to Seymour. "You go back in time like you're thinkin', your atoms are gonna be in two places at the same time. That makes Isaac Newton very very mad, not to mention the universe. So, the universe, it boots you over to some parallel timestream and everyone's happy 'cause your atoms ain't in the same place twice no more. You can go back in time with a time machine, sure; you just can't go back in *your* time, see?"

He didn't—*professors!*—but eventually I browbeat him into signing on with the Agency and paying his protection money like a good little chump.

"Good, good," I said, taking the pen out of Seymour's half-tranked hand. I folded the signed contract and stuck it inside my jacket. "There's just one more thing to take care of before I un-trank you and leave."

My hand lingered inside my jacket.

"What's that?" he asked, not liking at all that my hand was lingering inside my jacket.

"The 'Or Else' codicil," I said.

I pulled out my gat and shot him point blank in the heart.

Seymour fainted, the big baby.

It was just a harmless shot of nanos that'd give him a cerebral hemorrhage if he tried to jump timestreams or if he didn't pay his fifteen percent like a good boy.

"C'mon, Maizie," I said. "We still got time to catch the Dodgers if you hurry your caboose."

ME, I blame it on one too many ballpark franks or maybe it was that last Coney Island dog giving me the pepto, my lettin' my guard down the way I did when I got back to the Agency. It certainly wasn't from that watered-down beer they serve at Dodgers Stadium. That stuff couldn't even get a Boy Scout drunk, let alone get me drunk.

Not like I hadn't tried after seeing in the first inning how things were going down, those magnificent bums. That new kid pitchin' for the Cardinals, that Paul Dunn, he pitched a perfect no-hitter. I actually resorted to using my augments—scanning everything from chrono to bio to X-Ray—to check out if *he* had any augments, him pitching like that, but nope. Just dumb luck, clean living, and his magic Mormon underwears. Kid that healthy oughta be off fightin' Hirohito.

So I was out-of-sorts and had the pepto and wasn't paying any attention like I shoulda when I walked into the Chief's office to report on our new client.

I'd dropped off Maizie down at the lab to turn in Seymour's recall gizmo. Me being in a bad temper, we'd gotten in an argument on the way back.

She had got to waxing philosophical again. "Say, Vincent," she asked. "You ever collar yourself in one of these other timestreams? One of your other selves, I mean?"

And that set me off. See, all the crumbs I ever meet in this racket are losers like Seymour, and I ain't no loser. I ain't never gonna be meeting some other me, on accounts them other mes are gonna be winners, too. They're me, ain't they? Sure, they might not be A-Number One Temporal Agent like I am, but whatever theyse racket is in their own timestream, they're number one at that.

So we got to yelling and arguing, and as a result she was sulking down in the lab and it was just me walking past Guido and Lenny flankin' the Chief's outer door.

Those twose an' me, we had it in for each other. Theyse was always schemin' of some way to bogart my number one spot with the Chief out from under me. Them guys is two of the reasons I got all them augments I ain't told nobody nuthin' about.

So I walked past them, them giving me the fish eye the whole way down the hall toward 'em and the door. Smirkin' like they knew something I didn't, but I was too out of it to pay much notice.

I step into the security vestibule between the outer door and the soundproof inner door. I give my special knock and step inside the office. That's when it happened. I get dropped like a rock from a trank gun shot by the guy sittin' in the Chief's chair who ain't the Chief.

As I ragdoll onto the floor, I see that the guy who ain't the Chief...is *me!*

Next thing I know, I'm trussed up in a chair like a turkey. The Chief, he's trussed up in the chair next to me, only I could plainly see from the bruises and blood on his face, he's been given the workover, and I didn't like the way his head was slumping like that none.

So I turned my attention to the other me sitting in the Chief's chair instead.

He's looking at me the way I'd look at a Seymour, clucking his tongue, and trimming the end of one of the Chief's *primo* cigars.

"Disappointed in you, Vincent," he said as he lit the cigar. "Never figgered one of you other mes would be such a sad sack. Just lookin' at you gives me the pepto."

It must have been the trank talking, cause I blurted out "Who—?" just like a Seymour.

"I'm you," he said, puffing away on the cigar. "I'm doing the same thing youse do, only you're retail, I'm wholesale. See, I don't handle that nickel and dime stuff you do. I don't go around putting the business on music writers and Hitler killers. Naw, I leave that up to chumps like you. What I do is put the business on *agencies* like you. Fifteen percent of your fifteen percent. And 'Or Else' nanos to make you behave like a good boy."

He took the cigar out of his mouth and examined it. "An' another difference between you and me: I don't hide behind some clay pigeon Chief and act like he runs the whole show and not me, shadow puppetin' him alls the time. That's what losers do. Winners run their own show." He hooked his thumb at the Chief.

"I had one of them when I started my first day in my Agency. Next day I was Chief and Jersey had some new landfill."

He stubbed out the cigar and started reaching under his jacket. "I figger your Jersey could use more landfill, too." He looked at the Chief, then looked at me. "Maybe even a double donation. See, I figger if I were you and you are, I'd be a bit too dangerous to leave around as a loose end, even shot full of 'Or Elses.' Your versions of Lenny and Guido outside were more than happy to agree to take over this chicken feed operation and run it for me once I told them I'd firmly ensconce you in a Jersey dirt mattress."

I tried struggling against my bonds, but the other me just laughed.

"Jitterbug all you want," he gloated. "I dialed up a special trank just for you and your augments." That's when I noticed that on the Chief's desk, along with my gat he's got a manila folder with my Agency files open in front of him on the desk. He'd countered them all with that special trank. No wonder I felt weak as a kitten.

He made a big show of looking at his watch.

"Time's up," he laughed.

His hand pulled his gat all the way out of his jacket. It looked exactly like mine only the trigger was a lot more worn, which didn't cheer me up none. This guy meant business.

"Too bad youse was so small-time and never learned to work wholesale. You coulda been where I'm sittin'." He cocked back the hammer. "*Arrivederci*, loser."

Maizie picked that exact moment to burst into her daddy's office, bless her heart, crying all the way through the door about what a jerk I'd been. The other me took his eyes off me to take in the US Navy for just a second, but a second was all I needed.

Didn't I say she was the best Distracter in the business?

I fired up my special augments, the ones neither my file nor that other me knew I had, the ones that weren't completely tranked. I burst those heavy ropes holding me like they wasn't nothing but tissue paper in a flophouse outhouse and leapt across the room before the other me could swivel his eyes back my direction.

Mid-leap I snatch up my gat and take care of him quick like. And by take care, I don't mean none of that sissy nano nonsense neither. I mean the Valentine's Day in Chicago kind of take care.

Maizie was a little slow on the uptake, her having only Agency augments and all. "What—?" she seymoured. "Who—?"

Then she saw the rictused face of the other me bleedin' all over the carpet. "Say, Vince, honey. He looks like you!" She peered closer. "He *is* a you!"

"Naw," I said, holstering my gat. "Just some loser wearing my face. I ain't never been a loser, have I?" I kicked the nearest foot of the dead carcass. "An' in answer to your previous question, I still ain't never met another me, present corpse included."

That's when Maize saw her father. "Oh, Daddy," she scolded, "You got beaten up and captured *again!*" She wet the tip of her hanky with her tongue and started dabbing at his bruises.

She gave me the fish eye. "Vince, honey, it don't seem right you letting daddy take your Chief lumps all the time. He don't know nuttin' about being no Chief. He needs to be down in Florida playing bingo and the ponies."

"Yeah, yeah," I mumbled like I was listenin' to her yammerings.

I kicked the expensive Italian shoe on my double again, stared at it for a minute, then started to laugh.

Maizie looked up from fussing with her father and glared. "Something funny wit' the way I talk or something?"

"Naw, Maizie," I said, smiling. "Just suddenly waxin' philosophical on the job. Think it's time to maybe start getting the pepto about who's president and such like."

ᴧ

It was my forty-fourth collar this month, and my last.

My last ever, I mean.

I had eased the Chief into retirement. It wasn't right to keep using him as a clay duck, and besides, I had to give up field work. Things were too busy with our new business model for me to play agent anymore. Only reason I was on this last collar was to run this trainee through an easy case to show him how it's done.

That other me had been right, the sonuvagun. I'd been chasing chicken feed with my agency instead of following the money.

The big money.

Maizie wasn't doing field work, neither. She was busy, too, knitting little booties for Vincent Junior and the stork. She yammers at home as much as I thought she would, but since a) being the Chief now, I can do something about that if I want to, and b) I kinda realized I'd gotten used to it. Go figure.

Anyways that's beside the point. It's my last collar, see, and I'm sitting in the Oval Office and the chump I got sitting tranked is behind the Resolute Desk—only here it's the Redoubtable Desk—and he's giving me the pepto.

He was doing the same drowning fish act as Seymour. At least this chump wasn't so beige.

New presidents just sworn in, see, they're easy collars on accounts of them always having the pepto up about Their Place In The History Books. Plus, this particular chump was from Chicago, so he oughta know how the rules go down.

Instead, he was arguing like a professor and trying to welch out on forking over his Initial Membership Fee—and him with the confetti from his inauguration still in his hair yet.

"—but I can't just hand over one-point-six trillion dollars to you. The public—"

"The public don't signify," I said. "'Specially not if they get their own cut of the action. Like I showed you, we got it all worked out for you."

I hooked a thumb at the holographic display I'd showed him of dozens of other timelines under our new business model.

He didn't doubt what I'd showed him was real, not with every Secret Service agent in the joint floating midair, time-froze in a glittery glob of chronoflux. He just didn't like being on the receiving end of the Chicago Way was all.

I sighed and went through it again, tryin' to remember them elocution lessons Maizie made me take so I sounded more Chief-like. "Look, you dress it up as a 'Stimulus Package.' Dribs and drabs here, dribs and drabs there. Make it hard to track down where it all went: like pork for non-existent Congressional Districts; overseas loans ta China maybe; phoney-baloney companies that don't actually make nothin'—solar power maybe. Nobody knows nuthin', nobody can trace nuthin', nobody squawks nuthin'. Just follow the script like we wrote down for you."

"But fifteen percent of federal outlays on top of that—!"

"Who cares? Not like it's *your* money, right? Don't go waxin' philosophical on the job. It ain't healthy."

I don't know from philosophical, but he started to wax all petulant and glowery.

I don't let chumps give me the fish eye, so I lowered the boom. Showed him with the holo what we could really do if he didn't play ball, showed him how we could easily change things up if we was a mind to so that what's-her-name wins his election instead.

That did the trick, you betchum. The Baked Alaska look on his face was priceless.

He reached for the pen.

"After all, Mr. President," I said, as my trainee scooped up the signed contract. "Nice presidency youse got here. Be a real shame if anythin' wuz to happen to it..."

SUPPOSE THEY GAVE A RAGNAROK AND NOBODY CAME?

INTRODUCTION

"Suppose They Gave a Ragnarok and Nobody Came?" originally appeared in the Fiction River: Last Stand anthology, and therein lies a tale.

In sitting down to plan how to approach the assignment, I figured that nothing could be more last stand-y than Ragnarok. I mean, Ragnarok is the Groundhog Day of last stands.

I also figured that everybody else and their little dog Toto would be submitting deathly serious do-or-die pieces. What nobody in their right mind would be writing was a comedy piece.

Sometimes you need a little change-up pitch to get the ball over the editor's plate. Like an old, wise Chicagoan once said: they pull a knife, you pull a gun; they pull a gun, you pull a banana cream pie. Pow! Right in the kisser.

Seriously(?!), though—underneath all the bad puns, wordplay, linguistic hijinks, mythological mayhem, and microwave pork rinds, there's actually a solid story. Enough so that readers later voted "Ragnarok" into Fiction River's Reader's Choice reprint anthology.

So yes, I've been paid twice for this nonsense. Three times now if you count this Heimdall—I mean Hemelein—collection. Who says crime doesn't pay?

Speaking of paying, "Ragnarok" let me pay a tangential tribute to both my family's Sanpete County heritage (Spring City was originally called Allred's Settlement), as well as to that beat-up copy of the Larousse Encyclopedia of Mythology I used to lug *around everywhere as a kid, even on camping trips. I think there's still a trace scent of s'mores stuck to its battered pages.*

I had a lot of fun writing this story; I hope you have even more fun reading it, even if it is a rainbow bridge too far.

W hen this whole Ragnarok thing started, the fact that I was punching down Cat 6 cables into a Leviton 48-port patch panel with my Klien punch down tool doesn't matter.

Nor does it matter that I was pulling all-nighters over the weekend because Corporate had decided to expand our office and lease the empty floor above us and now needed the Voice Over IP premise wiring in place by next Monday so the new hires would have phone and Internet.

The only thing that really matters in telling how this Ragnarok all got started is that I was standing behind the seven-foot-tall Ortronics server rack with my face and hands hidden from view and only visible from the waist down when the stranger walked in. He saw my legs and feet, so he knew I was in the room, but he couldn't see me, if you know what I mean, which you will in a minute.

I didn't hear him step into the comm room. I was busy silently cursing the chicken scratches on my scrawled cut sheet and didn't hear him enter.

But boy, did I smell him!

He walked in and a cloud of funk saturated the room. He smelt like he hadn't bathed since Moses was a little pharaoh.

Look, this is San Francisco where seemingly half the population is homeless and the other half Nob Hill *bitterati* who think that bar soap and modern flush toilets are evil cis-normative patriarchal oppression, and, look, Electric Yggdrasil is a game software company and dress codes and personal hygiene standards for programmers is, well, a little lax even for Silicon Valley, but *Geez Louise!* That guy stank!

So I therefore wasn't totally oblivious to him when he walked in, cleared his throat, and said: "You are Thor Thorsen, yes."

He had a Danish accent even thicker than his funk of stunk.

I should know. Both my folks were first-generation Danish-Americans. Thanksgivings and Christmases with both sides of the grandparentage present tend to sound like Copenhagen on a Saturday night.

As for the other three hundred and sixty-three days of the year, well, our family lived in Ephraim, Utah, which only has two claims to fame.

First, it's the turkey farm capital of the nation. If you've ever eaten a turkey on Thanksgiving, unless it was some localvore free-range tom, odds are about 99 to 1 that you ate an Ephraim bird.

Second, Brigham Young colonized Ephraim nearly exclusively with Danish Mormon converts (along with a few Swedes and Norwegians thrown in in a vain attempt to civilize them). Even today, kids in Ephraim grow up pronouncing their gerunds as "-ingk" and generally sounding like a roadshow production of *Fargo*. Took me years and a hitch in the Air Force to scrub my accent.

So the way this stranger said it, it came out "You are T'or T'orsen, ja."

And I said, without looking around the patch panel, "I am Thor Thorsen, yes."

And he said. "I am god Tyr, sent to find you. Only toget'er can we save Yggdrasil and stop Ragnarok."

Stupid Corporate and their hiring binges! In this economy, all the crazies come running.

"Look, buddy, I'm sure "Godtear" looks great as a forum handle and all—I didn't know gods cried, BTW—and I'm happy you want to save Yggdrasil, but a) the company doesn't need saving; and b) contrary to LinkedIn, I don't do the hiring around here anymore. Human Resources does. Go see them. On Monday. Nobody here on weekends but me." Well, me and a few programmers playing games.

Funk Stunk wasn't buying any. He just plowed right ahead. "Yggdrasil not needingk resourceful humans, Yggdrasil needingk Aesir warrior-gods. Me and you."

"Look," I snapped, "I appreciate you classifying me as a fellow gamer-god, but I wouldn't mention Acer computers when you go see HR if I were you. Our HR person just came from Acer. Let's just say she wasn't a good corporate match over there." She wasn't much of a match here, either, to tell the truth, but I'd let him find that out on his own.

Funk Stunk started to get his little Danish up. "You are Thor Thorsen," he said testily. (I'm going to stop writing down his accent; I'm sure you can fill it in yourself.) "I am having right person. You are seventh son of seventh son, all the way back to Vikings, yes?"

This was starting to get a little creepy. Looking me up on LinkedIn is one thing; combing some online genealogy site for my family history is quite another. I started getting my little Danish up, too.

I dropped my cable and came out from behind the server rack fists bunched, and ready for action, Jackson. If this guy wanted god tears, I'll make him cry, *ja*.

As I walked out, we both got an eyeful of each other, and neither one was what the other expected.

Him, he was well over six feet. Barrel-chested. Arms to match. Bandy little legs, though. All in the upper body, like a blacksmith. This Godtear could have been my body double as far as our shapes went, only unlike me, he looked like he really did work out in the gym. With me, it's all pure genetics. I don't have much time for the gym. I'm sure somewhere between forty and fifty all this body mass of mine will move from the shoulders and arms to my waistline.

But it wasn't his physique that surprised me. He'd really gone whole hog on this Godtear forum handle persona: he was dressed head to toe in old, mangy furs, like an ancient Viking come to life.

Not only was he wearing enough furs to give PETA the vapors, most of them still had body parts attached! Legs, feet, tails. Worst of all was the fur hood he wore pulled up over his greasy, braided blond hair: a complete wolf head, right down to the taxidermied eyes and mouth. Only he must have rigged up the eyes with servomotors or something because the eyes swiveled like it was looking at you and the tongue lolled, too, and I'm not talking LOLed.

And that axe he carried! Fifty pounds of razor-sharp pig iron. Definitely no movie prop. This thing would chop trees as easily as it'd chop necks.

Whatever this Godtear was, he wasn't any game forum personality. Or employment seeking programmer. My fists unbunched real fast and I suddenly wished I hadn't left my phone behind the rack so I could call 911.

Or maybe the National Guard.

Or maybe even the Super Friends.

Be that as it may, though, I imagine my appearance surprised him even more than his did me.

I get that a lot.

Yes, my name is Thor Thorsen, and I talk over the phone with a faint Danish accent, and I'm the seventh son of a seventh son etc., but my mom only gave birth to six kids.

I was adopted.

From Mali.

Let's just say I'm a Norse of a different color.

He looked at me and blinked. Then he relooked at me and reblinked. Then he asked again, "You *are* Thor Thorsen, yes?"

"Thor Thorsen, yes."

"Holy smoke!" he exclaimed, only in Danish so it came out " høly smøkeh" even though it's spelt the same in Danish as it is in English (look it up).

He reached under his fur tunic with his non-axe hand and came up with a ball of spun brass wire of curious workmanship. He pointed it at me. I expected some death ray or something, but nothing happened except the wind chime sound of crystals tinkling against each other.

He got a puzzled look on his face. "No, yoost like I thot. It point to you. No mistake, you bet. You Thor Thorsen I look for, but not Thor Thorsen what I expect."

"I'm adopted," I said helpfully. Make the nice axe man happy, Thor. Maybe he'll go away.

He slipped the brass globe back under his tunic and pulled out a stone tablet carved in enough Old Norse runes to be in a Tolkien movie. He squinted at it the way I had my cut sheet.

"Hmm. Nothing *ja* or *nej* about adoption in legends."

How about showering? I thought to myself. *Anything in there about that?*

But of course I didn't say that. Not to a guy with an axe.

Godtear put back the tablet. "Thor Thorsen. You are different from others."

No duh, Sherlock. This was San Francisco. Try parking a pickup with military vet plates and faded and peeling Romney stickers in your Marin County driveway and see what the neighbors say. Let alone *you know*. The whole melatonin thing.

"You not believing Tyr, you bet," he said. "I show you, *ja*."

Tear-boy suddenly dropped his axe and literally pounced on me. He grabbed my right forearm hard with both his hands, gripped tight, and pulled in opposite directions.

My skin split—painlessly, much to my surprise!—and there beneath my mortal melatoninated epidermis—even more to my surprise!—shone the divine glow of an immortal god of Aesir.

"See? You really god. You god Thor."

Sunuvodin, so I was. I must be. I gulped.

He let go of my skin and it smoothed back into shape, covering the glow.

I looked at him with new eyes. "Who'd you say you were—?"

"Tyr."

Of course! Tyr. T-y-r, not "tear" as in baby crying.

Stupid English and its homophones!

I gulped again, "So, when you said the two of us have to save Yggdrasil, you didn't mean the company—"

"Company of what?"

"Never mind," I said. I felt like sitting down.

Me. Thor. Pagan god of thunder.

They were going to love this in my Sunday School class.

And Ragnarok.

I didn't like the sound of that.

From what little I knew of Norse Mythology, and I didn't know too much—in the entertainment biz, you don't go very deep into mythological source material, just strip mine it for game ideas—Ragnarok wasn't a very pleasant event at all.

A losing battle one could never win.

Still, I believed Tyr's crazy tale, what with my glowy underskin and all.

I pulled us both up a chair. "So, uh, Ragnarok. What's the scoop, Skip?"

He gave the frail plastic and chrome ergonomic chair the stink-eye, but sat on it.

He then gave me the stink-eye. "Odd you not remember all now that you know you are god Thor." He shrugged. "Vell, it being coming later, I sure. Mostly likely slow because of new plan."

He cleared his throat and began half-reciting, half-chanting the legend of Ragnarok like he was barded at some ancient evening campfire.

"Ragnarok. Twilight of Gods. Cycle Never-ending," he intoned. "Aesir ever-destined to fight, ever destined to lose. World ends. World reforms. Fight again. Over and over. Second verse, being same as first."

"Doesn't sound very fun."

"Is *not* being fun, yes." He stroked his blond, braided, stinky beard. "That is why this time Odin decided enough is being enough. *This* time we not let Ragnarok happen, not then have to be fighting it."

"Sounds like a plan."

"Of course is plan. Odin plan. He fix it so I awake early. I then find you. Then together we be stopping cause of Ragnarok: death of most handsome god Baldur by mistletoe."

I definitely didn't remember any of this. Where was a copy of Bullfinch when you needed it? "*Mistletoe?* What, Mr. Handsome gets kissed to death under it at a Christmas party?"

Tyr's eyes narrowed. "He being kissed alright, by golly! Kissed by arrow of mistletoe sprig. All fault of Loki Trickster."

Well, at least I knew about Loki. The superhero movie glut is good for something.

"This time we get to Baldur in his mortal guise before he awakens. Before *Loki* awakens. Hide Baldur away. No death, no Ragnarok."

I shrugged. Sounded logical. If I was going to have to do this whole Thor thing anyway, much better this than fighting a losing last stand.

Plus, if we found this Baldur god quickly then I could get back here in time to do the cutover Monday morning when the new LAN cables went live.

I stood up. "So how do we find this Baldur guy, anyway?" I doubted Norse Gods show up on Google Map street view.

Tyr got to his feet, too. He pulled out that brass ball globe thingie again. "Same way I find you. With this."

He handed the whatzit to me.

The spun-brass globe was lightweight and hollow, about the size of a grape-fruit. Inside were two crystal spindles that moved on their own. They floated in the air, tinkling like a wind chimes. "So, uh, how does this work?"

"Be thinking in mind, 'Baldur, Baldur.' Spindles then point way. You will know where. You will *feel* where. Now Baldur, most fair of Aesir, most handsome of Aesir, most all-time-record-of-being-murdered-every-Ragnarok-cycle Aesir."

I concentrated and sure enough, the spindles moved and pointed. I felt, I knew exactly where they were pointing.

"Cool," I said. "So what's this finder pointy thing called, anyway? I don't remember it from Norse mythology."

Tyr hung his head in shame. "Not Norse. Odin plan very spur of moment. No time to fashion Norse compass. We be borrowing from other pantheon. It called a Liahona."

I looked again at where it pointed. "Well, it's more a Liar-hona, 'cause it's pointing to somewhere in this very building and that can't possibly be true."

The only people in the building beside Tyr and me were some of the programmers over in their warren of cubicles playing computer games.

And none of them remotely matched the description of most fair, most handsome anything, let alone an Aesir god.

We're talking programmers, after all.

TYR WOULDN'T TAKE impossible for an answer, though. "Am impossible you being blond Thor, *ja*? So. Baldur possible here then, too."

So the both of us headed over to the programmer's area of our cube farm, me rechecking the Liahona every step of the way.

As we approached I could hear the *tik-tikka* of keyboard keys and nerd-rage trash talk. I knew those voices.

The Three Stooges, just like I'd thought.

The Three Stooges were our three lead game coders. In fact, they were my first three hires back when I started up Electric Yggdrasil (I should have never sold the company to some conglomerate!).

One of them the handsome god, Baldur?

Don't make me laugh.

Mix-and-match any two out of three stereotypical physical characteristic of a computer nerd, then throw in advanced cases of early male pattern baldness, and you had the Three Stooges.

The Stooges were playing our own online MMO game, *MechaVikings* where you pilot giant Japanese manga-ish robots in combat between skyscrapers in the great cities around the world. A fun game if I do say so myself. Maybe not as big as *War of Worldcraft* or as revered as *Heroic City: Capes and Masks*, but it's a good game and we make a decent chunk of change, enough so that we were staffing up for our huge new expansion release, hence my current wiring chore.

The true test of whether a game's good or not is if the developers play their own game as avidly as customers, and ours did. Shucks, I played myself on weekends when I wasn't pulling all-nighters to sling Cat 6 cable.

The Liahona guided me to the Second of the Stooges. George, his first name was.

I suddenly got a sick feeling in the pit of my stomach.

Me and the old crew were the only ones who referred to them as the Stooges. The newer Yggdrasil employees brought in after the corporate buyout referred to the trio by the various stages of the three's receding hairlines: Bald, Balder, and Baldest.

Balder.

Baldur.

And Balder was getting his butt kicked in-game.

Tyr must have sensed my unease. "Not to be worrying. No mistletoe for leagues and leagues. I make sure you bet. We are in time. We beat Loki here."

And then I heard the bone-chilling laugh of a fourth programmer, smelt the Old Spice, and knew we were not in time after all.

Brantley T. Stokey III, the fourth programmer. Recent hire. A real Eddie Haskell type. The higher ups loved him. Around them, butter wouldn't melt in his mouth.

But around the rest of us, particularly the original Yggdrasil "Keen Fourteen" crew, well...he backstabbed us early and often. In the military we'd call somebody like him a Blue Falcon.

The higher ups, though, had their own name for him because of his fake no-hassle, no-fuss demeanor: "Low Key" Stokey.

Loki.

We were too late.

With a cry of triumph, Stokey launched a sudden in-game attack on poor Balder.

I watched helpless as the computer monitors showed his giant robot lift its right foot and point it at Balder, launching a deadly point black fusillade of boot rockets.

Balder's robot character "died" instantly.

Killed by a missile-toe.

Loki stood up in his cubicle and cackled. "See you on the Field of Vigrid, suckers!" He vanished in a puff of brimstone, ozone, and Old Spice.

Ragnarok was on!

Loki had murdered what Tyr called the "seeded essence" of Baldur's true Aesir form when he struck down Balder in-game.

But more than that. At the same moment Balder's defeated robot died, Balder's physical body vanished as well.

Baldur's mortal guise, the flesh-and-blood I knew as George, had only been a disposable shell, merely a tin-foil wrapper on a stick of gum.

If George had never really been real, then what did that make me?

Was I, too, not real?

When the Aesir essence of Thor finally fully awakened inside me, would what I knew as Thor Thorsen be as casually thrown away as well?

I jerked myself back from that mental abyss.

That was not a path to go down. First things first. Like how I was going to win the unbeatable Ragnarok.

Or how I was going to explain George's sudden disappearance to Corporate, not to mention the police.

I then looked back at George's cubicle. Completely empty. So was Stokey's. As if both had never existed.

The remaining Two Stooges kept playing *MechaViking* as if nothing had ever happened. When I asked them about George, they looked at me like I had two heads. "George who?"

Tyr placed a meaty hand on my shoulder. "Is magicks of Aesir," he said as if that explained it. "Do not be worrying about the milk what is spilt. Must instead be girding for battle."

Tyr's belly rumbled.

"And also must be eating roast boar and making the plans," he said. "Odin plan be laying the egg like a Swedish hen. He make mistake but maybe Loki, he make one too, you bet."

Another belly rumble.

"But first, friend Thor take Tyr to nearest spit where boar is being roasted, *ja?*"

We headed for the employee break room and the closest roast boar I could think of.

Sitting in the break room, I had a wild idea. What if...what if I went back and undid Baldur's death on the game server itself? Do a little retroactive GMing. Would that bring him back to life? Bring back George, too?

I tossed the idea out immediately. MMO online games aren't like home computer games where you can save a point in time and go back and redo things. MMOs are real-time games.

Sure, GMs—"Game Master" in-game customer service reps—might restore game items lost by a computer glitch, but something so raw as to reverse an outcome of a non-glitched battle between two players—Loki hadn't even cheated or used a god-mode exploit or anything, it'd been an honest pwning of Baldur—if word leaked out, the person doing it, even the game's creator, would get the banhammer for sure. Banhammered from the game, the fan base, the game industry itself.

Besides, how could I change the results of George's fight if any trace of George no longer existed?

Like I said, wild idea. And a useless one.

Ideas like that needed the banhammer themselves!

I sighed and drowned my sorrows in a can of Fresca from the vending machine.

Tyr, on the other hand, was busy experiencing for the first time the joys and smells and tastes of microwave pork rinds, complete with monosodium glutamate, maltodextrin, and plain old garden-variety dextrin.

He thought they were the best thing since willing Valkyrie maidens.

I didn't mind him eating and enjoying them so much, to each their own but feeding pieces to the living wolf-head was an entirely different matter.

In a more perfect world, hats would not eat junk food.

Several microwavings later, Tyr looked glumly at all the empty pork rind wrappers piled in front of him, all the vending machine had had. End of the roast boar phase of our plan.

Now what?

"So," I said.

"So. We gather up what Aesir we can, and fight anyway."

"Even though we're foreordained to lose?"

He stood up. "The sooner we lose, the sooner we can try Odin's crazy plan again next time."

I tossed the Fresca can into the recycle bin.

"Great," I muttered. "In other words, your entire plan is straight out of an old movie: we're on a mission from the Gods to put the band back together."

Only unlike some movie, I didn't think this former orphan was going to save the day.

Not when that day was named Ragnarok.

RIGHT FROM THE start we were behind the Nordic eight-ball in our search.

Our big gun, Odin, my supposed true pappy (one I still could not remember) was not one of the "seeded essences" this go-around.

We had to make do instead with his two sidekicks, the crows Hugin and Munin, the avatars of thought and memory.

The way things had been going, I half-expected Hugin and Munin's mortal guises to be Native Americans of the Crow tribe or something, but they turned out to be regular wing-and-feather bird-type crows. In fact, they didn't even have a mortal guise, they were just their usual Aesir selves, hiding in plain sight, posing as mortals crows chowing down on bread crusts in some small indie book publisher's parking lot when we found them.

Pro tip: when talking to Aesir crows, never refer to them as Heckyl and Jeckyl. Crows peck.

Anyway, when we pulled up to the parking lot the Liahona pointed us to, Hugin and Munin flew into my truck cab and parked atop the dashboard.

"So," Hugin (Thought) cawed. "You tried old Odin's cockamamie plan and came up a cropper."

"I told the old fool it'd never work," Munin (Memory) added. He preened some chest feathers. "We had a perfectly good plan, but did Odin want to use it?"

"I gather he didn't," I answered.

"'Odin All-Father, not crows,'" Munin mimicked. "'Odin be havingk the plans. Crows not be havingk the plans.'"

Hugin looked me up and down, then turned to my stout stinky companion. "Hmm. Tyr—why is this mortal still mortal?"

Tyr shrugged. "God Thor not wake up yet. I be peeling back the skin and everything—peek-a-boo, Aesir is you—but his essence still be not waking."

Munin cocked his head, crow fashion. "Might work better in our favor at that. God Thor isn't the sharpest hammer in the shed, if you remember."

Hugin looked me over some more. "So, mortal—you don't seem too freaked out about talking crows."

"Well," I said with a shrug. "Corvids are pretty smart, after all."

Smartest birds there are. Brighter than cats, maybe as bright as dogs. We're talking cocker spaniel-bright. Why, just normal crows, ravens, magpies and the rest of the *Corvidae* family can be trained to talk like parrots. And they can think, too. They can puzzle out tool use on their own to open up food—nuts and things —and their back toes essentially have the grip of opposable thumbs.

They can talk, think, and thumb. If they ever form a union, mankind is doomed.

"What makes you think we haven't?" Hugin mind-read me. "We're in the very process now of forming the International Order of Crows, Ravens, Rooks, Blackbirds, Magpies, Jackdaws and Other Fell Birds—or IOCRRBMJOFB for short. We're localing every murder of crows, train of jackdaws, parliament of rooks, unkindness of ravens, pie of blackbirds, and tidings of magpies in Vahalla."

Munin dipped up and down in a nod. "We're fed up with being Odin's flunkies and saving his bacon."

"Fed up? Bacon?" Tyr asked, perking up hopefully.

"Look," I said, rather exasperated. "Back on track, okay? Ragnarok. What can we do?"

Munin gave a little wing-shrug. "Not much at this point. A ragnarok's gotta ragnaroll. Now if we'd been following *our* plan instead of Odin's—"

"And your plan was?"

"Instead of futilely trying to protect Baldur, do unto Loki first. Kill him before he kills Baldur."

Yikes. "Kind of bloodthirsty," I said.

Hugin laughed. "Why do you think we're called a *murder* of crows?"

I drummed my fingers on the dashboard. "Well, Loki's already flown the coop for someplace called Vigrid, so we're too late for that, too. What would your Plan B be, assuming we'd been following your Plan A? Who's the big bad second banana of Ragnarok?"

"They're all pretty nasty, but I'd have to say Fenris," Munin said. "Giant wolf that chases after the sun, eventually catching it and devouring it."

Tyr scowled. "Stupid Fenris wolf. Always giant evil wolfie be biting my hand off in Ragnarok battle. My good hand axe, too. My right one. I be liking my right hand. Does he be biting off my *mærkværdige* left hand? No he be not!"

Fenris wolf. Wolf. Why did that name sound so familiar? Was I getting back my god Thor memories, maybe?

Tyr was still going on about his hand. "Aesir not like you pampered mortals, not-yet-awake-Thor. Not be inventing the toilet paper." He waggled his left hand. "For that we be using—"

"TMI, Tyr," I said, cutting him off myself, if you'll pardon the expression.

Then I snapped my finger.

Fenris the Wolf! Of course! *Fenner* T. Wolfe, the solar power industrialist millionaire-inventor.

Wolfe was the Elon Musk-Bill Gates-Steve Jobs of renewable energy.

Only evil.

His big project at the moment was chasing after fusion energy—the power of the sun. Only he didn't want to develop it, oh no. He wanted to stop research on it, destroy it. Cheap, workable fusion power would put the kibosh on his solar panel scheme.

I knew just where to find him. Everybody in the Bay Area did.

I didn't need a Liahona. His big Marin County mansion lay on the other side of the bay, across the Golden Gate bridge.

I started up the truck.

"Hang on, crows," I said. "We're going Wolfe hunting."

WE PARKED in front of his big security gate.

I was somewhat at a loss on just exactly what to do next. Unlike Mr. Stinky Fur seated beside me, I wasn't a head-chopping barbarian. At least, not yet. Not until that other Thor's memories overwrote mine and *he* took over.

Tyr had ideas, though. He smiled and ran his finger lovingly over the rim of his axe blade. "Now I chop off doggie's paw and be seeing how he likes those lumps, *ja?*"

I eyed the stout gates again, and their state-of-the-art security camera system. "Careful, big guy. Mortal shell or not, you mess with this Wolfe and you'll get your hand lopped off here on Earth, too. You may have an axe, but he has lawyers."

I turned to Hugin. He was the most likely to have an idea of what to do now. Munin was great at things in the past. Things now? Meh, not so much. "Any bright ideas floating around in that corvid brain of yours?" I asked.

"Let's try tapping, rap-tap-tapping. Ring the bell and nothing more."

Smart crows are one thing. Smart aleck crows, however...

Before I could say anything, Munin flew over to the gate post and pecked the call button with his blunt black beak.

"Ah, my good Munin," a sepulchral voice intoned over the speaker. "Sssso very nicssse to sssee you and your friends."

"Nighogg!" Hugin cawed. He flapped his wings and feathers flew.

"I'm afraid friend Fenrissss hassss already left for Vigrid. Jusssst missed him. Only me in the houssssse, I'm afraid. I'm about to leave, too, to have a little ssss-nack. Care to join me? Yggdrassil bark soup is jussst sssso tasssssty."

Tyr bailed out of the pickup in a flash and shook his axe at the speakerphone. "Foul worm! I be whumping on your head this time, you bet! You'll not be gnawing Yggdrasil world-tree down this cycle!"

The snake only hissed with laughter and cut off the speaker.

I grabbed the Liahona. It showed that the giant snake, too, had vanished from Wolf's house.

The spindles spun and pointed a new direction. Next stop, the field of Vigrid. The battle of Ragnarok had begun.

I EXPECTED Hugin and Munin to use Aesir magic power or something to transport us to this Vigrid field place. Instead they just cawed at me to put the pickup in gear and drive.

I drove.

Even from Marin County I could see the mythical Yggdrasil world tree growing out of the San Francisco.

Location? Vigrid, venue for the big battle, was the fifty-yard line in Candlestick Park.

This time, Ragnarok would be local.

I pulled into the parking lot and we hurried into the stadium.

The scoreboard had us listed. We Aesir were visitors. The Jotunn, the forces of evil, were Home Team.

Well, it's San Francisco, after all.

The good news was that Odin's plan must have caught the bad guys flat-footed. They hadn't pre-seeded many Jotunn essences, either. They had only Loki, Fenris, Nighogg, and a garden variety assortment of giants.

Also, like me not yet awaking to my god Thor self, much of the Jotunn's powers were mere mortals. Loki may have been his usual God of Lies and Nighogg his usual scaly god-self, but Fenner Wolf was just a crooked executive in a tailored suit. And all those Jotunn frost and fire giants? Just Giants.

San Francisco Giants.

Mortal baseball players. Hundreds of them, maybe, but still just mortal.

Of course they had all baseball bats. And murder in their eyes.

On the other hand, the bad news was we Aesir only had the crew that had driven over in my pickup truck. A pork-rind eating god, a mortal, and two crows great at thinking and remembering and pecking, but fighting not so much.

We faced a hideous tree-eating giant serpent, God of Lies, Mr. Wolfe, and a bullpen of burly ballplayers.

And me without Thor's hammer.

Or even a spear and magic helmet.

Again, as I had over and over in this whole misbegotten adventure, I asked, "What do we do now?"

"Kill the bad guys. Prevent the snake from eating the World Tree," Hugin said.

"Protect hand," Tyr said.

"Remember Pearl Harbor!" Munin crowed.

"You guys are a lot of help," I said.

It was up to me, the mortal, to come up with the plan to save the day.

I thought frantically.

The ultimate goal was protecting the Yggdrasil world tree.

I could relate to that. That was something I did every day in my mortal guise, why I hung around my Yggdrasil after the conglomerate bought it, even if that meant doing manual labor on weekends instead of sitting with the rest of the VPs in the boardroom.

Maybe that was the key. Maybe that was why I was still Thor Thorson, not Thor God of Thunder.

Protect Yggdrasil.

Nighogg was already slithering toward it.

It was a stupefyingly gorgeous entity, this World Tree. Golden branching boughs reached high into the sky. Silver branching roots tunneled deep into the earth.

It almost looked like a computer network diagram.

Naw, it couldn't be.

Maybe it could.

"Hugin, Munin! I need an interface for Yggdrasil. Keyboard, tablet screen, anything."

Tyr scowled at me. "This is being no time for your mortal playthings! Pick up a hammer and fight!"

"That's just what I'm doing," I said. "Hugin, Munin. *Now!*"

The crows *were* pretty smart. They saw what I was thinking and conjured up a mortal server terminal, Acer brand, of course. Keyboard and flatscreen monitor.

A login screen appeared

User name. Password.

The only perk I still had at Electric Yggdrasil was that I still had my old master administrative privileges for the *MechViking* live game servers.

I typed those in.

Welcome to Yggdrasil, the screen emblazoned. *Hello, World Tree.*

I opened the administrative menu and found what I was looking for.

I looked up from the screen and smiled.

"Hey, Nighogg!" I yelled.

The giant snake looked up from the mouthful of Yggdrasil bark it was chewing.

"Bye, bye, snakey!" I yelled.

I stabbed the "Ban User" button and slammed Thor Thorsen's all-powerful banhammer down on username "Nighogg."

The snake—followed quickly by the rest of the Jotunn team—vanished like poor George.

ᚾ

THERE ISN'T much to tell after that.

We'd won Ragnarok for the first time ever.

Tyr and the crows headed back for the true realms of the gods and some much deserved rest and relaxation. I at least got to say goodbye to them before they left. I even took Tyr over to Sam's Club to pick up a couple cases of microwave pork rinds first.

As for me, I went back to my normal everyday mortal life. I never did awaken to god Thor, and I hope I never will. I like being just Thor Thorsen—melatonin, Danish accent, all-nighter stints and all.

But every once in a while, usually during some stupid staff meeting with those idiots from Corporate, I'm tempted to peel back my skin and let the magic banhammer fly.

PIRATE GOLD FOR BROTHER BRIGHAM

INTRODUCTION

Back in the '90s when I was first trying to break in professionally, I was part of a Provo-based writing group called Xenobia. We met every Saturday evening to critique a story one of us had passed out the week before.

Late one Saturday afternoon, however, the writer due to be critiqued that night had to cancel, leaving us with no reason to meet. M. Shayne Bell, the group's unofficial leader, got the bright idea to phone us all up and propose we each dash off a story to read to each other.

Two hours before the meeting, no less.

Being a young writer and not knowing any better, I wrote a silly little 2000 word piece about pirate ships plying the Great Salt Lake. I read the story at the meeting, and promptly forgot all about it. (There's no market for silly little 2000 word stories about pirate ships plying the Great Salt Lake, I assure you.)

Only come 2010, there was indeed a market.

Peculiar Press wanted Mormon-y monster-themed stories for their Monsters & Mormons *anthology. I dusted "Pirate Gold For Brother Brigham" off, expanded it out into a full story, and sold it. It saw print the next year.*

When I expanded "Pirate", I decided to keep it set in the same timeframe I'd written it in, a little frozen time capsule of the Utah Centennial period of the late-1990s. The Arctic Circle restaurant featured in the story, for example, was my study hangout during my BYU student days. Nice, clean, quiet, well-lit, tasty food, budget prices. Perfect place to study.

Unfortunately, Arctic Circle is also the originator of the bane of my existence: fry sauce.

Hate the stuff. Bad enough when only Arctic Circle served it, but the contagion has spread; it's now the default condiment throughout Utah.

I thought I'd escaped after I moved to the Oregon Coast, but right after I moved, supermarkets started stocking it on their shelves there, the dirty traitors!

If you can get past the fry sauce, you'll find a story about Spanish conquistadors, ghost pirates, ghost galleons, cursed gold, and annoying friends. You'll even learn (shudder) what the "sands" of the Great Salt Lake shore really are made of!

Utahns have this really sick habit. It's called "fry sauce," a disgusting pinkish gray goopy mix of ketchup, mayonnaise, and pickle juice that they insist on dunking their French fries into. Thank goodness I grew up in Oregon, that's all I can say.

I mention fry sauce for two reasons: first, in order to believe the rest of my story you'll need to believe really strange things happen in Utah, fry sauce being only one of them; and second, it was because of fry sauce this whole chain of events started.

We were sitting, my friend George and I, in a booth at the Arctic Circle on State Street, kitty-corner from University Mall in Orem. Arctic Circle is the drive-in hamburger chain that invented fry sauce. We've met for lunch on Saturdays at this Arctic Circle nearly every week since we were college roommates. George insists on eating there solely because of their fry sauce.

The thing about George is that he's an extreme Utahn; he puts fry sauce on *everything*. His burgers, his fries, his tossed salads. He hasn't tried putting fry sauce on Utah's other culinary masterpiece, green lime Jell-O, but it's only a matter of time.

So when he just sat there with his fry sauce still untouched, oh-so-lonesome in its little paper condiment cup, I knew something was wrong.

So I asked him what was wrong.

He didn't answer for a moment. Finally he asked, "Have you ever seen something you know you saw, but you also know you couldn't possibly have seen it because, well, because it's just plain crazy?"

I nodded. I opened my mouth to say "Fry sauce," but I never got the chance. From behind, a voice boomed: "Yeah! My mother-in-law!"

Ralphy.

Ralphy was George's cousin—second or third cousin, I forget which. Utah families get rather complicated. Ralphy was the kind of pest who never gets the hint he's not wanted. That's why he slid into the booth next to me. "See, this one time my mother-in-law actually said she was glad to see me—"

I should mention here that Ralphy does not have a mother-in-law. He is not now nor has he ever been married. Probably never will be. As I said, a lot of strange things happen in Utah; Ralphy is three of them.

"No one's ever glad to see you, Ralphy," I said.

"That's not what you said last time you needed your Plymouth jump-started." My new 1997 Plymouth had a bit of a battery gremlin.

Ralphy stole one of George's fries and dunked it in that pink Utah goo. "Cut it out, Ralphy," George said. "I'm being serious here."

"You certainly are," he said. "Serious looking that is." He popped the stolen fry in his mouth.

Ralphy had a point, much as I hate to admit it. George is the most serious-looking man I know. He even looks dour when he's rolling off a chair laughing. Comes a bit from his looking so much like old Brigham Young. Almost a dead ringer, now that George's grown out a Brigham-style beard. Of course, it's not too surprising that there's a resemblance. He's a direct descendant of Brother Brigham.

Then again, half the state is.

George sat quiet for a while, maybe hoping like I was that Ralphy would take the hint and leave, but Ralphy, as I said, never takes a hint.

Shrugging, George started up with his story again. "Promise me you won't laugh." We promised, although it took Ralphy a couple more lame jokes to get to that point.

George looked us dead in the eye. "I saw a pirate ship on the Great Salt Lake."

RALPHY PUT George's half-eaten Bounty Burger up on his shoulder like a parrot and in his best Long John Silver voice said: "Arrgh, Matey! 'Tis the scourge of the Seven Seas we be."

"You're a moron, do you know that?" George growled.

"*Brraa-waahhk!*" Ralphy's burger parrot squawked. "Mutiny on the Bounty Burger, me hearties. Walk the plank, walk the plank!"

George looked to me for moral support.

"Um, parrots aside," I said, "I think I'm with Ralphy on this one."

"I tell you I saw it!"

"You saw something, I'll grant you..."

"Don't give me any 'weather balloon' guff. You're not the only one who went to college." Did I mention Utah's over-educated? More degrees per capita than any other state. Half the truck drivers in the state have at least a bachelor's degree. Half the auto mechanics, half the plumbers—even Ralphy had one. In what, he's never said.

"Look," George said, "I know what I saw. It was a pirate ship. It had sails. It had a pirate flag."

I tried to calm him down. "When did you, um, see this pirate ship?"

"Last night about midnight. I had a blowout on I-80 just off the Saltair exit." George drives a Pepsi truck for Birnelli's bottling plant in Salt Lake City. About three times a week, he makes a run across the salt flats, past the Great Salt Lake, out to Wendover. "I got out of the cab and the moment I did, I saw it there on the lake."

I shrugged. "Must have been a sailboat from the marina sailing around." If you can believe it, they actually have a marina on the Great Salt Lake.

"At midnight? In this weather?" he asked.

I shrugged again. Myself, I couldn't imagine being crazy enough to get anywhere near that stinky lake, day or night, winter or summer—the stench of dead brine shrimp was enough to gag a maggot.

"And what about their pirate flag?" George persisted.

"A joke. Maybe a fraternity prank. You know the 'U.'"

Ralphy hissed at the mention of our archrival school, the University of Utah. Once a Cougar, always a Cougar. Just ask that greedy BYU Alumni Association. Did I mention Ralphy works for them? Now you know why your Alumni fund drive letters are so pushy.

"And what about all the men on deck, dressed like pirates and waving cutlasses?"

"I think the plural is 'cutlassi,'" Ralphy said, consulting his burger, which, in his so-called mind, was now a half-eaten dictionary.

"Maybe they had fishing poles and you just thought they were cutlasses?" I said.

"Yeah, right," George snorted. "Going fishing in the dead of winter on a dead lake with no fish. Not even tourists are *that* dumb."

Ralphy wiggled his burger, now a parrot again, vigorously. "Brine Shrimp off the port bow, Cap'n! It's Moby Dick—Arrgh, Matey. From heck's heart, I stab at thee! Harpoons away!" Ralphy hit me right between the eyes with the end of the paper wrapper blown from his soda straw.

The people sitting three tables away got up and left, looking at us and muttering as they left. I was about to follow them when George reached in his coat pocket and pulled out the Polaroid photo.

He SLID it across the table. "Does this look like I'm crazy?"

You've all seen that old grainy photo of the Loch Ness monster. Compared to the photo George showed us, that Nessie portrait is crystal clear. George's photo was all out of focus. One of his fingers covered the upper third of the picture. Still, there was something there. Fuzzy, white, and vaguely pirate ship-shaped.

Of course, it was also vaguely Bounty Burger shaped. Truth is, it could have been almost anything.

"Um," I said. "Everybody knows ghosts don't exist."

"Everybody also knows you can't take pictures of them, either. Looks like everybody can be wrong."

Like everybody in Utah on fry sauce, I muttered to myself.

Ralphy grunted at the picture and popped the last of George's fries into his mouth. "So what you want us to do about it, big guy?"

George leaned back in the booth. "I was thinking about going back out there tonight and getting a better picture. Maybe even take along some video equipment."

He paused and we both looked at Ralphy.

The Alumni Association has all that top-of-the-line video and camera equipment just sitting in their closet waiting for the next big BYU-U of U game. And Ralphy had the key.

"Why's everybody looking at me?" Ralphy asked. "Flip!"

Did I mention Utahns use "flip" and "fetch" for a certain other word used in the other forty-nine states? If really agitated, Utahns will add "you picker!"

"You pickers!" he added.

∩

It WAS ABOUT eleven p.m. when we pulled off I-80 and coasted into the deserted Saltair parking lot. Nobody in their right mind would be on the lake this time of year. Cold as a University of Utah football fan's heart and just as windy.

We unloaded the Suburban. We had more cameras and photography gear than that guy in *Bridges of Madison County*. I'd brought along that old beat-up telescope of mine, too. That was our cover story should the Utah Highway Patrol ask us what we three fools were doing out there on a cold winter's night. *Just looking at Jupiter, officer.*

We hunched up like frozen penguins and waited. A quarter-mile away, a constant stream of semi-trucks roared down the interstate, their drivers snug and warm inside their trucks. The pickers.

At least the night was bright. A full moon, of course. What was it about the supernatural and full moons, anyway? The moonlight reflected off the lake's calm, waveless surface. The light played across the white sandy beach.

Well, it's not exactly a sandy beach.

All that glinting white sand of Great Salt Lake beaches? Another weird Utah thing. Those smooth itty-bitty agate-looking sand grains aren't sand at all. They're what are called *oolite*. Layer upon layer of calcium carbonate formed around the chewy nougat of a brine shrimp fecal pellet.

That's right. We were standing on petrified shrimp poo.

It's a Utah thing.

George was munching on Doritos and fry sauce, and Ralphy was sipping at a thermos of hot Postum. Ralphy asked if we could at least turn on the radio and listen to the last of the Jazz game. We promptly told him to shut up.

"Like ghosts are afraid of the radio," he muttered, but for once he actually sort of shut up.

Three minutes to midnight, we saw the pirate ship.

She was a Spanish galleon, one of those huge lumbering behemoths Sir Francis Drake so loved to sink. White and faint—you could almost see right through it—and slightly luminescent. As she approached the Saltair docks, she hauled down her Spanish Cross flag and hauled up a black pirate Jolly Roger in its place. We could see men on its deck. Some of them looked like pirates, and some of them had on Conquistador armor. The ship glided across the Lake, right toward us, right toward the dock.

Right toward George.

The ship's captain stood on the poop deck. He held a captain's speaking trumpet. He put it to his mouth and called out something in Spanish. I only caught part of it—the name "Brigham."

He called once, twice, three times.

And then he, they, and the ship vanished.

"Oh my heck," said a shaken Ralphy. "I forgot to take any pictures."

WE ARGUED on the drive back.

George insisted we try again. "What for?" I snapped. "So we take the pictures. Then what? We say anything about this, people'll think we've cracked. Let's just forget all this happened."

Ralphy had been sitting in the back seat with all the photo gear, very quiet. Not like him at all.

"What do you think, Ralphy?" George asked. "Did you get any of that Spanish they were shouting?"

Like half the male population of the state, Ralphy had been a Mormon missionary. He'd gone to one of those Latin America countries, I can't keep them straight. Sometimes when I'm feeling charitable, I blame his irregularities on the endemic dysentery he had throughout his mission.

Sometimes.

Ralphy stared out the window, ashen-faced, watching the brine-crusted telephone poles flash by. It was the first time I'd ever seen him serious. "He was calling out for Brigham. Brigham Young." He turned to face us. "He said he'd brought gold for Brigham's temple."

"Flip!" I muttered. "Not another Lost Rhoades Mine ghost story."

Some weird Utah things are too weird even for Utahns to believe. The rumor about the Lost Rhoades Gold Mine providing the gold for the Salt Lake Temple's Angel Moroni statue is one of them. If you haven't heard the story, I'm not going to bother explaining it. Look it up on your library. I'll add this: it was Utah-weird enough Hollywood made a Gregory Peck western about it: *Mackenna's Gold. Sans* Utah and Angel Moroni, of course. Hollywood isn't *that* weird.

Looks like ghost pirates are, though.

Ralphy pointed at George. "They think George is Brigham Young."

George almost swerved off the highway. "What?!"

"It's not the full moon at all. It's George. That's why they've shown up. They think they've finally found Brother Brigham after all these years."

ᴧ

A FIERCE ARGUMENT ERUPTED. It was me against George, George against Ralphy, and Ralphy against himself.

I whistled to get us all to shut up. "Quiet, you pickers!" I cleared my throat. "Now. It's obvious we need to know more before we decide *anything*. Like maybe find out who these pirates are and how in the heck they're showing up in Utah."

"I've never heard anything about pirates in Utah."

"It *is* a landlocked state, George," I said dryly. "There were plenty of Spanish running around here in the old days. Maybe we can find a connection that way."

"At least *one* of us can." They both said.

It was my turn to have everybody turn and look at me.

"You pickers!" I moaned.

"You have access to all sorts of old records at the 'Y,' don't you, professor?" Ralphy said.

In other parts of the country, when you say the 'Y,' you mean the YMCA. In Utah, the 'Y' always means Brigham Young University. BYU. I'm not even sure they *have* YMCAs in Utah.

"Look, enough with the 'professor' stuff, already. I'm just a lowly adjunct instructor." The Y had another tenure cap going on. "Besides –"

"And what *you* can't find," George continued, ignoring me, "you can get from some of your historian friends up at the Church Office Building? Right?"

I offered dozens of perfectly valid excuses. They weren't having any.

"Flip!" I Utah-swore. "Flippity-fetch-fetch!"

IT TOOK me two weeks of digging, but I finally found the connection. I didn't find it at Church Headquarters or the 'Y' or even the YMCA. Instead, I found it over at the Utah Historical Society over in the old Rio Grande train station in downtown Salt Lake.

Seems back in 1540, the conquistador Francisco de Coronado's expedition reached all the way up to the Colorado River. In this account I found, Coronado expelled a handful of his men from the party. Coronado had discovered that the men had once been part of a galleon's crew who'd mutinied and turned pirate. They'd joined the expedition partly to slip out of sight from the Spanish authorities, partly to get their grubby little hands on the gold of El Dorado.

Juan Jose Avila, the captain of the mutineers, offered a bag of gold—booty from the pirated galleon—to Coronado if he'd only change his mind and let them back in the party. Coronado refused, swearing an oath at them, putting them under some sort of curse. Exiled into the wilderness, Avila and his men were never seen again.

At least not until George saw them.

"They must have made their way up through the desert, past the Indians and the crickets and the seagulls, to the Great Salt Lake," I told the rest of the guys. We were back at Arctic Circle, planning what to do next.

Ralphy had spent his time studying up on ghosts – watching umpteen cheesy cable TV shows and reading a stack of *Goosebumps*. "According to my sources," Ralphy said, "ghosts are just spirits who've got unfinished business on earth. Once they get that done, they can go to their final rest."

I stirred my straw around in my Diet Pepsi (twice the sin with only half the calories). "So what you're saying is old Jose's trying to atone for all that gold he stole by giving it over to a holy cause."

"*I'm* not saying it," Ralphy said around a half-chewed French fry. "I'm just saying that that's what my sources would say, but that's only if you believe in that false Purgatory stuff, which we know if we read our good ol' Bruce R. that—"

I held up his hand. "Let's hold up on the McConkie for a bit." Any time a conversation turned Gospel-ish, Ralphy would drag out his battered copy of *Mormon Doctrine* and cite it like was the Fifth Standard Work. I just wish good ol' Bruce R. had proclaimed fry sauce to be against the Word of Wisdom.

"Yeah," George nodded. "What I want to know is how that pirate ship figures in, genius. Did they haul that thing around with them on Coronado''s expedition?"

"Not to mention the Jolly Roger flag hadn't been invented yet in 1540," I added.

"Sometimes ghostly apparitions are symbolic rather than literal," Ralphy answered. I didn't even know he knew words that big, let alone could string them together in a sentence.

"So then, building on this R. L. Stine theory of yours," I said, "since the sin was piracy, they have to atone as pirates." I took a sip on my straw. "Seems simple enough. We just let them give their gold to Brigham"—I hooked a thumb at George—"and they can go off and rest in peace."

"I am *not* Brigham Young!" George harrumphed.

"They think you are."

"Yeah," Ralphy chimed in. A calculating look came to his eyes. "We give them Brigham, and they give us the gold, and then we—"

"*I'm not Brigham!*"

"Uh, hold on a minute there, Ralphy," I said. "Rewind the tape. Just what what do you mean by 'they give us the gold?'"

Ralphy, mouth full of fry sauce, looked at me like I was a simpleton. "They give us the gold. *Duh.* Now, I was thinking a forty-thirty-thirtysplit, since I'm the one who thought of it, but if you're going to get all sulky about it—"

"Oh, no!" shouted George. "I'm not keeping any haunted stolen pirate gold. I don't want blood on my hands!" George must have been reading some of Ralphy's *Goosbumps*, too. Or maybe he'd seen *The Mummy's Curse* last night on *Creature Feature*.

Ralphy glared at him. "Then I don't see any reason for us to stick our necks out for a bunch of goldy oldy moldy ghosts."

"We could always just do it just for curiosity's sake," I offered. "'Discovery of the unknown' and all that."

"I get all of that I want at my Singles Ward," Ralphy sniffed.

I had one last arrow in my quiver. It wasn't very *Mormon Doctrine*-y, but desperate times and seasons called for desperate measures.

"Well, then," I asked, "how about the chance to save some poor lost souls suffering in Purgatory?"

Ralphy rose up in full Bruce R. high dudgeon. "There's no such thing as Purga*story*—"

I cut him off in mid-dudge. "Why, Ralphy!" I indignified. "I'm surprised at you!"

"*Huh?!*"

"You of all people! Don't you believe in the Eleventh Article of Faith? Or free agency?"

"*Double huh?!*"

"'We allow all men the same privilege, let them worship how, where, or what they may,'" I quoted. "Even pirate ghosts."

"But—"

"But, nothing! Doesn't Bruce R. himself speak of missionaries going forth to preach in the spirit world?"

"And during the Millennium," George added, not knowing where I was leading the discussion, but Georgishly crossing all the Ts and jotting all the tittles and threading all the camels through needles.

"Spirit missionaries means non-member spirits, right?" I asked, not giving Ralphy time to answer. "Non-member spirits with Eleventh Article of Faith free agency, right? Even good ol' Bruce couldn't begrudge some Catholic spirits trying to atone and get back to God's presence according to the measure of light they possess—"

"But—" Ralphy whimpered.

"—And didn't the Prophet George A. Smith say, 'Keep all the good that you have, and let us bring to you more good, in order that you may be happier and in order that you may be prepared to enter into the presence of our Heavenly Father?'"

Paper takes stone, stone takes scissors, and a Prophet takes a study aid, especially when that prophet is George's namesake forbearer. George is a one-man walking DUP genealogy tree.

Ralphy agreed without another whimper. Live by the Bruce R., die by the Bruce R.

So WE WENT BACK out to Saltair the next full moon. Yes, I know, the full moon business wasn't necessary, but we weren't taking any chances. Besides, the light was better.

George stood on the end of the pier. We'd borrowed a costume from James Arrington's one-man show. James is a friend of mine. I've done research for him from time to time.

George looked just like Brother Brigham, cane and all.

"C-couldn't you a g-gotten a warmer costume?" he said through chattering teeth. The costume was made of lightweight material. Stage lights get pretty hot.

"Just hold on, George. Only a few minutes to midnight," I said.

The pirate ship arrived right on schedule. It stopped short of the dock and the crew lowered a ship's boat. Avila and his men rowed up to the pier. They climbed up the rope ladder, hauling a large wooden chest with them.

George stepped up to meet them. He was a braver man than I, I'll give him that. My knees were knocking and not just from the cold.

George extended a hand toward the captain, but Avila declined to shake. Rather, he opened the chest to reveal a king's ransom. Precious jewels and Spanish doubloons glinted in the moonlight.

Avila whispered something lengthy in Spanish.

"*For the temple,*" Ralphy translated. His three word translation seemed a bit truncated to me, but maybe Ralphy's Spanish was as rusty as my Thai.

George nodded at Avila's words like he knew what the ghost was saying and patted a hand on the open chest lid.

Avila and his men vanished, leaving only a smile. Cheshire Conquistadors. Who'd have thought?

Ralphy ran to the chest. "It's real!" he crowed, running his hands through the treasure.

I slammed the lid.

"Fer rude!" Ralphy muttered, rubbing his hands to check if he still had all his fingers.

George laid a hand on Ralphy's shoulder. "Now, Ralphy, remember what we agreed?"

Ralphy looked down at the chest. "There goes my chance to be richer than Bill Gates. Jon Huntsman, even."

HERE's another Utah geographic fact: the Beehive House, Brigham Young's old historic home, sits just a half-block east of Temple Square. It sits there just as handy at two in the morning as it does in broad daylight. Even handier if you're leaving a pirate chest full of gold on its front steps without being seen.

A Volvo with California plates and an "RULDS" sticker sped past on South Temple, honking at us as it passed. Even at two in the morning, there was still traffic in the heart of downtown Salt Lake that night. The Jazz must have won. When they lose, Salt Lake's a ghost town, if you'll excuse the expression.

"Geez, we're in plain sight here. And we're parked in a no parking zone.

We're gonna get caught," Ralphy whimpered. Ralphy was huffing and puffing. We all were. That chest was *heavy*.

"Yeah," said George. He pointed up at the ugly slab-white modern skyscraper just to the north of the Beehive House. "I thought we were leaving this over at the Church Office Building."

"This is Brigham's house," I answered after I got my wind back. "It's Brigham's gold."

"Pirate gold for Brother Brigham." George shook his head as if he still didn't believe it.

We took one last look at the chest and drove off.

∩

I CHECKED the newspapers the next day for any mention of the chest or the gold or anything, but there wasn't any. Not that day. Not the next day. Not ever. That week, though, the Church announced a slew of new temples, triggering yet another *Time* magazine cover story on how rich the Mormon Church was.

"Richer than they think," Ralphy said. We were back at Arctic Circle. This time George was slurping down fry sauce without a care in the world.

"What do you mean?" I asked Ralphy.

Ralphy cleared his throat. Always a bad sign.

"I didn't entirely translate everything Avila said at the time." He played with his straw. "Avila said something to the effect of, 'Here is a *second* chest of gold for your temple.'"

"*Second?*" George and I looked at each other. "You mean—?"

"I think the real Brigham Young once met Avila at the shores of the Great Salt Lake. You're the historian, professor. Remember Church history? The Church was broke once. Flat broke. And suddenly we weren't."

George choked on his Sprite.

Ralphy's grasp on history was about as firm as his grip on reality, but even a broken clock is right twice a day. My digital watch chose that exact moment to chirp the top of the hour.

∩

WE DIDN'T SAY any more the rest of that lunch about pirate ships or gold or anything else. In fact, we haven't ever been back to that Arctic Circle since.

George and I, however, did run up to Salt Lake and visit the Beehive House a few days later. The docent, an elderly lady who'd been there years and years and years, led us through the tour. In Brigham's bedroom, we saw an old wooden chest identical to the one Avila had given us. I asked the docent how long the chest had been on display.

She gave me a rather odd look. "As long as I've worked here. It sits right where Brigham left it."

Ralphy had said Avila had said *a* second chest. Not *the* second chest, just *a* second chest. I don't know about Spanish, but in English it can make a world of difference. Those old treasure galleons sometimes held dozens of treasure chests.

I looked at George and George looked at me.

The next full moon the Church announced another slew of new temples.

WHERE NOTHING LIVES BUT CROSSES

INTRODUCTION

The Mormon Lit Blitz is an annual contest for flash fiction—fiction 1000 words or under—publishing winners and finalists online.

It takes a certain amount of skill to write any type of fiction that short, doubly so with adding in a Mormon aspect. Double that again if you persist, as I do with my entries each year, in cramming sci-fi/fantasy into your Mormon-themed flash fiction.

"Crosses" was my entry for the 2014 special Hallowe'en contest the Blitz folks held, a contest specifically for monster-y Mormon flash fiction. For this special contest they graciously upped the word count limit to 2000 words, which in my opinion makes a world of difference. "Crosses" earned a finalist slot and publication.

The story is set in my "Stakeholder" story series. They're tales about a Stakeholder, a human/vampire hybrid who is unwillingly bound to a Rookery of vampires. Basically, he cleans up their messes for them, slaying rogue vampires who poach on others' territories, vampires who go crazy with blood lust, or otherwise threaten the vampire community's shadow existence.

The story idea for this particularly came to me decades ago, long before I'd even thought of becoming a writer.

A common trope in the vampire legends are the effect of a cross on a vampire. Mormons, however, for theological reasons don't wear crosses.

What happens when a vampire meets up with a cross-less Mormon? You're about to find out!

Comfort's in heaven; and we are on the earth,
Where nothing lives but crosses, cares and grief.

—Shakespeare, Richard II, *Act 2, Scene 2*

T he railway car lurched unexpectedly as the clattering train rounded yet another curve on the switchback westward course through the Berkshires of western Massachusetts. The specially chartered train was three days away from its terminus in the deserts of Utah.

Private railcars weren't all that uncommon even in the America of 1932, an America ravaged by the Great Depression. This railcar, however, was uncommon because of the two men who occupied it conversing with one another, only one of whom was alive.

December's chill seeped in through the railcar's windows, a chill hardly offset by the woolen blanket around Nathan Fairchild's legs or the burbling coffee pot at his side. The Austrian nobleman, recumbent upon the red satin divan, wanted the car's interior kept cold as a tomb and so it was.

Raab, as the Austrian styled himself, idly tapped a Turkish cigarette on the back of his hand. The hand was marked by an only partially healed burn mark in the shape of a cross. Raab placed the cigarette in his mouth and lit up. Acrid blue smoke wreathed his head in a tenebrous fog.

Baseborns rarely smoked—and bloodborns all but never—but, then, Raab was hardly one to abide the conventions of either baseborn or blood. If he had, the *Krähenhorst*, the ancient vampire rookery of Vienna, would not have exiled him here to the New World.

Iconoclasm was all well and good—vampire society was less a society than a loose grouping of solitary predators—but that iconoclasm had to stay within permissible bounds. Fairchild's rookery, headquartered in San Francisco, was not altogether certain that Raab would confine himself so. Fairchild had thus been assigned as Raab's minder rather than a normal human adjunct.

As if reading his thoughts, the Austrian smiled, baring his fangs ever-so-slightly. "You actually believe you could fell me *yourself*, human? In Vienna, it sometimes takes an entire pack to bring down even a baseborn such as myself."

Fairchild poured himself another coffee. Warmth spread through to his fingers as he cradled the mug with both hands. "I've heard of your famed Wild Hunts." He sipped. "Here in America, we tend to do things a little differently."

"So I was led to believe," Raab said. His eyes flicked to the painful burn mark the dockworker's silver cross necklace had seared into the vampire's hand.

Boston Harbor, and not two minutes off the gangplank of the ocean liner.

Raab had insisted on hunting immediately for fresh game. That the first dock-worker he'd waylaid into a dark alley turned out to be Irish Catholic...

"What did you expect in Boston?" Fairchild asked.

Raab sniffed. "As if one miserable human city—or even continent—differs from the next."

Still, once the Austrian had hurled away the offending pendant, he had fed deep and long. The sated vampire would not need to feed again for many days, not until after he'd reached his destination.

The rattle of an eastbound train passing in the opposite direction drowned out further conversation. As the relative quiet of the railcar's passage down the track returned, Raab blew one last stream of smoke, then stubbed out the remains of his cigarette. He sibilated the desiccated hiss that passed for laughter among his kind.

"Vienna would say that *this*," he held up his burnt hand, "only underscores their view that they were right and I was wrong. Faugh." He looked sharply at Fairchild. "Do you know why those *graubärte* exiled me?"

"The High Council doesn't confide in mere humans." And if Fairchild limited his information sources to only the High Council or his immediate boss, the Judge, he would have been dead long ago. No, Fairchild knew, knew more than Raab did.

Raab steepled his fingers. "Tell me, human. Do you believe in the constructs of Good and Evil?"

Fairchild felt the comforting weight of the tension steel stakes holstered under his brown leather jacket. Oh, yes—he believed in Evil, all right. And the presence of Evil presupposed the existence of Good, though Fairchild had yet to meet it face to face. The closest to Good Fairchild had experienced was the solid chunk of sharpened steel hammered through a vampire's beating heart.

"Merely the constructs of the human mind," Raab said, airily waving his fingers, "and yet, have you ever considered why their feeble minds evolved in such a way to possess it?"

"Evolved?"

"But of course. Have you ever heard of any human culture that had not developed some notion of Good and Evil and Gods? One must account for it by evolution or else join in the silly belief that some God actually exists."

He went on. A vampire holding court cares not for a response from livestock after all. "For all their tools and machines and clever little monkey thumbs, humans are powerless against us—save for this imaginary construct of Good and God and Holiness they fetishize in their odious religious symbols."

He nursed his burnt hand again. "Good and Evil. *Faugh!* Merely a chance evolutionary proto-phrenic defensive mechanism that reflects our own psychic abilities back upon ourselves. But would those fools in Vienna listen to me?"

The train clattered down another mile of track before Raab spoke again.

"Seventeen million head of livestock dead from the Kaiser's foolish Great War," Raab spat. "And perhaps an order of magnitude more from the *Spanische Grippe*. Europe's peasants are disillusioned, doubting in their imaginary God. It would take only a little push using the levers of power the *Krähenhorst* wields and we could free ourselves from those accursed silver trinkets forever!"

Raab extracted another cigarette from his inlaid silver case. "But no, the old fools aim instead to de-God the *elite* of human society." He tapped the cigarette on the back of his hand again. "As if we fed on them —those who would be missed—instead of safely draining the nameless, faceless masses." He exhaled another long stream of smoke.

Fairchild hid his disgust behind a tightly gripped coffee mug.

The war's disillusionment of Europe's populace was already waning, and left to their own devices the common man might recover. Vampires played a longer game.

The disillusioned elites of shattered Europe—the statesmen and the poets, the writers, the artists, the filmmakers, even the clergy itself—those whose gift and duty was the channeling and dissemination—the control—of thoughts and ideas were proving fragile reeds in the aftermath of industrialized Armageddon. They were sloughing off the stays and guides of the time-tested moralities for the modern hedonisms and glittering raw power the *Krähenhorst* secretly proffered. The elites would in turn suborn, legislate, and mock into extinction the common man's convictions of the divine.

Already it had begun in Italy with that strutting stone-jawed oaf and his Blackshirts, and in Germany also, with its little beer hall corporal.

Turning the masses through the elite might take years, might take decades, but the decadence would be permanent. Hadn't they played the same game with Rome a thousand years before?

Raab's true crime against his nest was not his rebellion or his alternative plan, but his rash impatience. And it would soon be the death of him. That had been arranged long before Raab set foot on American soil. That is why Stakeholder Nathan Fairchild, sanctioned slayer of those unsuitable to the rookery, had been ordered to lead the unwitting Raab to the killing field.

Raab idly dragged on his cigarette. "Tell me about this new domain of mine."

"Hunting ground we call them here," Fairchild corrected.

Raab smiled sardonically. "Ah, yes. I've heard of these Americans' predilection for deluding themselves that they run their own affairs, when the truth is they are nothing but—what is that delicious Americanism?—free range cattle."

He blew another stream of smoke. "My new...'hunting ground.' It is what I asked for?"

Fairchild nodded. "Yes. We actually had a vacant territory with a substantially low amount of *Kreuzenträger*." The term for cross-wearing humans. "Not one in ten thousand, in fact."

Raab smiled as he took another drag on his cigarette. "That low? Good, good." He hissed again in vampiric mirth. "You Americans really are mongrels, aren't you? Too debased even for proper shrivenings. I shall enjoy hunting on my new preserve without those *verfluchten* crosses to vex me."

Fairchild smiled, too, but only to himself. It never occurred to Raab to ask why such a seemingly prize territory was left permanently vacant. It never occurred to Raab to realize he was being led to his doom.

TEN MILES NORTH OF ST. George Utah, Fairchild let his Model A truck coast to a stop. A dusting of early April snow glinted in the Saturday morning sun. By noon it'd be soaked into the red sandstone dirt.

Grabbing a three-pound sledge hammer, he got out of the truck.

The door of the rancher's cabin was ajar, just as the frightened rancher who'd told Fairchild his story had left it. It hadn't been difficult to track down. Not difficult at all.

The rancher had left his radio on. Fairchild could hear the scratchy sounds of the KSL station out of Salt Lake City. Its fifty thousand watts of broadcasting power was enough to carry down here in the southeast corner of the state. They were broadcasting some annual meeting the Mormons held in their holy Tabernacle.

Fairchild crunched up the gravel trail to the cabin. He made no attempt at stealth. He could smell the vampire now; what's more, he could smell the blood of jack rabbits and mule deer upon its breath.

Animal blood held only an illusion of sustenance for a vampire. A vampire attempting to subsist solely on animal blood would slowly starve, the lack of human blood not only killing him but slowly driving him mad the way mercury-laden fish would a human.

But what other option had Raab in his new domain, but to scavenge from the four-footed beasts? For he could not feed on its people.

Over the radio the Mormon preacher was slowly, methodically answering a common question asked by the outside world: why didn't Mormons wear crosses?

Raab lay huddled, shaking in a corner of the cabin, too weak, too maddened, too feral to even recognize Fairchild or the danger the stakeholder presented to Raab. Raab's swollen mouth gabbled in pain and insanity.

Every inch of the vampire's naked body was burned and scarred with the same burns a cross would make. He must have tried to feed a dozen times before he realized the truth, the trap he'd been lured into.

As much out of pity as duty, Fairchild hammered a steel stake through Raab's heart. In its convulsions, the heat of the vampire's over-taxed super-oxygenated blood—the same blood that gave a vampire its power—consumed the vampire in a gout of flame.

Fairchild dropped the hammer and turned back for his truck.

The radio preacher concluded: "Just as we Mormons worship neither a dead nor dying God, we do not connote our faith in Him through the symbol of His death. What symbol, then, do Mormons use? None, for no earthly emblem, sigil, or token could possibly suffice. Rather, our very lives—our very beings—can and must become that symbol, a living symbol, a living testimony of the Living God."

Raab had tried to feed in the heart of Mormondom where every living person was a cross and held its power.

A land where nothing lives but crosses.

NEW ENGLAND'S GOD

INTRODUCTION

"New England's God" is one of my newest stories, having just recently seen print in Pulphouse Fiction Magazine #13.

What do one obscure battle, one very obscure non-battle, and a choir instructor have in common? Aside from the American War of Independence, what they have in common is their being a textbook example of how I come up with many of my stories.

I read a lot of non-fiction, mostly history, and in my reading I'll often come across various historical oddities and inexplicable events. Or inexplicable if you're limited only to mundane history, but very idea-sparking explicable if you're a fiction writer like me. Smoosh two or three of those oddities together until they start to explain each other and you have a Lee Allred story!

I was about to say that every schoolchild knows the story of Lexington and Concord and the Shot Heard 'Round the World, the April 1775 starting point of America's War of Independence, but given today's schools that might not be true.

What isn't so universally known—even among historians—is that the British under General Gage attempted a similar weapon-grabbing raid on the Massachusetts town of Salem just two months prior (February 1775).

Gage sent a column of British troops by sea (hence Paul Revere's later concern: "One if by land, two if by sea") to march on Salem and seize not mere muskets but privately-owned cannon. (If that little factoid changes the complexion of certain current event conversations, so be it.)

The British arrived in Salem but were stymied at the North River bridge by an assemblage of ready-to-brawl Massachusetts militia. Unlike Lexington and Concord, no shooting took place luckily. No cannon-seizing took place either, however.

Accounts on exactly what happened at Salem that day vary widely. But what is known is that the British slunk back to Boston empty-handed. (The Salem Raid probably explains the intransience on both sides at Lexington. The British were resolved not to back down again; the Americans were convinced they would.)

My story's depiction of that day's events—up until the parley—follow a blend of the varying historical accounts.

Astute readers remember that Salem, home to the infamous witch trials, served as a real-life geographic template for H.P. Lovecraft's fictional town of Arkham. The near-battle, therefore, takes place on the real-world analog of the Miskatonic River. This has some bearing on the story.

Another story element is a famous song from the Revolutionary War: "Chester" (from which lyrics I've pulled my story's title). The general public might know it from its use in the church scene early on in the John Adams HBO mini-series, albeit its use there was ahistorical (the song hadn't been written at that point, a little error I nod at in my story).

But those of us geezers around during the Bicentennial were quite familiar with the song. It practically served as the theme song for the Bicentennial, just as it served as the theme song of the Revolution two hundred years earlier. Then, and for many years afterward—well into the mid-Nineteen Century, in fact—"Chester" was considered the unofficial American national anthem.

"Chester" is both a choral hymn and a fife-and-drum martial march. You can find recordings of both choral and instrumental versions. I find the arrangement played by the "President's Own" U.S. Marine Band especially striking.

Even more striking is the song's composer, William Billings. Billings is probably the oddest prominent American who ever lived. A grotesquely deformed gargoyle of a man —blind, lame, withered—with atrocious personal habits and hygiene, Billings was nonetheless the Father of American Choral Music.

A tanner by trade, with no formal musical education whatsoever—indeed, almost no education at all—he nevertheless became America's first published hymnist and first professional composer of any type. He formed the first church choir in America and much of his life was spent as a singing master—despite having a mangled bullfrog voice and not being able to hold a note on key. He even authored perhaps the most influential instructional book on choral singing in this country.

A third story element is the Battle of White Plains, New York on October 28, 1776 just three days shy of Hallowe'en.

At White Plains, the crack British Army defeated (almost annihilated, really) Washington's ragtag footsore amateur army—and would have gotten away with it, too, *if it hadn't been for that meddling Hudson River. Washington just barely managed to slip across it to safety.*

The battle has one additional feature of interest in this story. It's notable for being the battlefield where a certain celebrated Hessian horseman lost his head, as "documented" by storyteller Washington Irving.

All these elements come together to form what my Pulphouse *editor called "an original fantasy story set in history unlike any history or any fantasy you might know."*

Or to put it as an elevator pitch: "National Treasure *meets* Call of Cthulhu *with* Sleepy Hollow *thrown in."*

October 1809
West Point, New York

Twilight had lost little of the day's late autumn heat, but the muggy October air was not the reason for the rivulets of sweat trickling down the faces of the three first-year cadets seated around the dining table.

The smell of a hearty meal filled the room. Lamplight and candles flickered gaily. Outside the thick brick walls, an impromptu choral of second-years could be heard crooning old soldier's tunes from the Revolutionary War. Despite such pleasant surroundings, the three cadets—theirs the faces of a funeral pallor.

Lt. Colonel Christopher Garrick (Ret.), their tormentor and instructor, smiled amusedly. A lean man in his late fifties, only his graying temples displayed any marked change in his appearance since he'd served as a young officer during the Revolution.

His sudden, unexplained smile unnerved his three victims.

Oh, the three had been safe enough during the meal, but now that the roast fowl had been plucked clean from the bones and carried away from the table by Garrick's manservant, the three knew they'd now be expected to make conversation with their Professor of Artillery and each of them knew full well their abysmal standing in his class. They had little doubt as to where the conversation must turn.

Taking pity on them, Garrick unstoppered the decanter of brandy. "Come, come, Mr. Showalter. Your glass, your glass!"

Young Showalter blanched. "I—I'm not much one for hard spirits, sir," he squeaked.

"Then it's high time you learned, Mr. Showalter," Garrick said, taking Showalter's empty glass from him and pouring an over-healthy draught. "An Army officer is expected to hold his liquor. But first you must learn to drink it."

Showalter stared at his brimming glass the way a sparrow stares at a cobra.

Then he gave a not-so-furtive glance down the table toward Garrick's fourth dinner guest, a magazine scribbler named Washington Irving from the city here at West Point to gather what he called local color. "He's not going to write about this, is he? It'd kill my father, reading about me getting drunk and my father a minister."

Irving, who had been slouched at his end of the table emptying his own decanter, drew himself up, straightening as best he could with rubbery reflexes. His long, square face turned toward the offending cadet.

"My dear young man, whatever your name is," Irving slurred, glossing over the fact that at twenty-six Irving was scarcely older than the cadet. "I'm an essayist, not some mere loathsome reporter. I deal not in facts, but in Truths. Rest assured that reporting on the banal commonality of some nobody taking to drink for the first time is beneath me."

Irving rubbed his high, gleaming forehead. "I traffick in the odd. The unaccountable. The strange."

At this, Garrick smiled and poured himself a splash of brandy. "Oh, I think the Point can accommodate you on that score, Mr. Irving. Indeed we can."

As if on cue, the cadets outside ceased caterwauling whatever ditty they'd been bludgeoning into unrecognizability and began to sing a tune so familiar that not even their untrained voices could hide its identity.

> Let tyrants shake their iron rod,
> And Slav'ry clank her galling chains,
> We fear them not, we trust in God,
> New England's God forever reigns.

Garrick tapped his finger in time to the tune. "What song is that, Mr. Showalter?"

Showalter goggled wide-eyed at him, as if Garrick had asked what nation were they seated in. "Why, 'Chester' of course," he said.

> Howe and Burgoyne and Clinton too,
> With Prescot and Cornwallis join'd,
> Together plot our Overthrow,
> In one Infernal league combin'd.

Garrick nodded.

"Chester". The fife-and-drum march the blue-coated Continental army had fought to, the chorale hymn the desperate Colonials in every pew in the land had beseeched God to. If the newborn Republic could be said to have a national anthem, that song was "Chester".

Garrick settled back in his chair and felt his waistcoat pocket for the small tin of tobacco. "I twice met the man who wrote it. William Billings. Queer little man. Born with only one eye. One arm withered, totally useless. Both legs clearly shorter than God intended, and one leg very much shorter than the other. Voice louder, more raucous than a drunken crow." Garrick retrieved his long clay pipe from a nearby side table. "He was a tanner by trade, stank so badly of tanning acids you couldn't stand downwind of him without your eyes watering. Addicted to snuff—not in small pinches—but great, heaping handfuls at a time."

Garrick pointed the long stem of his Churchwarden pipe at Irving. "You wanted strange, I suggest you start with him."

Irving shook his head. "A Massachusetts man, I believe. Boston or Salem or some such. My purview's strictly New York."

"The second time I saw him was in New York." Garrick lit his pipe and puffed deeply to get it started. "Battle of White Plains, in fact. But I suppose I should begin at the beginning."

He exhaled a long blue stream of smoke. "Mr. Showalter, when would you say Chester was written? Come, come, man. You're father's a minister. If he doesn't have Billing's *Singing Master's Assistant* stacked in his pews, I'll eat my hat."

Poor young Showalter's mouth worked like a beached cod. "Uh, seventeen seventy-eight? At least that's the year the Assistant was published."

"So no later than seventeen seventy-eight." Garrick turned to one of the others. "Mr. Ford, the song mentions various British Generals. Gage, Burgoyne, others. What's the earliest those lyrics could have been written?"

Cadet Ford, who'd managed this far to escape attention during the evening, stammered. "Uh, uh—" He shot a panicked look at the other cadets.

"Seventeen seventy-six," Cadet Vernal offered. Vernal, a complete and utter clot as far as mathematics or artillery went, was a fiend for historical dates. "Lord Cornwallis didn't arrive in the American Colonies for the Carolina campaigns until June of 'seventy-six, so the song couldn't have been penned until after that."

Garrick blew a smoke ring. "What if I told you I heard Billings himself sing those very lyrics in February of seventeen seventy-five before any of those battles happened?" Another smoke ring. "Strange, wouldn't you say?"

Irving fished out a well-worn pencil stub and a small note book as if in answer.

Leaning back in his chair, Garrick, amidst wreaths of blue smoke, began his tale: "It all began in Boston Harbor where I served under General Gage as a young captain of artillery—"

"You were a British officer in the War?" Showalter squeaked.

Garrick smiled. "Everyone makes mistakes..."

February 1775
Boston, Massachusetts

AMERICAN RABBLE-ROUSERS NORTH of Boston were gathering cannon, for what purposes our General Gage, pleased to be appointed by King George III the military governor of the rebellious Province of Massachusetts Bay, knew not.

Where they were getting them posed no mystery: Dutch ship captains conducted a brisk trade of selling off "surplus" and "worn out" ships' cannon at smaller Massachusetts harbors like Salem and Kingsport.

What the Americans were doing with these Dutch cannon now was also firmly established: colonial foundries were even now fitting them with the new lighter and faster gun carriages the Americans seem to have an unholy knack for designing.

What they intended on doing with them afterward kept our Governor-General Gage up at night with fevered imaginings.

Gage had four thousand British regulars in Boston Town, along with the makings of a small naval fleet under Admiral Graves docked in Boston harbor. With such a force, there were many things Gage could have done about those American cannon. Smart, sensible, decisive things.

Instead, this is what he did do.

On a cold and blustery winter's day (is there any other kind in Boston?) in late February of 1775. Gage summoned us to his ill-heated office in the miserable and drafty stone mausoleum known as Castle William, perched on the damp maw of Boston Harbor.

Three of us stood before the ill-tempered Gage: my commanding officer in the 64th Regiment, Lt. Colonel Alexander Leslie, tall and stiff in his best red coat; some Royal Navy captain I was not familiar with—some slump-shouldered graybeard wearing a faded uniform just as worn and tired; and myself, a newly promoted captain at the time, having just taken command of the 64th's equally newly formed rump artillery battery. I had the office; what I didn't have was the cannon or the men, save for a handful of guardhouse-bait doughties.

We stood there on shivering. The Governor-General had a roaring fire going, but almost all the heat went straight up the flue—a pernicious little draft that repeated caulkings had failed to plug, and we three stood right in its gelid path.

Fortunately for once, General Gage got right to the point. "Gentlemen," he said, unrolling a large map, "these blighted 'Patriots'—" he sneered at the word "—have gotten hold of some several pieces of cannon and are fitting them with army carriages for some future mischief. Intolerable."

He smoothed the map flat and pointed. "Here. This miserable flyspeck named Salem."

"The one with all the witches?" Leslie blurted.

"I don't care if it's home for the Devil himself, blast it!" Gage roared. "I want you to march in there and seize those cannon."

"That's maybe twenty miles, sir," Leslie protested. "The colonials will find out I'm coming long before I get there. They'll hide those cannon, scatter them across the countryside. The Army'll look right fools."

Gage jerked his chin in the direction of the Navy captain. "That's why you're sailing out of Boston instead of marching."

The Navy ship's captain cleared his throat. "I certainly hope you're not expecting me to dock in Salem harbor so you can disembark your troops one-by-one in the face of a hostile mob. They'd never clear the gangplank alive if any shooting starts."

Gage glared up at him. "That, captain, is why I'm proposing you sail here." Another finger stab, this time at a small deserted cove on Marblehead Neck, just a few miles from Salem itself. "Tomorrow's Sunday. You'll lie off the cove until the Marblehead locals are all oh-so-piously in Church. Leslie will be able to disembark, form his columns, and march into Salem before anyone's the wiser."

I hadn't said anything, I hadn't even blinked through all of this, but Gage fixed his glare on me anyway. "You have something to say, Mr. Garrick?"

"Well, sir," I said. "Won't a troopship sitting off shore for several hours arouse some suspicion?"

"The men will be kept hidden below decks until the last moment," Gage said. "All they'll see is a ship. A ship is a ship. It could be the Pasha of Cathay's royal barge for all those ignorant Colonials will know."

A ship is a ship.

Marblehead was a fisherman's town. Those ignorant Colonials made their living at sea, but you don't tell a general that. Not General Gage, who as a general knew better than any mere captain of artillery, and as a highborn English gentleman knew better than an entire continent of American Colonials.

For the next ten minutes, Gage curtly and succinctly laid out the detailed plan of how Leslie was to proceed with two-hundred-and-forty picked men. Colonel Leslie was the type of British officer who needed a detailed plan, even to put his boots on in the morning. A gentleman but hardly a scholar.

The plan explained, Gage dismissed us.

"Not you, Garrick," he said. "A word with you."

I stood at attention in front of his desk.

"Garrick," he said, "I'm sending you on this mission because you have a slight modicum of knowledge about cannon, which Kind Providence knows is more than that fool Leslie has."

"Sir." There wasn't anything I could say to that that wouldn't get me into trouble.

Gage picked up a quill pen and began idly bending it like a bow. "But that's not the primary reason I'm sending you as an advisor to Colonel Leslie. I'm told you seem to have a canny understanding of these Colonials. What they will do, what they will think. I shouldn't wonder." He bent the quill a little too far; it snapped like a twig. "Like calls to like."

"Sir?"

Gage began toying with a second quill, twirling it. "There are two kinds of people in this world, Mr. Garrick. Those who need to be led, and those, through breeding and temperament, who are born to lead them."

I spoke before I could stop myself. "Meaning us, sir? Meaning you?"

The twirling stopped. "The world is as it always has been, Mr. Garrick. As God created it, as God rules over it."

"It would seem the New Englanders mean to worship a different god," I observed.

"New England's God is the same God that governs England. There can be no other. Would you have them rule themselves? Madness! This continent is peopled entirely but by the dregs and gutter sweepings who couldn't make a go of it in Britain proper."

"They seem to be making quite the go of it here, sir." Again my words poured out before I could stopper them up.

"Things are not always what they seem, are they, Mr. Garrick?"

The tip of Gage's quill pointed directly at me.

"Army officers exist to be obeyed and lower ranks exist to obey. This is the natural order of things. Officers are gentlemen of breeding and distinction while the ranks are the kennel sweepings of our society. The Army sets the price of a commission steep enough to keep out riffraff. Oh, once in a great while we commission someone from the lower ranks, stiffen up the bloodlines as it were, but it is our decision, not the upstart's."

The general stared at me and his eyes flashed with the same intensity they took when he spoke of the Colonials. "I don't know how you gulled your way into an Army commission—no doubt your adroitness at the card table—but I know you for the gutter-dregs you are, Garrick."

"Sir, if you've a complaint about the service I've rendered as—"

Gage pounded the desk with the flat of his hand. "You will listen, I will speak."

Cold winter air whistled up the flue.

"I intend to use you, Garrick, as I would use a plowhorse. This Salem expedition. If it succeeds, that ninny Leslie will garner the credit. If it fails..." He flashed a shark's smile. "I rather suspect your superbly honed sense of sense of self-interest will see to it does not. Dismissed."

I saluted and spun on my boot heel. I had not yet made the door when Gage added: "I'm paying out enough rope to let you hang yourself, guttersnipe. If not today, if not tomorrow, then soon. Breeding always tells."

WE SPENT that cold winter night, Saturday, February twenty-fifth, rowing out in small boats to the troopship in great secrecy—no lanterns, oars muffled, men forbidden to even speak. We slipped out of Boston Harbor and sailed up the coast to the designated cove where we weighed anchor and hid below in the stifling lower decks. We waited.

And waited.

I spent those long hours going over in my mind Gage's tirade.

Oh, he'd been right about me.

I had started life as a street urchin, a shoeblack at one of London's leading opera houses. It was there that I learned to ape the mannerisms and speech of my betters. It was also there that I learned that indeed Gage had right about the other, too, that the world was divided between slave masters and slaves.

Irrespective of my lack of any galling chains, I was a slave. Did what I was told, lived like I was told, and made to grovel in gratitude at the feet of those who gave those orders.

I'd not wish to be any sort of slave master, but I would not be a slave—and there was no third way.

My observations of the high and haughty at the opera house had also taught me that the vast, uncrossable gulf between me and my betters was an artificial one. That they were no better men, no wiser, no smarter, no more pious than I, only that they had two things I lacked: money and standing.

Money I could scrape up. As Gage said, I had a certain ability with the pasteboards, and—even more importantly—an even greater dexterity ferreting out those who did not.

But standing? How was I to gain that? My low birth precluded me from all other paths save academe or the clergy, which my personal habits closed off just as securely. No, the only path to standing was the military, and one needed influential friends to rise in the Navy.

That left the Army. I soon had the price of an ensign's commission—400 pound—and my theatrics and glib patter would allow me to imitate being a "gentleman" long enough to purchase it, but I knew I was bound to be found out as a fraud soon after.

If I stayed in England.

But if I took a commission in a regiment leaving for the Americas, I'd be too far away to have my made-up background exposed. By the time I returned to England, my actual career in the Army would see me through.

And so it had until Gage ferreted me out.

In the dark of the hold, I glanced over at my commander, slack-jawed and green as the anchored ship slowly rolled and dipped with the waves. I had to ensure this ninny, as Gage had so aptly described him, this seasick ninny succeeded in this fool's mission if I were to keep my grasp upon my new life above the gutter.

We disembarked at two o'clock and by two-fifteen we were marching up the Neck Road to Salem. No scouts, no flankers. Just quick-marching as fast as possible toward our goal before the locals could react.

The few short miles flew by in near-silence. The tromp of boots, the jingle of brass buckles, the hollow thonk-thonk-thonk of wooden canteens slapping against bayonet scabbards. Our heated breaths steamed white in the cold winter air.

A Colonial rider from Marblehead overtook us. He cantered past our column, doffing his hat and pausing to chat with Colonel Leslie for a moment.

Some Loyalist acquaintance he knew—a Tory named Pederick, Leslie explained. I tried to tell him he could trust no Tory out of his sight, but Leslie ignored my warning. After a brief chat, Pederick cantered off. He pulled ahead of our column and rounded the corner. By the time we had rounded that same corner, Pederick was nowhere on the road to be seen.

He had galloped ahead to warn the townspeople of Salem, just as I had feared.

The townspeople of Salem were ready for us when we arrived.

Their militia, their vaunted Minute Men, lined the opposite shore of the

North River. They had raised the drawbridge over the river, blocking us from entering the town.

The foundry where the cannon were hidden lay only a short distance from the drawbridge. I could see the locals dragging away the cannon into nearby fields, covering them over with hay and leaves and branches and even shovelfuls of dirt.

Leslie, fool that he was, saw nothing but the impediment of the river before him, balking his entry.

A few boats, dinghies and such, lined the bank. He ordered some of our men to seize them, but the locals were too quick. The raced ahead of our men and knocked the bottoms out of the boats with axes.

Across the bank, the Colonials mocked and jeered us as our stymied men stood and shivered.

"They must be fiddlers, they shake so!" yelled one.

"Red jackets, lobsterbacks!" yelled another. "Cowards!" yelled still another.

More ominously, it was one of their leaders who yelled "Damnation to your government!"

Your government.

This was the start of a bloody rebellion only a match away from igniting.

Leslie, of course, began forming up ranks. He meant to begin shooting, striking that match.

The locals began forming their own lines, reading to return fire.

It was at this point that the town's militia leader, a Colonel Timothy Pickering, arrived. A ruddy-jowled man in his late fifties.

Leslie, still issuing preparatory orders, either did not see or pretended not to see the white flag of parley Pickering's aide held aloft. When I pointed it out, Leslie sniffed, "A ruse, a Colonial trick to make us lower our guard."

It was no ruse.

I saw a desperate Pickering adopt a curious square-elbowed posture, a gesture. The Grand Hailing Sign of Distress of the Masons.

Leslie was no Mason, but I was.

Like my Army commission, the Masonic Order was means to an end. A path to genteel society open for me, one where I could garner acquaintanceship with the influential.

"Sir," I urged, explaining the gesture, "no Mason would play false with that. I beg you. If you think it some trick, send me over to parley with him. I'm expendable."

My urgency was, for once, heartfelt. I knew what Gage would do with me if Leslie failed here at Salem—and starting a war was indeed, failing.

Leslie thought, and I could see the brass clockwork gears ratchet 'round in his head. A successful parley would give me the glory instead of him. "No. You shall accompany me as I parley with them."

Leaving his second-in-command in charge of the troops, Leslie and I rode over in a small skiff provided by Pickering.

Hurriedly stepping in front of Leslie, I shook hands with Pickering, giving him the Grip and the "will you spell it/halve it" and all the other folderol to establish my bona fides.

"I doubt there is anything to discuss. I am here for your cannon," Leslie said, brushing aside any pleasantries. "I mean to take them back with me. The only thing to discuss is whether my men slaughter your men first before I do so."

Pickering wrung his hands. He was frightened, I could tell, but it was not Leslie's threats that frightened him. I could tell that, too.

"I ask but an hour. One hour to show you something first." His head lowered. "After seeing what I have to show you, if you still want the cannon, you may take them. We will not resist."

I urged Leslie to agree. We had still had plenty of daylight. An hour wasted was a cheap price to pay to accomplish our mission without bloodshed.

"Very well," Leslie said, marking the time shown on a nearby clock tower. "One hour."

"This way," Pickering said, leading us into the foundry.

A man met us inside, a disheveled man wearing a greasy leather tanner's apron. More gargoyle, than man—William Billings, as I described him earlier. One-eyed, one-armed, and standing on mismatched legs. He reached inside a pocket under his leather apron and pulled away a handful of snuff. With a great gaseous honking noise like flatulence in reverse, he inhaled as much of it as his nostril could pass. The surfeit he jammed back into his pocket.

"They've woken It," he rasped in his crow-loud voice. "The trampings of their boots. The trampings of their minds."

"Brother Billings will guide you down into the chamber," Pickering said. "You must hurry. If what he says is true, haste is essential."

Λ

Down a long, rickety wooden circular staircase we descended, down a narrow cylindrical shaft cut into the living rock of the earth's sacred crust.

Down, down, down we went, farther than any miner ever dared, farther surely than any biblical lake of fire and brimstone.

At last we reached the end, the last treads of the staircase bottomed out into a fantastic cavern with walls of faceted gem.

"Diamonds?" I whispered, running my hand across the faceting.

"Mere glass," Pickering said. "It grows naturally down here, like salt crystals on a string suspended in a glass of brine."

"Not mere glass," Billings crow-rasped. "Peer deeper."

I did, staring it the facets more closely. Suddenly I saw movement across the face of the glass, like movement in a mirror, only this was no mirror. What I saw were scenes of war. Bloody, violent war. War between red-coated British soldiers and blue-coated Colonials. Whole armies crashing against each other.

Scenes shifted, one after another. I saw General Gage. More scenes. I saw a General Burgoyne, a General Prescott. I saw Lord Cornwallis.

More scenes. I saw another general, General Clinton ordering his troops. I saw Colonel Leslie following those orders, his troops advancing across a white plain toward a broad, blue river.

I saw myself directing the loading of cannon in that same sanguine battle.

"The future," Billings rasped. "Your future, my future, our countries' future."

I could not help but notice he emphasized the plurality of countries.

Pickering, stolid sensible Pickering, broke the spell. "Hurry, gentleman. This way."

If the first chamber was fantastical, there are no words in the English language for the main chamber we entered.

Huge. So huge. One could put all of Parliament Building inside it and still have room left over for much of London. That strange living glass also adorned its cavern walls. Light from some unknown source caused the facets to blaze.

A company of men clustered around the near wall. Mason, stone masons I mean, with hammers and chisels, attempting to cut a round sphere whole out of the living glass. The task must have been a near-impossible one, for scattered about their feet were dozens, no hundreds, of shattered previous attempts.

But it was not the stone masons that first drew my eyes. It was the cannon— a Dutch a six-pounder polished like new, brother to the ones above being hidden away—manned and pointed directly at the center of the cavern.

Flanking the cannon stood a choir of men in Masonic regalia softly singing hymnodies.

My ears may have lingered on the hymns, but my eyes followed the trajectory of the pointing cannon's muzzle.

It pointed to a large hole in the floor of the cavern.

At first I thought my eyes were playing tricks—a deep, deepening shadow seemed to twist and gyre above the hole. But the more I stared, the more certain I was somehow that indeed that fell shadow did move and coil and writhe

"Get back!" hissed Billings, pulling us to the cavern's wall. "It awakens!"

A bugle sounded and the crew manning the cannon sprang to action. They rammed powder down its bore as quickly and surely as any British artillery crew I'd ever seen, but it was not a lead cannon ball they loaded next.

No, it was a faceted sphere of that living glass hewn from the cavern walls.

Suddenly, with no warning other than the chill of Death brushing its way down my spine, an immense creature—a thing—burst out of the hole, burst out of the writhing shadow into the light.

Tall it was, taller than any steeple. Broad it was, broader than any building. I attempted to ascertain its shape, but somehow the shape of the hideous thing shifted and contorted, never staying one thing constant.

Limbs it had. Great coils of tentacles lined on the underside with gaping suckers like a monstrous octopus, the tips of which were shaped like the head of an eyeless moray eel, all teeth and jaw and rending death.

Legs it had, the churning cloven hooves of the devil itself, centipedal in endless, changing numbers.

It wore the T-shaped head of a gigantic hammerhead shark, horrible insectoid compound eyes poised on the ends of the cranial crossbar. Its open mouth held not teeth but more of those writhing tentacles serving as squirming, squamous cilia.

Its lumpen torso proved perhaps most horrible of all. It looked as if it once had been covered in a sickly beige fur, but only a few scraggly patches remained. Instead, the dead-fish white of its skin was choked with pestilent, pustulant, cancerous boils so rotted with death and decay that I marveled that the thing could still live.

But live it did, and it radiated a numbing feeling of age. Older, more ancient than the Earth, of God's Creation itself. But more than that it radiated sheer Evil, Evil so vile to be beyond the ken of the Devil himself.

It stared at us, we puny mortal Men—the stone masons, the choirmen, the cannoneers. At me.

And then it lunged.

It crossed the great space of the cavern in a trice, faster almost than I could blink. Its tentacles reached out hungrily for my flesh, for my soul.

I am not ashamed to admit that in that moment I screamed, paralyzed.

And then just before it reached me, it suddenly faltered and slumped.

Above the scraping wheeze of the thing's bellow-like breath, I heard this— the notes and words of the song I now know to be "Chester"—

Let tyrants shake their iron rod,
And Slav'ry clank her galling chains,
We fear them not, we trust in God,
New England's God forever reigns.

On and on the verses flowed, telling of the future battles I had seen in the living glass, telling of not only of hope but of eventual victory over this foul thing.

With each new note, the creature's form solidified, as if the laws of nature, the laws of God's creation, of mortality, finally took dominion over its alien nature.

Yet it persisted, continued to twitch, to slowly advance toward me.

Once solidified, however, it could now be targeted.

With a roar the cannon fired its crystalline shot. The glass sphere struck it true, stunning it finally into quiescent submission.

Unconscious, the creature underwent a final metamorphosis. It lost solid shape altogether, revering back into that liquid tenebrous shadow-matter I'd seen earlier. The liquid flowed back toward the hole and down it like a drain.

The thing had been contained once again.

The hymnists had switched to a gentler, less martial tune. The cannoneers swabbed out their gun.

Billings mopped his greasy brow with a rag only slightly less greasy. "One hundred-and-twenty hymns I wrote before I finally found one that neutralized it."

"W-what—" Colonel Leslie croaked, his throat parched from sheer terror, "what was that thing."

"That," said Billings, "is New England's God." He pocketed the rag. "At least that is what we've grown to call it."

"But what is it?"

Pickering, the militia leader, placed a hand on our red-coated shoulders. "The personification of slavery, of servitude, of subjugation for the sake of subjugation. It feeds off these, both thought and deed. Of one man seeing himself to be above another. Of seeing others as beneath him.

"Aye," said Billings, digging out another handful of snuff. "It awakened during the Witch Trials. Cotton Mather and all his tergiversations and falsehoods, his infernal need to cast down others to parade his own self-righteousness."

Pickering nodded. "And now you British with your need to grind us under your heel have stirred it up again."

Luckily, Colonel Leslie hadn't heard him through Billing's snuff-snorting honk. "We must kill it," Leslie said. "We must destroy that foul thing."

Pickering shook his head. "It cannot be destroyed. The best we can do is keep it at bay. That is why we need those cannon. Not to fight you, but to fight it."

"But you already have a cannon down here," I said, pointed it.

Billings wiped his running snuff-coated nose with the back of a snot-encrusted hand. "This isn't the only cavern it can emerge from, if it gets hungry enough. Twenty-four others. Twenty-four cannon."

"I see. I see, indeed," Leslie said. "But will even that be enough? If that thing should break to the surface—if it should walk abroad upon all the land—"

"Not all the land," Pickering said. "It cannot cross running water, at least not major rivers. It's constrained to New England, thank Providence, hemmed in by the Hudson to the west and the St. Laurence to the north."

Leslie straightened his shoulders. "Colonel Pickering, Mister Billings—you shall keep your cannon."

"And if General Gage objects?" I asked.

"After seeing that?!" Leslie snapped his fingers. "A fig for General Gage. We'll simply tell him there weren't any cannon here to be found."

"Excellent," Pickering said. "And now, I believe your hour is almost up. Brother Billings, lead the colonel back up before his troops get nervous."

Leslie and Billings strode off toward the staircase.

Pickering pulled me aside. "He'll quickly forget what transpired here. A mind not warded with the frequent repetition of Masonic rituals soon cannot hold the memory of the physical representation of It very long."

"Will I remember?"

Pickering nodded. "The rituals work. Even for a Mason who no more believes in them than he believes in the uniform he wears."

I gave Pickering a startled look. Had I really been found out twice in the space of less than a day?

"Be at ease, young man," Pickering said. "I've no deep insight into a man I've only so briefly met. I'm merely repeating the words I've seen myself utter so many times in the living glass. Those words, and these:

"You think that to avoid being a slave, you must grudgingly become a slave master, that there is no third way. But there is. You have seen into the glass. We are building that third way here, on this continent, a nation where all men are created equal and endowed by their Creator with unalienable Rights. A nation where New England's God shall never hold sway."

October, 1809
West Point, New York

"And so we sailed back to Boston and told Gage we'd found no cannon. Gage thought, because we'd 'forced' the locals to allow our inspection, we'd won. The non-Masonic Colonials who knew nothing of the cavern, well, they'd thought they'd won because we'd left without their cannon. And so neither side backed down two months later at Lexington and Concord."

Garrick set aside his pipe and refilled his brandy glass.

The three goggle-eyed cadets stared at him in dead silence.

Irving, who'd scribbled not a single word during Garrick's story, refilled his own glass. "You said you'd met Billings twice."

Garrick nodded. "So I did."

He relit his pipe. "The second time should interest you, Mr. Irving, as it happened in New York. Upon the field of battle at White Plains, to be exact..."

October, 1776
White Plains, New York

AFTER LEXINGTON and Concord and Bunker Hill, General Gage had managed to get himself replaced by General William Howe, for which I was eternally grateful. Shortly thereafter, Howe marched us off New England soil and sailed us to Nova Scotia, for which I was infernally grateful.

Come July, when the American Congress was scribbling their Declaration of Independence, Howe landed the British Army in New York harbor, determined to crush Washington's puny little Continental Army once and for all.

By October we'd taken Staten Island, Long Island, and the southern portion of Manhattan. We were now poised on the broad flats of White Plains to drive the ragtag remnants of Washington's army straight into Hudson River.

Colonel Leslie was now Brigadier-General Leslie. He was such a well-bred ninnyhammer that of course the British Army would see him as perfect general material. The only decision he'd made as general that I'd agreed with was appointing me to his staff.

On the night preceding the twenty-eighth, we gathered around a farmhouse table, staring a map by lantern light. The map showed the Hudson to our west. Washington's main lines were to the north, but a significant portion of his men were to our immediate west, atop an insignificant hill wedged between the river and our lines. Howe had ordered Leslie to storm that hill.

Either we would push the Colonials atop it into the river or Washington must come down to succor them, in which case the Howe's main body of five thousand crack regulars would smash them upon their anvil.

Either way, in the morning the American Army would be destroyed, and with it, their stillborn republic.

The mood in our requisitioned Tory farmhouse was jovial. This would be the last night of the war and the recent unpleasantness would soon be behind us. We faced an easy battle ahead. A reconnoiter of Chatterton's Hill had revealed that the Americans had little in the way of cannon or even musketry. Indeed, our scouts had reported seeing the some Doodles reduced to carrying makeshift spears and pikes.

"We'll reduce them to carrying twigs and dirt clods!" Leslie roared and his staff laughed with him.

Leslie swept the map with the tip of his sterling-tipped riding crop, his latest affectation. "I will want our Hessians under von Donop here on the right flank, our British regulars on the left. We will sweep up the hill directly westward—" he flicked his crop thusly "—and drown them in the river."

Aides heads bobbed.

Leslie looked around. One of his aides was missing. The Hessian interpreter. "Dietrich. Where is Dietrich?"

Luckily for him, Lt. Dietrich Knackenbucher chose that moment to step through the door. A bluff, hardy Hessian with a barrel chest and broad shoulders, he hardly looked like a studious "book cracker," which is how his name translated. Dietrich was a holy terror on horseback. Indeed, he seemed to think that the only place for an officer in battle was atop a horse. I had tried to warn him of frontier Colonials whose long-distance prowess with their Pennsylvania rifles was matched only by their hatred of Prussians, but he scoffed at the danger. I continued to be amazed that he hadn't been potted yet.

Dietrich waved a sheet of paper and unleashed a stream of excited, guttural German. Eventually switching to English, he said, "The Americans are getting sehr desperate indeed!" He passed around the paper. "They are offering bribes for any of our men—Hessisch oder Engländer—to switch sides. Two pigs and a cow! Ha! As if my men would settle for such a ridiculously low sum!"

I grabbed at the printed broadside, tilted it to read it by firelight. It was true. Two pigs and cow. And for officers, a land grant.

Someone else reached for the sheet.

Numbly, I handed it away.

I staggered out of the tent.

All this time, ever since the cavern and the creature below, I had lived in a dark cloud of despair. I had seen with my own eyes the foul being I truly served by wearing the redcoat uniform of King George.

My driving ambition to not call any man master had led me down the path of masterdom myself. And by the time I learned there might be a third path, it was too late.

The Americans would never welcome me after my having led troops against them. No, I was trapped on the English side, where renouncing my officer's commission meant sliding back down into London's gutters.

And now I find out, on the eve of the American's destruction, that they would have welcomed me gladly after all.

It was not the offered pig or cow or land that I craved, but the proffered hand of equality.

Morning came and the battle began. First a skirmish here, then there. The crackle of muskets. Blue gunpowder smoke wafting up, mingling with the white moist breath of the men in serried ranks. Then the full weight of the two opposing armies smashed together and the battle began in earnest.

The Hessians on the left flank attacking up Chatterton's Hill were having a hard go of it. They were learning that sharpened spears and bladed pikes were no laughing matter when their wielders sheltered behind stone walls impervious to musket fire. It meant bayonet work where one blade was as effective as another.

The Americans—Smallwood's Marylanders—suddenly rose and counterattacked down the hill. The Hessians were undone.

General Leslie snapped his brass telescope shut. "It's Bunker Hill all over again. We must relieve pressure on the Hessians. Our right wing must press harder. One good hard push and those people will give way—I feel it!"

His head swiveled side to side, looking for a runner. He'd already sent the lot. His gaze fell on me. "You. Garrick. Get to the 35th Regiment. Tell that sluggard Colonel Carr he is hereby relieved. Take command of the 35th yourself and get them started up that hill!"

He had just given me a colonelcy—a field promotion in the heat of battle, the battle of all battles in this war—and very likely a medal in the bargain.

I had achieved my place at last. I was now permanently ensconced in the ruling class irrespective of my gutter-bred origins.

I saluted and turned to sprint across the field.

At that moment, the earth shook and the sky darkened.

A great tearing sound could be heard, an unearthly keening like that of a host of lost souls under the lash.

And then suddenly there it was, looming above the battlefield—the foul shifting evil of New England's God. The vile creature had fed itself, gorged itself on the thoughts and deeds of seven thousand British troops gathered to drag an entire continent down and affix the clanking chains of subjugation.

It had broken free of its cavern, broken free of the Masons, and now its evil walked abroad upon the land.

It roared its triumph in the cold autumn sunlight.

And then its myriad legs and hooves rushed it straight toward Chatterton's Hill.

The American lines broke.

But so did our Prussians and British regulars.

Victor and vanquished, subjugator and subject—it did not seem to matter. Both sides were terrified of the monstrosity's primal fury.

Nothing could stop it the Evil thereto.

No. One thing could.

One thing could stop it, nullify its powers.

My throat dry with fear, my lungs paralyzed in terror, I nonetheless lifted up my voice:

Let tyrants shake their iron rod,
And Slav'ry clank her galling chains—

The thing paused, looked at me in confusion, perhaps even in pain.

From across the lines of battle, the fife and drums of the American bluecoats picked up my feeble song. Quickly the hilltop echoed in the sounds of American voices sounding their hymn of salvation: "Chester."

The creature writhed in unaccustomed pain, stymied, flummoxed, but not defeated. I knew that in only moments it would shrug off the effect of Billing's song.

Suddenly there they were, standing at my side. Colonel Pickering, in his American bluecoat, and William Billings, in his grimy tanner's apron. They were bruised and bloody, but they had managed to follow the creature up through whatever Stygian underground passage the creature had emerged from.

Billings held the cannon ball carved out of living glass in the crook of his one unwithered arm. "Quickly," he croaked. "A cannon."

Nodding, I led the two to a nearby British cannon, abandoned in the chaos and terror. Pickering and I served as powder monkeys, officers unaccustomed to the actual work of loading cannon. We somehow managed to ram down first the powder charge and then the precious crystal projectile. Billings stood by the match hole as we sighted the cannon at the hulking form of the screeching evil thing.

"Now!" Pickering shouted his eye squinted at the target.

Billings touched the match.

It was at that moment, between the touching of the match and the lighting of the powder that Dietrich Knackenbucher, that idiot Hessian horseman, saw an American bluecoat commandeering a British cannon and spurred his horse forward toward us, bent on riding down a perceived enemy.

The cannon roared.

The glass cannon ball arced across a trajectory carrying it straight into the vitals of the monstrous creature.

But not before it first smashed through Dietrich's skull, decapitating him in a fraction of a second. So quickly in fact that the rest of his body continued to sit astride its terrified steed, galloping westward with all possible speed down the Tarrytown Road. I was told later that the gruesome corpse managed to stay in the saddle all the way to the nearby hamlet, whose name is Sleepy Hollow, if I remember correctly.

As for New England's God, the instant the living glass cannonball struck it, it dissolved again into liquid shadow and sunk once more deep into the subterranean bowels of this weary Earth.

Like before, the memory of the creature quickly faded in the minds those who'd seen it. In the confusion, the beaten Americans atop the hill instead of being driven into the river to drown managed to avoid capture and slip northward to rejoin the main body of Washington's troop, that said body then retreating north into the hills and safety.

Guided, no doubt, by Pickering's Masonic brothers whose minds, like mine, were not aided with the fog of forgetfulness.

We British had won the battle, but not the war. Washington's Army still lived.

I did not relieve Carr of his command or get that colonelcy, but then I did not care anymore about such things.

That night in the dark, I slipped past the British pickets and, printed broadside clutched firmly in hand, I crossed over to the American lines.

Within the hour, I was standing before General Washington himself, and within a fortnight, I was a bluecoated colonel in the Continental Army fighting against New England's God and all its evil work.

I did take that land grant, of course. I'm not entirely an idealistic fool.

I did make sure, however that it was west of the Hudson River and not in the New England domain of a creature that, however subdued, is never really defeated.

⋀

October, 1809
West Point, New York

"AFTER THE WAR," Garrick said, "the Army and the Mason destroyed twenty-three of those twenty-four glass caverns. Only one was kept to entomb the creature in. To this day, the Masons keep watch below while the Army keeps watch above."

"Th-the Army?" Cadet Showalter blurted.

Garrick took a long drag on his pipe. "Why do you think the Point is situated on the Hudson's west bank, Mister Showalter? Why do you think its cannons continue to point east toward the opposite bank?"

Clock chimes sounded the quarter of the hour. Garrick put down his smoldering pipe.

"Almost lights out," Garrick told the three wide-eyed cadets.

Reluctantly, they made their thanks and made to leave.

Showalter turned, clearly embarrassed. "Ah, that was a pretty good story, sir, especially about us still keeping watch. You almost had me believing in it."

"Story?" Garrick asked. "What makes you think it was only a story?"

He nodded toward a polished walnut armoire standing against the far wall. "If you will check that large cabinet door there in the middle, you'll find one of the glass cannon balls we keep on hand."

Showalter started toward it, hand outstretched, then realized what he was doing. His face flushed bright red from ear to ear. "You almost had me, sir."

The cadets filed out, the other two teasing and jeering Showalter.

Irving, still seated at the far end of the table, put away his pencil and pad. "I'd better be getting back to that tavern I'm rooming at. If I hurry, I can get there before they close the bar."

Garrick shook his hand in farewell. "I trust the evening wasn't a total loss."

Irving smiled. "I told you I traffick in the odd, the strange, the turn of a phrase. I found the image of a headless Hessian galloping into a town named Sleepy Hollow a striking one, and the name Dietrich Knackenbucher whimsical enough I could put it to good use, though I'd have to render it into Manhattan Dutch first: Knickerbocker, perhaps. Yes, a Knickerbocker tale."

He settled his fashionable civilian hat upon his head. "But my dear, dear Colonel—please leave the wild Hallowe'en storytelling to us professionals."

Garrick closed the outer door and latched the bolt. He returned to the dining room. He'd leave it for his manservant to clean in the morning. The brandy, however, he better put away now.

He stoppered the bottles and carried them over the armoire. He opened the large middle door and set them next to the cannonball carved of living glass.

CAN SUCH THINGS BE?

INTRODUCTION

"Can Such Things Be?" is the second story I wrote for my "Clockwork Deseret" chthonic-steampunk-alternate history series, and the first chronologically. It's the origin story of the Republic of Deseret's supernatural-battling spy agency, the "Correlation Department."

"Such Things" appeared in A Mighty Fortress, the fourth and final volume of Immortal Works' Mormon Steampunk series.

I had a lot of fun with this one, doing the research on 1880s Price, Utah and its attendant mining communities. It's truly amazing what you can dig up on the internet. (I think back on my beginning writer days of library book stacks and card catalog files and shudder.) I particularly enjoyed coming up with the monster for this one, as well as the idea of a fourth see-no-evil monkey.

In "Such Things", I formally reveal the identity of the Correlation Department, the man who works under the nom de guerre of Nate Sabbas and whose real name can be anagrammed into "Creameries Bob": Ambrose Bierce, noted proto-sf author famous for mysteriously disappearing without a trace.

Charles Fort once snarked of Bierce's disappearance that maybe somebody was collecting Ambroses. If by somebody he meant science fiction authors, then somebody certainly has.

I first encountered Bierce in Heinlein's Lost Legacy novel (a criminally underrated work, in my opinion) where he'd collected up Ambrose for a tale of paranormal abilities *and mysterious doings at mysterious Mount Shasta. "Such Things" is a nod to Heinlein and Mount Shasta in my own collecting up of poor Mr. Bierce for fictional purposes.*

I described Bierce as a proto-sf author, but actually Bierce's stories read surprisingly modern. He was Weird Tales *before there was a* Weird Tales, *and his influence on many Golden Age SF writers is well deserved. I've tried to pay a little homage to his work, not only directly using one of his story titles, but also using others of his titles for section heads.*

Steam buckboards and chthonic coal mines, magic bullets and magic mountains— "Can Such Things Be?" They can in the pages of the following story...

I. The Secret of Macarger's Gulch

March 12, 1888
Macarger's Gulch Mine
Price City, Republic of Deseret

Mormon Apostle and First Vice President of the Republic of Deseret George Q. Cannon carefully stepped down from the steam buckboard into coal-dirty snow. The shift in weight caused the wagon to flex on its springs, shattering the thin rime of ice formed from the dense fog. Shattered ice tinkled like tiny wind chimes.

Cannon stamped his half-frozen feet in an attempt to warm up. The ride from Price's train depot to the mining camp had been a long, cold one. Even his graying beard had started to form its own rime of ice.

His eyes and throat burned. Much of the heavy fog was coal, thick enough in the air to taste. Chimney smoke from the town, coal dust from the mine, from the tailings, from the mountains of heaped coal waiting along the rail lines for shipment.

If he hadn't had an audience, he might have spat some of that acrid taste from his mouth, but an audience he did have.

Besides a second wagon of government agents, there were two local men. The locals came up to greet him: Jean Pierre Arceneaux, the local bishop, and Tom Williams, representing the mine. Both men carried lever-action repeating Ogden-Browning rifles. They looked dead on their feet. White bandages swaddled Williams's head above his bruised and cut face.

Of the miners themselves, none had shown up, although Cannon could feel them staring at him from the putative safety of their tarpaper shanties.

Cannon couldn't blame them, if only because of the bitter cold.

Blizzard of '88, they were calling it back East. Out here in the West, folks' teeth were chattering too hard to call it anything but cold. Frosts early, crop season cut short, granaries emptying rapidly—much of Deseret would be a mite hungry by and by.

Cannon already had a long list of things to worry about. He didn't need *things* like what had happened added to that list as well, and yet—if he didn't take care of it, who would? Deseret had nobody else to do it.

Bishop Arceneaux stepped up and offered a hand in greeting. Cannon's own hands were so cold, he couldn't pull his glove off. He had to bite the finger of it to pull it free. Arceneaux pumped the Apostle's hand in the usual over-vigorous Mormon handshake.

"Don't know whether to call you Elder Cannon, Brother Cannon, or Mr. Vice-President," the French convert said with a weary attempt at a smile. The man had his own list of local worries.

"Vice President will do," Cannon said. "This falls more under my wheelhouse in Home Office than my ecclesiastical duties."

"You'd rethink that, if you'd seen 'em," Williams muttered. Williams had a face like a squoze lemon and a voice with all the dulcet tones of a wood rasp. "Straight from the fiery pits of Hell they were—"

"Tom," Arceneaux gently chided his companion. "What happened was bad enough, no need to embellish it."

Williams fell into a sullen silence.

Behind Cannon, his government men clambered down from the stake-bed wagon. They shrugged on curious overalls, rubberized like gum boots.

"You received my cable?" Cannon asked.

Arceneaux nodded. "We left one of them lay so you could get a look at it like you wanted."

Williams eyed the government unloading ropes and tackle and huge canvas tarps. "More than a look, I'd wager." He jutted a chin at the stake-bed wagon with its large, flat bed. "Plan on hauling it back with you, ain'tcha?"

"Back to town in the wagon, then from there by train back to Salt Lake."

Williams snorted. "You're gonna need a bigger wagon."

"We'll see. If need be, they can cut it up." Cannon's men had also brought a couple steam saws along. "Now where—?"

"The minehead." Arceneaux took Cannon by the elbow. "This way."

Cannon let himself be led. The fog was thick, the snow-packed ground treacherous, and Cannon knew he was not a young man anymore.

The walk to the minehead didn't take long. Arceneaux stopped next to the office shack that sat at the mouth of the mine. "Here." He pointed.

Arceneaux needn't have bothered.

Fog or no, nobody could miss the monstrous giant rattlesnake coiled and curved across the cold, cold snow.

A rattlesnake Mother Nature never conceived.

A hundred feet long if it was an inch. Its tail forked out into a brace of rattles, each the size of a nail keg. And as for the head...

Heads, plural.

The foul thing had two heads, spade shaped and fanged. Dear heaven, how they were fanged. Its poison must also have been an acid of some sort. The red-brown dirt under its jaws boiled and sizzled under the still-dripping venom.

A true cold-blooded reptile could never have functioned in this temperature, but the snake hadn't frozen to death, that was for sure. Scores of holes pock-marked the entire length of the corpse. The locals must have shot bullet after bullet into the creature in an attempt to bring it down.

Worst of all—worst because it proved beyond a shadow of a doubt what Cannon and Deseret faced here with these monsters—the snake's corpse had begun to revert back to its original form—a ribboned seam of black, bituminous coal.

Cannon toed it gingerly with his boot. "Hard to believe this thing was ever truly alive."

"Alive enough to kill six men," the dour-face Williams snapped.

Arceneaux sighed. "Easy, Tom."

To Cannon, the Frenchman said, "Williams was down with the men when it happened, you understand. He's still a little shaken."

Cannon smiled, a smile as cold as the frosted air. "Myself, I'd be *more* than merely 'shaken.' Please tell me what happened down there."

Williams gave Arceneaux a sideways glance, as if expecting another reprimand, then began to relate his tale. "Like your bishop said, I was down there with them Greeks—"

"Miners, Tom," Arceneaux gently chided. "Miners."

Like most mining towns in Deseret, Price was predominantly Gentile. And, like most such towns, that caused friction. That the miners here happened to be mostly Greek and the local Mormons mostly French didn't help matters. Nor did the fact that Williams, judging from the interplay between the two locals, furnished much of that friction personally.

Williams sullenly continued. "Like I said, I was down there with the *miners*. They'd ran into a coal seam so rich, the way they described it, it didn't sound possible."

"Tom's a mining engineer," Arceneaux said, "So—"

"Will you let me tell it?" Williams snapped. "Yeah, mining engineer—as if that made them Greeks ever listen to me. So anyhows, old man Macarger, he's the mine owner, he sends me down to check things myself, see if them Greeks were making things up or lying or maybe just drunk."

Williams's voice trailed off as his gaze wandered over to the government spreading the rubberized tarp on the ground next to the monster. "You really gonna try shiftin' that thing, ain'tcha?"

"Please, Mr. Williams," Cannon said, "my time is limited. Pray continue. And remember, I'm more interested in snakes than ethnicities."

"Oh, snake. Right. Of course," Williams said. He rubbed the white bandage around his head. "Anyhows, so me and half of first shift, we're standing there at the rock face of number one shaft, staring at the richest coal seam I've ever seen —richest one in the entire world—when all of a sudden, bang, it happens!"

"Bang, *what* happened?" Cannon asked.

White breath curled in the cold as Williams struggled to find words to explain it. "Gonna sound crazy, I know, but that coal seam began shimmying and shaking, just like a live snake, and started shining brighter than the morning star."

He made an undulating motion with his hand. "And then all of a sudden like, that coal seam just slithered right out of the rock face. Right out. Just like a living snake. It *was* a living snake." His voiced faltered. "Fanged two of us before we could bat an eye."

Williams wiped his brow. Sweat dripped down his face and neck just remembering it. "Me and the Greeks, we hightail it for the surface, that thing just a slitherin' right behind us. Lost four more before we made it topside. I rang the alarm—" he pointed at the rusty steel triangle dangling on a rope tied to the eaves of the shack "— and grabbed me a rifle." He scuffed his foot in the snow. "Me an' the pit bosses, see, we sorta keep some rifles in the shack in case the miners ever have a difference of opinion with old man Macarger."

Cannon frowned. He spent a growing amount of his time trying to keep a lid on disputes between miners and mine owners. That they needed each other— and that Deseret needed them both—was something of which Cannon had had great difficulty persuading them.

"Where is Mr. Macarger now, by the way?" Cannon asked.

Williams clammed up.

For once, Arceneaux looked as sour-faced as Williams. "Mr. Macarger felt the best way to handle the situation was to leave on the first train out of Price."

"Naw, that ain't it." Williams scowled. "Macarger didn't light out, he just hopped a train to San Francisco so as to bring in Chinamen for the mine." He hooked his thumb in the direction of the tarpaper shanties. "On account of them Greeks refusing to go back down."

"Mr. Macarger needn't have bothered," Cannon said. "Nobody's going back down. I'm ordering the mine dynamited in the interests of public safety."

That set both locals back on their heels.

"Macarger's not going to like that much," Arceneaux said with clear under-statement.

"I don't know *I* likes it much," Williams said. "Maybe Arceneaux here," he pointed at his companion, "he might not care. He's still set with his dry goods store down there in town and all, but me? Means *I'm* out a job—right alongside them Greeks."

"Might be a blessing in disguise, Tom," Arceneaux said. "The Fisk brothers have been hounding you to go work for them anyway. I'd rather take their money than Macarger's any day."

"They're down Emery way, though. Not sure I want to pull up stakes."

"Better stakes than snakes."

Williams grimaced. "You got that right."

Simpson, the lead government man, walked over to Cannon, his awkward rubber boots *scrunching* in the snow. "We're ready to start bundling it up, sir, any time you say."

"Just a few more minutes, Simpson," Cannon said.

Simpson shrugged. "Getting dark soon. I'd prefer doing this while we still have light, if you know what I mean."

Cannon knew what he meant. Strange things happened in the dark these days. "Just a few more minutes."

He turned back to the mining engineer. "Please continue, Mr. Williams. You just sounded the alarm and laid hands on a rifle—"

"Yeah, yeah," Williams said. "I'd stopped running and grabbed me my rifle. Them Greeks, though," he turned his head and spat in the snow, "they just kept running."

"That isn't fair, and you know it, Tom," Arceneaux said softly. "Most of them came back after they'd seen to their wives and kids. You know they did."

"Okay, so some of them did," Williams said. "Some of them even had the mother-wit to bring their own guns." He spat again. "Not like that did a whole lot of good. Here, let me show you."

Williams held up his repeating rifle. With a quick back-and-forth levering of its handle—*chak-chak*—Williams ejected a round. He caught the ejected round in his hand and held it out for view.

Just a common .40 caliber lead slug. *Lead.*

Williams fed the round back into the receiver.

"We musta pumped a hundred lead rounds into that thing," he said. "All that did was put a lot of fool holes in it. Lead didn't hurt it one bit. Not one iota." The rasp of his voice softened. "If it hadn't've been for your bishop here..."

Arceneaux shrugged. "I just happened to be in camp at the time. Besides my

main store in town, I run a small cash store here in camp maybe one day a week."
He pointed off in the fog where the cash store must lie.

He continued. "I heard the alarm, we all did. First I thought it was a cave in,
but then I heard the fleeing miners shouting about a monster."

The Frenchman shrugged again in that Gallic way of his. "Then I remembered those crazy instructions the Brethren sent last month—" Arceneaux's face
suddenly flushed, realizing who he was talking to.

One corner of Cannon's mouth turned up slightly. He'd written the letter
himself. "Not so crazy-sounding now, I'd wager."

"I'd fight any man who tried to say it was," Arceneaux said, with an
exhausted attempt at a smile. "Anyway, I grabbed that carton of cartridges that
came with the letter—"

"The copper-jacketed slugs," Williams put in.

"The copper ones, like Tom says," Arceneaux agreed. "Well, they seemed to
do the trick."

Williams snorted. "Seemed to do the trick. Let me tell you, after me and the
Greeks shootin' the barrels off our rifles with no effect, your Bishop here walks
up and calmly as you please puts a single copper slug into that snake and it
immediately keels over and dies."

Arceneaux's face clouded with the memory. "That's when—"

"That's when them others all slithered out," Williams finished. "The baby
snakes." He snorted. "If you can call thirty-foot snakes 'babies.' Over a dozen
of 'em."

"We counted fourteen of the smaller snakes later after it was all over," Arceneaux supplied.

"Evidently you stirred up a nest of them," Cannon said. That wasn't good.
Wasn't good at all.

Williams spat. "You ain't foolin'! And them Greeks? When the smaller ones
showed up, them Greeks all run off a *second* time."

"Georgiadis stayed."

"Okay, Georgie stayed," Williams admitted. "And maybe the Kokolakis kid,
too."

"Did lead bullets have any effect on the smaller ones?" Cannon asked.

Both men shook their heads.

"Like spittin' into a furnace." Williams said. The mining engineer tapped the
receiver of his rifle. "Now, I may be slow but I ain't stupid. I shucked out my lead
bullets fast as I could lever and reloaded with those magic copper ones of yours.
Got them two Greeks to do likewise."

Williams shook, and not from the cold. "Twenty cartridges in a carton don't
go all that far among four shooters, especially when you're so skeered you

couldn't hit a barn door. W-we were down to our very last copper slug when we managed to put the last of them down."

Bishop Arceneaux laid a comforting hand on Williams's shoulder. "We did it, though. We killed them all."

He turned to Cannon. "But could you please tell me *what* we killed?"

Cannon looked at the two local men. Hurt, tired, but proud of what they'd done. And scared they'd have to do it all again.

Nests of them.

And neither the Brethren nor the government had the answers as to how such things could be—why the laws of nature and reality were suddenly shifting and breaking.

He could, however, answer at least one thing.

"Coal Rattlers," Cannon said softly. "That's what we've taken to calling them."

"Taken to—? Sweet heaven above," Arceneaux breathed. "You mean this wasn't the only—"

Cannon shook his head. "Park City and Coalville confirmed. Rumors of other places."

The locals fell silent and stared at each other. The mountains around Price were lousy with coal mines.

The Apostle toed the snake again. "You burn those other snake corpses?"

Both men nodded.

"Just like you cabled," Williams said. "Ground's too cold to bury 'em, so we just threw 'em down an abandoned shaft. Poured kerosene and quicklime on 'em and set 'em ablaze. Burned them down to ashes, that did. They was mostly back to being coal again by then, anyways. They burnt up real nice."

"Good. But I'd like to make sure. Before we dynamite the mine, I want you to pour salt on those ashes."

"Salt?"

Cannon tilted his head in the direction of the wagons. "We brought some fifty-pound sacks with us. Seems to work like copper does on them." Salt taken from the Great Salt Lake, at least. "We don't know why, exactly."

Salting the very ground. Maybe those ancient Romans knew more than they put down in their histories. The evils of ancient Carthage never came back, that was for sure.

Arceneaux cleared his throat. Concern lined his face.

"President Cannon," he said, "we were lucky this time, but what do we do if there's more of them?"

Williams nodded. "Yeah, sure, maybe you're dynamiting *this* mine, but we got a heap load of other coal mines around here."

"Your letter—this policy of having the local ward leaders handle these things," Arceneaux said, "it won't work. Maybe once, maybe twice. Not in the long run. We're just plain folk, family men. We're not soldiers. We're not gunmen."

And that, Cannon knew, was a very good point.

Yet, who else did Deseret have?

Cannon had no answer.

∩

II. The Realm of the Unreal

That evening
Deseret Pacific depot yard
Price City, Utah, Republic of Deseret

THE VICE presidential train sat on the rail siding, its engine chuffing steam in great clouds of white that drifted upward to join the lingering fog. Gas lamps lit the dark fog-shrouded night in fragile cones of white-wisped light.

George Q. Cannon stood on the end platform of his private saloon car watching the government men tie down that giant snake carcass to the flatbed hooked between his car and the caboose.

Engine, coal car, saloon, flatbed, caboose. All for just one person: him.

Cannon still felt a bunch of foolishness, an entire train just to haul him around, but he didn't begrudge the extravagance this time. Time had been of the essence.

The government men had tightly wrapped the snake in that rubberized tarp back at the minehead. They'd had to chop it into sections with their steam chainsaws after all. Now the men, finally out of their rubberized overalls, were lashing a second tarp over it, securing the cover tarp to the flatbed railcar.

Simpson, their leader, jumped the distance between flatbed and saloon.

Must be nice to be young.

"Just about got it secured, sir," Simpson said, white breath pluming with every word. The temperature must have dropped another ten degrees since they arrived back at the station. "Why don't you go inside and warm yourself up. You can't help anything by standing out here watching and fretting."

Cannon chuckled sourly. "I'm in your road, is that what you're trying to say?"

"I wouldn't say that, sir," Simpson said, "but the Good Lord provided Franklin stoves and warm railway cars for a reason."

"Alright, alright," Cannon sighed. "I'll go inside and get out of your hair."

Simpson sighed. "All due respect, Mr. Vice President, but you've said that before." Simpson opened the door into the railcar and gently chivvied Cannon into the car's small entry hallway, closing the door firmly behind them both.

After being in the bitter cold so long, the cherry warmth of the car near staggered him. Simpson began to peel layers of clothing off Cannon. His heavy outer jacket and the woolen muffler around his neck were still rimed with ice.

Cannon pushed away Simpson's hands. "I'm not decrepit yet. Quite capable of removing my own coat."

Simpson smiled, ducked his head in a clumsy bow, and exited the car to resume supervising his men.

Cannon, coat and scarf over his arm, stepped into the car's main parlor.

The furnished compartment was much too ostentatious for Cannon's tastes. Gilt metal fixtures, red velvet wallpaper, overstuffed chairs—but that expected pomposity came with a vice president's high office. Cannon preferred working while he traveled rather than luxuriating, so he'd had a desk dragged in as well.

The man who oversaw vice presidential security felt the same way about work. He'd had a second, smaller desk brought in.

He sat behind that second desk now, a withered shell of a man in a high-backed wheelchair writing with an almost clockwork precision.

The working surface of the desk was as Spartan-sparse as its owner: a pad of telegraph forms, a pen holder, an electric buzzer. Only one decorative item sat upon the desk: a wood carving of the Three Wise Monkeys, each monkey in turn covering eyes, ears, and mouth.

See no evil, hear no evil, speak no evil.

Without even looking up from his writing, the crippled man asked Cannon, "Simpson finally chuck you inside where you belong?"

"Your men are far too cheeky, Samuel." Cannon held his hands over the compartment's Franklin stove to warm them.

"My men are doers, not crawlers," Samuel Peck said, making one last scrawl on a pad of telegraph forms. He pressed an electric button on his desk, sounding a bell, and a fresh-faced young man—boy, really—popped in from one of the back compartments.

Peck tore the top sheet from the pad and gave it to his runner. "Get these code groups off," he snapped.

The young man immediately dashed out of the saloon. Seconds later his head streaked past the saloon's window as he headed for the train station's telegraph office at a dead run.

Peck set down his Waterman fountain pen. "Wanted to get that off before we pull out of the station. Confederates are stirring the pot again. Running guns to the Cleburnites this time."

Cannon winced. Deseret's southeastern region was rife with disgruntled Gentiles who thought the Mormon's northern half of New Mexico should really belong to the Texas Republic. What the Confederates had to gain from it, heaven knew.

"It never ends, does it?"

"No," said Peck. "It never does." Peck looked far, far older than his actual sixty years. Ravaged as much by the crushing strain his job as head of Deseret's intelligence service brought him as by his injuries.

The train's whistle blew a warning. It was ready to leave. Evidently Simpson's boys had finished tying down their tarp.

As if in echo, the steam kettle on the stove whistled, too. Peck spun his wheelchair around and rolled it from behind his desk over to the pot-bellied stove.

"Sit down, Mr. Vice President. I'll fix some chicory to warm us up."

Peck carried the kettle to a little side table where he spooned a roasted mixture of ground sugar beets, rye, and chicory root into a couple of mugs, then poured in the scalding water. He carried the cups in a lap tray over to where Cannon sat in his favorite overstuffed chair.

The train whistle blasted again, the engine started chuffing and puffing. The train slowly pulled out of the station.

Cannon spoon-stirred his hot drink. "Bishop Arceneaux is right, you know." He took a sip. The warmth felt good, even if it tasted nasty. "We can't just keep relying on the local congregations to handle these...*things*." The incidents were growing more frequent. And more deadly.

"No, you surely can't," Peck agreed, sipping his own chicory. "So, what do you plan to do?"

Cannon finished off the last of his drink. He'd never cottoned to the coffee substitute, but he'd drunk his share of it in winter. This winter, well, this winter Deseret ought to be using every sugar beet and grain of rye for *food*.

What to do, indeed.

Soldiers weren't the answer. The Nauvoo Legion didn't have enough troops to guard every coal mine, and even if they did, posting soldiers in the powder keg of a mining town wasn't a viable solution.

Only one path open that he could see.

"Hand it over to your Beehive 5," he told Peck. "Increase your appropriations, have you recruit up some—"

"No," Peck said.

"—more men—"

"No."

"— more teams—"

"*No.*"

Peck put aside his mug of chicory. "No, Mr. Vice President. It won't work."

The crippled man angrily wheeled his chair back around behind his desk. "That telegraph I just sent? Do you know what it says? Do you know what it means? It means the traitor Jim Bowie Cleburn won't live past the week. *I* sent that in a cable. *Me.*"

Cannon's mouth hung open. "You ordered a cold-blooded *assassination*—? That's *monstrous.*"

"Yes, it is. And that's my point," Peck said.

He picked up the pen he'd written the telegraph with, then set it down again.

"Oh, I didn't order *my* men to kill him. Merely made it look like Cleburn was double-crossing the Rebs so they shoot him themselves. But he had to die one way or another to protect the Republic."

The clatter of the moving train filled the silence.

"As you say, monstrous," Peck said at last. "That's what this job is. That's what I am, that's what my men are."He sighed. "You need men who fight monsters, Vice President. Not men who *are* monsters."

CANNON AROSE from his chair and placed his hand over Peck's, patted it. "You're not a monster, my friend."

After another silence, Peck picked up the carving of the three monkeys. His finger ran along the carving's rightmost edge, jagged and knife-hacked.

"There used to be a fourth monkey," Peck said, "sitting with his hands in his lap. Do no evil."

He set the carving back down. "I keep him in my safe where his idealism won't be tainted."

Peck rolled his chair to the window. He watched the sandstone canyons roll by.

"The hardest battle," Peck whispered over the clatter of the rails, "the hardest battle I fight behind this desk is preserving my last shred of decency still doing the job this desk requires."

He spun his chair around. "And you want to give me *more* power? *More* authority? You know what happens when you give a man even just a *little* authority!"

Cannon knew all too well. "Then what should we do?"

"Not that. It's all my men can do not to think of our flesh-and-blood enemies as inhuman monsters. Training them to fight *actual* monsters...they soon won't make any distinction."

Cannon frowned. "I repeat, then—what should we do? These unnatural incidents grow in number and strength. Not just coal snakes but the Meadow revenants, the hungerers at Donner Pass, that lake creature high in the Uintahs..."

Peck wheeled back to his desk and took up his pen.

"What's needed is a new organization," he said. "One parallel to Beehive 5, one a mirror opposite of Beehive 5. Instead of spies—and, yes, assassins—composed of shining knights and dragon slayers instead."

On the back of a telegraph form Peck sketched out an organization table of sorts.

"You'll need scholars to master the old forgotten alchemies; engineers and scientists, the steam power and the sciences. Inventors to combine them both into new tools, new weapons. Field agents to wield them."

The pen nib came to a halt, then resumed writing one last line with a flourish.

"And to lead your new dragon slayers, a St. George."

He handed Cannon the piece of paper.

Cannon frowned.

The organizational structure was there in the chart, alright. But the neatly labeled boxes were empty. No names, no particulars, not even where or how to find them.

Even the organization's name had been left blank.

Only one box had been filled in. In the topmost box, signifying the head of this new bureau, Peck had penned in: "Our new St. George."

"And where shall I find this St. George?" He looked at Peck. "Where shall I find this other you?"

Peck leaned against the high wicker back of his chair. "Not me. My talent lies in rooting out dishonest men, not honest ones. But if and when you do find him, tell him I have a monkey for his brand new desk."

Cannon stared at the chart.

He'd start putting what he could in place, do all he could, but—it would all be meaningless without the right man at the top. Cannon knew in his gut he could comb the whole of Deseret and not find his St. George.

Some say the Lord will provide, but mostly what the Lord provided was two hands, a brain, and a strong back to pull the handcarts, to dig the irrigation ditches, to dig out the coal, to build the steam engines, to carve an independent Mormon nation out of a barren desert.

Cannon would do all he could, even if it was hopeless. For Deseret, for the men of the mines like Arceneaux and Williams and the Greeks. He'd do all he could, and maybe then the Lord would provide.

But if the Lord planned on providing, he'd better do it soon.

III. The Moonlit Road

April 5, 1888
Near Mount Shasta
Upper California, United States of America

FOUR NEWSPAPERMEN SAT around the hunting cabin's roaring fireplace. The cheap booze and the cheap talk flowed freely. There was one from each of the Four Americas—Ramon Gallegos from Texas, William Shaw from Dixie, George W. Kent from the original United States, and drunken Barry Davis, a Jack Mormon from Deseret.

The four traveled with US President Grover Cleveland on his nationwide tour of a proposed Continental Park system that encompassed scenic sites of all four nations, but even the most determined scribbler could only write "Fat Man Looks at Local Scenery" so many times before ennui set in.

So here they were, the four of them, up in an old hunting cabin on the foot of the Shasta slope rather than down in the main lodge with presidents and potentates and their hangers-on.

The four newspapermen preferred it that way, to be honest. The company was better, after all, for they were with their own: a fifth reporter of the group and the second most newsworthy personage in the traveling caravan, the celebrated author, poet, and columnist Ambrose Bierce.

Bierce stood, elbow resting on the fireplace mantle, the center of their attention, warming himself as much in that adulatory glow as that of the fire's. Ambrose Bierce in the flesh was the same Ambrose Bierce of the penny postcards: a leonine head atop a leonine body. An unruly mass of dark hair, a bristling moustache, a set of bushy brows perched above a Jovian glower. At rest or in animated conversation, Bierce's face inevitably took on a misanthropic mien of utter contempt for the human race.

In short, he looked like this year's model of a new Mark Twain.

In fact, one of the company mentioned that; Shaw, it was, from the *Picayune-Democrat* out of New Orleans. "Heard tell some folks say it's not only his looks you're trying for, you're trying to *be* the next Mark Twain."

Bierce only laughed, a hearty chuckle that tapered into an asthmatic wheeze. "Back when I was younger—and a bit more foolish—I once thought to myself, why not? Why not be another Mark Twain? Alas, I realized I lacked the most essential ingredient of a Mark Twain—a cracking good pseudonym."

He struck a lucifer against a fireplace brick and lit his cigar with it, a foul-smelling five-center. "Oh, I tried on every name I could think of in my attempt to come up with a good Twainish pseudonym. Even tried anagrams made out of my own name."

He puffed long and hard and blew out a greasy blue cloud of smoke. "Only anagram I could come up with that wasn't pure gibberish was 'Creameries Bob'."

The circle of newspapermen laughed, even the ones who'd heard it before.

"No, gentlemen, I could never be a Mark Twain—or even want to be one. And why's that you ask?"

Bierce hooked a thumb in his vest pocket. "Because Mr. Clemens has achieved his goal—fame and fortune. And, having achieved that modest goal, he has now settled back into a long, comfortable semi-somnambulance to await eventual expiry. A wait he affects with the least possible effort expended. I wish him and his porch swing well."

Bierce extracted the cigar from his mouth and examined its smoldering end as if it held the secrets of existence. "As for myself, I desire far, far more. I seek a cause worthy of my talents." He stubbed his cigar out with quick, angry stabs. "So far I haven't found it."

Reaching for his overcoat, for the night was windy and chill, he said, "And now if you gentlemen will excuse me for a moment, I must see a dog about a horse."

And with that, Ambrose Bierce stepped off stage and through the door of the cabin.

∩

AWAY FROM THE CABIN, hidden in a copse of evergreens that Bierce made double sure was out of earshot, Ambrose Bierce, the great man, bent over double, hacking and wheezing, trying to draw in his breath in long, agonizing asthmatic gasps.

The cold, clear night air bit like burning daggers in his lungs.

Those infernal cigars. They'd be the death of him yet.

He checked the white cloth of the handkerchief he'd coughed into. No blood. No TB, at least. At least he was spared of that.

Somewhere in the struggle for breath, Bierce had shot out a hand against the rough bark of a tall pine for support. The crackled bark stabbed his palm. Astringent resins smeared his fingers.

He pushed himself away from the tree and stood on his own two feet.

He scooped up a handful of snow and washed as best he could his pitch-sticky hand.

The night wind soughed high in the trees. Bierce looked up at the sound and saw the glories of the night sky. The bright twinkling stars, the pale of the moon, the glow of the snow-capped cone of legend-shrouded Mt. Shasta.

For the mountain did glow.

Not just a reflection of the feeble, friable light of moon and stars, but a true glow—a glow blue-white and eerie, a glow that seemed to pulsate in time with his now-calm breath.

"Balderdash," he wheezed at the glow. "Poppycock."

A trick of the light. An aurora borealis. Or an undigested lump of potato, as Dickens might say.

But only a potato and no Marley, for the world as Bierce knew it held no chain-dragging ghosts or admonishing holly-wreathed spirits Yet to Come.

And no glowing mountains.

Breath regained, reality reimposed, Ambrose Bierce, the great man, stomped his way though the crusted snow back toward the hunting cabin.

That the mountain, as if not to be denied, started calling Bierce by name in the moan of the soughing night wind was something Bierce deliberately paid no mind.

⋀

When Bierce returned, the cabin's candles, none too tall to begin with, had all guttered out. The only remaining light source lay in the flickering red flame of the fireplace.

The other reporters sat around it, their backs against fitful pools of shadow capering across the room. Savages huddled against the ancient terrors of the night. Children clustered around a campfire trading spooky tales. Middle-aged men picking apart the rumors and legends surrounding Mt. Shasta out of boredom and malice.

That last was the last thing Bierce wanted to discuss—that brooding mountain outside—but he was chilled to the bone and the lambent warmth of the fire too inviting to resist. He pulled up a chair and joined them.

Fat-bellied Kent of the *New York Telegraph-Sun* spoke of the old Klamath Indian legends, about the sacred mountain being home to both the mighty Spirit-Above-Ground and the Spirit-Below.

The southerner Shaw spoke in his characteristic drawl of dead men walking its slopes the way they do in the hoodoo camps of the Louisiana bayous.

The aristocratic Gallegos of the *Austin Star Courier* lectured them in that dismissive, high-and-mighty *hidalgo* tone of his. He spoke of the writings of modern so-called alchemists, of the Shasta mountain being the last abandoned outpost of sunken Lemuria, of it being a nexus of ley lines, lines of force from the unseen worlds rubbing up against our reality.

But Davis of Salt Lake's *Gentile Vedette* said nothing, only slowly and methodically consumed the last third of the bottle cradled in his tremoring hands. Yet it was Davis who turned to Bierce and asked, "And what does our i'lushtrush...illustriush...our eshteemed celebrity think on the matter?"

"I think you've had enough, friend," Bierce said with a knowing smile, and reached over and plucked the bottle from Davis.

Davis made a clumsy grab and snatched it back.

Gallegos laughed. That condescending patrician laugh of his. "Don't you know, Davis? Mr. Bierce, here, doesn't believe in such things. He is the world's leading agnostic."

"Agnostic," Kent quoted, fingers clasped together atop his sizable paunch, "is what an atheist calls himself in polite company."

Bierce reached in his pocket for another cigar. "Did I really say that? If not, I shall have to steal it and use it."

"But surely," Shaw said, "you cannot deny the veritable storm of recent strange events. Monstrous winged cuttlefish off the shores of your Massachusetts, your own Yankee army fighting off hordes of fishlike men in Kingsport!"

"I can and I do deny such things," Bierce said.

"But the affidavits, the photographs—great heavens, man! I *myself* have seen *zuvembie* shambling through the moonlit bayous!"

"After which, you sat down with them and shared Davis's bottle," scoffed Bierce.

Bierce rose from his chair and once again took center stage, leaning against the fireplace mantle, for he felt an oration coming on.

"As for photographs and affidavits," Bierce said, settling into his subject matter, "didn't that old fraud P.T. Barnum have plenty of both testifying to the veracity of his Cardiff Giant? Yet this one truth remains: a concrete statue is still only a concrete statue and will always remain but a concrete statue."

Bierce lit his cigar. He waved the sulfur-tipped match to extinction. "Oh, I don't deny we may have recently encountered heretofore unknown specimens of flora and fauna—this is still a vast, virgin continent, in the main, uncharted even — but to assign mere heretofore unknown cryptozoological specimens some supernatural or infernal attribute—this I do categorically deny."

Gallegos sniffed. "You Yankees! You don't believe in anything you can't jingle in your coin purse."

Bierce fixed upon him a haughty stare. "If by that you mean I admit only in the rational, the tangible, the provable, then you surmise correctly. We live in an age of science, gentlemen. With every turn of a locomotive's wheel, every revolution of its engine, we travel further down the track to rationality, leaving further and further behind the old ignorances and superstitions."

Davis looked up owlishly from his bottle. "You don't believe in God, then."

A long, blue cloud of cigar smoke streamed from Bierce's mouth. "I hold the question of God's existence in abeyance. Mortal senses cannot detect Him, who if He does exist, seems hell-bent on using His Omnipotence solely to hide from us."

Bierce held up his hand to quell the inevitable uproar.

"As for religion itself," he continued, "I need only point to Davis, here, to show the value of *that* flummery. Behold the fruits of dime-store prophets and do-it-yourself gold Bibles."

Davis set aside his bottle and made to stand. When he realized he couldn't, he clutched his bottle again. "My—my failings don't mean the Church isn't true." His voice lowered to near inaudibility. "Only means *I'm* not."

Bierce blew another cloud of smoke. "Hear how he phrases it? His church is 'true.' How can any form of Christianity be true, predicated as it is, on untruth."

He swept his hand at the circle of men before him. "You all are newspapermen and a newspaperman is the greatest student of human nature this world has ever produced.

"It is our stock in trade to know the high and the mighty, the poor and the destitute. To tear the public masks off presidents and popes and ploughmen and expose what's underneath. Have you ever once—once—encountered a man who became his utter and exact opposite in the space of a single heartbeat like the supposed Saul of Tarsus on his road to Damascus? Can sinner become saint, persecutor become protector, all in the flash of a blinding epiphany? Can such things be?"

Bierce exhaled a wreath of smoke that swirled around his head.

"No, by thunder! They cannot! And your own lifetimes of experience tell you so. No such Saul—and thus no such Paul—ever could or ever did exist. That story is no more real than dead men walking the slopes of Shasta. No Saul ever traveled down any moonlit road."

Gallegos snorted. "It was broad daylight."

"See?" smiled Bierce. "The falsehood doesn't even make good fiction."

Silence fell over the cabin, the only sounds that of crackling pine logs burning.

Bierce lost himself in a creative reverie, composing in his mind the column he would write on tonight's discussion. He thus was only dimly aware of the scrape of Davis's chair against the floor as the man pushed back and stood.

The drunken Deseretan stepped over to the larder cupboard and uncorked a new bottle of hooch with his teeth. He brought the lip of the bottle to his mouth, then slowly lowered it and recorked the bottle.

It was that motion, so uncharacteristic of the man, of human nature, that caught Bierce's attention.

"You talk a lot, Bierce," Davis slurred, "but I don't see you doing anything to prove what you say."

Bierce took the cigar out of his mouth. "Eh? What's that? The drunk speaks?"

Davis swept his hand in the direction of the mountain outside. "I mean, here we are on the slopes of Mt. Shasta where from all accounts you can't take ten steps without running into the preternatural, and you can't be bothered to get up off your duff and take those ten steps to prove it or not."

Davis pointed the neck of the bottle at him like Gabriel's fiery sword. "You say such things do not exist. Well, walk up that mountain and prove it!"

Shaw chuckled. "He's got you there, Ambrose."

Bierce bristled, stung as much from an inferior—and a southerner—taking the liberty of addressing him by his Christian name as by Davis's drunken challenge.

He thought of pointing out the absurdity of trying to prove a negative, then realized the others would see it as cowardice.

Bierce threw the stub of his cigar in the fire. "Very well. I'll leave right now." Far from entrapping him, a hike up Shasta would put the perfect cap to his column.

Portly Kent struggled to his feet. "Now hold on, A. B.," he said, "it must be after midnight now. You can't go out in the snow and cold at night. Why, your lungs would never stand it."

Bierce shrugged on his heavy coat. "The devil take my lungs, sir, not that my lungs are any of your business. As for it being night, aren't those the normal business hours for ghosts and ghoulies?"

He gathered a few things from the hunting cabin, a few slices of cheese and some hardtack wrapped in a bandana, a canteen of water, a small knapsack to put them in, and a heavy hardwood walking stick.

He made Gallegos dig out the alchemist's book he carried and dutifully marked with an 'X' on his trail map the confluence of the dozens of supposed ley lines that intersected on Shasta.

Packed up and ready, Bierce stepped out of the cabin and into the moonlight. The four others followed him out.

"At least let us accompany you, Bierce," Shaw pleaded, shivering in the cold. "You can't go out there alone."

Bierce waved them off. "These things only seem to show themselves if a man's alone. The supernatural must have a visceral dislike for corroborating witlessness."

Bierce settled his pack strap and gazed up the moonlit trail. "Adieu, gentlemen. Save a chair at breakfast for me."

The four reporters watched him round the first curve of the trail and disappear behind the snow-covered pines.

AND THAT WAS the last the world ever saw of Ambrose Bierce.

Search parties the next day quickly found the spot on the map Bierce had marked. The spot turned out to be a small hollow ringed by lava boulders. They found his walking stick and knapsack neatly placed against the rock face.

Searchers swore that only one track of footsteps in the deep snow led into the hollow. None led out.

Afterward, for years and years, reports came in that Bierce had been sighted here or sighted there: Bierce walking arm-in-arm with the Mormons' prophet on the grounds of their Temple Square; Bierce manning a steam harpoon aboard a whaler off Kingsport, Massachusetts; Bierce deep in the voodoo-ridden swamps of the Louisiana bayous; Bierce walking the moonlit roads of Appalachian coal country carrying bags of salt upon his shoulders.

These reports were all dismissed as testimony of cranks and crackpots.

No, Ambrose Bierce died that morning. However the remains of his body had managed to vanish, one thing was certain: the man known as Ambrose Bierce died upon the slopes of Mount Shasta.

On that, even Ambrose Bierce could agree.

IV. Postscript

April 6, 1888
Salt Lake City,
Republic of Deseret

GEORGE Q. CANNON sat straight up in bed, gasping for breath. A *skritch* of a match revealed not quite five in the morning on the hands of his bedside clock.

His wife Charlotte murmured, "George?"

"Go back to sleep, dear," he told her. "I'm just going into the office early. General Conference this weekend."

She murmured again and rolled over, back asleep before he finished speaking.

He stroked her long braided hair in apology. While perhaps not a lie, his words had been a prevarication. Work was not the reason he quickly dressed and climbed aboard his steam buckboard and motored it onto the dark, deserted streets of the city.

Cannon was the practical one of the Council. The doer, the organizer, the administrator. Let the Wilford Woodruffs of the Twelve dream their dreams. Cannon was the feet-on-the-ground one.

He didn't dream dreams.

But he'd awoken from one.

In truth, not a dream, though, a nightmare.

He dreamt he had been a monkey trapped inside an airless box, pounding and pounding on cold steel walls to get free, gasping for breath.

Cannon spent his drive deep in thought. When at last he slid his buckboard to the curb, he found he'd driven, not to his Church office on South Temple, but his Vice-President's office at Council Hall on First South.

Quickly climbing the stairs to his office, the first thing Cannon did was spin the dial on the heavy document safe in the corner.

There inside the cold steel walls sat Peck's fourth monkey statuette, given Cannon "for safekeeping," Peck had insisted. The little fellow still had his paws folded snugly in his lap. The bland expression carved on his face showed no sign of ever gasping for breath or desperately pounding to be free.

For no reason Cannon could think of, he took out the monkey and turned to place it on his desk.

That's when Cannon saw the stranger.

Shock white hair on a leonine head, white eyebrows, white moustache. The stranger's face somehow seemed to glow, and his facial features were slowly shifting as if a new face was settling into place.

The man wore a heavy coat and had snow upon his boots.

The stranger espied the one sheet of paper that never left Cannon's desk these days, the organizational chart Peck had scribbled that night on the train. Cannon had made no progress on fleshing it out.

"Quickly," the stranger said, "a pen."

Cannon handed him the one from his pocket.

Taking it, the stranger hastily began to fill in the chart. At the very top of the page, the stranger wrote "Correlation Department" and then proceeded to fill in the empty boxes. Precise names of agents to hire, precise names of scholars to recruit, precise items of equipment to design and build.

The stranger scribbled furiously, racing as if to finish before the glow about him faded, before the virtue had gone out of him and the vision of what he saw dimmed.

Finished at last, save the topmost box, the stranger paused. His newly shaped face had dimmed of all epiphanic glow.

He thought for a moment, then in the box where Peck had facetiously written "Our St. George" as leader of Deseret's new legions of dragon slayers, Ambrose Bierce—given at last a cause worthy of his talents—scratched that out and penned his New Name.

TRACTING OUT
CTHULHU

INTRODUCTION

My elementary school library was housed in what they called "the annex"—a long wooden "temporary" World War 2 training structure built to train wartime telephone switchboard operators. In fact, the old training switchboards and Bakelite headsets with braided cotton insulated cords were still kept in a disused back room.

Despite its creaking punky-wood floorboards and peeling exterior paint, the annex library was a magical place. That's where I discovered science fiction in the form of Heinlein's The Rolling Stones.

It's also where I discovered alternate history, but not in the way you'd expect.

I discovered it in the non-fiction section.

Shelved on the south wall of the library's southeast corner with the rest of the history books sat a slim book on the history of the American West. Not a very remarkable book in itself (I don't even remember its title), but it changed my life.

There on one of its pages—don't ask me why, it wasn't a big enough book to go that much in depth with the Mormon migration—was a map of the State of Deseret: a magnificent blob shape covering Utah and Nevada, the Mormon southeast corner of Idaho, a slice of Wyoming, the eastern half of Colorado, the northern halves of Arizona and New Mexico, and the eastern slopes of California's Sierra Nevada Mountains as well as chunk of southernmost Southern California.

And best of all, the page had a little squib caption explaining this Mormon home-land really, truly once existed.

I won't say I experienced a euphony complete with choirs of singing angels, but it did open up a vista of possibilities in my mind and dreams of a world where Deseret still existed.

Without ever having heard of the alternate history genre before, I stumbled onto the concept by myself. I spent much of my grade school days from then on doodling maps of alternate Americas, alternate Earths, and even far future alternate alien planets.

Since then, I've been a total fiend about Deseret. Not in any crazed wacko secessionist homeland movement sense, I assure you, but merely in a crazed wacko alternate history buff sense.

In fact, the first professional story was "For the Strength of the Hills", a novella detailing an alternate history Utah War and the birth of the Deseret of my childhood dreams. Much of whatever power is in that story derives that library-born epiphanic enthusiasm.

I've since revisited that alternate timeline (what I call my Beehive 5 universe) since then. My pre-WW2 tale "Subject To Kings" saw print in States of Deseret, *and I've also drafted a few unpublished pieces and story fragments. But in the main, I've done quite a bit less with the Beehive 5 universe than I'd hoped to do, and far less than some emailing readers had hoped, as well.*

The problem is when I sit down with my author hat on, I have a hard time maintaining a viable enough suspension of belief to write convincingly of an independent Deseret.

Deseret, my Deseret anyway, has too much land for too few people, and contains too many juicy resources whilst surrounded by Mormon-hating hostile nations, each of which is up for a little land grabbing. Worse, Deseret hasn't enough iron or bauxite deposits to build the weapons of modern war (even if she could scrape up the manpower to man her army anyway).

So my reaction to the announcement that Immortal Works was opening a Mormon steampunk anthology (once I'd stopped laughing at the sheer absurdity of Mormon steampunk) was that of relief. I could transfer all that worldbuilding I'd already done about Deseret and the Four Americas over to a steampunk-and-magic setting.

In a world with alchemic magic, I could transmute Deseret's abundant copper to steel alloys, I could field ranks of steam-powered automatons for an army. I could launch fleets of eldritch dirigible warships preventing hostile invasions.

I could Deseret not only as alternate history now, but I could write action and adventure and alchemy and chthonic monsters and all kinds of pulp hero fun.

The result what I call my "Clockwork Deseret" story universe.

My inaugural story in that universe, "Tracting Out Cthulhu", was simply the most fun I've had a writing prose fiction.

I sold "Tracting" to Immortals' initial steampunk volume (All Made of Hinges), *then followed-up with selling its prequel "Can Such Things Be?" to their fourth and final volume* (A Mighty Fortress).

"Tracting" is a world of CTR magic combat rings, Mister Mac robots, zombie replacements of world leaders, and pairs of combat elders fanning out to search old Tokyo for hidden Elder Gods. It's a story of airships and magic portals, Japanese folk magicks, evil brains in jars, and super-powered Japanese schoolgirls with huge folded combat paper fans.

That grade school kid wandering the book stack of the annex library would have loved it.

March 1903
Consulate Row
San Diego, Mormon California, Republic of Deseret

The evening's reception in the marble-lined Netherlands Consulate glittered as brightly as any event could, hosted by dour, stolid Dutchmen serving dour, stolid Dutch cooking.

Still, drinks flowed and guests mingled, tongues wagged and the band played on. No diplomat ended up shot or stabbed, so no new wars were likely to be declared the following morning. By the generous standards of diplomatic circles, the night's affair qualified as a roaring success.

Holland boasted such famed living physicists as Hendrik Lorentz, Van der Waals, and Pieter Zeeman. Perhaps that is why they preferred their reality classical, their sciences natural, and the subject of alchemy imaginary claptrap.

Perhaps that was why they were slipping as a colonial power.

At any rate, no Geared Science apparatus could or would be seen anywhere inside the opulent confines of their consulate-generals, which made Dutch parties popular with a certain subset of the international scene. These people preferred, when discussing certain matters, the ability to do so away from Geared or Alchemical eavesdropping.

Why else would one go to a one of their parties? Perhaps the people of Holland were slyer than they were given credit for.

Hisato Nozaki, member of the Japanese trade delegation to the Four Americas, and some said the eyes and ears abroad of the Emperor himself, disliked the Dutch, but no more so than he disliked all *gaijin*.

Just as his revered Emperor did, Nozaki knew the sole path for the Yamato people and their nation to survive was to embrace the ways of these *gaijin*— their sciences, their arts, their culture. If that meant having to stoop to occasionally mingling with Europeans and Americans, so be it.

Dressed in a well-tailored business suit, Nozaki projected a modernity equal to any Westerner in the room. If not quite the powerful warrior he had been in his youth, the grey-haired septuagenarian still prowled the room like a lion in winter.

The room stank of bland, over-cooked and over-fatty *gaijin* food and the cloying sweet smell of Cuban cigars. Nozaki threaded his way through the milling crowd and the noise which felt as much a palpable barrier as the throng itself. He angled toward a tall, athletic-looking man with weather-beaten skin standing off to one side along the far wall.

The lean man's invitation card had read "Smith" which Nozaki supposed might even actually be the man's true name. Every other *gaijin* in the Four Americas seemed to be named Smith, especially here in Mormon Deseret, if he wasn't a Young or a Snow.

Smith or not, the lean man certainly wasn't a businessman after a Dutch East Indies rubber consignment like the other Mormon Smiths in the room. This man's face had a hard-used look, the same look Nozaki knew his own face had during his younger samurai days.

Nozaki snagged two drinks off a passing serving tray and offered one of the drinks to 'Smith.' Nozaki sipped on his delicately—the cloying taste of *jenever* didn't agree with him—then said, "The snows recede, the cherry blossoms bud."

Smith replied, "Ah, but do they truly blossom or only herald gaudy Spring?"

Sign and counter-sign exchanged. Nozaki relaxed. "And intriguing question, Mr. Smith. Perhaps if we were to step someplace a little more quiet, we could discuss the weather?"

Smith eased a corner of his mouth upward in a knowing half-smile. He set the untouched drink on a bookshelf.

"This way."

He led Nozaki through the maddening crowd to a balconied terrace outside.

ⵔ

As part of Consulate Row, the Dutch Consulate sat on the Sunset Cliffs overlooking the warm Pacific. Red and green running lights of surface vessels entering and leaving the harbor gleamed fairy-like in the dark. Hundreds of feet overhead, the dim glow from dirigible gondolas danced; air freighters heading out over the Pacific to all points east, carrying goods from Deseret and the Four Americas to Asia and beyond.

The night air felt cool but pleasant. Wind soughed in the top fronds of palm trees. The gentle waves of low tide susurrated as they rolled to shore. The air smelt of salt spray and hibiscus from the small garden below the terrace.

Nozaki took a small object from his waistcoat pocket, a small sheet of *mino washi* paper he'd intricately folded many times into the figure of a swan.

Usually Nozaki folded cranes to serve as his *shikigami*. The use of a swan was pure whimsy on his part, a play on the erroneous legends that those birds were mute. Then again, the art of *kamigami-do*—"the way of spirit-paper"— depended as much on the mood and mind of the caster as the end shape of the folded paper.

Nozaki placed the paper swan on the wooden rail running the length of the balcony. The noise of the surf and wind abruptly hushed.

"We may speak freely now," Nozaki said. "No unwelcome ear will eavesdrop."

Smith pulled out a small brass box the size and shape of a deck of playing cards. Hidden gears inside whirred, and a tiny antenna telescoped out. The muted background noise quieted even further.

Smith placed the brass box on the railing beside the paper swan. Again he gave Nozaki that half-smile. "Not that I don't trust yours, but I prefer my own acoustical baffle."

Smith then slouched against the railing in a typical American posture. "You called this morning, said you wanted to talk. Okay, talk."

Americans. Always so direct.

"Five years ago," Nozaki began, "shortly after the explosion of the battleship *CSS Mame* and the commencement of the Spanish-Confederate War, New Orleans and Cuba both experienced *zuvembie* outbreaks. The Confederates later concluded Cuban *bokors* in the pay of the Spaniards summoned them as part of their war effort."

Smith shrugged. "I'd say that's pretty general knowledge. You going somewhere with this?"

"What isn't general knowledge, is that during both outbreaks, pairs of young Mormon men were reported going house-to-house throughout the affected sections of the two cities."

Smith shrugged again. "Sounds like some of our missionaries got a little over-eager. Nothing like a *zuvembie* attacks to get folks thinking about the afterlife."

It was Nozaki's turn to smile. It was not a warm smile. "Ecclesiastical missionaries don't carry shotguns and pistols. No, Mr. Smith, these were *your* men—Correlations Department agents."

He held up a hand to forestall Smith's next deflection. "And no, you weren't there to surreptitiously help fight off zuvembies, despite what Richmond believes. You went in to find the Tendrils."

Smith no longer smiled or slouched. He stood erect, poised, wary, his right hand eased itself under his jacket toward the gun holster, well-tailored not to show.

Nozaki nodded to himself. Japanese translators had long agonized over guessing the precise word, the precise term the Deseretans used amongst themselves. From Smith's reaction, they'd hit upon it precisely. Smith would now believe Japan knew much more than it in fact did. Nozaki's mission had a chance of succeeding.

"Relax, Mr. Smith," Nozaki said. "Your secret has not been uncovered, least of all by Richmond." The Confederates were just foolish and haughty enough to try *using* a Tendril, rather than destroying it. "We know because in Japan we have long known from ancient texts the existence of the ancient malevolent entity that sleeps and dreams under the sea: the *Koudai-kodai Ika*."

Smith silently remouthed the term Koudai-kodai Ika—vast ancient cuttlefish—and that amused half-smile returned to Smith's face. Like many compound words in Japanese directly translated into an inferior gaijin language, the word-string sounded a bit comical. But as with most compounds the end-concept had its own gestalt, one much greater than the simple sum of its parts. The Koudai-kodai Ika was far more than a simple sea monster.

The shock worn off, Smith eased back into his slouch. His hand, however, remained in reach of a quick grab at his hidden weapon. "The cultists of the Legrasse bayou south of New Orleans called your cuttlefish 'Cthulhu,'" he said.

At the utterance of that name, the paper swan flickered in the wind. For the briefest of moments, the full roar of wind and surf returned.

"Cultists which *you* personally stopped from their mad attempt to wake the Sleeper," Nozaki said, speaking only after the noise dimmed again. "The Tendrils and the zuvembie outbreaks they unwittingly caused were mere accidental discharges emanating from the Koudai-kodai Ika's stirring mind. The world was supremely fortunate those illiterate Cajuns knew so little about the forces they tampered with."

Smith's eyes narrowed. "You're selling something. Spit it out."

Two more rolling waves broke upon the darkened shore before Nozaki spoke again. "There's been a new attempt to awaken the Koudai-kodai Ika. A Tendril has appeared somewhere in Tokyo. And whoever these new acolytes are, they are *not* illiterate backwoodsmen."

Nozaki turned to face Smith. "They are *using* the Tendril, manipulating it not to randomly spawn zuvembie but to...compromise...government leaders and the key elite of our society. The rot has spread far and fast. Roughly one-third of our governing class is now...We need your help, Mr. Smith. I *beg* your help. Before...before..."

Nozaki's voice faltered, failed him.

Smith's hand snaked out to the humming brass box on the railing. He boosted his mechanical protective device to maximum gain as if mere silence could shield him from the ears of a waking Koudai-kodai Ika.

"Japan has its military, its own agencies," Smith whispered. "Surely your equivalent of our Correlations Department, your Steel Angel Layer could—"

"The *Wakou Tenshi-Sou?*" Nozaki growled, fist clenched. "There is no more Wakou Tenshi-Sou! The Tendril struck there first!"

Nozaki bowed his head and his whole frame sagged.

"I am its last untainted member."

∩

A GLEAMING black Vettius-Dama limousine waited for Smith—for Smith was his actual name, Kennicott Fielding Smith—at the front of the Dutch Consulate.

The Italian steam job was a luxury import, but a necessary one for the Correlation Department. Deseret's indigenous automotive firms built to market, the domestic market—farm vehicles and vehicles for large families. ZCMI Motors made cheap, rugged Woodies—wooden framed sedans—that made great economic sense in iron-poor Deseret, but nothing that could be readily rendered proof against alchemic attacks or sabotage. Wood proved even more porous than air against Alchemy and Geared Science.

Northern Italy's iron mines in her Val D'Aosta region sat upon nearly as large and potent a juncture of Ley lines as did Deseret's legendary Bingham copper mine. The cold steel made from their iron and the Vettius-Dama automobiles made from that steel could be easily runed and warded. Its enclosed cab could be made a veritable fortress, cheap at the price.

Smith nodded at the chauffeur as the man opened the curbside passenger door for him. He eased his lanky frame inside, grabbed the door handle himself, and shut home the door behind him.

Even before Smith finished seating himself in the rich Cagliostron leather, even before he spoke to the limousine's other passenger, Smith reached out with a brass wand-like apparatus. At the flick of a button the heated wand oozed a dab of sizzling hot wax across the door crack. The stink of melted wax filled his nostrils. Smith pressed the signet on the head of the wand into the cooling wax, imprinting a defensive rune.

The car pulled into traffic with the sibilant silence of a steam-engined vehicle.

Smith eased back into the polished leather upholstery. It squeaked as he settled in. The rest of the interior looked just as fancy. Even the bullet-proof calxiglass windows were etched with Art Nouveau curlicues that would have made Alphonse Mucha proud.

The other passenger raised an eyebrow at the wax wand cooling in Smith's hand.

"Two shikigami circling overhead, flapping their little folded paper wings," Smith explained. "They might belong to our friend, but they might not."

The other passenger nodded. With his shock-white hair, bushy brows, and a drooping mustache he looked like, in his own words, a cut-rate Mark Twain. He went by the palindromic alias Nate Sabbas. Sabbas had once borne a different name, a famous name known all across the Four Americas. He'd walked away—literally—from that name and the celebrity life attached to it and now served unseen in the shadows as head of Deseret's Correlation Department.

The way Smith had heard it, when a General Authority once complained about the obvious artificiality of Sabbas' name, Sabbas told him he'd thought about using an anagram of his actual name instead, but the only anagram he could come up with was "Creameries Bob." Sabbas he remained.

Sabbas gestured at the Dutch Consulate receding in the rear window. "Bad as we thought?"

Smith nodded. "The Tendril's shifted to Japan and it looks as if it means to stay." He gave a quick rundown on what Nozaki told him.

"Makes sense," Sabbas said, his reedy voice wheezing with the asthma that soon would prove fatal. "For all the frenzied modernizing, Japan's still very much a feudal top-down society. Blind obedience to authority. Emperor worship. Perfect setup for whoever it is opening the Tendril." Sabbas drummed his fingers on the seat leather. "You'd better give me a full report." He pulled a stubby pencil and small paper notepad from his pocket. A lifetime working for newspapers died hard.

"Don't," Smith said. He took the notepad away from his boss. "Nozaki is a practitioner of kamigami-do. He knew things he could only have known from reading our paper archives. Reading them long distance through his art is my guess. We must assume *anything* we put to paper is now compromised. And that the corrupted members of Steel Angel Layer are all paper-mages, too."

Sabbas swore a Gentile oath, another newspaper habit.

Smith shrugged. "The news isn't all bad. There were obvious gaps in what he knew. The True Name of the squid, for example. Things we keep at Brass Level and above."

Sabbas swore again. "Don't tell me we're going to have to put *everything* on brass plates." The most potent, the most malevolent secrets of the Dark Arts safeguarded by the Correlation Department were transcribed onto wafer-thin plates of sanctified Bingham copper brass.

Smith shook his head. "I think there're some easy fixes. Going forward, we use only special paper impregnated with iron ore dust—or maybe Bingham copper—in the rag content. Existing archives we can maybe spray with some sort of iron ore emulsion. In the meantime, we keep all paper records in filing cabinets made of cold steel, runed and warded."

"I'll make of note of that," Sabbas said. His hand fumbled at his pocket, then stopped. "No, I won't."

THE LIMOUSINE PULLED up to the Naval Jetty. Choppy water slapped heavily against the concrete pier. A small navy launch lay to, its throaty diesel engine coughing up blue clouds of acrid stinking smoke.

Halfway across the harbor lay the Coronado Island naval base. Dazzling searchlights speared upward in the dark, illuminating a gleaming silver airship descending majestically like a magnesium cloud.

The *Haun's Mill* was a new design, first of its class fresh from the builder's yard. Powered by inexhaustible pitchblende-fractionate engines, propelled by closed-system turbines, lifted by ballonets of half-charmed helium, the lithe craft could slice through the air at speeds over a hundred knots while her coal tar-engined, water-boilered, hydrogen-bagged rivals could only wallow at speeds below sixty.

Freed of the need to lift huge water tanks for ballast and waste steam, the gleaming hammered-leaf surface of white-gold orichalcum boasted not lifting runes, but alchemistic symbols which deftly warded off the fury of wind and rain. No storm existed that the *Haun's Mill* could not glide through. No spot on the globe lay too remote to reach in mere days.

Sabbas turned from staring upward to stare at Smith. One bushy white eyebrow rose questioningly.

Smith met his stare. "Nozaki contacted us early this morning. The meeting wasn't until this evening. You didn't think I was just going to sit on my hands for eleven hours, especially when we knew most of what he was going to say anyway."

"The Air Branch isn't going to be too happy about you requisitioning their new toy."

Smith placed his hand on the door handle. "After you brief them on kamigami-do, the Air Branch, the Navy, the Nauvoo Legion—they're all going to be far too busy panicking about their paperwork to worry about one little airship."

He yanked open the limousine door and stepped onto the concrete. Grit crunched underfoot.

Sabbas cleared his throat with the ragged wheeze of an asthmatic. "Good luck, Ken," he said gruffly.

Smith paused. "Up against an elder squid god, luck's a little outgunned."

Without looking back, he swung the car door closed. He stepped down into the launch, maintaining perfect balance as the wooden boat rolled in the swells.

"Cast off, sailor," Smith said. "I've got an airship to catch."

SMITH BLINKED against the actinic blue of the electric lights illuminating the tarmac and the frantic bedlam boiling beneath the grounded airship.

The helter-skelter of bodies and machines only seemed a disorganized madhouse as base personnel prepped the *Haun's Mill* for a trans-Pacific flight.

Leather-lunged chief petty officers bellowed orders at work details of sailors replenishing potable water, rations, lubricating oils, and all the other normal sundries consumed in flight. Wooden crates of small arms ammunition waited to be loaded, too.

Civilian employees of the Grumman Works, airship designers who'd been aboard the *Haun's Mill* on a test flight when she'd been unexpectedly diverted to San Diego, screamed blue bloody murder—less at being shanghaied than at the abominations being committed on "their" poor airship.

Snarling arc welders flung glowing red-orange rooster tails. Shipfitters were welding into the cargo hold a specialized ten-by-fifteen foot command-and-control center known to Correlation wags as a "portable mission home." The damage the electrician's mates were doing to the airship's electrical system in their hasty, jury-rigging attempt to string power to the C-and-C cab made the Grumman men cry.

They came streaming over to Smith to complain. Several dozen people, in fact, were hectoring Smith for his attention, but Smith had only two people he needed to speak to.

The first was Field AP Curt Roundy, the ranking Correlation combat elder. All of thirty-eight—old for a CD field agent—Roundy stood leaning against the meals-on-wheels counter, the portable field kitchen serving up refreshments to the work crews: deep fried scone-bread along with steaming hot cocoa for the Mormons, coffee for the Jack Mormons and Gentiles. The sizzle of scones in the bubbling oil and its homey aroma made Smith's mouth water.

Roundy began wolfing down a scone, but then he could afford to. He wouldn't be spending the next forty-odd hours in a bunk comatose from an IV-administered hypnogogue with a Sleep Learning Nyctalope wired to his skull. Roundy already knew Japanese from previous hypnogoguing. With the leg wound he picked up in last month's little kerfuffle in Romania, he'd be restricted to the shipboard support echelon, so he wouldn't need to hypnogogue any tracting maps of Tokyo. You don't hypnogogue on a full stomach.

Roundy swallowed the last of the scone and hastily wiped his hands on his trouser legs when he saw Smith coming. "Sorry, boss. Just catching a bite while I could." He picked up his chalk slate from the counter in anticipation of Smith's first question.

Good man. Word had already come down channels to avoid paper. Smith hadn't even thought about using chalk slates instead. Should have. Roundy had.

"Let me see how you set up team rosters," Smith said, taking the slate from Roundy. Twenty-five pairs. Fifty combat elders total. Long-standing pairs were teamed together, SOP. Pretty much like Smith figured. "How many of them already speak Japanese?"

Roundy scrunched his face in thought. "About half. Twenty-two."

"And all paired together."

Smith shoved the slate back at him. "Redo the roster. Parcel out those who already know the language one to a team."

"That's going to cut into combat efficiency," Roundy said, frowning.

"Can't be helped. Tokyo has the most difficult street system in the world. Even locals don't understand it. It's *got* to be hypnogogued by at least one team member, and that's a forty hours course. And everyone's got to have the language on this one—and that's another forty hours. Not enough time for both. Parcel 'em out, Roundy."

"Yessir," Roundy said. "Uh, that still leaves six non-speakers, three teams of odd men out."

Smith's turn to frown. "Throw 'em into threesomes, then." He put up a hand. "I know, I know, it cuts down the number of teams and you'll have to redraw your map assignments. It'll give you something to do on the flight over."

"Yessir. Guess I better grab another scone and get to work then."

Smith cast a covetous eye at the bubbling oil vats. "Scones any good, Dave?" When Roundy, mouth already full, nodded vigorously, Smith sighed. "They would be. None for me, I'm afraid. I'm spending the flight hooked up to the machine, too."

Roundy blinked. "Sir? Thought you already had the language. And the maps."

"So I do," Smith said. "Thing is, I'm meeting the Emperor as soon as we touch down and from what I understand Imperial Court Japanese is almost its own separate language. So I get to enjoy a twenty-hour supplemental instead of a bellyful of scones."

"Hard luck, sir."

Smith allowed himself a smile. "Hard luck is having to talk to *him*." He hooked a thumb at the squat fire-plug of a man glowering incandescently at the foot of the airship's boarding ramp.

The captain of the *Haun's Mill* was *not* happy.

∩

AIR BRANCH CAPTAIN Josiah Turley stood five-feet-naught in tall-heeled boots. Sixty-five years old and bald as an egg, the dour Yankee transplant had been skippering airships since the days of Thaddeus Lowe and airscrew Montgolfiers. Rheumy eyes, sunk deep in a corrugated face, followed Smith.

Turley turned his head every few seconds to spit tobacco juice on the tarmac. The whole area near him gleamed slick with the brown greasy stuff. The last expectoration nearly splattered Smith's shoes. Turley must've had a spittoon sitting on the lip of the baptismal font when he took the plunge.

Before Smith could open his mouth to speak, Turley opened his. The smell of chaw on his breath made Smith's stomach roil.

"You the jackwall who hijacked my ship out from under me?" Turley punctuated this with another spit of juice.

"I'm the Correlation Department Presiding Field Agent who requisitioned the *Haun's Mill*, yes," Smith answered. "When will she be ready to lift?"

Hock. Spit. Splatter. "Maybe an hour. Plus however long it takes you durned fools to drag that monstrosity you've been welding back out of the cargo bay. I won't be lifting with it throwing off my trim. No, by thunder." *Hock. Spit. Spatter.*

"The C-and-C stays," Smith said. He pulled out his pocket watch. "Now, you will lift ship at the top of the hour. That's fifty minutes from now."

"I will, will I?" Turley turned and expelled an extra-large glob.

"Yes, you will. And then you'll get us to Tokyo in forty-eight hours." Smith glanced again at his watch. "No, forty-seven hours from now."

Turley choked as he swallowed chaw juice. "Forty-eight hours?!" he wheezed. "Why, man, it must be six thousand miles to Japan!"

"Five thousand five hundred and eighty-nine statute miles to be exact."

"It can't be done. Not in my ship. Not in any ship."

"The design speed of the *Haun's Mill* is one hundred and twenty knots. Do the math. Completely doable."

"Are y'daft, man? That's *maximum* speed. You can't sustain maximum speed for forty-eight hours. Not with her brand new and her engines not even broke in. You'll fly her to pieces!"

"Then fly her to pieces," Smith said. "But get us there."

Turley hooked a finger in his mouth and pulled out the dripping wad of chaw. He flung it to the ground. "I won't do it, y'hear me? I don't care what fancy legal papers you wave at me, you jumped-up civilian clerk. I'm an officer of the Air Branch and *I'm* the captain of the *Haun's Mill*."

Smith stared at the little man one heartbeat. Two. Then he said, "Captain Turley. I am the Presiding Field Officer of a declared Condition Carthage emergency. As such I supersede all civil and military authority save Governor-President Wells and the Prophet Joseph F. Smith. I outrank your entire chain of command. *I am your chain of command.*"

He paused and Turley shrunk under his gaze.

"Your file says you're steady under fire," Smith continued, "that you're a man who gets the job done. Normally, those would be plusses in my book, but for this trip all I need is a streetcar to get me down the block. When I board a streetcar, I don't very much care *who* the driver is. Now you will either fly me to Tokyo, or I'll relieve you of your command and turn the fastest, sweetest airship in the world over to your first officer and *he* will fly me to Tokyo. Do you understand me?"

Turley stared at his toes. "Oh, you'll not be wanting to do that," he muttered. "That daft boy'd land you in Australia, like as not."

The airship captain fished out his stick of chaw and bit off a healthy-size bite. He looked up at Smith. "So I guess I'll fly for you," he said around the mouthful of tobacco. "And I guess I'll shave off another hour to boot."

43 hours later
Tokyo, Japan

THE RENTED motor launch shot northward, its prow cutting across the cold dark waters of Tokyo Bay. Kennicott Fielding Smith turned his head to look back at the *Haun's Mill* moored among the rows of cargo airships, a barracuda among beached whales. The orichalcum of her outer skin gleamed white-gold in the morning sun.

Tokyo's famed Gaijin Field with its rows and rows of foreign airships lay at the end of the far southern hook of Tokyo Bay in the sleepy little outskirt village of Haneda. Foreign traders who wanted to travel into the City proper needed to travel the eight miles by steam rickshaw or, if they were in hurry, by motor launch across the bay.

Smith was in a hurry.

Already his teams of combat elders were fanning out by rickshaw and boat toward the city to tract out the hidden Tendril. Captain Turley had done better than he'd promised—Grumman had built the *Haun's Mill* better than they knew

—and the airship had suffered only a thrown propeller shaft on number three starboard in the last hour of her wild ride.

The extra hours Turley bought might just make the difference.

The *Haun's Mill* gleamed brightly but only, Smith thought, because of the protective runes of Reformed Egyptian carved into its skin. Everything else on this warm spring day seemed clouded, shadowed.

The sun seemed dimmed, and the blossoming cherry petals gave off no scent. The very air he breathed seemed slimy and viscid. The new factories lining the harbor belched not just thick coal smoke but tangible gloom and despair.

Smith had traveled many times to Japan. It never had been like this.

The Tendril corrupted not only the leaders of the country, but the country-side itself.

Perhaps those extra hours wouldn't be enough.

Standing there at the boat's gunwale dressed in the formal clothes of a diplomat—black morning jacket and waistcoat, dove grey striped trousers, silk top hat, patent leather shoes—he suddenly missed the comforting bulge of a shoulder holster under his left arm. He'd be going in to see the Emperor without so much as a penknife in his pocket. Alone.

Smith turned to the embassy official who had met him at the landing field. Brenford was only a Third Secretary, but he seemed to have a good head on his shoulders, a welcome change from most of the Gentile Nations Department embassy officials Smith seemed to encounter in the course of his missions.

Only he and Brenford were aboard. The diplomat stood at the wheel, piloting the rented motor launch. Smith had insisted Brenford rent the boat rather than hire it. The agent had things to discuss he didn't want any local to hear.

"Grant know we're here?" Smith asked.

Brenford shook his head. "We managed to con Ambassador Grant into a survey trip of Kyoto to assess expanding the mission field into the Kansai region. He'll be gone all week." Apostle Heber J. Grant not only served as the Deseret ambassador to Japan, but as the Church's mission president here as well.

At least the real Heber J. Grant did.

The lookalike *thing* that had somehow taken his place...

"Do the Japanese know? That Grant's been—?"

Another shake of the head. "Not that we can tell. Or if they do, they're not saying."

Just as we weren't saying that we knew of maybe a dozen countries where the Tendril lanced in and out and replaced one of their top leaders with a doppelganger.

Nozaki had mentioned a "corruption." Smith didn't think he'd meant it actually replaced Japanese officials, but more a tainting and suborning, like unto what had happened with the countryside, the cherry blossoms, and the spring air.

The motor launch neared the city docks.

Brenford cleared his throat. "Uh, sir? Things have gotten a little...*strange* here the last couple days," he said. "You going in alone and unarmed...I don't—"

Brenford fumbled in one of his pockets. "Please take this. I know it's not much, but—" He held out a tiny one-shot derringer of all things.

Smith did his best to not even smile. Brenford meant well. The best he knew how. "Thank you, son, but they'd detect that first thing. *We* would. No, my only option is going into the lion's den barehanded."

This time Smith did smile. "But not unarmed." He pulled out of his own pocket a strange object of brass and leather. At first glance it looked like an archery glove gone horribly wrong. There was a palm piece of tooled leather, but no glove-fingers at all. Instead, the palm piece attached to a man's finger ring, a simple unadorned circlet of Bingham copper brass.

Smith slipped the ring on the ring finger of his right hand and pressed down the adhesive-backed leather to fit snugly against his palm. "Palm of Gilead, we call this," he told Brenford. "A little something we borrowed from the Bar-Giora."

"That Jewish group fighting the Ottoman Turks?"

Smith nodded. Deseret funded much of the active Zionist quest for a homeland.

He held out his hand, fingers spread and palm to Brenford. The device glowed slightly then *phased*, meaning it sunk—brass ring, leather, and all—into his hand. "Undetectable because there's nothing to detect. If Ottoman *djin* can't find these, the Japanese can't either."

Brenford stared open-mouthed at Smith's seemingly empty hand. "But what does it do? Shoot magic lightning?"

"Something like that," Smith said.

Brenford chopped his throttle and the motor launch slopped against the worn-out rubber tires hung off the pier as bumpers.

Smith clambered up onto the dock. He saw the Japanese government limousine waiting for him. He also saw the Japanese official presumably assigned to be his escort.

"Good luck, sir," Brenford called.

Any luck Smith had allowed himself to believe in had just dried up.

The man standing there—standing impossibly there—was the man Smith had left five-thousand five-hundred and eighty-nine statute miles behind in San Diego.

Hisato Nozaki.

ᑎ

THOUGH DRESSED in nearly the same colors as Smith, Nozaki in his formal kimono of greys and blacks and five family crests and the white *haori-himo* tassel mock-chrysanthemum looked the elegant peacock next to Smith's dowdy gaijin-jacketed sparrow.

Nozaki smiled with his mouth, but not with his eyes. "Mister Smith—you look as if you've seen a ghost."

Or a doppelganger.

Retreat or attack? Smith stepped forward. "You couldn't have gotten here this fast."

Nozaki's smile broadened. "You did. You arrived in the manner of the West—gears and cogs and clanking great machines. I arrived in the ways of the East—elegant, simple, the path of least effort—superior in every way."

Unlike at the Dutch Consulate, here Nozaki stood on home ground. His careful mask of neutrality slipped. Each and every word he spoke dripped with disdain for the gaijin West.

And Smith relaxed out of his combat stance.

Such a petty, oh-so-human frailty was beyond the ken of any doppelganger. Nozaki was who he appeared to be.

"You'll have to show me your parlor trick someday," Smith said.

He opened the passenger door of the limousine and climbed in.

ᑎ

NOZAKI'S STEAM limousine was of Japanese manufacture. Workmanlike, but Automobile Shokai's attempt at copying bolt-by-bolt the elegant Vettius-Dama hadn't quite succeeded. Built of cold steel it might have been, but the iron from Hokkaido's Kamaishi mine lacked any confluence of Ley Lines. Still, it was an iron box and protective wards of Japanese kanji carved into the paint would serve somewhat to deflect unwanted attention.

Rather than wax, Nozaki affixed a white slip of paper marked with hand-brushed kanji calligraphy to the seam of the passenger door, a Shinto protective seal of some sort. "I have attempted to duplicate the conditions that so frustrated my shikigami in San Diego. I believe we are safe enough to discuss matters here."

The car rolled through the narrow streets not-so-silently, honking all the way as it threaded its way through the packed mass of kimonoed pedestrians. The midden stench of an open-air fish market seeped into the less-than-airtight compartment.

Smith settled back into the slippery red silk upholstery. "My teams are already tracting out the city."

Nozaki grimaced. "So. They are already deployed? It would have been better to wait until after our meeting."

"Time is not on our side," Smith replied. "A city of one-and-a-half million, pretty big haystack. It could take days, weeks to find that needle."

A deep frown from Nozaki. "We do not have days. We do not have even *hours*."

Pretty much what Smith thought, too.

"Still," Nozaki said, "it would have been better for you to wait. The purpose of this meeting—an Imperial Rescript expanding your ecclesiastical proselytizing in our country—was meant to provide cover for the sudden appearance of your combat team pairs."

Distain crept back into Nozaki's voice. "Without this play-acting, without this—how you say?—*fig leaf* to explain away your men, your blatant accomplishing of what we could not will be a great loss of face and might endanger our final success. Many in power still smart from the loss of face suffered from Commodore Perry and his black ships and will stop at nothing to prevent another such disgrace."

Smith shrugged. "*Shikata ga nai.* Can't be helped. What's done is done."

He removed his top hat and ran a hand through his sandy hair. "We've got a more immediate problem. One between you and me."

Nozaki cocked an eyebrow.

"Spent the trip boning up on Court language and etiquette," Smith said. "Seems ninety, ninety-five percent of everything the Emperor says or does in public is scripted out to the letter by this iron-clad etiquette. You could play a Victrola record and only be off a word or two."

Thunderstorms brewed in Nozaki's eyes, but he nodded reluctantly. "Setting aside your insulting gaijin bluntness, much of what you say is true." His eyes narrowed. "Be reminded the same strictures apply to those appearing in the Emperor's presence."

"That's the rub. I'm going to deviate from your script."

Nozaki's hands balled up into fists.

"You mean to insult the Emperor?" he hissed.

"See? This is why I said we have a problem," Smith said. "Relax. I'm not going to dishonor your precious Emperor. It'll only look like I am. All I need from you is to do nothing about it."

"That will be...difficult."

Smith sighed. "You're telling me. Look, you see me do something upsetting, all I ask is that you count to ten first. Count to ten and watch the Emperor for *his* reaction. If you still think I'm in the wrong after counting to ten, go ahead and lop my head off."

"Now *that* I can agree to."

∩

Nozaki's limousine pulled in front of the wooden Provisional Diet Building.

"Our audience with the Emperor is here," Nozaki said, stepping out of the automobile.

"Not the Imperial palace?" Smith asked.

"At the Palace, the Palace Guards control security. Here, my organization, Steel Angel Layer, does."

Smith got out of the car and took a survey of his surroundings.

The unimpressive wooden building hardly looked like a nation's seat of power; in fact, it looked more like an elongated two-story Kansas schoolhouse only with pagoda roofs. Smith knew it to be only a temporary make-do until the permanent building, a gargantuan pile of granite designed by the finest German architects, was built.

That granite building's exterior neared an early completion. What would have taken decades using human laborers had taken mere months utilizing mechanical men. Scores of lumbering automatons swarmed the building's exterior, hauling and fitting into place heavy blocks of granite.

The air rang to the clangor of pistoning limbs and granite blocks scraping along each other. A worksite filled with mechanical men could hardly be called a quiet place.

Called by a variety of names according to the country of origin—automated persons, Capeks, Rossums, automatons, gear-goobers, avtomats—the machines had first been invented in the Confederacy as a wholesale replacement of their servile blacks. The use of mechanical men in industry spread to other countries, mostly for dangerous mining and industrial factory tasks. Attempts at adopting them for military uses had proven less than successful.

Other nations saw mechanical men as vaguely sinister, a necessary evil. Labor-strapped Deseret with her tiny population saw them as a boon. Mormons designed theirs with cheery, children's toy features and called them Mister Macs. Many Mormon households adopted a Mister Mac as sort of a family pet.

Smith himself owned one, although his was an Ingram Bros. Mac-10, a rejected military experimental model he'd taken a shine to. It sat an ocean away, on its electrical charger back in his office in Salt Lake.

Smith turned to Nozaki. "I thought you said your entire organization except for you was tainted."

Nozaki began climbing the short flight of concrete stairs. "They are. But I still have some control of their duty roster, tainted or not. Would you rather face just two of my men? Or four entire companies of tainted guards at the palace?"

"Can't argue with that arithmetic."

Smith followed him up the stairs and into the building.

∩

IF THIS WERE TEMPORARY OPULENCE, Smith would hate to see what the permanent Diet Building would end up like. The flawless hardwood floors gleamed. Centuries of man-hours must have gone into the intricate carving of cypress wood wall panel murals and delicate cedar *ranma* transoms.

And yet...

And yet that same taint he'd sensed in the harbor seemed intensified here.

A dark haze permeated the room, blurring the beauty of the wood carvings. White and lavender chrysanthemums, arranged so artfully in vases, gave no fragrance. Sound seemed deadened in the building's hallway, and a deep sense of foreboding seeped from the very walls.

Smith knew he shouldn't be surprised. What better place for those using the Tendril to taint than the seat of governmental power?

Nozaki turned right. Down the long corridor lay a room elevated to the height of a half-flight of stairs. Red carpet ran up the stairs to the heavy door flanked by two white kimonoed *Wakou Tenshi-Sou* agents, young men fit and strong.

"The *Gokyuushou*," Nozaki explained. "The Emperor's resting place—his working office in the Diet building. He awaits us within."

Smith followed Nozaki down the corridor and up the stairs.

At the top, mere footsteps before they reached the frowning Angel Steel Layer guards, Nozaki flexed his arms and out of his voluminous sleeves two sheets of paper the size of a playing card fell into his waiting hands.

Without warning, Nozaki flung the papers, the sheets refolded themselves into throwing stars, cutting into the chests of the two men. The paper *shuriken* sunk deep into their beating hearts. They clutched their blood-soaked chests and collapsed noiselessly to the floor.

"Quickly," hissed Nozaki as he bent and grabbed one of the dead men. "The sentry's alcove." He gestured at a small side door with a jerk of chin. "Drag them in there."

Following Nozaki's lead, Smith dragged the second corpse into the small side room.

Nozaki wiped the blood from his hands on the kimono of his victim, staining the pure white silk. His face lacked any trace of emotion or remorse.

"They were tainted. They meant to bar our way," Nozaki said. "Their new masters thought I would not strike them down."

Smith wiped his own hands till they looked clean at least. They still felt tacky as treacle. Nozaki must have thought Smith squeamish and felt the need to explain. He needn't have bothered. Smith had done things just as raw in the service of Deseret.

"They thought wrong, then," was all Smith said, but Nozaki must have heard his words as a Westerner's smug reproach even so.

Nozaki turned to him. "You think I enjoyed killing *my own grandsons?* We must find the Tendril at all costs." The old man's head bowed. "The cost so far is too high as it is." With that, he regained his composure and exited the side room.

Smith looked down at the dead men. Each of them clutched in their hands the same squares of paper Nozaki had turned into shuriken. Nozaki had struck before his grandsons could.

Smith caught up to Nozaki at the double doors leading into the Gokyuushou. Nozaki set his hands on the doorknobs. "Now go," he said, "and commit your gaijin indignities upon my Emperor."

CRYSTAL CHANDELIERS. Gemstones set in lacquered wood. The glory of the Gokyuushou was Celestial to the outer hallway's mere Telestial.

Smith's attention, however, focused on the man who sat at the end of the room behind a polished L-shaped desk: the Emperor Mutsuhito, to be styled in Japanese fashion Meiji after his death.

A solid man in his forties with jet black hair frosted with silver, he sported a broad, drooping chevron moustache and a short Van Dyck beard. Thick black eyebrows slanted down into a V, giving his otherwise bland stare an angry, accusatory glare.

In portraits, the Emperor always wore ornately-trimmed black hussar uniforms, covered in orders and saucer-sized medals and medallions. Today the Emperor wore a simple new-style khaki Japanese military uniform styled on the British khakis adopted in their war with the Boer. He wore no orders or ribbons or medals, as if an envoy from lowly Deseret was beneath any attempt to impress. The Emperor's military service cap—what Nauvoo Legionnaires referred to as a "bus driver's hat"—lay tossed contemptuously upside down on the short arm of the desk.

One step ahead of Smith, Nozaki approached the Emperor. Six paces short, he suddenly prostrated himself upon the parqueted marble floor and shouted an announcement of Smith's arrival, pitched so high and fast that even with hypnogogic sleep training in Imperial Court Japanese, Smith could hardly understand any of it.

Smith stepped up even with Nozaki.

"Bow, you fool!" hissed Nozaki from the floor.

Instead, Smith deliberately remained upright while taking another step forward. "Your Imperial Highness," he said in a steady voice that penetrated the room even through the sound-muffling taint. "I stand before you as living proxy both of my nation's sovereign ruler and of the prophet of my people's God. I therefore speak to you sovereign to sovereign without the bowing and scraping of this fool beside my feet."

Nozaki sucked in air through his teeth in shock and anger, sounding for all the world like a hissing garter snake. He'd raised his face, however, just enough to stare at his Emperor.

Shock and anger and deep humiliation should have been the Emperor's reaction as well. Instead, the man's head canted at an unnatural angle, devoid of any reaction save a dull confusion. The Emperor's jaw worked as if trying to summon a response, but finding none, as if Smith's words were so foreign from any anticipated conversation as to be utterly incomprehensible.

Smith took another step forward. "'Twas bryllyg, and the slythy toves...'"

At these nonsense words, the Emperor's head canted still further. His frame began to shudder.

Smith took another step. "Duty is heavier than a mountain," he said.

This steadied the Emperor. These words from the Imperial Rescript that he himself had written were familiar to him, part of the pattern of his mind. The Emperor's head straightened, and his face took on a less blank air. "Death is lighter than a feather," the Emperor said, finishing the couplet.

Another step forward. "Lighter than a feather," Smith repeated.

"Heavier than a mountain," the Emperor replied like a phonograph needle skipping a groove and only playing part of a phrase.

Another step. "Feather," Smith said.

"Mountain," the Emperor said, the needle skipping again.

One last step and Smith had reached the desk. "Duty."

"Death," said the Emperor.

As sudden as Nozaki had thrown his two shuriken, Smith reached across the desk and grabbed the Emperor's tunic. Cloth bunched in both fists, Smith tore it open in a great ripping noise, exposing the Emperor's bare chest.

Or what should have been his bare chest.

Revealed lay a striated white waxy torso that looked all the world like the root of a man-sized daikon radish.

Nozaki, who had already launched himself up from the floor to attack Smith for laying hands on his Emperor, gasped. "*Mandrake!*"

The paper square in Nozaki's hand twisted itself in the signature weapon of the Steel Angel Layer, the *harisen*—a three-foot-long slapping fan. Kamigami-do hardened the paper into iron, sharpened its pleated fanfolds into steel razors.

With a high-pitched Japanese war cry, Nozaki swung his harisen in a flashing arc, chopping the not-Emperor horizontally in two. The blow fell so fast and sharp the not-Emperor's lower torso remained seated at the desk even as its upper body flew across the room.

The severed torso thudded to the floor.

No blood. No gobbets of flesh. No internal organs and strings of intestines hanging out.

Smith bent down to poke at it. Just a solid mass of fibrous vegetable matter. A giant radish root. That's all its waxy-white cross section was.

Smith rose. "We'll have to work fast. Show this to whatever contacts you have left who aren't tainted. Luckily, we're in just the building to do that."

Nozaki stared down at the dissevered vegetable. "You *knew*."

"Let's just say I suspected," Smith said. "They've done this to one of ours, and a Japanese Emperor is a lot easier to script than a cantankerous Mormon apostle, especially when surrounded by a palace retinue that's been tainted. Our doppelganger tripped himself up within an hour of the swap."

"You knew and said nothing," Nozaki repeated.

"As if I could trust somebody who just pops up six thousand miles away from where I left them and won't say how. You don't exactly inspire trust, Mr. Poker Face."

Nozaki toed the dead thing on the floor.

"*Amaterasu*," he said at last. "The technique is called an *Amaterasu* after the sun goddess. You create a mirror of aether that reflects where you want to go and then you step through to the other side. The procedure is difficult and can only be done sparingly."

"Just like mandraking," Smith said. "Otherwise we'd all be vegetables by now."

He eyed the old man. Nozaki had opened up a bit, but can I really trust him? I can't do this without trusting *somebody* in the Japanese power structure. Nozaki looks to be my best bet.

Root hog or die, as Smith's forebears had said.

Smith cleared his throat. "Key figures in a dozen countries have been swapped with these talking turnips, but haven't tainted anybody else. Our guess is that they mean to take over your country outright, build up a power base. Swap your Emperor—that's all you'd really need—and taint whoever else was necessary."

"And those other gaijin mandrakes?"

"Done, we think, to spoil any foreign response to the takeover until it was too late."

"So." Nozaki's face clouded in thought. "You are right. We must show this mandrake to the elite of my country who have not yet been tainted. Stay and guard this. I will go fetch those I can within this building for a start."

"Right," Smith said in a sour voice. "And the first person to walk in while you're gone will see me standing over the rutabaga and think the gaijin did it. No, thanks."

Smith picked up the gold-plated telephone on the Emperor's desk. "What say we use this newfangled contraption?"

Nozaki reached for the receiver and all Scratch broke out.

ꓵ

BLINDING light coalesced into a shimmering oval hanging a foot in the air. The oval materialized in front of the double doors to the hallway, blocking the exit.

"*Amaterasu!*" Nozaki shouted, dropping into a combat stance.

The oval expanded large enough to drive a team of horses through. Hordes of screaming, gibbering old madmen and crones—their elderly wrinkled bodies naked and rotting—shambled out of the mirror.

Limbs, body parts, and rotted fragments of flesh dropped away as they slowly advanced.

"Zuvembie?" Nozaki asked.

"Worse. *Struldbrugs.*"

"Strudel-bugs? How do I kill them?"

"You don't. If they could be killed, they wouldn't be struldbrugs. The bodies are dead already; it's their brain that can't die. Decapitation does deprive them of a body, though."

"And because of my blind mistrust, you stand here weaponless," Nozaki said raising his harisen fan overhead in a two-handed grip. "Then stay back. I will separate their brains from their bodies."

He leaped into the first wave of shambling horrors and began lopping off the heads of screaming half-rotted geriatrics, clawing and clutching at him.

The more he chopped the more came through the Amaterasu.

This didn't bode well.

Zuvembies were but mindless, soulless, purposeless corpses reanimated through alchemic means with no more mind than a pithed frog. And like a pithed frog, galvanized into twitching by electric current, their dead flesh twitched to the inductance of Ley Line energies. Their decomposing bodies kept upright and shambling forward solely due to muscle memory.

The poor fools who became struldbrugs very much had minds. Minds, volition, purpose, and most of all anger and pain. They who feared death more than they feared the consequences sought immortality through alchemy. But alchemy could only keep the brain eternally alive. When bodies ran to their allotted time and expired, mind and soul were still shackled to a rotting, putrefying corpse. Alchemy let their brain tap into Ley Lines to twitch their corpse in a parodic semblance of life, but could never truly grant it.

There were always alchemists who claimed they could, and always desperate struldbrugs who would enslave themselves to them in the vain hope of the impossible.

Whoever gathered these wretches had gone for quantity of servitor, not quality. Many destroyed themselves just by moving.

Even so, they pressed Nozaki hard. Extremely fit for a seventy-year-old, he nevertheless *was* a seventy-year-old and he began to tire rapidly.

"Fall back, Nozaki!" Smith yelled over the screaming rage of the struldbrugs.

For a wonder, the proud warrior obeyed. He executed one of those seemingly impossible *ninjutsu* backward leaps. He landed feather-light on one bended knee. Sweat ran in rivulets down his face and his breath heaved in and out raggedly.

The struldbrugs advanced across the room toward them. More continued to pour out from the glowing portal.

"Though I am loath to say it," Nozaki wheezed, "there may perhaps be too many of them."

"And they keep coming," Smith said with a nod. "Well, let's see if I can thin the herd a little."

Smith held his right hand to the square and concentrated. His palm began to glow and the Palm of Gilead emerged into view. The glow intensified, expanding much like an Amaterasu. A pistol materialized in his grip, a compact automatic pistol chased in Bingham Mine Pit copper and Rhoades Lost Mine orichalcum-gold.

Smith pulled back the slide of the Browning-Odgen Pocket Hammerless, chambering a round, then let it snap back.

"Maybe I can't portal people in and out like you, but I can transpose certain objects from anywhere around the globe."

Nozaki, chest still heaving, glared at the dinky .32 and its paltry seven-round magazine. "A larger weapon might have been more advantageous," he grumbled.

"Only works with objects I have a deep attachment for." The little pocket gun, the one he normally carried in his shoulder rig, had saved Smith's life a dozen times.

Smith swung the pistol into a firing position and squeezed off a shot. It struck the nearest shambler dead center in the windpipe. The bullet explosively obliterated the creature's neck entirely and its head went flying, screaming in frustration the entire way.

The rune-inscribed alchemic loads Smith carried in the little gun weren't exactly the normal wadcutters you buy over-the-counter at a ZCMI.

"Seems to do the job," Smith said, shifting aim to the next closest shambler.

The line of struldbrugs paused. They were thinking, rational beings and none of them wanted to be decapitated by a foe they couldn't reach. Decapitation meant eternity as a head in a jar. Let the other struldbrug bite the bullet.

The mass of horrors began backing up in a screaming, angry panic.

The crush of their oncoming fellows from the portal pressed hard against them, though. Unwillingly the front rank slowly pushed forward.

Smith aimed and shot again, de-bodying another one.

The front rank redoubled their retreat and for a moment the mass of horrors once again pushed backward.

Again and again, for the remainder the magazine, Smith held the line of struldbrugs at bay, until finally, with the last round, the slide of the little hammerless pistol locked back in the open position.

Empty.

Smith didn't have enough emotional attachment to interchangeable magazines to transpose any with the Palm.

At least he'd bought time for Nozaki to catch his breath.

"Yes. A much better tactic," the old man said, rising to his feet. "Fighting at a distance. An old fool like myself should not have fought them directly. This time I shall leave that to my shikigami."

With that, Nozaki threw open his kimono jacket, exposing its inner lining. Attached to the lining, shingled like snake scales, hung hundreds of folded paper cranes. Nozaki barked forth a single word of command and the flock of cranes flew up like a murmuration of starlings, wheeling, circling, diving into the approaching struldbrugs.

Razor-sharp wings sliced again and again. Evisceration by a thousand cuts. Withered limbs and crabbed-face head fell away. Bodies stacked by the dozen, the fallen forming a barricade blocking the progress of their ever-arriving replacements.

Yet, with each slice, the paper cranes lost a portion of their virtue. The shikigami began shedding scraps and shreds of paper until, fully spent, they faltered and fluttered to the floor inert.

Worse, the quality of the incoming struldbrugs rose. No longer the putrid rotting corpses they'd faced at first, these new reinforcements stepping through the Amaterasu were the freshly-dead. Their controlling minds were sharper and smarter and less-crazed with pain.

And even these new-dead gave way to fresh bodies partially replaced with mechanical limbs and parts.

"Only a dozen of my shikigami remain" Nozaki said, his face gray. The strain of controlling an entire cloud of shikigami telling.

Smith looked about, seeing bookshelf after bookshelf of leather bound books with gilt lettering on the spine. "If it's more paper you need—"

Nozaki shook his head. "The paper must be *mino washi* paper from Gifu, and then only when blessed by Shinto priests through certain rites." He exhaled a breath as another crane fell to the floor. "Not that it matters. These new type built of cold steel are largely proof against my weapons."

"Suggestions?"

"None, save we fight until we fall."

"I was hoping for another option," Smith said.

The stream of struldbrugs had slowed down to a trickle. They'd stopped sixty to seventy shamblers leaving only a dozen or so clankers to deal with. The newest ones had had their bodies entirely replaced by metal parts, a total fusion of alchemy and geared science. The immortal brains of the metal men floated in a jar of bubbling liquid.

"There is none," Nozaki said, nearly drowned out by the cacophony of clanking steps and questing, snapping metal claws.

Smith raised his right hand to the square again. "Then maybe I can make one. Don't even know if this is going to work, but if these guys want to play with metal men, maybe just maybe—"

The Palm of Gilead glowed once more. Streams of light flared and grew until that glare became bright as the sun. The Palm sizzled and started to smoulder. Smith bit back against the pain.

The streams of light consolidated into a ten-foot globe of light and heat, then the globe vanished in a blinding flash and a peal of thunder. In its place stood Smith's beloved mechanical Mister Mac.

The Mister Mac's light-bulb eyes lit up. Its electrical system whirred to life. "Greetings, Brother Smith," it honked. "How can I serve?"

Smith winced against the burns on his hand. The Palm had exhausted itself completely and had flaked away to burnt charcoal. With his left hand, Smith pointed at the approaching clankers. "Acquire targets: all moving objects in an arc constrained by the walls of this room. Mark."

"Parameters set. Targets plotted." Belt-fed Mormon-Maxim machine guns popped out of the automaton's thick forearms and swung into position.

Smith gave a shark's smile. "Mister Mac: Code Boggs. Repeat. Code Boggs."

"Extermination order received," Mister Mac said, mechanical voice devoid of emotion. "Commencing Code Boggs now."

The two guns spit out such a deafening stream of fire that the entire mass of attacking struldbrugs, metal clad or not, simply disintegrated. Mister Mac's arms swung back and forth in precisely calculated arcs, hosing down everyone and everything in front of it. The violence of the attacks such that even the Amaterasu portal-mirror shattered under the impact of the high-powered .303 steel-jacketed shells.

Smith's shark smile grew wider. Nothing like a MAC-10 Mister Mac. Nobody Boggs the way they Bogg, nobody shells the way they shell. Nobody.

The only problem was—

And even as Smith thought this, his Mister Mac ground to a shuddering halt. Its head and arms drooped lifeless and the electric glow in its bulb eyes dimmed, then died completely.

The only problem was the stubborn design flaw that had cancelled the line and had driven the engineers of Ingram Bros. around the bend. After about forty service hours in the field, its batteries would no longer hold more than a three-minute charge. Even swapping out the batteries for factory-fresh ones fixed nothing; three minutes and they were drained.

Mechanical, alchemical, electrical—the designers argued the root cause amongst themselves. Smith thought it deeper than that. He thought his metal friend's Babbage-brain calculated not only targets and trajectories, but costs and consequences. He thought his metal friend had a conscience.

Heaven knew Smith's conscience had long since atrophied.

Ω

IN THE AFTERMATH OF BATTLE, Smith's ears rang like an entire chorus of anvils from the Maxim fire. He coughed, his throat raw from the acrid gun smoke and the choking miasma of necrotic, shredded flesh. He gagged on the unbearable stench.

His blackened, blistered right hand throbbed in pain.

Nozaki stepped through the riddled bodies of their attackers. Footing was tricky. Minced flesh and splattered gear oil slicked the floor like an ice rink.

"Your metal friend was too efficient," he said, scowling. "It would have been best to leave the Amaterasu intact and functioning. The portals work in both directions. Those behind all this were surely on the other side."

Smith patted his poor depleted metal friend with his good hand. "Who's a good boy?"

To Nozaki he said, "Sorry I saved our lives."

Nozaki eyed him. "You are wounded," he said, his tone softening just a little.

Nozaki crooked a finger at his last remaining shikigami and it fluttered its paper wings toward Smith. It alighted on his burnt hand, perched there for only a moment, then refolded itself into a long bandage strip and wrapped itself several times around Smith's hand.

Immediately the pain left his hand and the flesh healed.

Nozaki went back to toeing the bodies of the fallen horrors. "Perhaps one of these is still intact enough to talk."

Smith looked up from his bandaged hand. "Try one of the all-metal ones."

"So," Nozaki nodded.

They found one. One of the clankers had had its metal body shot to ribbons, limbs all blasted away, but the fluid-filled glass jar holding its floating brain remained undamaged. More importantly its audio and visual inputs and speaking voder were still intact and functioning.

Nozaki gave it a good kick. "You. Monster," he said. "Speak."

The burbling brain said nothing.

Smith cleared his throat. He pointed down to the Cyrillic labelling on its metal body's dials and switches. "It's Russian. I don't think it understands you."

"So," Nozaki said. He gave the brain jar another kick and spoke in Russian, "Where did you portal from? Where is the Tendril? Who are your masters? You will tell us everything or I will smash that glass jar of yours and watch you flop around like a jellyfish and die as the fluid drains away."

The floating brain chortled through its voder apparatus, a hideous, hollow metronomic sound. "Ho ho ho. That would not kill me."

"Then I will slice your brain into a million slices."

"That would not kill me either. Only destroying the Ley Lines would kill me and to do that you would have to destroy the planet itself," the brain said. "You cannot kill me, you cannot threaten me, you cannot coerce me."

Nozaki's face darkened with anger.

Smith laid his bandaged hand on Nozaki's shoulder. "You're going about it all wrong, buddy. Let me try."

Smith bent down and unscrewed the jar unit from its shattered machine torso. One of the jar's two microphones that served as the brain's stereoscopic "ears" dangled loosely on a braided wire.

Smith held up the jar and stared into its camera "eyes."

"Do your worse," the brain laughed. "You cannot kill me, either."

"I have no intention of killing you," Smith said in Russian. "I mean to do something far worse, and see to it that you stay alive."

Smith grabbed the dangling microphone and yanked hard, snapping it off at the cord.

"I'm going to rip off your eyes and ears one by one. Then I'm going to encase you in a cube of cement six feet square. Then I'm going to drop that cube of cement into the Pacific Ocean. Not just any spot in the ocean but the Marianas Trench. You'll spend eternity trapped down a watery abyss five thousand fathoms deep—blind, deaf, and helpless, but ever-so-much alive. And you won't even be able to scream because I'll have ripped out your voder."

Smith grabbed one of the jar's camera-eyes and snapped it off. "Talk!"

The frightened brain couldn't spill its non-existent guts fast enough.

Nozaki left the interrogation of the discorporal struldbrug to Smith.

Smith's bloody-minded ruthlessness underneath that insipid Western congeniality of his had surprised Nozaki. Perhaps there was a place in Japan for gaijin methods and gaijin toys after all. And for gaijins themselves. There certainly was a place for men like Smith.

But first, Nozaki must secure the Gokyuushou.

He stripped his regrettably dead grandsons of their squares of mino washi paper. Rearmed, he dealt with the Diet guards and Diet members only now beginning to cautiously poke their heads into the Gokyuushou. It was not so much they might be cowards as that the Gokyuushou belonged to the Emperor, making it sacrosanct.

Nozaki had the guards set up a perimeter, then made sure the politicians got a good look at the mandrake imposter. He also sent for the Diet photographer and his camera. Nothing could stop the news from spreading that the Emperor had been defiled, a massive setback for the enemy.

None of the arriving responders and onlookers carried the Tendril's taint. Questioning revealed that those guards and politicians who did had fled the building en masse after the shooting stopped. Or rather, after the Amaterasu had shattered.

Very good news. That meant the enemy had limited resources and was unable to fashion another Amaterasu portal at present.

Miraculously, the gilt telephone on the desk survived unscathed. Nozaki telephoned the nearest troop barracks and ordered a company of riflemen as reinforcements.

The barracks reported that they, too, had suffered a mass desertion of men and officers, running pell-mell down the street. The enemy must be regrouping its forces.

Nozaki sent two paper cranes soaring out the window. One flew overhead, providing reconnaissance of the immediate area. On the other, he'd scrawled a hasty message before sending it speeding toward its destination.

Smith must have finished questioning the brain. He handed it over to one of the palace guards who dumped it in a large canvas mail sack and pulled the drawstrings taut.

Before he handled it over, Smith tore off the remaining microphone-ear.

"You promised—!" the horror squawked through its voder, its voice quickly muffled to impotent silence at the bottom of the thick sack.

Smith turned to Nozaki. He grinned. "No sense letting it eavesdrop."

"Did it know anything useful?" Nozaki asked.

"Only the general location of the Tendril," Smith said with a tired smile. He accepted a proffered water canteen from one of the arriving troops and drank deeply.

"Old Floating Brain said it was within a mile radius of someplace he called 'Kilometer Zero,'" Smith said.

"The center of Nihon Bridge. It is the starting distance-measuring point for our railway system."

For a moment, Smith's face took on a faraway look, visualizing a map of Tokyo. "Nihon Bridge. Nihonbashi business district. Got it."

"We must strike now," Nozaki said. "The enemy is off-balance. Its forces are in disarray." Nozaki told Smith of the panicked retreat of the enemy's tainted assets.

Smith nodded at his assessment.

"Just get me back to my airship, then. I'll vector in my combat elders," Smith said. "Your limo still out front?"

Nozaki smiled. "I think I can do better than that."

As if on cue a glow of light coalesced into an Amaterasu. Out stepped a dozen teen-age girls. They each wore a long, red pleated skirt and a white *haori* kimono jacket. They carried a variety of martial weapons—*naginata* halberds, *katana* swords, and even the asymmetric *azusa yumi* longbow unique to Japan.

"They are *Miko*—shrine maidens—of the Nozaki Clan," Nozaki explained. He indicated the oldest girl, a girl of eighteen who instead of a weapon carried a *haraegushi*, a wooden wand with a folded lightning-bolt paper stream attached. "My granddaughter Yumiko."

Yumiko bowed deeply with all the solemnity of an adult. Her embarrassed smile, flushed cheeks, and quick glances at the exotic gaijin Smith were those of a young girl in the springtime of life.

"We will form an Amaterasu to your airship at Gaijin Field," she said, "and from there accompany you and Grandfather to the Tendril."

Nozaki dipped his head in brief acknowledgment of her plan. Already one of the shrine maidens had started the chant to open the new portal.

"When it was founded, the Steel Angel Layer—over my objections—was quite adamant in its refusal to accept female adepts into its ranks," Nozaki said. "It is now Japan's great and good fortune that the oversight was committed."

Smith started chuckling.

Nozaki's eyes narrowed. "You find it amusing my nation having to be saved by teenage girls?" he asked sourly.

Smith waved away Nozaki's anger. "Relax. It's just that in Mormon culture," Smith said, still smiling, "if you *really* want to get something done, you send in the Sisters."

ᑎ

Approximately one kilometer NE of the Nihon Bridge
Tokyo, Japan

WHEN HIS PARENTS died suddenly of Tremonton Fever, they left the three-year-old boy who would someday grow up to be Staff-Senior Field Agent Shupe with exactly two things: a patched flannel blanket that had seen better days and the unfortunate name of Johann Sebastian Boxelder Shupe. Shupe lost the blanket, but kept tight hold on the name.

The name—Shupe insisted on using the entire triptych, not initials or diminutives like "Joe"—caused a lot of teasing and constant fights in the Kearns-St. Ann's orphanage. Shupe grew up a six-foot-two-inch strapping youth, quick with his fists and slow with words. When he turned nineteen and the time came as it did for all young Deseret men to choose between an ecclesiastical mission or a two-year hitch in Deseret's military, Shupe chose the Correlation Department instead.

"They do a lot of fighting," he said in explanation. "All they do is fight."

Which suited Shupe just fine and, from Shupe's unbroken string of superior-rated efficiency reports, it suited the Correlation Department just fine, too.

Now, walking the narrow claustrophobic streets of Tokyo, Shupe wanted to fight this instant. He wanted to punch his junior companion right in the kisser.

Shupe felt all turned around. The funny-looking wood buildings with paper doors and windows all looked the same and the narrow streets jutted out at irregular angles and lengths. He felt like a clumsy giant walking in the crowds of the short skinny locals, and he didn't really understand any of their rapid-fire babbling speech. Hypnogoguing never really seemed to take with him.

Worst of all, when the boss had swapped the roster around back in San Diego, they'd taken away his usual junior companion and stuck him with Junior Field Agent 3rd Class Yoshida Clayton, the greenest greenie Shupe had ever teamed with.

Junior Agent Clayton knew where they were; his father worked for a Deseret trading company and he'd grown up in Tokyo. Junior Agent Clayton knew what the crowd was saying; his mother was Japanese, and he'd used the language since he was in the cradle.

That was the problem. Clayton knew. He knew it all.

He'd never even been on a combat op before, but he knew more about how one should be run than Shupe or even the boss, Presiding Field Agent Smith. If you didn't believe it, just ask Clayton himself.

Right now, he was gassing on about hypnogoguing. "...doing it all wrong, I tell you. It doesn't do any good they way they're going about it." Clayton's voice was thin and reedy, and his English had an accent to it from living in Japan all his life.

"S'that so?" Shupe muttered, trying to keep his concentration on the little ball of spun brass wire in his hand. The Liahomer's tiny gyroscopic spindles attuned to Cthulhuchthonic intrusions. So far, the device had not so much as even quivered the whole morning. "That's another block checked. Call it in."

"...what they really should be doing..."

"Call it in."

"...is put someone like me in charge to..."

"Call it in," Shupe growled, "or I'll shoot you in the leg."

Clayton blinked. "No need to get rude about it."

Greenies. You just had to know how to handle them.

Clayton pulled the leather messenger bag off his shoulder and rummaged around within. His hand came out clutching the corded microphone of the portable Marconi sender. "Team Brigham Five reporting. Block 8 of Nihonbashi Horidome-Chuo cleared. Moving on to Block 9."

Clayton didn't even wait for acknowledgement before shoving the microphone back into the bag and continuing where he left off. "See, the main deficit of your current sleep-training method is..."

"I don't care," Shupe said. He looked across the confusing five-way intersection. "Now which one of these is Block 10?"

"That one," Clayton said, pointing. "Now as I was saying, the chief deficit is that the current setup is only teaching language. Vocabulary, grammar, a few basic idioms. What it's lacking is culture context. Folk tales, children's rhymes, history—a whole ingested lifetime of absorbed details that mere vocabulary and grammar can't convey."

Shupe frowned. He thought he'd seen the Liahomer twitch.

There. It did it again. To the left.

Shupe wheeled to the left, too, instead of following the clockwise search pattern they'd used on each block previously.

"Hey!" said Clayton who'd continued lecturing for several paces before he'd realized Shupe had reversed direction. He jogged over to catch up. "You're going counter-clockwise. Breaking the search pattern leads to inconsistencies, redundancies, and uncovered areas, not that the current search pattern is all that optimal. What we should be doing is searching in concentric circles spiraling in toward the center—"

"Zip it, kid," Shupe barked, focusing on the lazily-twitching spindles of his Liahomer. *Close, but no banana* as his old trainer used to say.

Clayton's Marconi started squawking. "Attention all teams," it said. Holy Heber, it was the Boss himself, calling from the airship's C-and-C. "Target believed to be within one-mile radius of Nihon Bridge. Converge on area with all possible speed. Revised area assignments as follows."

One of the regular C-and-C dispatchers began a long litany of new search area assignments for each team.

What a time to have to depend on this Clayton for map details. Not for the first time this morning, Shupe wished he'd gotten map-hypnogogued instead; maps took good with him.

Shupe rummaged in his own messenger bag and pulled out a folding map printed in English he'd picked up in Gaijin Field's terminal building. He unfolded it and squinted. The type was tiny, and the map made no sense at all to him.

"Nihon Bridge—that's near us, isn't it?" he asked Clayton.

Clayton looked at him as if Shupe were stupid or something. "Only our starting point this morning. Only one of the most famous cultural locations in all of Tokyo. We've been working the north bank of the Nihonbashi River all morning. We're a little more than a mile northwest of it now."

Shupe refolded his map and checked his Liahomer again. "Right. This way then." He pointed further north and to the east.

"That's the wrong way!" Clayton squawked. "Our new area's back that way!" He pointed back the way they'd come.

"We covered that area this morning. My 'homer is pointing this way. We go this way!"

"You're going to get us in trouble!"

Shupe just laughed. "You've been complaining all morning about the way the Department runs things. Now we start doing things my way."

He held out the Liahomer and followed the twitching spindles.

The satchel Marconi-sender kept squawking at them. "Team 5b, report in. Team 5b, report! I know you can hear me, Shupe!"

"We'll report in when we're ready," Shupe muttered to himself. The spindles were twitching like mad. Block 9 had been another bust, but Block 10...

Block 10 was mostly a block of merchant shops catering to the Japanese business class looking to buy gaijin items. Building 15, the building the Liahomer was dancing at jig to, seemed to sell an eclectic mix of European bicycles and gramophone records.

"What's the sign say above it?" Shupe asked.

"Niho Wing, Ltd.," a sulky Clayton answered. He wasn't happy about haring off in the wrong direction and cringed every time the Marconi squawked at them. "Wing's the name of the bicycle brand. German, I think."

"This one's it," Shupe said, slipping his 'homer into his bag.

"Call it in?" Clayton asked hopefully.

"Not until we've eyeballed the inside to make sure," Shupe answered. "Sticks out."

Both Shupe and Clayton pulled out their leather-bound Standard Works to maintain the illusion of their ecclesiastical cover story.

The interior of the shop looked dank and dismal. A line of German bicycles stood gathering dust. Wagner gramophone records lined one shelf.

Shupe stepped toward the odd little shopkeeper behind the counter. "Hello. We're interested in some bicycles. Mind if we look around?" Shupe said, hoping his sleep-trained Japanese was even remotely intelligible.

"We're not open for business," the odd little shopkeeper snarled. "You'll have to leave at once."

"But we just got here," Shupe said as he stepped toward the counter.

The Liahomer in his bag was oscillating to beat the band. He could hear it repeatedly smack the sides of his canvas bag in its frantic churnings.

"Leave at once!" the shopkeeper ordered. The motions of his mouth seemed to not match the words he spoke.

The Liahomer spun even wilder.

Shupe swung up his hand and pointed the crested pewter ring on his finger right in the shopkeeper's face. Not just any ring, but a Correlations Deparment CTR ring—Combat Tactical Ring.

The press of a thumb and the ring's crest flipped open on a hinge, revealing a tiny atomizer nozzle. A squirt of consecrated oil hit the shopkeeper right in the kisser.

The shopkeeper's face melted away. The being's true face beneath the dissolving mask proved not in the least bit human.

With a shout, a trio of disgusting creatures bearing the same inhuman face boiled out of the back room.

Difficult to see in the dark shadows of the shop, but to Shupe they looked like nothing less than man-sized snapping turtles walking erect on their hind limbs. They bore the same face as the shopkeeper, predominated by a raptor-like razor-sharp turtle's beak. They had a Friar Tuck tonsure ring of black-green hair that looked like coarse strands of seaweed. Instead of a bald spot on top of their heads was a bowl-shaped white ceramic plate of some sort.

Shupe held his Bible in his left hand. His right hand grabbed the Departmental .32 Browning-Odgen Hammerless out of its shoulder rig. Shupe fired point blank twice into the storekeeper's chest.

The bullets *spanged* and *spinged* off the turtle shell like they were bouncing off alloy steel.

He fired three more times to no effect.

His partner Clayton backed away from the newcomers. "It's a *kappa*," he shouted. "You can't kill a kappa that way."

"Like this, then?" Shupe shifted his aim at fired at the creature's face. Again, it bounced off.

"No, no, no," Mr. Know-It-All Clayton shouted. He'd edged around one of the bicycles on display, putting it between him and the nearest kappa. The angry kappa leaned over the bike, reaching for him. "You have to smash the plate on its head."

"Plate?" Shupe asked as he fired his last round in frustration.

"Like this," Clayton said and in a double-handed swing, smashed his leather-bound Triple Combination hard against the white ceramic plate on the creature's head. The plate shattered into a thousand shards of pottery, kappa brains splattered everywhere, and the dead kappa slumped to the ground.

Shupe downed the next kappa, proving a pistol butt to the plate worked just as effectively.

With the storekeeper down, Shupe could turn his attention to the remaining two kappa double-teaming his junior. He reloaded a fresh magazine and aimed.

Turned out a bullet worked even better than a pistol butt.

Shupe ducked inside the back room for a quick look. Frowning, he stepped back to the shop floor.

Clayton was brushing kappa gore from his suit jacket as fastidiously as a cat shaking snow from its paw. "See? I told you the hypnogogues need to include folk lore and mythology."

"Yeah, yeah," grumbled Shupe. "Call in, will you? Give 'em our location and tell them we've found the Tendril."

Smith had soon been apprised that there were several limitations on the art of casting Amaterasu portals. Not only did the act of casting one require several hours of complete rest afterward by the caster, but the caster could only fashion a portal to a destination the caster was already familiar with. None of the Nozaki shrine maidens had ever set foot in the Niho Wing store.

Luckily, however, one of the girls shopped quite frequently at a bookseller a couple blocks away. As was common for the Nihonbashi area that catered in all things gaijin, the bookseller carried magazines depicting the latest in gaijin women's fashions.

Such were the little things battles hinged on. For the sake of Nozaki's already battered pride, Smith kept from laughing.

Smith entered the bicycle store with Nozaki and his gaggle of teenaged shrine maidens in tow. The miasma of taint choked the room. This was the place.

And this time he came properly armed.

In those anxious minutes spent back on the airship, waiting for his teams to call in, Smith took a couple minutes to grab a proper combat kit.

He rubbed the polished stock of his "Hot Cat" automatic rifle, Browning's fix of the abysmal French *Chauchat* light machine gun. Smith carried an ammo bag with plenty of 20-round half-moon magazines. The Hot Cat spat out .30-06 Springfield rounds. If the enemy had any more metal-bodied struldbrugs, he'd be ready.

Smith's eyes flicked between the two combat elders. It was easy telling which was the senior.

The senior companion, the tall beefy one named Shupe, seemed hardly surprised in the least by Smith's far-too-timely arrival or that he was accompanied by an old man in a dress or a costume party of teenage girls swinging around medieval weapons. Life in the Correlations Department jades a man quickly.

The only thing Shupe seemed concerned about was that Smith hadn't brought more combat elders.

"They're on their way," Smith told him, "but they'll have to catch up. Speed is our greatest weapon right now. We need to strike *now* with what whatever we've got."

Shupe didn't look happy about it, but he gestured toward the backroom. "The Tendril's in here."

They entered the backroom. Even an electric torch could hardly penetrate the dark gloom. Jumbled wooden shipping crates and piles of trash covered much of the hardwood floor. The room stank of death and decay and last week's spoiled cabbage.

In the center of the room lay the Tendril.

If an Amaterasu was a coalescence of light, the Tendril was a concentration of shadow and ancient evil. A pine-green blacker than black, an inky tenebrous substance neither matter nor energy, but something far older and far fouler. Its knotted, gnarled shape generated an impenetrable fog, and the Tendril seemed to vanish into some far distance outside the plane of reality the storeroom itself resided in.

"We destroy it, sir?" Shupe asked. "Like you did in Cuba?"

"Negative, Senior Agent," Smith said. "That won't get us back Brother Grant or the Emperor."

Nozaki nodded. "This thing must lead to wherever they are. Destroy it now and we lose them forever. We follow the root, trace it back to where our enemy lurks."

Shupe frowned. He holstered his little pocket pistol. "Clayton," he called to his companion. "Guess scripture chase is over. Looks like we're going to need our other sticks." He held out his book of scriptures and triggered it. The books acted as a rudimentary Palm and transposed with the combat elder's standard-issue battle weapons, Krag-Jorgensen bolt-action repeating rifles. They already carried ammo reloads in their messenger bags.

Smith nodded. "Okay, then. If everybody's ready, follow me."

Smith started walking down the length of the root-like Tendril and off into the never-never non-existence it led to.

AFTER A LENGTHY STRETCH, the nebulous shadow-fog seemed to solidify into an underground cavern. The floor, if it was a floor, seemed a series of steps downward like some naturally-occurring lithoid staircase.

Natural to what, Smith didn't know. The shapes of everything he saw looked completely askew, as if Euclidean geometry held no sway with whatever universe they now existed in. Angles and distance held only arbitrary meaning and seemed to shift about.

But they continued to descend—down, down, down.

Smith felt a slight tug on the back of his jacket. He looked over his shoulder to see Yumiko, the leader of the shrine maidens, delicately clutching his jacket for reassurance. She stared down at her feet. She trembled.

Nozaki whispered. "A brave girl in battle. It is just that my granddaughter does not deal well with dark and confined spaces."

Smith cleared his throat. "Listen up, people," he said in a loud, commanding voice. "We can't afford to get lost or separated in this crazy place, so everybody link up. Put your hand on the shoulder of the person in front of you. You shorties, if you can't reach their shoulder easily, just grab on to the back of their jackets."

Nozaki nodded his thanks and stepped backward to join the human chain.

After an unknown amount of time—minutes? centuries?—the strange cavern led back to human reality and the mortal planet Earth. As reality returned, the tunnel angled up, not down. Sunlight beckoned at the end, framed in a post-and-lintel doorway that looked to be some lost artifact of ancient Egypt or perhaps Babylonia.

Smith freed himself from Yumiko's butterfly grip. "All of you wait here while I take a look at what we're getting into."

He padded silently up the stone stairs toward the opening, Nozaki right on his heels. Toward blue sky and the keening wail of the sheering gull.

The doorway opened to an ancient abandoned temple, built much like the Acropolis in Athens. Open-air, the roof supported by fluted stone columns, carved stone friezes depicted scenes from a ghastly mythology Smith had never seen. Smith wanted to shudder each time his full gaze fell upon the carvings.

"Over here," Nozaki hissed. He was crouched down at one of the pillars on the far side.

Smith scuttled over to him.

The temple, or whatever it was, sat atop the peak of a small island. Looking closer he saw that the stone was not volcanic, but some sort of strange oolitic sandstone. Aeons of wind and wave, water and storm had worn away the surface into bizarre shapes—but not the jagged, random Karst landscapes associated with limestone. The erosion here looked unnatural, almost purposeful.

The bulk of the island sat like a stack of giant-sized children's building blocks tumbled into one great pyramidal heap. Jutting up to form blocks at irregular intervals were a series of carved stone plinths, obelisks, and pylons. Something—surely neither wind nor wave—had carved strange foul-looking runes onto the stone facings.

Down below at the shore line of the island, Smith saw evidence of other men. He pulled his coggles from his satchel, and set them, pince-nez-fashion, on the bridge of his nose.

The brass coggles were much like a slimmed down optometrist's phoropter, only instead of the various corrective lenses that clacked into place with ratchet-dials to adjust for poor vision, the lenses of a coggle adjusted for various light spectra—infrared, ultraviolet, light-gathering nighttime lenses—as well as dialing in various telescopic strengths.

Smith thumbed the coggles for high magnification.

He sucked in his breath. Halfway up the side of the mountainous island stood a long row of glass capsules filled with a viscous blue-green fluid, like what the struldbrug brains floated in, only holding the missing world leaders: among them Brother Grant, the Japanese Emperor, that upstart young British PM Winston Churchill, and that poor arm-withered German Crown Prince Wilhelm.

Air bubbles leaked from their mouths. They must still be alive in that fluid. Closer inspection showed a great number of pumps and generators attached the bank of capsules and a handful of technicians tending to them.

Down at the shoreline, an armed yacht lay anchored a short distance offshore. The armed yacht bristled with Maxim guns and even sported a one-inch quick-firer. Various rough looking men armed with rifles patrolled the deck.

On the shoreline another couple dozen armed men moved, escorting two men and a struldbrug-like machine man topped with a glass jar. From their strut, they were likely the leaders of the island expedition.

Smith cranked his coggles to maximum magnification.

The brain in the mechanical struldbrug was not a brain at all, but an entire head. There was no mistaking his identity. The leonine hair and beard belonged to Karl Marx, thought dead for twenty years. Lenin, the Russian agitator, marched by him. Smith didn't know who the shorter Asian-looking man was.

He passed the coggles over to Nozaki.

"Tsuji," he grunted with distaste. "General Masao Tsuji. A fanatic who wanted to bring back the Shogunate. With him as Shogun, of course. Driven out of the Diet and into foreign exile."

Smith took back his coggles. "Looks like he's switched from Shogunism to Marxism. Quite the reversal."

"Hardly surprising. Whatever would put him on the Chrysanthemum Throne, that would be what he'd espouse," Nozaki said. "That answers the question of who formed their Amaterasu."

Smith took a closer look at the yacht. There, flying from a mast was a red flag emblazoned with the hammer-gear-and-pestle of the *Das Arbeiter-Thaumaturg-Kollektiv*—the Worker's Thaumaturge Collective. Smith wondered if the irony of the world's leading communist organization operating a yacht had escaped its owners.

Smith lowered the coggles. "Well, now we know who we're facing. Question is, what do we do about it?"

Nozaki had shifted over to another side of the temple. "Perhaps nothing."

Smith crept over and looked down that side of the mountain. He didn't need coggles to see what lay down there. Huge steam cranes lifted a gigantic object partially out of the water in a web of sisal rope. The slime-green oblong object was nearly the size of the Salt Lake Tabernacle and similar in shape.

"The *Koudai-kodai Ika!*" Nozaki snarled.

Smith nodded. Old sleeping Squidhead himself.

The Tendril they had followed from Tokyo slithered a trail down the mountainside to root itself in the exposed portion of the sleeping elder god's skull.

"What can we do?" Nozaki said, uncharacteristically despairing in the immensity of the ancient great evil below him. "If we attempt to rescue those trapped in the capsules, their guards will fight, and we cannot risk killing even one of them lest the human sacrifice awaken that great sleeping evil. The Sleeper must *not* awaken."

Awaken.

A smile spread across Smith's face. "*We* don't battle the guards. We let someone *else* do it."

He sketched out his mad plan to a disbelieving Nozaki.

∩

SMITH, Nozaki, and Senior Agent Shupe crawled down the side of the mountain toward the steam cranes. They carried sharp-edged naginata halberds borrowed from the shrine maidens.

Once the Herculean task of winching up the sleeping Cthulhu out of the water had been completed, the comatose horror must have given them no trouble. Only one bored mechanic was posted near the crane to keep watch.

"I've doped out why they had to lift the Cuttlefish," Smith said as he crawled carefully down the strange landscape. "They couldn't create their Tendril in diving suits. They needed to work in air, and that meant exposing part of it to the atmosphere."

Nozaki nodded, then put a finger to his lips. They were only a dozen yards from the bored guard, nodding in his chair under a tarpaulin makeshift marquee.

Nozaki released a paper crane. The shikigami fluttered over to the guard. Just before it reached him, it unfolded itself and reformed as large square of paper. The paper plastered itself over the guard's face forming a skintight seal.

The panicking guard clutched at his nose and mouth, but he couldn't pry off the shikigami. He tried to shout a warning, but no sound emerged. He spasmed as his burning lungs could draw in no more fresh air. A moment later, he collapsed. The shikigami fluttered off his face and away.

The unconscious man's lungs heaved, and he started breathing again.

"Quickly," Smith ordered, and each of the three men ran to a different crane. At Smith's signal, each of the men swung their rune-inscribed naginata and severed the braided steel cable wound tautly around the take-up reel.

With a mighty slash, the Koudai-kodai Ika dropped into the briny water.

It stirred.

"*Run!*" Smith screamed as he sprinted for the sheltering cover of the giant stone blocks. His companions fled just as fast.

Much like a buzzing fly disturbing a sleeping child, the sudden shock of the water against its skin roused the somnambulant Ancient One. A three-fingered claw the size of a log cabin rose from the water and brushed at the sudden irritation, severing the Tendril attached to its skull-top.

This sudden sharp pain roused the creature further. It rose out of the water, tall as a New York building, its sleepy eyes barely open. From its great height it could see the bulk of the moored yacht and the ant-like men milling about it.

Those men panicked at the first sight of the giant horror looming up over the side of the mountain. Screaming in terror they rushed onto the boat. Water churned at the boat's stern as the yacht's diesel engine roared to life and its prop bit deep into the sea. The yacht inched forward.

Halfway up the island slope, the sobbing capsule technicians begged and pleaded for them to come back.

The yacht wallowed into an arc that would point its bow away from the giant fiend wading toward them.

Suddenly a large circle of light coalesced in front of the boat and the boat vanished into Masao Tsuji's hastily cast Amaterasu portal.

Deprived of its prey, the still groggy Cthulhu sank again beneath the wave to resume its dreaming, just as an awakened man will roll over and fall back to sleep.

It took mere moments for Junior Agent Clayton and the shrine maidens to overpower the distraught technicians and secure the capsules.

SMITH LEANED back in his chair and swallowed the last of the Japanese soda pop Yumiko had handed him.

"I didn't *know*," Smith answered Nozaki. "I only hoped the Cuttlefish would go back to sleep."

He, Nozaki, and the others who'd traveled to Cthulhu's island sat relaxing under a large canvas marquee the military had set up outside the Diet Building.

The overhead canvas, rippling in a swelling breeze, made great flapping noises like a great bird of prey preparing for flight.

Smith and the others had uncorked the kidnapped world leaders and portaled them back to Tokyo in one of the canvas military tents outside the Diet Building. The leaders were a little worse for wear, but no permanent harm seemed to have been done.

Unfortunate in the case of some of them, if you asked Smith, but of course nobody did.

The Tendril's taint, which had blighted the minds of so many Japanese, also proved temporary. The high and low were all recovering nicely, and things were getting back to normal.

Some things were.

By befouling the Emperor's very person, however, the Arbeiter-Thaumaturg-Kollektiv had awakened a permanent enmity against them in the hearts of the Japanese people.

They'd also pushed Japan and Deseret closer together. Already diplomats were hammering out new trade treaties and military compacts.

Part of that new relationship included a growing rapport between their two respective counter-alchemic intelligence agencies: the Correlation Department and the Steel Angel Layer.

Smith swallowed the last of his *ramune* soda. He rattled the marble stopper around in the bottom of the distinctive blue glass bottle then handed the empty to Yumiko. *Not bad.* The lemon-lime flavor tasted pretty good and just uncorking the drink was like playing with a toy.

He'd have chat with Sylvester Q. Cannon when he got back home. Cannon Cola might want to license the stuff.

Nozaki frowned. "You gambled the entire world on a mere *hope?*"

Smith shrugged. "More of a hunch. It occurred to me that maybe the reason all those previous attempts to wake the Cuttlefish failed because he doesn't want to wake up," Smith said. "Maybe he just wants to remain asleep, dreaming of lost domains. If so, he'd resent mightily any attempt to wake him. "

Nozaki could only shake his head. "And what if you'd been wrong?"

Smith splayed out his fingers. "No alternative. It was only a matter of time—maybe only moments—before the ATK woke him under their thrall. They really thought they had some means of controlling him after he woke. I didn't dare guess otherwise."

He suddenly laughed, "But then, their dogma wouldn't allow them to admit they couldn't, would it?"

Nozaki's eyes narrowed. "What makes you say that?"

"'From each according to his ability, to each according to his need,'" Smith quoted, "And brother let me tell you—old Cuttlefish has a lot of ability."

Yumiko shyly offered Smith another ramune. Smith set the bottle atop the folding map table and banged the marble stopper protruding from the bottle's neck down hard with the heel of his hand, opening it.

"I don't know, sir," Agent Clayton said, rubbing a splinted arm. He'd retreated just a little too enthusiastically when the Cuttlefish had started thrashing and had taken a tumble off one of the basalt blocks. "Each according to his needs? That doesn't sound too bad."

Smith fixed a cold eye on the boy. "Who assesses that need? It won't be you, it won't be me, it won't be some poor farmer out in his field. It'll be the ATK leaders. It'll be their thugs with the guns."

Nozaki nodded. "A slaveholder's assessment of ability, a slaveholder's assessment of need," Nozaki said. He polished off his own drink. Warm sake. He'd snorted in disgust as Smith had chosen a kiddie beverage over *man's* drink.

One of the Miko maidens rushed over to pour another round of sake in the flat little cup Nozaki held. Sake cups looked like milk saucers to Smith, but too each his own.

"At any rate, what now, Smith?" Nozaki asked, downing the heated rice wine in a quick gulp. "Marx and Lenin are surely dead. And maybe that traitor Tsuji as well. He had not completely rested before forming that last-ditch Amaterasu. Bad things happen if you attempt one too soon after a prior one. They may have even ended up in the center of the Earth's core."

"I doubt we'll be that lucky. Those types always seem to survive somehow. But that's a problem for another day," Smith said.

A combat elder suddenly handed him a dispatch. Smith unfolded the telegraph and frowned as he read it.

He shot to his feet, shoving the crumpled dispatch back into the hands of the startled elder. "Right. My compliments to Captain Turley and tell him I need him to prepare to lift ship immediately. I need to be in Samoa yesterday."

"Trouble?" Nozaki asked, arching one eyebrow.

"Some fool German down there woke something he shouldn't have," Smith said, slipping on his jacket. He buckled on his Palm of Gilead. "A *tenifa* shark monster from the sound of it. Nothing I can't handle."

Nozaki was already on his feet. Yumiko, too. She held her haraegushi at the ready, her shy face serious as a shield maiden's.

"Nothing *we* can't handle," Nozaki corrected.

JESTING PILATE

INTRODUCTION

There are certain characters in literature which ascend to iconic stature, creating whole media empires and inspiring a raft of imitators: Sherlock Holmes, Tarzan, Horatio Hornblower, Dracula, Conan the Barbarian.

A lot of us young readers grow up to be young writers yearning to play in the sandbox of their favorite iconic characters, continue their adventures. Some of us are lucky enough to manage it. I've been extremely lucky in landing comic book gigs to write Batman, Dick Tracy, the Fantastic Four, *and other comic book touchstones of my youth.*

Such opportunities of working with licensed characters are rare, however, even in an era of IP media saturation.

Some iconic characters you're free to play with, those which were published long enough ago they've lapsed into the public domain. If you want to write Dracula *(1897), for example, or* The Three Musketeers *(1844), knock yourself out.*

But other old characters you'd think would surely be in the public domain—Sherlock Holmes (1887), for example—are still out of bounds, thanks to Mickey Mouse meddling (literally) with the already convoluted copyright laws.

For those characters, as well as for those inarguably under copyright, a writers only option sometimes is to create your own analog. That raft of imitators I mentioned? I could reel off, for example, a list of ten, twenty, thirty or more imitation Tarzans appearing Golden Age comic books. (Marvel Comics still uses one of theirs: Ka-Zar.)

Horatio Hornblower has spawned not only maritime fictional doppelgangers

(Patrick O'Brian's Aubrey-Maturin *series), but even a land-based ground-pounder Army type (Bernard Cornwell's* Richard Sharpe *series). There's even faux Horatio Hornblowers in space, notably David Weber's* Honor Harrington.

Sometimes even the imitations spawn imitations. O'Brian's Aubrey *books served as the template for David Drake's* RCN *novels,* Honor Harrington *the template for Mike Shepherd's* Kris Longknife.

I've occasionally dabbled in creating homage characters myself. My Victorian sleuth in "The Curious Case of the Ha'Penny Detective" is a Holmes stand-in, even to the point of relitigating by proxy Holmes' first case, A Study in Scarlet.

And this next story, "Jesting Pilate", features in one Jacobian poet-playwright James Talmage an amalgamation of two singular fictional characters: Robert E. Howard's sword-and-sorcery Solomon Kane and Edmond Rostand's flamboyant poet-cavalier, Cyrano de Bergerac.

I'm far from the first to imitate either character.

Cyrano has a cameo in Heinlein's Glory Road *and appears in modernized form in Steve Martin's movie,* Roxanne. *Marvel Comics has an extradimensional Pilgrim-hatted demon hunter character running around in their books.*

For my character I smooshed together these two iconic swordsmen, poet and demon-slayer, in a story of Shakespeare's London during the early reign of King James, of plays and palace intrigues, creatures of evil and men of letters, iambic pentameter and rapier ripostes. (I've even snuck in my own twist on the Francis Bacon Theory of Shakespeare for those of you of a literary bent.)

Take a seat and sit back as the house lights dim, the players trod the boards, and our play begins, the very thing to catch and keep safe-fast the conscience of a king!

The cobblestone alley narrowed until it barely spanned a man's shoulder width. Thick London fog muffled the footsteps of a balding man in doublet finery and starched linen ruff wandering the night alone after curfew.

Or not quite alone.

Two men followed him. The first was a cutpurse, padding silently only three paces back. Behind the thief, equally as silent, a tall lean man dressed in a gray that blended into the fog. The tall man silently drew a sword, a whippet-thin rapier of the finest Spanish steel.

The balding man had proven trebly foolish. First, for braving the night after curfew. Second, for not hiring a linkman—Devil take the curfew! And lastly, for wandering the back alleys of London head down deep in thought, mumbling to himself, oblivious to the danger behind.

The balding man had one piece of luck: the cutpurse timed his strike two paces too late.

The alley unexpectedly opened into a small courtyard between buildings. As if panicked that his prey might escape, the thief abandoned stealth. In his haste, he slipped on offal from an emptied chamber pot. A loose cobblestone underfoot clattered past the balding man, breaking the balding man's reverie.

The balding man whirled, peering into the dark and fog. His eyes widened at the sight of the ha'penny knife and the ha'penny thief behind it. The balding man scrabbled backward. His steaming breath—perhaps his last—shot upward in the damp and cold.

The thief moved in.

Before he could strike, a voice called out behind the cutpurse, a voice solid and strong as if trained for the stage, a commanding voice:

A little man with a little knife
Means to cut a little purse
From a man whose pen flashes bright with life
As it cuts a matchless verse.
And so is ask'd which the greater task:
The sword or the mighty pen?
It doth depend, my cutpurse friend,
On whose blade does the flashing first!

The swordsman stepped forward, his gray cape swirling. His gray garb as plain as the balding man's clothes were gaudy. The swordsman's face lay shadowed under the wide brim of a tall-crowned Puritan hat.

The thief, not only stripped of his element of surprise but surprised himself, had the choice of fleeing past his intended victim or confronting the tall stranger with the sword.

He chose poorly.

With an effortless flick of the rapier's tip, the swordsman flipped the knife from the advancing thief's grip, then, continuing the blade's arc plunged it unerringly into the scoundrel's heart.

"William," Jacob Talmage said as he wiped his sword blade clean on the dead man's own clothes before slipping it back into its scabbard, "your nighttime wanderings with your Muse will one day lead you to your death. You should leave off nocturnal wanderings when lost in your composing. I cannot always be walking so providently behind you."

William Shakespeare smiled and shook the gloved hand of his friend and creative rival. "Would you have me waste the time it takes to stroll from Cheapside to Blackfriars? Should my mind, otherwise unengaged, not be about its own task while my feet perform theirs?" He kicked the dead man's corpse. "Still, I thank you for your rescue, friend Jacob, as I do not thank this ruffian. He made me drop a line."

He looked up at Talmage. "And if I might speak of lines, yours were, as well as poorly scansioned, poorly timed. Leave be your little impromptu compositions *after* you dispatch a foe, and not before, or mayhap you find your own daemon Muse lead *you* downward as well."

Talmage smiled. "Mayhaps, but not tonight." He gripped his friend on the upper arm and pushed him along. "Come, the scene is over, let us quit the stage. This thief was only gallows' bait, true, but I would forego the pleasure of speaking to the night watch. I take it from the direction of your travel, you make for the Goat and Bagpipe as well?"

Shakespeare nodded. "The Goat, the Bagpipe—and the Bacon."

Talmage's eyes narrowed. "Aye, our newly spurred Sir Francis Bacon and his thrice-dammed Rosicrucians."

THE RAUCOUS NOISE of the tavern guided them in long before the warm fireglow through mullioned glass lighted their way in the fog.

Rather than entering the tavern, Shakespeare pointed to a rickety side staircase. "I keep a small room here," Shakespeare muttered, "not wanting to write certain lines in open company at the Globe."

Talmage nodded. Good Queen Bess had been dead only one scant year. The murky lines of power and authority and intrigue swirling around the new King James in the Year of Our Lord 1604 still roiled and churned. Precautions such as these were wise for a writer who touched upon the lives of kings and queens.

The upstairs room was small and cramped. Its only heat against the riverside dank was the small beef tallow candle Shakespeare lit and the body heat of the two men themselves. Shakespeare blew on his hands and then quickly scratched his quill over a sheet of foolscap, putting down the lines he'd composed along the way. The name he penned in ownership read "Fr. Bacon" rather than his own.

Talmage laughed. "*Et tu?*" He produced a sheaf of paper from under his cloak with a similar false Baconian appellation penned in Talmage's hand. "Since first hearing the man speak, I suspected he penned not a single word that bears his name. They say the new King is 'the wisest fool in Christendom' but our Wise Bacon treads close on His royal heels. I wonder how many others he has gulled into providing him his seeming wit."

His host bade Talmage to sit upon the room's only chair, a spindle-shanked castoff, while Shakespeare examined his rival's work, Talmage's counterfeit entitled *Of Truth*.

"Gulled or paid or blackmailed, whichever best suits Bacon's catchpenny purposes," Talmage said softly.

Shakespeare smoothed out Talmage's top sheet upon the desk and tapped the first lines with the back of his hand. "I like this, Jacob. It has your voice. '"What is truth?" said jesting Pilate, and would not stay for an answer.' But 'tis too fine a line for Bacon. Pray save it for one of your own plays. The Globe and the wider world will know it yours anon they read it anyway."

Talmage stood to retrieve the sheets from his friend's hand. He refastened the roll with ribbon and slipped it under his cloak. "'Tis the point, William. I tire of Bacon's game, and would let Truth out, knowing full well that blathersgate savant will fail to see my jest. Tonight my servitude ends. Like jesting Pilate, I mean to wash my hands of it."

Shakespeare rolled up his own work. "You dice an expensive game, my lord. Those of us with but workaday lives who have not freebooted with Drake and Grenville and shared their treasures must play a cheaper hand. Sir Francis Bacon is the King's new passing Fancy." He rubbed his bearded chin. "Still, I find I'd fancy watching his be-baconed eyes bulge wide at the two of us entering paired, a gift for him in both our outstretched hands. Those dice I *can* afford."

Talmage gathered his gray cloak and resettled his hat upon his head. Shakespeare clucked his tongue at the gray felt tall-crown, wide-brimmed Dutch-manner like the Puritans favored. "I dislike hats that slouch so. And the color! When will you come down on one side or another, my friend? Your gray is too black for surpliced Christendom, too white for black sheep dissenters. Too Puritan for safety's sake and too cavalier for dour pieties."

"I'll gladly dye it once I find plain Truth's hue." Talmage said as he unlatched the door. "And this I promise, my good friend: unlike Pilate, whence e'er I finally do hear sweet Truth, I'll stay fast to heed its call."

TALMAGE DESCENDED the side stair and entered the tavern's front door first, his scabbarded sword a welcome weight upon his hip. The firelight from the tavern's roasting fire was not as cheery inside as it looked from the outside looking in through the leaded mullions. The flames capered like Satan's imps, casting unnatural shadows across the faces of the assembled guests seated at one long table, or rather, at several table pushed together to form one whole. Sir Bacon sat at its head, flanked by two dour-faced Rosicrucians. A motley of players and fellow scribblers filled out the rest of the ale-sopped benches.

Roughhewn beams of darkened oak held up the room's low ceiling. Talmage muttered a curse for its low construction as he stepped in, cursing more for a man his height having to stoop to save his head against the beams, than the limit of movement it would place should he have to draw his sword.

Shakespeare followed him in, close behind.

Portly Ben Johnson saw both of them enter, but had eyes only for his balding friend. His fat bricklayer's fist pounded the table, bouncing the earthenware mug set before him. "Will!" he roared at Shakespeare a pace behind the taller man. "I was but in the midst of regaling our host about our own part in Bishop Miles' and his Royal Patron's great project—"

"Your grape-born regalements will wait, Master Hodman," Sir Francis Bacon said, his stentorious voice silencing the babble around him. Only the elderly Rosicrucian seated on his left continued his low-pitched monotonous chant of nonsense words. "Or more happily wither on the vine altogether, for I see my two great and good friends have brought me gifts bearing Greek."

He reached out for the ribbon-bound papers. "I take it these are the texts I hired you to proof? I wonder what it is I have to say tonight?" He quickly scanned the texts, passing each sheet in turn to the fox-faced Rosicrucian on his right.

The fox-faced man bedecked with collar ruff and feather-plumed hat frowned at the top sheet in Talmage's hand and whispered in the ear of his master.

Bacon's eyes narrowed for the briefest of moments, but he waved for Talmage and Shakespeare to sit at the foot of the table. "Join us, my two good friends. Our revels are yet not ended, and our players have yet to leave the boards."

"I must decline, Sir Francis," Talmage said, his hand edging to the hilt of his sword. "I find the environs here less to my likings than your haunts of old. A soul could stand to his full height at Grey's Inn, and the full frame of his body could follow. Besides," he added, pointedly looking at the Rosicrucian, "I likest not your newfound company of rosy-crossed players."

"Nay, stay!" Bacon called. "Hear my thought for a new play. It concerns a foolish man who would fain leave his jailor. He finds he never can, however. What say ye of that?"

"I say a new playwright should be best found. I have ever preferred my plays to have the ring of truth."

"'What is truth?'" Bacon quoted sneeringly, his fingers caressing the top sheet in Talmage's hand. "I am the King's new favorite, and Truth is what I say it to be."

Bacon's eyes shone with the guttering flame of the firepit. "Oh, I will publish this new work you've proofed tonight, my dear Talmage, and I will continue to publish those proofings that follow. For they *will* follow. And that foolish man in my play? E'er will he safevouch his jailor's words for he shall never leave his jail. Never."

"Mayhaps the shadow who capers upon the proscenium of your imagination will thus be amenably disposed, Sir Francis, but as for myself, the hour is late and I will take my leave."

As he turned for the door, Shakespeare made as if to follow. Talmage placed his hand on his friend's shoulder and shook his head. "'Tis not a storm a workaday ship from Avon should sail in, Master Will," he softly said. "Stay on your life and your future words. But, take care. 'Tis such a tavern and such a company of rosy crosses here as poor Kit fell from in Deptford. I truly wonder at how many have danced to our host's goatish pipes and for how long."

He stepped to the door. The room was silent save for the crackling of the pit fire and the keening murmur of the old man's chants.

"Godspeed, my jesting Pilate who will not stay for his answer." Bacon laughed behind as Talmage stepped into the fog. "'T'would be a shame should you run afoul of the watch this late past curfew."

∧

THE FOG CLOSED in around him as Talmage briskly strode away. The streets were dank and silent save for the leathered scrapings of his boots. Once thought he heard the soughing pad of feet behind him. He ducked inside a side alley, and waited, shadowed and silent, but no man passed by. He resheathed his sword, but crept out the back of the alley and altered course. The fog grew thicker.

Somehow he found himself returned to the backstreet courtyard where he'd dispatched Will's cutpurse although he should be several streets away. The corpse lay undiscovered still, pooled in its blood and evacuated effluvia.

Bacon's laugh echoed against the courted walls.

Talmage drew his sword but saw no one at all.

Again he heard the keening of the old Rosicrucian's chant. Tendrils of fog swirled and curled above the dead man's corpse and solidified into a man-shaped mockery with eyes that glowed with the guttering flames of Perdition. Another being of fog and smoke formed, and then another and another. Their wraith-gray claws stretched out as the four creatures advanced toward the slowly backing Talmage.

Many a man would have dropped their sword and many a man's mind would have gibbered in madness at the sight. Talmage but gripped his sword's hilt all the tighter and sprang forward, his Muse racing as was its wont:

Creatures of Smoke or creatures of Flame,
Devils or Men, 'tis surely the same.
Courage of steel and mettle of heart
Shall with Christ's blessing
Cause—thee—to—part!

On each of the four last words, he stabbed out at the four mockeries in turn. His sword met not wisps of fog, but solid flesh. As each creature of fog clutched its vaporous breast and fell, the veil of fog and smoke vanished and what once was each a creature became uniformed soldier of the King, falling to the dew-slicked cobbles.

The fog lifted as if it had never been, and the full moon shone over the courtyard. Talmage found himself facing a small army of the King's Yeoman of the Guard. A ring of pike points hemmed him in.

Their captain stepped forward. He had the same fox-face as the Rosicrucian at the tavern, and a dangling red-painted crucifix. Impossible that he could be the same man, but there he stood.

"Jacob Talmage, known sometimes as James Talmage," he intoned, "I have the King's Warrant for your arrest." He smiled, and Talmage thought he saw a flash of the Goat's pit fire behind the man's eyes. "The charges are unspecified, but the murder of these four guards will do."

The captain wrenched the sword out of Talmage's hands. He swished the air with it a stroke or two, as if examining its balance, then rammed it home in Talmage's own belted scabbard. "By all means, keep your sword. It will amuse His Majesty mightily to be presented it in Court by your own hand, drenched as its blade is in the blood of His Own Guard."

∩

By the time it took to be marched to Whitehall Palace, the hour neared cockcrow and yet the Great Hall was ablaze with light and the King sat on his throne, attended by his courtiers, as if they'd spent the entire night awaiting Talmage's arrival.

Two burly Beefeaters, liveried in the Crown's scarlet and gold and armed with heavy halberds, met Talmage at the door and flanked him as he trod. No other weapons were evident. No nobleman in the room wore so much as a dagger. The new King's terror of a naked blade was known far outside the confines of the court.

What game was Fox Face playing, leaving Talmage possession of his sword?

Each step down the mat of plaited rushes laid atop the hall's flat stone flooring took Talmage closer to the monarch. Courtiers lined both sides, staring slack-jawed not at him, but at some unseen focus. The faces of the blank-eyed women were rouged as current custom; those of modest means rouged with carbonate of lead, which slowly drove a constant user mad, while those of greater wealth rouged with tinted bear fat, which surely drove the bear mad.

Talmage treasured the tiny smile the flitting thought-jest brought him; likely he would live to smile no other.

The King's throne sat upon a dais, centered under the mullioned panes of a brooding oriel window through which the dawn's light was not yet due. The King's pudgy frame showed itself weak in every little nervous twitch at the approaching halberdiers. His bulging, protuberant eyes darted this way and that. His narrow-chinned face lay scarred by pox. One got the sense that the King could have been a great man had he but tried, but that that he did not try—at that or at any other ambition other than maintaining his seat upon his throne.

Flanking him right and left were eight Rosicrucians—seven Fox Faces as alike as if cast from a mold, with one more the twin of Bacon's companion at the tavern. No, he *was* the companion at the tavern, for Sir Francis Bacon stood at the King's own right hand. How they had arrived ahead of him, Talmage could not say.

What Talmage could say was there no doubt now where the power lay in the Court. The same King who had written obsessively of fell powers in his Scottish *Daemonologie*, who had his royal self tortured dozens of young girls falsely accused of witchcraft, had himself been bewitched by the chanting *Rosenkreuzers*.

Brought within two paces short of the King, Talmage now could hazard why that Fox-Face had taunted him by leaving Talmage his blade. The same chanting that undoubtedly had left these courtiers mindless husks and bewitched the King also left Talmage weak and almost unable to move. He could no more draw his sword and spring to attack than he could jump over the moon.

Bacon bent down and whispered in his monarch's ear. The King's eyes steadied, as if focusing for the first time. "So," he said, crossing his leg. "This is the playwright who dispatches four of Our yeoman with naught but a blade and a well-turned Alexandrine."

He snapped his fingers and a young page brought a gilt finger bowl. The King dipped the tips of his fingers in it, then motioned it away. Court gossip said James' skin lay soft as taffeta sarsanet, made so by the monarch never truly washing. Talmage could well believe the latter part of that gossip; being this close to the King smelled like standing near a midden on a hot day's sun in Billingsgate Market.

The King fixed his bulbous eyes on him. "Do you think you may chop down

Our men like so many trees in Birnam Wood?"

"Nay, your Majesty," Talmage said, his voice a mere squeak. Any mention of the creatures he had fought would only lead to charges of witchcraft.

"We should think not."

Again Bacon whispered in the monarch's ear.

"Our good friend Sir Francis suggests that, like Christopher Marlowe before you, you have contracted the pen-scribblers complaint: hiding sedition and treason inside the seeming merry lines of your plays, most specifically your *Tamerlane and the Turtledove*. What say ye?"

Talmage found anger-fueled strength enough to place his hand upon his sword hilt, but no more. "I say I performed that play in this very Great Hall on the very command of your August Self. It had no more treason in it now than it did then—"

"Impertinence!"

"—when your own August Self clapped and praised it!—"

"Impudence!"

"And I also say that it is for the *King* to decide what treason be and not some ear-whispering Court sycophant!"

Red pulsed on James's cheeks as he fought for regal control.

Once calm, He reached his bleach-white fingertips and softly caressed the gold-threaded doublet of Sir Francis. "We'll not have it thought Our granting favors to Our supporters a defect," he said, too softly for comfort, "for even Christ Our Lord did the same, and therefore We cannot be blamed. Christ had his beloved John. I have Sir Francis."

The King dropped his hand and leaned forward in his throne, the red in his face returning. "And as for Law, do not presume to tell Us about Law! Kings arose before the estates or ranks of men, before any parliament, before any laws made, and by Kings was the land distributed, which under God's Grace was wholly Theirs to begin with. So it follows of necessity that Kings are the authors and makers of Laws, and not the laws of the makers of Kings!"

"I have no quarrel with your claim of Divine Right, my King," Talmage answered calmly, "only with Sir Francis asserting such a claim to it as well."

James pounded a soft fist upon the lacquered arm of his throne. "*You* have no quarrel with My *claim*? Who are *you*, little man, to decide what claim a King might have?"

He rose to his feet in anger.

"I am God's Hand on Earth and you will fear and obey Me as you would Him. All of this wretched isle was given to Me by Him to mete out as I please! I hold title on it all and everything and everyone within! Everyone—body and soul! Do you hear? *Body and soul!*"

The King's mercurial outburst caused even the Rosicrucians to catch their breath. For the barest moment, the chanting stopped.

And that moment was all Talmage needed. With a shout he drew his blade as the Muse bubbled up inside him once again:

As Kings are wont, They often flaunt
As They forget atop Their Throne
Where Divine Right ends
And Greed begins
(Unfettered oncost beknown)
And so miscount in vast amount
The sums They think They own:

A subject's troth and, aye! his oath,
And heart if One can cajole.
But one things lacks
In this Kingly tax
The thing no King can toll—
For a King can't claim what is God's in name,
And that is the immortal soul!

Before the first line fell silent, Talmage had dispatched the two Beefeaters with a quick stroke, left and right. He leaped forward to strike, not at James, but at the tavern *Rosenkreuzer* now fumbling at his blood red cross hanging pendent on his chest. Talmage could ill afford to give these rosy crossers time to begin their chant anew. He feared the ancient's chant the most and so struck him first.

One, two, three, they began to fall to his blade, offering almost no resistance at all, so great their surprise. By the fourth, they began to gather their wits and began chant again and even to shout, but to no effect. The words that tumbled out of Talmage's mouth, given to him by his Muse, seemed to counter any shouted witcheries.

As the last fox-face fell, Talmage turned his blade to Sir Francis. Before he struck, he toyingly flung aside with a mere wrist-flick the crimson obscenity hung around Bacon's neck. He then plunged full the rapier's reddened blade into Sir Francis' heart as he shouted his final line.

His Muse-given virtue spent, Talmage dropped to a knee before his King, offering his reversed sword hilt-first in surrender as the loyal subject he ever was. Whatever happened now, at least James and the Kingdom were safe from further witchery.

A babble of voices rose behind him as the assembled courtiers came to their senses and their own volition. The babble turned into cries of "Guards! Guards!" as they saw at last the bloody tableau before them, and the wretched little man on the throne cowering at the sight of the blade and screaming, "Take it away! Take it away!"

Yeoman of the Guard burst into the hall to arrest Talmage.

Whatever happens, Talmage thought as they surrounded him, *at least England is safe.*

The guards hauled him to his feet.

To Talmage's horror, one by one the dead Rosicrucians rose, too. They rose from their pooling blood like string-pulled wooden puppets and took up their chanting anew, again ensnaring King and courtiers alike

The last sound Talmage heard as the guards dragged him away was that of the King shouting at His mindless Court, "Why don't they dance? Why don't they dance?" The last sight he beheld was that of the slain Sir Francis rising to his feet and beginning to caper like a motley fool to please his captive King.

⋔

THE GUARDS TOOK him not to the Tower as he supposed they would, but dragged him down passage to passage in the meandering hulk of Whitehall Castle, through Chapel and Presence Hall and thence to the King's Guard Chamber and the Great Chamber below. Down and down into finally the cellar underneath, down into the brick-arched undercroft that once served as King Henry's Great Wine Cellar.

A dozen sconces burned brightly. Smoked meat and wheels of Danish cheese lay stacked on shelves between the wine casks. A dozen bottles of the finest Spanish sherry from Montilla kept company beside a hundred Welsh hogsheads of commoner vintage.

The guards chained Talmage to a heavy iron ring newly fastened to the far wall of a small alcove. He wondered if this be a sick jest on the part of the King's Rosicrucian puppet-masters, to chain Talmage just out of reach of the finest victuals while they fed him his daily slops.

The Rosicrucians were not done with him yet.

Within moments, dozens of hodmen began delivering their loads of brick. A team of bricklayers, stout as old Ben Jonson, mixed up a trough of mortar and began to wall the alcove shut, brick by brick.

They meant to execute him by immurement! By the barbarian practice used only by the Mongols and Mahometans who reived along the edges and boundaries of civilized men!

Vainly did he struggle against his chains as the wall went up, chafing the skin under collar and manacles raw and bleeding. Vainly did he shout and curse and snarl at the bewitched brickmen.

In precious little time at all, they settled the last brick into place and Talmage's world fell dark.

Bacon's words echoed : *He shall never leave his jail. Never.*

Ո

TALMAGE STRUGGLED until his strength left him. He recited lines of poetry to keep his sanity until his parched voice left him.

He dreamed fitfully, nightmares of himself and Will and old fat Ben, and of other English scribblers of note, captured and hag-ridden like Bacon, and set to by the rosy crossers to writing lines for Miles Smith and the King's new Authorized Bible, removing plain and precious truths and adulterating the rest while Fox Face looking on in nodding approval.

He awoke with a start, convinced by he knew not what that so long as he slept not, as long as he dreamt not, it would not happen.

He fought to keep awake until unslaked sleep at last came to claim Talmage for its own.

Ո

"DRINK THIS," a soft voice entreated as its owner pushed a cup of clear cold water to Talmage's cracked lips.

Talmage opened his eyes. He lay unchained upon the floor of his alcove tomb. Three men knelt by his side somehow, in a space that should scarce fit Talmage alone, as if the bounds of the room bound not the three men. Light filled the room, but from whence it came Talmage could not say, unless it came from the plain-garbed men themselves.

He drank greedily, then swallowing wrong, coughed the water up great racking coughs.

Whatever he was, he was not dead.

He sat up. They had tended his wounds and clothed him anew. His scabbarded sword leaned propped against the bricks. The midden filth of his confinement gone, the scrubbed floor laid out with clean rushes.

And *still* he was trapped inside the vault.

Who were these men? *What* were they? Their breaths steamed in the cellar's chill and he felt their bodily heat as they wrapped arms about to lift him to his feet. Their booted heels whisked softly upon the floor-strewn rushes. They were not ghosts.

"Nor angels," the first one said, as if hearing Talmage's very thought. "We're men like you, perhaps a little further upon our journey is all."

"'Tis not meet to give names in this fell place," the second said, again knowing Talmage's mind. "Instead describe us by what we are. Three who tarry. Three who endure until the end. Three who march as guidons, but cannot enter battle."

"Our bounds are set." The third one nodded. "We can but give a hand up from the mud here, set a traveler on his way there. We are tarry-ers for the Lord, but not terriers to fight His rats. That task is yours, brother."

Talmage eyed his sword but did not buckle it on. "For all the good my fighting did. I could slay those Rosicrucian rats a thousand times; they'd just rise up anew."

The second chuckled. "It is not Rosicrucians you truly face. The Rosicrucians are but foolish little men consumed with intricate counterfeits of Truth—a zealotry which served only to loose your true foe. The corrupted spirit some call the Gadion who now usurps his benefactors' forms and that of your friend Bacon abroad the land."

"And soon intends to usurp yours as well," the first and leader said. "That is the purpose of this bewitched immurement. The Gadion has within his power to animate a man's remains in any shape he chooses in a grotesque semblance of life, but he needs the innate spark of Man to do so. He draws it from those he immures—not quite dead, not quite alive."

"There are others bricked up in this cellar as you were. Your task is to free them and end this evil," the second said.

"The Gadion will not freely give up his source of power. He will fight you once you step out from these bricks, so take up sword in hand," the third said.

"We must take our leave," the first said sadly. "We cannot further help save in this: 'Ye shall know the truth, and the truth shall make you free.'"

And then they were gone without telling him what that Truth be or freeing him from his prison.

Slowly the light that abided with them faded, too.

"And would not stay to answer," Talmage muttered bitterly in total dark.

He took stock. He was freed from his shackles if not the walls. He had his sword close by. He felt rested and fed and hale.

He felt along the new-built wall for an opening. He pounded his fists against it in the dark to no avail. "Take up my sword, indeed," he spat.

Take up sword in hand. The only direct command they had given him, save to free his fellows.

He quickly buckled his sword belt around him and drew his old friend rapier, its cold steel singing in release of its confinement. The fell-enchanted bricks tumbled in a heap, releasing him. He felt the power of his old Muse arise within him as he stepped forth a free man past the tumbled bricks into the cellar proper.

With a banshee's scream, the fox-faced Gadion in all its power leaped toward him, long bloody talons extended.

Talmage managed to kick the fiend away. He sidestepped into the clear and held his sword at the ready. The Muse bubbled up inside him again:

> To know what is Truth, know the warp and woof,
> The Sum of all that Is.
> But to know its source is the better course—

"*Silence!*" the creature screamed, slamming into Talmage and knocking the swordsman across the room. "You'll not name Him here!"

To Talmage's horror, the fox-face melted like candle wax as the Gadion adopted Talmage's own form. His own form, aye, and worse—it counterfeited his own Muse!

It advanced with a twin of Talmage's rapier. "*Men but sneer,*" it began in guttural tones—a mockery of Tamalge's own voice:

> Men but sneer "What's Truth?" as they claw and tooth
> Their way through this mortal coil,
> As they fight and war, gamble, dice, and whore,
> Pillage, rape, and ruin, and spoil.
> Never pond'ring much 'til Death's cold touch
> Comes to place them in the soil.
>
> 'Tis the mien of Man to waste out his span,
> Squander life 'til his time runs down.
> First heavens will fall and this wide world sprawl
> And the seas they will run aground,
> Dark the stars will wink, down will planets slink
> Ere Man will his soul turneth 'round.

Talmage fought desperately, but the fiend matched him move for move. Talmage was forced back and back until he slipped on the loose-piled bricks and lay sprawled at the creature's mercy.

"*You are nothing!*" the creature with his face hissed, flushed with the power of Talmage's Muse usurped. "Men are nothing! You're just another plaything in your Creator's toybox. Worth no more than the mud from whence you sprang."

Talmage had but strength to wipe at the blood seeping from a slice above his brow. "If we're such nothings, why do expend such great effort to do us ill?"

The creature looked taken aback.

"Yes," continued Talmage, rising to his knees. "If we're but only another creation, why do daemons not spend similar effort clawing the rocks down from the hills or felling each sparrow in flight? Why is it only man they seek to harm and twist and bend?"

He rose to his feet, his wounds forgotten, the virtue of his Muse returned triumphant:

> *I am but a Man, made from slime-caked mud—*
> *Up from earth cometh I!—whose fleeting breath*
> *From nostrils flared is bellowed but by God.*
> *Called only by grace His Child, and yet—hath*
> *Ever Father sired Gets not of His kind?*
> *Nay, the Child is but the form of the Man!*
> *If be His Child indeed, then what shall we*
> *Be when fully grown into our Manhood?*

Talmage held forth his blade. The Gadion cowered and dropped his to the ground.

"Be gone! I say!" Talmage commanded. "You have no power here. Not over one who knows Truth at last!"

> *So this is the Truth and its warp and its woof,*
> *The Sum of all that is known.*
> *Be gone ye false mold, for ye haven't a hold*
> *On a God-Child knoweth by His Own!*

With a piteous cry the once-fell creature, reduced to its withered true form, slinked back on all fours into the shadows cast by the flickering wall torches and faded away. Talmage felt its hold over King and England burn off like morning dew before the summer sun.

Jacob Talmage sheathed his sword and set to unbricking the walls that held his playwright brothers: Will and Ben and Francis. Aye, even the old toothless Rosicrucians, now harmless in their folly.

The cellar torches had all but guttered out by the time the last brick was pulled away in time and the Truth set free.

LUMP OF CLAY

INTRODUCTION

I've written a number of Civil War stories. No doubt I'll write more.

The Civil War was a war like no other. Freedom or Slavery, waged for all the marbles. True, the war had other causes that both sides latched onto then and latch onto still today, but as Lincoln stated in his Second Inaugural Address, all men knew then and know now in their soul: "that this interest [slavery] was somehow the cause of the war."

And so the war came.

And is with us still.

Do not think for a moment it ever ended at Appomattox.

The desire to be slave master over others is ever, ever with us. There are those who would rule over others and there are those who would rule over no man but themselves. Much if not most of our current societal strife is a clash between those two mutually-exclusive philosophies.

It is a point I touch on again and again my fiction. See this volume's "Jesting Pilate" and "New England's God", for example. If there's a mystic element in these stories in regards to that struggle, it is no more accident than the mystic element present in my other Civil War stories such as "And Dream Such Dreams" and "East of Appomattox" printed elsewhere.

There is an inescapable mystic—almost holy—quality to the Civil War itself, this American Götterdämmerung, this American Ragnarok. The speeches and songs of the period reflect that. The "Battle Hymn of the Republic" is not so much a call to arms as it is a call to prayers. Lincoln himself is more prophet than president.

It is a Lincoln as prophet, not politician, who said when delivering his farewell address to his beloved Springfield, the home he would never see again: "I now leave, not knowing when, or whether ever, I may return." It is prophet, not politician who closes that same speech in prayer-like supplication: "Trusting in Him who can go with me, and remain with you, and be everywhere for good, let us confidently hope that all will yet be well."

Is it surprising then, that into this mystical struggle I blend an ancient Jewish legend whose whole crux (if I might use that word) is the fashioning of a slave? For that is the sole very purpose of the legendary creature—to be naught but slave to its master, a master who literally holds the power of Life and Death over his slave in the shem he inscribes?

You are about to meet crippled Union Army soldier Max Levy, a young man shattered of body and spirit. Max returns from battle only to find himself in a new battle. He must confront the metes and bounds of that ancient Jewish legend of Master and Slave if Freedom and the Union and the remnants of his very soul are to prevail.

September 30, 1862

Max Levy drifted out of the laudanum-tinctured dream he'd been having of a blood-soaked cornfield and the meaty slap of a Minié ball striking a young, frightened boy.

He awoke, sweat-soaked, to find himself once again home in his own bed, buried under the warmth of an eiderdown quilt. The shades were drawn over an open window. The horse-clop traffic sounds of Washington, D.C., at night drifted in, carried by the cool autumn breeze. On the wall hung the dark shape of his Union blue uniform where in a rare moment of lucidity during his fever, he'd demanded it be placed.

His leg ached, somewhere between the flat spot under the eiderdown and the corn-field farmer's barn where a Union surgeon had sawn it off and tossed it with the others in the pile.

Max heard voices in the front parlor: his father and old Isaac Stampel, *hazzan* of the city's tiny Hebrew Congregation synagogue.

"...and how is the boy?" Stampel asked.

"As well as can be expected," his father said in the English he had struggled so hard to acquire, accented though it might be.

"And you?"

Chair legs dragged on the floor. "For eighteen years, I have been practicing for unpleasant conversations I might one day have with my son. If he should come to me and say, 'Papa, I wish to marry a Gentile,' or 'Papa, I wish to turn my back on my people and its teachings,' for these I had a ready answer. For these I was prepared. But to have my son come to me and say, 'Papa, I wish to fight to free another man, to free an entire people,' what does a father say to that? What words are there?"

A floorboard squeaked. "And then to see my son, my own son..."

The laudanum enveloped Max and lowered him down into dreams once again.

November 17, 1862

MAX SAT on his bed and stared out the window at the bustling city outside. His two crutches lay on the lumpen mattress beside him. Wagons and carriages clattered down the street. Small clusters of soldiers, such as he used to be, occasionally marched past on their two strong legs. A light snow began to fall.

He heard his father and Stampel sitting in the parlor talking once again. The bedroom door was thin and their voices carried plainly.

Mild anger warmed Stampel's voice. "You know it is only a matter of time, Joseph. The others feel the same. We cannot continue to go down this road that Przibram's reforms would have us travel. Our traditions—"

"And I say not now," his father replied, his voice perhaps less heated but just as firm. "After the war, perhaps, but not now. We are few enough as it is. Now is the time for unity, not for breaking apart. Yes, I, too, miss the old ways, our traditional ways; I think them only proper. Yet, for now, these reforms serve our cause too, if they gather in these new Sephardi arrivals where we can teach them the proper Ashkenazi ways."

Max heard the soft clang of the wood stove door opening, and the rattle of the iron poker.

"I will wait for now, Joseph. But not forever. Now, what of the boy?"

The floor creaked as his father crossed the room. "He is not happy with our decision."

"He is a boy. What boy is *ever* happy with the decisions a father makes for him? We will need a rabbi of our own when we break away, you know that. I cannot leave my shop to study, you cannot. The boy can. Besides, what other use is he without a leg? This is as much for him as it is for us."

The heat leeched entirely from his father's voice. "So I have argued with him. At length."

"Still, you are his father. He must do as you say. Now, as to his education. I have written to friends in Philadelphia and—"

The stove door clanked shut. "I was thinking of asking Berliner."

"The Kabbalist?" Stampel exploded. "He would have your son dabble in superstitions! Ten magic words and clay statues that move—!"

"I have spoken with him. He will teach my Max only what we wish taught," his father said. "And he would hold the boy's interest. Better to have him learn from Berliner than to reject learning at all."

More silence.

"Very well, Joseph," Stampel muttered. "But no good will come of it. You shall see."

Outside Max's window, the snow began to fall in earnest.

January 5, 1863

MAX PULLED the collar of his wool coat tighter. His breath steamed in the cold winter air. Each jounce of the buckboard wagon sent red hot needles through the stump of his missing leg. Would what was left of him ever heal?

Next to him on the buckboard's jouncing seat sat old man Berliner, gently holding the reins in age-crabbed hands. The old man still dressed in the ways of the Old Country, not as they did here in America. Bespectacled, bewhiskered, as old as Moses, there was a hidden power behind that craggy face, behind his soft-spoken words. No wonder the boys of the shul and the gossipy women assigned Berliner strange powers. No wonder dour reactionaries like Stampel warned against him, muttering of magicks and superstitions.

Berliner drove the wagon past the Capitol building. Workmen were erecting a new set of scaffolding atop its newly finished dome for the placing of the huge bronze statue which sat under an oilskin tarp amidst the busy construction area. Berliner's small clapboard house sat to the north on the outskirts of town, atop a small rise above the muddy banks of Rock Creek and within sight of the great white dome rising above the trees.

Max's meager belongings lay in the back of the wagon. A bundled roll of clothes. A wicker basket of food from his mother. Other young men his age already had much more to show from grabbing their own futures.

Max had bled his future out in a Maryland cornfield.

"They tell me you are a soldier," Berliner said. Age had given his voice a raspy edge. Harsh, but not unfriendly. As calm as the gentle falling snow.

"Was a soldier," Max said. His own voice was too flat for even bitterness.

"You sound as if you regret your choice."

Max felt his cheeks flush. "I regret nothing—only that I can't be back there. I sit here a useless cripple, while others—"

"It is a fine country to fight for."

"You bet it's a fine country!" Max said. "Papa's told me what life was like in the Old Country. Here, why right here in Washington itself, Congress itself gave our very own Hebrew Congregation the same rights Christian churches here in the city have. That'd never happen in the Old Country."

Berliner said nothing for the space of several hoof clops. "Yes," he said finally, "I was in that very building watching the day they signed that piece of paper. All 'rights, privileges, and immunities.' It was a fine thing."

"You bet it was."

The old man shook his head sadly. He sighed, the puff of air fluffing his unkempt beard. "I did not think it possible, but perhaps there truly are disadvantages to *not* having lived with the hate and the fear and the burning torches of the Old World..."

The old man fell silent.

The horse nickered and shook its reins as it plodded down the frozen, rutted streets. Clumps of mud-stained snow kicked up by its hooves splattered against the angled board on the wagon's front.

"Yes, what Congress did was a fine thing, a great thing, but what is greater is that they have not signed such a paper for any other *shul* outside of this city. Nowhere else in this nation."

Silence once again.

Max knew himself to be bright, bright enough to recognize the old man's alternating obliquity and silences formed a teaching method, but Max had also spent the last two years being instructed by rote by screaming sergeants even in the simplest things. The old man's obliquities—but even more so his gentle silences—unnerved Max. Unnerved him greatly.

"I do not understand," Max finally said, grudging every word.

Berliner nodded once as if acknowledging an important step had been taken.

"Maximilian Levy, the study of the Talmud is the study of law. Not just the Talmud, but all Law. Where does Law come from?"

He turned for the first time to look Max in the eyes.

"When you know the answer to that, you will be able to solve the riddle I have set before you about what a fine thing the Congress did that day and why it is an even finer thing it need not ever be repeated elsewhere in this nation."

Not another word was spoken for the rest of the journey to Berliner's home.

The two-story clapboard lay north of the city near the wooden banks of Rock Creek. The house looked as if it sagged under a great weight.

Less than a quarter mile away, able-legged union soldiers tramped about the makeshift barricades of Fort Stevens, one of a series of emergency fortifications ringing the nation's capital.

Falling snow and distance muffled the faint cadences, but Max felt each tramped march step in the leg he no longer had.

Berliner ushered Max inside.

At first glance it did not look like the iniquitous den of a furtive magician, as the whispered stories about the old man would have it. It looked altogether all-too-ordinary. No, not even that. It looked old and shabby. As old and shabby as Berliner himself.

Scuffed floorboards creaked underfoot. They were met by a stern-faced housekeeper, a rail-thin widow who glanced at Max with disapproving eyes. What she did to earn her hire, Max couldn't say. The entire house groaned under the weight of laden bookshelves. Nearly every flat surface in the house lay strewn with haphazard stacks of books.

Berliner had converted his large front parlor into a classroom. A long, sturdy oak table with carved trestles as thick as Max's remaining leg would serve as a desktop for both Max and Berliner. Berliner had placed the chairs so that they would face each other. Books and papers lay strewn across its surface, or rather, half its surface. Such disorganization offended Max's Army-trained need for order and method.

Even through the house's thick wooden walls, the bellow of a leather-lunged sergeant could be heard. The voice, its tone and memories, tugged at Max.

Berliner's sharp eyes saw this. He gestured solemnly toward Fort Stevens. "Out there, out there you learned to be a man, but you also lost yourself."

His arm swung to encompass the oaken table and its mass of books. "In here, you will learn once again to be a man. To be whole. To be made whole."

Berliner placed Max's carpetbag on the floor of the parlor and gestured at the chair Max was to sit in.

"Let us begin."

July 2, 1863

THE FATE of the nation and four million chattel slaves were being decided at a tiny Pennsylvania crossroads town less than a hundred miles to the north. Inside Berliner's front parlor, however, the night seemed like any other quiet summer's eve.

Cicadas buzzed. Flames of the kerosene lantern hissed inside the soot-streaked glass chimney. Boiling cabbages bubbled in the back kitchen, a late night meal being prepared by the housekeeper. The chipped and battered grandfather clock brought from the Old Country kept perfect time with Max's droning recitation in Hebrew.

Berliner removed his reading spectacles and shook his head sadly. "Enough for tonight, Maximillian," the old man said. "Enough and, sadly, never enough."

Max looked up from the page. He blinked against the lantern light.

Berliner shuffled over to the front door. It lay open in a vain attempt to coax a cooling breeze through the house.

The old man stared out into the night.

"Maximillian," he said at last, "the Talmud is not something one can simply march across in lockstep, in perfect tempo like a soldier."

"But my father and Stampel say—"

"No doubt, they do, fixed as they are on tradition," Berliner said. "Tradition is fine. Tradition is the framework, the skeleton of Judaism, but only a skeleton. Not its muscle. Not its flesh. Not its beating heart. Knowledge gleaned from the Talmud must also at times come in flashes of insight, in leaps of faith."

"I don't understand," Max said. He pushed the book away. "If I get it wrong, you are angry with me. If I get it right, you are angry with me."

"I am not angry, Maximillian. Saddened, perhaps..."

Berliner turned to face him.

"Tell me, Maximillian. Your leg. This foolish cause you sacrificed it for. Who told *you* to free the slaves? Where is it written they *must* be free? Where is it even written that God *wants* them free?"

Max felt the familiar cold anger returning to his heart, the anger he held that day he walked out of his father's house, the anger that not even that bloodied cornfield in Maryland could drain away. The anger that one man could think that he could own another. "My heart, old man. It's written on my heart."

Berliner nodded. "Just so. God's Law is always written on one's heart."

Max pointed at the sprawling pile of books on the study table. "Then what are these?"

"There is law and then there is *Law*," Berliner said. "Those, those—" He shrugged. "If we could hold God's Law in our heart and completely obey it, we would have no need of these lesser laws. But since we are imperfect beings, since we are mere unruly children in the sight of God, He gives unto us make-work rules, training rules, the kind of childish rules you give to *kinder* in kindergarten."

"If Isaac Stampel ever heard you say that, or my father..."

"Why would I ever waste such words to men so unready to hear?"

"But you say them to me."

"You are not Isaac Stampel. You are not your father."

Max sighed. "I just wish my father understood that."

"All fathers see in their children the continuations of their work and their hopes for the future, the same as God sees in us, his children. Fathers are often disappointed. But sometimes not. Sometimes, gloriously not."

Berliner dimmed the table lamp. "Now, enough for tonight. Let us eat. In the morning, we will resume. Perhaps you will find it easier to focus after this mighty battle to the north you fret about has been won."

"You really think we'll win?"

"Whose Finger was it that wrote upon your heart the slaves must be freed? Do you really think that that Finger, having writ, merely moves on?"

A growing breeze in the deepening twilight soughed in assent.

A warmth from within rose inside Max. For the first time since the bloody fields of Antietam, Max Levy found his face could still smile.

July 4, 1863

MAX GLANCED FURTIVELY over his shoulder. It was Saturday. *Shabbat.* He should not be sitting here in the kitchen table, reading the housekeeper's newspaper.

Max could not help it.

The news was too great. His joy was too great.

The Union Army had won at Gettysburg. General Grant had taken Vicksburg. The war was as good as won. The slaves were as good as freed.

Max's sacrifice had not been in vain.

The door from the parlor quietly swung open. Berliner stood in the doorway.

His face suddenly warm as a coal stove, Max guiltily dropped the newspaper.

The paper's banner headlines shouted to all the world the battle victories in type so large even Berliner could not have helped but scan them, even on Shabbat.

"The battle is won then, as I told you it would be. Perhaps now you will be in a better frame of mind to learn."

April 1, 1864

MAX STARED out the front parlor window. Soldiers had strung a telegraph line to nearby Fort Stevens. The line of makeshift poles past Berliner's house leaned crazily, the wires sagged. The soldiers had not cared of neatness, only speed and functionality. That is the way of war.

Inch-tall mounds of April snow capped the pole tops. Too-soon-returned robins, feathers fluffed against the cold, clumped together on the sagging wire, a line of fuzzy balls with beaks and bird feet.

Far from the robins, a solitary bird sat on the wire's end, a lonely crow. Ugly, fell, grotesque—it lacked the graceful lines of the robin, the delicate voice. It sat alone, unwanted, unneeded.

Berliner barked Max's name, startling him out of his reverie. The birds scattered to the sky, as if they, too, had heard the old man.

"Maximillian!" Berliner repeated. His gnarled finger tapped the opened passage he had quizzed Max on all morning. Berliner sighed. "You will find no answers out that window."

"I won't find them in here, either!" Max pushed himself away from the book-stacked table, away from his studies, away from the incessant, endless, meaningless droning of the old man.

Max snatched up his crutches and stumped out of the room, out of the house.

The next few moments passed in rage-fueled blur. When Max came to his senses, when Berliner finally caught up with him, Max found himself at the woodpile, standing there without his crutches, precariously balanced on his leg. A billet of wood lay placed on the old tree stump that served as Berliner's chopping block.

Max had been trying to chop it with the large clumsy axe.

Max stared down at the axe in his two hands. He was too empty for tears.

"I have the strength in my arms to swing this," Max heard himself say. "But I haven't the footing. If I swing, I fall. If I use one hand to steady myself, I can't swing with enough strength with only the other. What is to become of me?"

"What indeed?" The old man sat down upon the woodpile. "You have the strength to learn, but you indeed lack the footing."

The old man pulled at his beard. "This is not working. This cannot continue. Write to your father. Tell him what he asks is a waste of time. I will talk to him further when next we go to town."

April 6, 1864

BERLINER HALTED the buckboard wagon outside Max's father's dry goods store. Max eased himself down to the muddy melted snow to tend to the horse, only to find an angry Isaac Stampel standing there, holding the horse's reins short by the bridle bit.

His father, looking just as angry, strode out of his store, making his way toward them past wooden crates and burlap sacks of feed.

"*Shalom*, Joseph," Berliner said, still seated high in the wagon. "If you would be so kind as to fill my usual order—"

"What is the idea, old man?" Joseph Levy bellowed. "What nonsense have you been filling my son's head with?" He wiped his clean hands needlessly on his white apron.

"Only the nonsense you hired me to teach him," Berliner said.

Stampel growled. "I told you it was a mistake to send the boy to this—this Kabbalist and his superstitions."

Joseph Levy wheeled. "Quiet, Stampel. Maximillian is *my* son. I will handle this." He turned again to Berliner. "Did you really tell the boy that studying the Talmud was a waste of time?"

Max flushed. "Father, that isn't what I wrote—"

Berliner held up a hand. "I will deal with this, Max. It is a time for precise words. Words have power. Words are how God constructs the Law, shapes the world."

To Max's father the old man said, "I told him it was a waste of time studying in the manner you demand he should be taught."

"It is how they do things in Philadelphia."

"They do a lot of things in Philadelphia."

Joseph Levy's face grew darker. "It is what I paid you to do."

"Ah, yes," the old man nodded.

Creaking with age, Berliner got down from the buckboard to face Max's father.

The old man reached in a side pocket of his jacket and extracted a gleaming twenty-dollar gold piece. "Your payment for this month's tutelage, Joseph. Unspent. Do you wish it back?"

"What I wish is for my boy to be taught."

"Your coin," Berliner said. His hand dipped again in the pocket and extracted its twin. "And here is mine. Take them both, Joseph. Buy railroad tickets, take your son to Philadelphia. Have the rabbinical scholars there test him. See if he is not their student's equal, if not their better. I have taught your son, Joseph."

"Taught him what?" the angry Stampel demanded. "Your Kabbalist superstitions, your magic words? You've taken the boy up into your attic, haven't you, Berliner? You've shown him that—that *thing*!"

"Attic? What attic?" Max asked, his head swiveling from Stampel to Berliner. "What thing?"

Berliner sighed. "You see? The boy knew nothing—until you told him."

"So you say."

Berliner sighed again. "Isaac Stampel. I suddenly remember all over again why when you were his age I sent you away and gave your own father back his money. Still you learn nothing, still you hear nothing. I gave Joseph my word I would teach his son only what he wished me to teach. I have kept that word. You and Joseph, on the other hand, gave me *your* word that I would have a free hand in how I taught Maximillian. Are you not men of your word?"

Stampel stammered. Max's father motioned him to be silent. "Old man, you know full well what our hopes for the boy are. He is to be more than just our rabbi. He is to be our bulwark against Przibram's insidious reforms. That is ultimately what we are paying you to do—mold the boy into what we wish, what we need."

"Mold him?" the old man asked. "As one would a lump of clay? He is not yours to mold. He is not clay and he is not a boy. He is a man."

"He is a boy."

"I am a *man*, Papa," Max said.

Max shifted on his crutches. "I have stood as a man and I have fought as a man. Even on one leg I stand here as a man. *I'll* decide *if* I study, *what* I study, and what course in life I take *after* that study, whether to be your bulwark or to choose my own path. I will make my own way. That is what you brought me into the world to do."

Berliner placed a hand on Max's shoulder. "'Today I am a man.' I was there the day your son spoke those words in solemn ceremony. Did you not believe them, Joseph? Or were they just words? Were they just...superstition?"

Max's father turned his face away. There may have been a catch in his voice when he said at last, "I'll go fill your order, old man."

THE BUCKBOARD RIDE BACK to Berliner's house passed in silence. As Berliner bustled back and forth to the pantry, carrying in his boxes and bags of supplies, Max— no cripples need help!—stumped his way awkwardly, painfully up the stairs to the top of the second-floor landing.

Now that he knew it existed, he could easily see the rectangular trace of the attic trap door up in the ceiling.

A thin pull cord affixed to the bottom of the trap door used to open it had been coiled and tied out of reach, but whether Berliner had done so to keep Max out or the old man himself out, Max couldn't say.

Balancing himself shakily on his single leg, Max snagged the loop of the cord with the crook of his crutch and pulled the trap door open.

The door opened on well-oiled hinges. A folding wooden ladder, cunningly and carefully crafted, lay folded on the revealed underside of the trap door.

"Stairs you've learned to manage, but a ladder is another thing entirely, isn't it?"

Max jumped at the voice. He hadn't heard the old man climb the stairs behind him. Shamefacedly, Max made to swing the trap door shut again. "I shouldn't have opened this. Sorry."

Berliner stopped him. "I can see you won't get any studying done today until I've satisfied your curiosity. Very well."

The old man ran his gnarled fingers over the varnished surface of the folding ladder. "I made this back when I first built the house, back when my hands could still do a little of what I wanted them to. Oh, I could carve a piece of wood in my youth. Oh, was my father upset the day I set down my carpentry tools for a scholar's life!"

"Fathers," muttered Max.

Berliner unfolded the ladder, locking its leg-ends firmly against the floor with a snap.

"In the Old Country, such things were not done," Berliner said. "In the Old Country sons took up the trade of their father, as their fathers had, and their fathers before them. In the Old Country, that was the dream a father had for his son. In America, a father's dream is for his son to become better than him." He shook his head. "This new country, this strange country."

"This *better* country," Max insisted.

The old man shrugged. "Here and not there, am I not? The mouth might disparage America sometimes. The feet? The feet have voted in favor. Always listen to the feet, Maximillian, never the mouth."

Berliner looked the ladder up and down. "Now, regarding feet. The question is how to get you up there. I know. Wait here."

The old man scrambled up the ladder, spryer than his years suggested. Max heard shuffling above as Berliner moved about, then a coil of a stout rope dropped down, suspended most likely from a rafter beam or something.

That made sense. Max still had two strong arms, arms strengthened by carrying his leg's burden through his crutches. He made ready to swarm up the rope hand-over-hand.

Berliner's face peered down from the trap opening. "No need to climb like a chimpanzee. Simply hang onto the rope. I pull you up on a pulley. Hand me up your crutches."

Max did so, then held on as Berliner pulled the rope up. As he reached the top, Max saw the rope was a block-and-tackle affair affixed to a swinging arm.

"When I build the house," the old man said, swinging the dangling Max over from the trap hole to solid footing, "I build so I can haul heavy items up."

Max blinked against the dim lighting. Stampel had created an expectation in Max's mind of some sort of wizard's secret laboratory, but all he saw was a dusty, jumbled attic full of books and the bookshelves to hold them.

The musty smell of old books filled the attic space. Row upon row of leather-bound books, so old their leather bindings had all but crumbled away. In the corner he heard the startled scurry of mice. Some of the leather book spines looked chewed as well.

Max barked a short, disappointed laugh. "You can tell my father I don't see anything up here to tempt me away from my *midrash*. All I see is books, and I have more of *them* downstairs to study than I want now. A lifetime's worth."

His eyes better adjusted to the gloom now, Max saw pinned against one wall a parchment diagram. Upon it had been drawn a sort of tree consisting of ten circles with crisscrossing paths between them, paths connecting each of the ten to their fellows. Hebrew words labeled the circles and the connections, illegible in the dark and the fading ink of olden days

"The *Sephirot*—the ten attributes of God," Berliner said, equal parts proud to show his secrets and anxious that he might spark Max's unwelcome interest. "The heart of Kabbalah. Through these we *Mekubbal* unlock the secrets of the Universe, the secrets of God."

Max grunted. "Stampel's 'ten magic words?'" He leaned in to read the faded script.

Keter, crown; *Chochmah*; wisdom; *Binah*, understanding...the list went on like that.

"A bit of a letdown for magic words," Max said.

He pulled a book at random off one of the shelves and skimmed through it. It seemed chiefly concerned with reducing words to numbers by adding up its letters as they appeared in the alphabet, and then using those numbers to find links, mystical or otherwise, to other word-numbers.

Max replaced the book on the shelf. "I'm inclined to agree with my father. It all seems like just so much superstition to me."

"And would you also write off the whole of Judaism on the basis of a single glance at a page of the Torah?" the old man asked, his surprise, and yes, disappointment, showing in his voice.

"A single glance of any of the books downstairs," Max said, "would tell me they deal with people. People and their daily lives. God's relationship to Man."

Max swept his hand to encompass the shelves of books. "All of this seems singularly devoid of Mankind. Sterile. It's not a universe I wish to know, let alone know its secrets."

"Not so, Maximillian," Berliner said gently. "We Mekubbal hold that Mankind is the focal point for the Creation. 'All of this' as you so put it is in part to teach us the totality of Man's relationship with his Creator. Indeed, the Kabbalah offers up the ultimate lesson of Man's creation. Come, I show you."

He led Max to the very back of the attic, back behind its furthest bookcase, back into its deepest shadow.

There in the shadow, sat a cloth-covered strange lumpen shape. Tall as a man. Taller.

"Yes, Max. That is the clay statue Stampel spoke of. That is my golem. As God created Man from out of the dirt, so, too, do we Mekubbal create a living being out of a lump of clay."

Max stumped over to it and removed the cloth. Beneath stood a crude man-shaped figure—misshapen, deformed, ugly, imperfect, carved out of clay and kiln-dried into brittle ceramic. Its face, if that horrible deformity could be called a face, lay frozen in a twisted grimace of agony. Mercifully, its bulging eyes were closed, shuttered by heavy eyelids clamped tight.

"I brought it with me from the Old Country," Berliner said, stepping up behind Max. "I foolishly thought it might be needed here."

Max ran his fingers over the surface of the creature. "This clay used for the creature—" An ochre-grey clay that did not match that found along the banks of the nearby Rock Creek.

Max instinctively knew this kiln-dried ancient clay came from the Old Country. It smelt of the dust of ages, the fear of centuries past, of pogroms, of death and burning, of soul-crushing ancient hatreds.

The same stench Max had smelt tramping with the Union Army through the slave pens of the South.

"Marsh clay from the Vltava river itself," Berliner said. "The same clay the great Rabbi Judah Loew ben Bezalel himself used to build *his* golem. Fired in the same kiln Rabbi Loew used, constructed according to the same method he used."

Smeared across the thing's forehead lay a thin finish of crackle-dry good red clay—local clay, Rock Creek clay, American clay. At the touch of Max's fingers, the reddish dust crumbled and fell to the floor.

"For the writing of the *shem*, the name of God," Berliner explained. "The *shem* activates the golem, brings it to life."

The old man, the wise old man Max had thought the epitome of rational thought and learning, actually believed he could make this *thing* come to life.

As if sensing Max's incredulity, Berliner said, "I show you."

He rummaged around in a shelf of jars until he found a certain earthenware one. He frowned. "It has been some time since I used this." Opening the jar, he nodded. "Sill moist. Good."

Berliner dipped his hand into the jar and came away with a large glob of creek bank clay. He smeared the red clay across the golem's ceramic forehead. "A clay tablet of sorts to write upon."

Gouging his index finger into the wet clay, Berliner traced out a word in Hebrew letters.

אמת

Emet. The word for Truth.

And what is Truth, if not another name for God?

The hideous creature's bulging eyes opened.

Blinked.

It ponderously turned its head to stare first at Berliner, then at Max. Its neck, which should have been an unmoving, unyielding ceramic and should have shattered at the torqueing movement, twisted in supple folds of muscle and skin as if it were a flesh-clad living object. It sounded like stones grinding against each other.

"I don't believe it," Max whispered, but his eyes gave him no other choice.

"Not bad for mere 'superstition', is it, Max?"

"It's all true," Max burbled. "The legends, the superstitions. Rabbi Lowe and the Golem of Prague."

"The legends exaggerate much, as legends always do."

Max stared at the golem staring back at him. "But his golem fought off the Emperor's soldiers, prevented the pogrom of the Viennese Ghetto?"

"A bit exaggerated, but, yes. Rabbi Lowe contrasted his creature with the thought that it could be a shield for our people. So served it."

Flashes of memory burned in Max's mind. Lines of blue-clad troops marching toward rows of waiting musketry. The snap and crackle of gunfire. The meaty thud of a lead ball striking limbs, rendering them shattered and useless.

"I would build me no shield," Max said coldly. "I would build me a *sword*. I would build a hundred, a thousand of these creatures and sweep the South clean of its slave pens and auction blocks."

Max's words triggered the creature. Its lopsided mouth opened and let out an inarticulate moan, the chilling sound of a tongueless mute.

It made to move toward Max. It moved as a glacier moved. Slowly. Inexorably. Its great meaty hands pawed at Max, as if demanding/asking/begging for something only Max could give.

Berliner stepped up. "And who gave you leave to move, you great dumb brute?" There was a snarl in his voice that Max had never heard before. The snarl of a master to slave.

The creature returned to its former stance, resentment in its dull ceramic eyes.

"You see the limitations of this lowly creature?" Berliner asked. "Mindless. Thoughtless. Needing instructions for even the simplest task. How God must see us so, too, eh?"

Berliner reached forth his hand again to the creature's forehead. "And now I think it best for the moment to return this beast to insensate somnolence. To do so, you simply do *this*."

His finger dabbed at the red clay, smoothing away the letter aleph from the word *emet*.

Emet—אמת—became *Met*.

מת.

Truth had become Death.

The creature's eyes closed. Its semblance of life faded away.

A final dab of the finger and even the word *met* was scrubbed away.

Berliner wiped the fresh clay from his hands with a cloth.

"You can teach me how to fashion one of these?" Max asked.

Berliner shrugged. "I could. The principles are not hard. The question is, should I? Your talk of turning these into weapons of vengeance. No good can come from it."

"No good can come from smashing evil? No good can come from *tikkun olam*? Repairing the world?"

Berliner laid a hand on Max's shoulder. "It is not your goal I question, but the method proposed."

"But Rabbi Lowe used it to—"

"Speak not of fashioning these beasts into swords. It cannot be done. You have seen how mindless it is. It is one thing to stand such a stupid creature in the confines of a narrow alleyway to block the passage of Emperor Rudolf's soldiers, to frighten them away, to send them scurrying back to the palace with tales of a monster that guards the Jews. Quite another to have a golem move with independence of thought needed upon a confused and crowded battlefield."

Max shifted his gaze toward the lifeless golem. "That is truly what you think of your creation? Mindless, useless, without the ability to think or act for its self?"

"I do not think, *I know*. You saw how difficult it was for me to control it."

"I saw."

Saw more than you think, old man.

Berliner shook his head ruefully. "The golem was difficult enough to handle in the Old Country. Here in this new one, where all things are so very different— so much worse it is to make it to obey."

"So much worse, indeed," Max nodded slowly. Acknowledging the old man's words, if not assenting to them. "I think I understand. You have my solemn word I will speak no more about fashioning golems to order them into battle. I've no wish to order them at all. I wish only to learn through them Man's relationship to his Creator."

Berliner pulled on his beard as he thought. "Very well, Maximillian. That much I am willing to teach you," he said, unaware he had taught Max so much already.

"THE PRINCIPLES for creating a golem are not hard," Berliner said, patting the head of the now-lifeless ceramic creature. "It involves but three steps.

"First, you fashion its form out of clay. Any clay should work. In theory.

"Second, you make sure you have created it with some sort of imperfection. Only God is allowed to create a perfectly formed being. Any imperfection will do. In theory.

"And finally, you inscribe upon its forehead the shem, as you have seen. Any of the infinite names of God will do. In theory."

Max frowned. "You say 'in theory.' But in practice?"

"In practice only Rabbi Lowe's methods seem to work. Otherwise," Berliner chuckled, "we would be up to our necks in golems created by any schoolboy from the shul, would we not?"

"So you used Rabbi Lowe's method to create this one. The same clay, the same kiln."

"The same clay. The same kiln. The same mathematically calculated imperfections painstakingly derived by Kabbalist numerology you disdain so."

Max laughed sourly. "Well, I won't be visiting the River Vltava for its clay anytime soon, so I suppose I won't be making any golems." His tone grew serious. "Although I find it odd that God would create such a miraculous universal lesson for all Mankind, then restrict it only to those fortunate Viennese living on the banks of the Vltava."

Berliner shrugged. "It seems to be the way things are. Well, we can have you learn to inscribe the shem—"

Max shook his head.

"No, I've changed my mind. I've no further interest in your golem."

Berliner blinked. "You do not wish to inscribe the shem yourself? Feel what the Creator felt when he breathed life into our lump of clay?"

Max swung on his crutches toward the light emanating from the opened trap door. "I've no wish to create a slave. Clay or any other kind."

July 11, 1864

Once again Max looked up from his studies to stare out the parlor window.

"Something's wrong," he said.

All morning Union troops had been marching past the house toward Fort Stevens, but not in any cohesive manner. A company here, a squad there. Even clumps of four or five stragglers—such as Max saw right now—kept moving past.

They all had the same set mouth, the same look on their face that Max knew far too well. They were marching into battle.

Max crutched himself out the door as fast as he could manage. "What goes, fellows?" he called.

The oldest of the four, a grizzled sergeant old enough to give Berliner a run for his money, stopped and spat on the ground. "General Early and the whole Confederate Army's just north of here. He aims to march right over the top of Fort Stevens and on into Washington. And there's beggar-all to stop him."

The old sergeant spat again. "They're emptying every stockade and green-as-grass training camp, trying to scrape up men for the defense."

A private with his head wrapped up in a white linen bandage nodded. "They even have Sarge here combing the hospitals. Walking wounded, invalids. You name it. He's rounding us up. We ain't even got ourselves a rifle."

Another spit of tobacco by the sergeant. "They'll be rifles enough at the fort, son, by and by. Rifles from men with no more further use for 'em. Same as we're sure to leave 'em later on for others." He spoke as a man headed toward his own death.

He eyed Max up and down, his gaze pausing long and hard on the leg that was no longer there.

"Antietam," Max said simply.

The sergeant nodded. "I was there," he said simply. "There and a hundred battles afterward. You were one of the lucky ones. You were able to stop at Antietam." He gathered up his three fellows with the sergeant's jerk of chin and the stragglers started back up the road.

"Get a hot meal while you can, son," the sergeant yelled over his shoulder. "If things go south as I think they will, I'll be back to fetch you for the lines."

A quarter mile away, the guns of Fort Stevens fired, sending outgoing shells high into the air.

Seconds later, Confederate cannon roared back. Max cringed as he heard that old familiar cloth-ripping sound of incoming shells shrieking through the air.

Max had been to Fort Stevens. His father had driven him out there once, bringing a load of dry goods. It was a fort in name only. A few wooden ramparts mounded over with earth. A few rusted, clapped-out cannon manned by men even more worn out and useless. The so-called fort wouldn't hold out for long.

He pulled out his pocket watch.

Three p.m.

Max wondered if the South would win the war by suppertime.

July 12, 1864

MORNING.

Somehow Fort Stevens had held on through the night.

Through the long dark hours its cannon occasionally boomed out. The desultory fire of a near-whipped army husbanding its ammunition.

The Union guns were silent now.

Confederate cannons still roared. Max cringed with each incoming shell.

Even old Berliner, seated in his customary chair in a house that now reeked of burnt gunpowder, seemed jumpy. "A quarter-mile is not all that much distance after all."

Max pushed himself to his feet.

"No distance at all," he said.

He hobbled to his room.

He had brought very little with him when he'd moved in with Berliner. A carpet bag with a few extra shirts, a razor, a daguerreotype of his mother.

The one thing he had made sure to pack was the blue uniform tunic he had worn as a soldier. They had cut away, thrown away his matching blue trousers when they had cut away his leg. Max would not see the tunic thrown away, too.

He quickly donned the jacket, buttoning its rows of brass buttons with practiced efficiency.

Berliner stood in the open bedroom doorway. "What are you doing, Maximillian?"

Max buttoned the last button. "Saving the sergeant a trip."

He picked up his crutches from off the bed. Clean sheets and eiderdown. A world removed from the hell he was heading back to.

"You can't. You mustn't. You—" The old man's mouth gabbled like a fish. The tears forming in his eyes were not entirely caused by the smoke. "You'd never make it anyway. It's a quarter mile—"

"No distance at all, as you yourself pointed out."

"I won't allow it." The old man grabbed each side of the doorframe, forming a human barricade.

Max crutched himself to the doorway where Berliner stood, blocking him. "Either I go out this door, or I go out the window. Your choice."

"Max, you have no leg. What possible use could you even be? You cannot walk, you cannot march, you cannot even run away if it comes to that."

"I can still shoot, old man," Max said. "I can lean against the parapet and shoot. And there won't be any running away from this one. We hold or the Republic dies, the slaves never seeing their freedom. I will not have it I sacrificed a leg in vain."

Berliner let go of the doorframe. His arms slowly lowered. "Come," he said, his voice catching. "You will not walk. I drive you."

ℵ

LIKE BERLINER'S HOUSE, Fort Stevens was in the countryside past the northern outskirts of the city, almost as far north in the District of Columbia as one could get without being in Maryland. The area held a few scattered houses, mostly cleared fields and trees.

One of those black oak trees lay across the road, shattered by cannon shot. Berliner had to climb down from the buckboard and lead the horse around the fallen log. The smell of green wood suddenly exposed to the air wafted up.

"Overshot," Max said, speaking loud enough to be heard over the crackle of musketry. "The Rebs must be using plunging shot to try to take out our guns."

When he saw that Berliner didn't understand, he explained. Now Max was the seasoned teacher and the old man the untried, nervous student.

"The fort's cannons are dug in too good for the Rebs to be able to shoot straight across normal-like and hit 'em. So they're shooting upward in a high trajectory arc so the shell falls down from straight above them."

Berliner nodded as he climbed back up into the wagon, but Max saw that the old man still didn't understand.

"It's all precise mathematical calculations," Max said. "Angles, trajectories, powder charges' velocities. The slightest error in your math, the wrong number, a transposed digit—it's very easy to be off a quarter-mile."

Max laughed at the kind of joke only combat veterans saw, the black humor inherent in the art of death. He stopped, sobered, when he saw his laughter disquieted his teacher. "Maybe your Kabbalah *is* right. Our world *is* ruled by numbers."

A ricochet zinged nearby. Berliner wiped at his brow. The late morning air had heated up rapidly. The day seemed poised to be a scorcher, even for July. "I am beginning to wish I had brought my golem. I could use a shield, Maximillian."

Max shook his head. "It would have done you no good."

He fell silent for a few clops of the horse's hooves, then turned to face his mentor. "Rabbi Lowe was very wise, and you are very learned. But if the golem is the ultimate discourse about Man and God, both of you failed the lesson."

Berliner sputtered, but Max cut him off. "Both of you created servants. Created slaves. By doing so you are in essence saying that God created *us* only as slaves. That is not *emet*—that is not Truth.

"Do you draw up a contract with the ox that plows your field? Do you bargain with the earthworms that till your soil? The God of Israel covenanted with Abraham's children, set out duties and responsibilities on each side, as you or I would contract with the other."

Berliner could only stare at him. "Are you saying that God and Man are—?"

"I do not discount the gap between us, the gulf. But it is of degree, rather than of kind."

Berliner shook his head. "You, my young friend, are more dangerous to your father and Stampel than I with my Kabbalah or Przibram with his reforms."

The crackle of gunfire grew louder as they approached the fort.

A NUMBER OF WAGONS—BUCKBOARDS, ambulances, even a fancy carriage—lay parked at the outskirt of the fort. To Max's eye, they marked the pell-mell rush by the Union army to man the fort. Anything that moved must have been used to haul men and ammunition.

A Union soldier, a private serving as picket, grabbed their horses' reins to stop their approach. He took one sneering look at Berliner's clothes and style of beard and spat a wad of tobacco juice at the buckboard. "And where do you Hebrews a'think yer a'goin'?

Max plucked at the blue tunic he wore. "I'm here to fight, same as all of you." He started the painful journey of descending to the ground.

The sentry spat again. "Well, we don't need your kind here. Git on back home!"

A thin, reedy voice came from behind the fancy carriage. "It's his country, too, private." The voice's owner stepped around where Max could see. Max knew instantly the tall gaunt man standing six-foot-four in frock coat and stovepipe hat: President Abraham Lincoln.

Lincoln turned to the officer accompanying him. "Colonel—?" He snapped his fingers, as a busy man would do in trying to remember the name of a man he'd just met.

"Lieutenant Colonel Oliver Wendell Holmes," the officer supplied. "Junior."

Lincoln nodded. "Colonel Holmes, get this man a rifle. I see a nice empty spot along that wall there where he can be posted."

The officer looked from Lincoln to Max and back again. "But Mr. President, that man is missing a leg."

Lincoln looked down at him. "I doubt seriously you're telling this boy anything he doesn't already know. Heaven knows we need every man here we can get."

Holmes opened his mouth to argue, thought better of it, and called for a sergeant instead. The old grizzled sergeant from yesterday showed up to lead Max to his place on the wall.

∩

MAX LEANED against the rough-hewn log wall, taking most of the load of standing off his leg. The earthwork pushed up against the log wall proved wide enough that Max could rest his elbows on it, rest the nine-pound weight of his Springfield rifle upon it, too.

He looked out across the distance to where the Reb soldiers must lie crouched behind cover. He could not see them, but he knew they were there, could feel that it was only a matter of time before they started marching *en masse* to take the fort. The fort's remaining cannon were down to their last shells and, anyway, they were sited wrong. The angle of fire they had from their dug-in positions did not bear upon the infantry in front of Max. There was an artillery revetment just behind Max with a perfect field of fire, but unfortunately no cannon had been placed there.

Max could see the occasional puff of black powder as here or there a Reb in the brush banged away. Smooth bores, not even rifled. Max had no fear of them. They couldn't hit anything.

It was the fellows in that stone house that fretted him. Sharpshooters. They had plucked off the men to either side of Max. Just then, a Sharp's bullet whined past him, missing him by gnat's breath. Forced to lean unsteadily against the wall as he was, Max couldn't even duck down.

He heard a shuffle behind him. It was old man Berliner.

"What are you doing, you old fool," Max growled. "You'll be killed up here!"

"And you won't be?" the old man said.

"You're no soldier. You've never even shot a rifle in your life!"

"I'm not soldier, but it is my country, too." He set a couple of fresh cartridge boxes on the earthwork next to Max. "I don't have to be a soldier to fetch for you. You fire the rifle. I will be your legs."

Max didn't like it, but he couldn't very well chase the old fool away.

Berliner peered over the parapet, his eyes squinting behind his thick spectacles. "I hear from the soldiers that more shells for the cannon arrive soon."

A puff of smoke from the stone house and another Sharp's bullet zinged. A soldier three places to the left of Max screamed in agony.

"Fat lot of good it's going to do if our cannon are sited wrong. They need to move one to that pit behind us."

The confederate sharpshooter fired again.

Max tried to spit but his mouth was too dry. "'Course, they can't shift one there because if they tried those fellows in that stone house would pot them like quail. Perfect line of fire."

Berliner wiped at his brow. "Surely with all these great cannon, they could blast away that house, yes?"

Max shook his head. "Shooting big rock only makes lots of little rock. Funny thing about rubble—it's even harder dig an enemy out from rubble than it is an intact building."

"My assessment exactly," a voice behind Max said. Max half-turned and saw that colonel and the President himself half-crouched behind him.

"This is the spot I was telling you about, Mr. President. We need to site a gun here, but we can't do it without clearing out that sniper's nest first."

"That stone house?" Lincoln asked.

"It'd take three hundred men to do it," the colonel said. "Three hundred men we don't have." He paused. "And beside, it'd be murder to send them out there. They'd never make it. Worse than Fredericksburg. Worse than Pickett's Charge."

"I see," Lincoln said. He straightened up to his full height to get a better look at the field.

The Sharps fired again and a .52-caliber slug punched through Lincoln's stovepipe hat, sending it flying.

"Get down, you blasted fool!" Colonel Holmes yelled, throwing himself bodily upon his command-in-chief and pulling him down.

Max half turned to see the commotion. He saw the president sheepishly dust himself off. The great man opened his mouth to speak—

There was a flash of light, the sound of explosion, and Max's world went dark.

ᴧ

MAX CAME to lying in a patch of wet clay. He'd been carried behind the line to the rear of the fort. His ears rang and his face felt scorched from powder burns. The bitter iron tang of blood filled his mouth.

Artillery shell. I've been hit by an artillery shell.

A near-miss or he wouldn't have survived.

He tried to move, tried to sit up, but there came a blinding pain in his left arm.

"Easy, Maximillian," old man Berliner said, leaning over him. The old man's face was cut and his glasses were missing, but otherwise he seemed fine. Better than Max. "You were hit."

No, not his arm, too!

"Just a nasty cut," the old man hastened to add. "You'll heal just fine."

Forewarned of the pain now, Max sat up. He checked his arm. A bloody gash just below the shoulder, but just a cut as Berliner had said.

He reached for his pair of crutches placed next to him. "I have to get up. I have to get back to the line."

Agony as he tried to put weight on his left arm.

"There is nothing useful you can do here now," Berliner said. "You cannot shoot a rifle like that. Let us go home, yes?"

Max gritted his teeth and managed to get to his feet. The pain was such he knew Berliner was right, but he could not, he would not leave. "I can at least man the wall and take a bullet meant for another who *can* fight."

"Maximillian, that is just crazy talk!"

The thin reedy voice spoke. "He's right, son. You've done enough." The president, hatless and muddy but otherwise no worse for wear stepped up with Lt. Col. Holmes in tow.

"How is the boy?" Lincoln asked.

"Aside from an acute case of stubbornness, he's fine," Berliner said.

The president chuckled. "I hear that is a common trait among your people."

"Common among *all* men, I'm glad to say. When the Lord fashioned us out of clay," Berliner said, nodding at Max, "He did not create quiescent slaves. He created us free men. Stubborn, willful, argumentative. Human."

Lincoln chuckled again. "That He did, sir. Although I'd have preferred it if He had fashioned our Southern countryman just a leetle bit less stubborn."

An orderly ran up to Holmes. Panting, he delivered his message. "Colonel, the Rebs—they're gathering behind the tree line, massing for their attack. I seen it myself."

"Gentleman," Lincoln said, his voice as dead as their chances. "They march, they'll take this fort. They take this fort, there's nothing to stop them from taking Washington and winning the war."

Holmes angrily kicked at the clay dirt beneath his feet. "All because we can't site one lousy cannon."

Lincoln set his jaw. "Colonel Holmes. Gather up your three hundred. I will lead them to that stone building myself."

"Sir, you can't do it!" the colonel pleaded. "Three hundred angels of the Lord himself couldn't cross that ground."

Max straightened his shoulder. "But perhaps one golem can."

He started tracing an outline with the tip of his crutch in the soft red clay. A crude outline of a man of gargantuan proportions.

His old teacher scurried after him, peering nearsightedly. "Maximillian! Maximillian! What do you think you're doing?"

"I'm making a golem out of clay."

Max traced a bulbous head, broad shoulders, long powerful arms, a barrel chest.

"Maximillian, this is crazy talk. You cannot—"

"You said any clay would do, right?"

Next were the legs and feet. He traced two good legs, short and squat, but strong. Splayed feet broad enough to support the weight of such a monster.

"But first you mold the clay, bake it. Tracing an outline is not the way you create—"

Max sketched out eyes and ears. He wanted the golem to be able to see him, hear what he had to ask.

"You mean that's not the way you did it in the Old Country," Max said. "I'm not creating an Old Country golem. I am creating one for *this* country."

Berliner persisted. "But the calculations, Maximillian. The imperfections have to be precisely calculated, measured, balanced according to the—"

Max turned for a moment. "By the very nature of my being human, anything I create will be imperfect. The greatest, most perfect masterpiece by the greatest artist ever would still be found imperfect compared to God."

Almost complete, Max saved drawing in the mouth for last. He drew an open mouth with teeth and tongue. His would be no mute beast. His would talk to Max as Man talks to God.

Berliner tugged at his arm. "At least let me write in the shem. You do not know the way it must be done."

Max shook him off. "I have seen the way it must *not* be done."

Carefully, Max wrote a single word upon the sketched figure's forehead.

As Max wrote, Berliner twisted his wrinkle hands together. "What are you doing, Maximillian? Even without my glasses I can tell you do not write the proper shem. You do not even write in Hebrew. You write left to right."

"I *am* writing the proper shem. Of all God's Ten Thousand Names, I am writing the only one that fits."

And with that, Max wrote the final letter.

Suddenly there came a noise unlike all others, a noise like the sound of heaven's gates opening, a noise like the sound of the veil between God and Man rending itself apart.

The ground trembled and the flat outline of the golem rose from the earth.

As it rose, it gathered the red clay about it, filling it, forming it into a solid three-dimensional figure, a misshapen monstrosity ten feet tall. Its surface was pebbled with leaves and sticks and stones and even the discarded brass button from a soldier's uniform.

It stank of excavated dirt, of field after the first spring planting, of a desert after a sudden rain. It moved with the ponderosity of a mudslide. It stared at the clutch of Gentiles staring back at it.

Holmes pulled at Lincoln's sleeve, trying to get him away to safety. The President shrugged him off. "If it means us harm, Colonel, we are as good as dead. But I do not think it does."

The creature turned its head toward Max and looked down at him. Its eyes glowed as if lit by the molten magma of the Earth's core. It opened its cavernous mouth to speak.

"Who disturbs my sleep? Who wrests me from the soil?"

It spoke with the voice of an earthquake.

Unafraid, Max stepped up. "I did, friend. I have great need of your help."

The creature's eyes narrowed. "You created me? You mean to order me about as my brethren have been?"

"I make no orders. I see no slave before me," Max said. "I ask only for help as friend to friend."

The creature thought. "You would call me friend?"

Max nodded. "I have called you here as such."

The creature thought again. "What is this boon you seek?"

Max took a deep breath. "We are fighting a great war upon this land to end the slavery of our fellow human beings. If we lose here today, the stain of slavery will continue on."

The creature growled with the sound of boulders smashing down a mountainside.

"There is slavery on this land? This soil?" It growled again. "This cannot stand. This is hallowed soil. This is a promised land. A land where all must be free."

Again Max nodded. "That is what we, too, have come to believe." He quickly described what needed to be done. "All I ask," Max concluded, "is that you go where we ourselves cannot survive and chase away the soldiers in that stone house."

"And afterward?" the creature demanded. "You will release me back to the soil? Or will you find me yet another task and another and another as your kind have always done with my brethren?"

"I will release you, if that is what you wish," Max said. "Or you can remain and go and do as you wish. I created you, but I do not own you. I created you with free will, as my Creator created me."

The creature pondered. "Slavery is a great evil, the slavery of my kind as well as of yours. But I find you are no slaver. You have created me free in the hope that I would free others. Very well. I will do this thing. But afterward I will return and we shall see if you do indeed tell me the truth when you say that I am free to choose my own path."

With that, the creature set out in great lumbering strides.

Max and Berliner, Lincoln and the colonel all rushed to the wall to watch the creature stomp across the killing field between the two armies.

At first, there came total silence from the Confederate lines, as if they could not believe what they were seeing. And then, when they realized that the impossible was indeed happening, they erupted in panicked, frightened screams.

But frightened or not, they remembered they were soldiers. They remembered they were men.

First one, then two, then a dozen, then every rifle on the line blazed away at the lumbering creature. The Confederate cannon joined in.

To no effect.

The rifle bullets merely sunk themselves deep into the soft red clay. The artillery shells gouged out gaping holes in the creature's clay body, but as soon as a hole appeared dirt and clay from beneath its feet leapt up to plug the void.

The creature reached the stone house. He did not even need to raise his titanic fists in anger. The Confederate soldiers hidden inside ran out of the building, scattering to the countryside.

The creature again opened its cavernous mouth and yelled out in a tongue shared with its lithic brothers, the tongue of earth and stone and bedrock far below. The very soil itself obeyed that voice. A great chasm opened up, the ground parting open like a grave, and the stone house sank down, down, down into the earth, the stones of the house returning at last to kith and kin.

The Confederates, should they ever return, would find no stone shelter to snipe from again.

With contemptuous ease, the creature turned and strolled back to the Union lines. The Confederates fired a few ragged shots, but their heart wasn't in it.

Indeed, there would be no attack now. Already the troops who had gathered to make the final push were dispersing, packing up to limp back home to the South.

The battle of Fort Stevens was effectively over.

The Union was saved.

At least for today.

PERHAPS THE ODDEST thing of the day's happening was that when the creature crossed over back into Union lines, there came no cheering from the Union throats. Instead, a hush fell over the men, men who had expected to die and see their nation die with it. They had witnessed something beyond their ken. The religious among them bowed their heads, and the more worldly silently wished that they, too, knew how.

The creature sought Max out.

"I have done the thing you asked. Will you keep the covenant you made with me? Will you release me back to the soil?"

Max nodded. "I will keep my covenant. *You* choose what happens next. Stay or go as you please. Or I can release you from the shem, although for my part I would wish to know you better."

The creature lowered itself, easing itself upon its back, upon the ground from whence it had sprung. "You and I are created from the same clay, we share a common bond. Listen in the quiet of the dark of night, listen to the still small voice of the heart, my not-quite-brother. You will hear me, we will talk. We will know each other better."

Max bent down. His finger hovered above the creature's forehead, the place where he had carved the shem, the one name of God out of all God's names that had proved truer than any emet.

His finger paused above the English word *friend*.

With a swift, sure stroke, Max's finger erased the first half so that only the word *end* was left.

The creature dissolved in a shower of dirt, reconstituted back into the free soil of a free nation.

NAUGHT BUT DEATH
STANDS FAST

INTRODUCTION

As the name itself might indicate, my "Clockwork Deseret" fiction universe focuses on Deseret and Mormon arcane secret agents, but it does so against a worldwide broader canvas of national secret societies each reflecting the unique characteristics of their respective country.

You've already met Japan's Steel Angel Layer in "Tracting." Mapped out for future tales are secret agencies from France (Société de la Rue Morgue), Imperial Germany (Grenzschließungsgruppe 13), and others. Closer to home, Deseret must contend with the North's Bureau of Alchemy, Science, and Firearms (BASF) and the Confederate South's Mummer's Troupe.

In this next tale, "Naught but Death Stands Fast"—a novella written expressly for this Hemelein story collection—we delve into the secret world of Britain's Domesday Chapter—a plucky band of gentleman-explorers, amateur experts, and hobbyists so typical of 19th Century Britain. The Chapter operates out of a certain Deptford tavern made infamous by the murder of Christopher Marlowe.

Globetrotting Mallory Millrace Tafford, big game-hunter, must contend with man-eating tigers, steam-powered cyborgs, corrupt colonial officials, rampaging fishmen, and a trigger-happy German Navy. Oh, and stave off certain world destruction by Cthulhu's Consort in the process of all that.

From the British Raj to the crowded streets of London or the equatorial heat of British East Africa, the Britannic sun never sets upon shepherd's pie, poetry, or pink gin in this adventure tale, shaken not stirred by the mysterious head of the secret Domesday Chapter: an ageless immortal who walks a bit on the Wilde side.

April 22, 1889
Sthanadharaka, India

T he stifling near-twilight lay hot and heavy. How India's humid air could simultaneously be both soaked-sponge saturated and yet gritty with red laterite dust was something only Vishnu knew. By all rights, the humid dusty air should coalesce into mud or even baked clay, hot as it was.

Hidden in the leafy green of his hunting blind, Mallory Millrace Tafford daubed the perspiration beading on his brow. He couldn't afford to get blinded by sweat, not now. A sliver of the sun behind him had already sunk beneath the horizon. If his prey was going to show, now would be the time.

Tafford had chosen his spot carefully. Not only did the orange-pink sun and its glare lay behind him, but the blind sat upwind of the wide spot in the Sthanadharaka River, the spot both animals and villagers alike used for a watering hole. Two reed-thin young brides, all of maybe thirteen, carried empty water urns on their shoulders, chatting away as they headed to fetch one last urn of water before the sun fully set and forest beasts prowled.

From their perfect serenity, you'd never know that a half-dozen villagers had been clawed to death at that very spot the past two weeks. But now the Great White Hunter sent by the District Constabulary was here, wasn't he? That he would slay the man-eating tiger was a given.

Tafford, the supposed Great White Hunter, wished he shared their confidence. A tiger would have been no problem. The creature preying on this village, however, was no cat-brained tiger but as smart and cunning as a man. Blinking with sweat, Tafford dabbed at his brow again and reseated rifle stock against his shoulder.

It was a lovely rifle, almost a work of art, chased as it was with gilt Celtic runes and Sanskrit *strotram*, a custom Pendles double-barreled game rifle chambered for Rigby's powerful Nitro Express. The bolt mechanism glinted in the pink-orange light stabbing through the leafy boughs, well-worn from use and well-maintained by habit.

In the time it had taken Tafford to wipe his brow, a third woman had appeared from out of the brush, the trailing the two-girls with cat-like grace. She, too, carried an urn upon one shoulder. It looked cracked and chipped as if discarded once, but picked up again out of desperate need.

The two girls reached water's edge and bent down to fill their urns. The third woman quickened her pace.

Tafford dared flick his gaze from his sights, centered on the base of the newcomer's spine to the tracks she left in the river bank's mud.

They weren't human; they were more like the marks of a jungle cat.

Tafford shifted aim. His crooked finger squeezed gently on the left barrel's trigger. A vicious hypersonic crack and the water urn upon the woman/thing's shoulder shattered. Pot shards exploded like shrapnel, cutting and slicing the woman/thing's face.

Shock, pain, and rage from being attacked undid the female Rakshasa's disguise just as Tafford intended. Her features flowed into a sleek bipedal hybrid of cat and girl—her true form.

Her delectable two-course meal forgotten, she whirled to face the direction of the gunshot. She blinked, blinded by the rubied setting sun. The green-branched hunting blind lay downwind and down-sun, but both her near-human intelligence and her animal instinct told the beast-woman that was where her tormentor lurked. She coiled herself in a crouch then sprang twenty feet in the air at the direction of the blind.

As she landed on her first bounding leap, her features flowed again, and she melted into her hunting form: that of a powerful four-legged true tigress.

One great cat spring.

Another.

Tafford, shoulder sore already from the first massive discharge, pulled the trigger on his remaining barrel. The .450 Nitro Express silver bullet, inscribed with druidic runes, caught the Rakshasa dead-center of her heart, killing the creature instantly. The still-snarling corpse landed a mere half-foot in front of Tafford. Outstretched claws, twitching in death, shredded the branches of the hunting.

Tafford shakily got to his feet, standing at his full 6'4" height. Big-boned as he was tall, even at fifty, Tafford still mostly possessed the same sturdy build he'd had in his Oxford rugger days. Usually his size proved an asset—anchoring for the recoil of a .450 Nitro discharge, for example—but not when squeezed inside the cramped confines of a hunting blind.

He walked stiffly around the blind. His joints felt like they would never bend properly ever again. How many hours had he been cramped in there so?

Tafford's eyes watered from the still swirling dust and power fumes. Rigby kept promising a smokeless power cartridge instead of its venerable black powder-and-cordite one, but so far hadn't delivered. He blew his narrow, wedge of a nose—the Tafford family nose, all the inheritance a remittance man like him would ever get from the family clan. He folded his sweat-soaked (and now snot-soaked) cloth and shoved it in a trouser pocket.

He toed the dead Rakshasa.

That had been entirely all too close.

He'd had had to wait, though, until the Rakshasa had taken tiger form to take his kill shot, otherwise hard evidence in the form of a bipedal corpse of Rakshasas actually existing would have spread across the whole of India within a fortnight.

Speaking of which...

As the ringing in his ears from the big rifle's discharge slowly subsided, he became aware of the wild cacophony of screams and yells coming from the thatch-walled village. Villagers were pelting out of its gates. The two young girls who'd been the Rakshasa's mealtime prey stood ankle deep in the river, quivering and shrieking.

The local Constabulary man, a Welshman named Poyner, trotted behind the rush of villagers.

Let him calm them down. Tafford had work to do.

He gently leaned his Pendles rifle against the bole of a tree and with a hook-nosed knife began gutting his kill. If he hurried, he could still make the night train to Calcutta.

Calcutta, India

TAFFORD DOFFED his grimy bush hat as he entered the muggy office of Calcutta's Deputy Inspector General of the Imperial Police, exposing a receding hairline had had sunk down the back of his head to the level of his ear lobes. Another family curse.

The Deputy Inspector General's room was well-lit and clean, its walls scrubbed and whitewashed to within an inch of their life. Mid-afternoon sunlight, hot and heavy, streamed in through the louvered window. A lemon tree stood directly outside, its pungent flowering scent masking the stench of effluvia and human waste that Calcutta reeked of.

Obsessive order and sprawling filth. The British Raj in a nutshell.

Deputy Inspector General Haines, a ruddy-faced man in mutton-chops and starched khakis, sat at his desk. His two servants stood their posts. A houseboy in a purple satin jacket dutifully fanned a palm frond in the direction of his lord and master. A native orderly in white police tunic, turbaned on top and barefoot as a newborn, manned the bar cabinet. The cabinet stood fully stocked, if you called nothing but Plymouth gin and Angostura bitters fully stocked.

Tafford accepted the proffered pink gin and sank into a rattan chair, grunting as he did so. The hunting life kept him fit enough, but at fifty, a man had a paunch no matter how fit he kept himself.

Eyes darting toward the two servants, Tafford surreptitiously slipped his free hand into his pocket and tapped twice on a runic talisman carved from dull gray Holyhead granite. Tafford knew for a fact that the *Thaumaturg Fabrikkollektiv* or the *Arbeiter-Thaumaturg-Kollektiv* or whatever the Russo-German thaumaturgic worker's conclave was calling itself these days had penetrated the Imperial Police. He just didn't know how or who. Neither did he know just how much English either of these servants spoke, but his trinket would turn whatever English was spoken in the room into foreign gibberish in the ears of any non-native English speaker. No sense taking chances, even if the servants were as innocent and pure as driven snow.

Calcutta had no snow, neither had it completely innocent servants.

Tafford sipped his gin and waited.

Eventually Deputy Inspector General Haines looked up from his eternal stack of paperwork. "Back so soon?"

Tafford sipped his drink. "She made it too easy. Immature female, too inexperienced to know to shift her hunting ground. Or to suspect a hunting blind upwind and up-sun."

Haines pushed himself up from his desk and stepped over to a wall map. The map held a number of paper-flagged stickpins. One pink-flagged pin, a dozen or so blue. Pinholes dimpled the map, suggesting that forty or fifty additional similar pins had been removed prior.

Haines removed the last pink pin and stared at it. "She was the last then?"

Tafford nodded. "Last known Rakshasa female." Another sip. "Oh, there's still a few elderly males about, high up in the Kush, ones too experienced and cunning for me to find. Without any breeding partners, though, they'll soon die out."

"Wither on the vine, eh, what? Good," Haines said with satisfaction, discarding the pin into a rubbish basket. He sat down again. "You seem to have worked yourself out of a job, though."

Tafford motioned to the orderly, who exchanged his empty glass for a full one. "I shan't mind." He sipped. "Terrible thing, wiping out an entire race of beings by culling their females. Leave it to London to be so bloody-minded."

Haines snorted. "I shouldn't feel too sorry for the Rakshasa, if I were you. Maneaters, every last one of them." He settled back at his desk.

"Not natural maneaters," Tafford said quietly. "We're an acquired taste." He sipped at his drink. "The Rakshasa say we taste like chicken."

Haines glowered at him. "All well and good for *you* to joke. *You* don't have London firing off telegrams right and left, breathing down your neck to do something about them. Savage brutes." Left unclear was just who Haines meant were brutes, London or the Rakshasas.

"Brutes, maybe, but not unthinking," Tafford said mildly, choosing to believe Haines spoke of the cat-people. "Likely we'll never decipher their written language now." The females were the conservators of Rakshasa arts and language; males couldn't be bothered.

"That's for future scholars to debate," Haines snapped. "All I'm interested in —all London's interested in—is the present. That the slaughter of villagers has stopped. The rest is frippery."

"More fool they, then," Tafford said behind the uptilted rim of his drink.

Haines crooked a finger at his orderly and took a glass of gin himself. "I do hope you policed up the kill, Tafford," he said after draining half the glass. "Carcass and so forth. That would be all we'd need, some clever yogi-walla picking up claw to make a trinket or talisman and using it for who-knows-what mischief. Mischief directed against us most likely."

The Sepoy Mutiny lay more than thirty years in the past, but every Briton in India felt bone-deep that could happen again at any moment. Uneasy lay the colonial crown of the British Raj.

"Carted it all back with me," Tafford wearily assured. "Hide, meat, bones, and two buckets of offal," Tafford said. "I'll need an indent for the freight charge."

Haines nodded, jotting a note. "That should be alright, I suppose." A thought occurred to him. "You say you took it in tiger form? I'm rather embarrassed to admit it, but I've had the most beastly rotten luck trying to get myself a rug. Game all seem to go on holiday whenever I have the odd weekend free to hunt." He paused and smiled a trifle too affably. "I don't suppose you could—"

Tafford knocked back the last of his gin. "If I let you have the hide for a rug, within a fortnight the rug would be strangling you in your sleep. You don't know how to cure a Rakshasa hide to leach the magicks out. My boys do." Tafford smiled maliciously. "First, you have to—"

Haines held up both hands, palms pointed out. "Enough, enough. I don't want to know." The official fished his pocket for his pipe, then realized it sat buried under papers on his desk. He retrieved it and filled it with tobacco. "I'm not even supposed to know the Tavern exists. Forbidden to know, actually. Same directive from London that ordered me to employ you, if you can believe that."

Tafford did. He knew Whitehall's opinions all too well. He also knew how desperately Whitehall depended on what they—like other layman—called the Tavern. What those who belonged to it called by its proper name: the Domesday Chapter.

Haines struck a lucifer with a *skritch* on the arm of his chair. A couple bellows-like puffs, and the Deputy Inspector General got his pipe going.

"Well," he said around the stem of his pipe, "Maybe London can afford to play silly beggars. But out here, magic exists." He exhaled a cloud of blue smoke. "No matter how much I wish the devil it didn't."

"Never believe it doesn't exist back in London, too." Tafford set aside his glass. "The better for England, I should think." Especially with the French and the Germans and the Russians having it.

Haines, mind too small to think that far ahead, snorted. All he saw was the bounties Tafford collected. "The better for *you*, I should think." He pulled open a desk drawer with a squeak. He tossed an envelope at Tafford. Bank draft for a hundred guineas, London's bounty on a female Rakshasa. "Though why I'm paying *you* a bounty..." he trailed off bitterly. "Your precious Tavern has a Royal Charter. In my book that ought to make you a public servant." And thus, ineligible for bounties, just as Deputy Inspector Generals were.

"Not *my* precious Tavern," Tafford said, slipping the envelope inside his cotton drill jacket. The tiny hourglass phylactery—the mark of Chapter membership—depending from his silver wrist chain gave partial lie to Tafford's flat denial. "I work for them on a piece-rate basis. A hired expert, if you will. What they have to do sits too heavy on a conscience." The image of the last Rakshasa tigress in the iron sights of his rifle flashed unbidden in Tafford's mind. *My own evils are bad enough.*

A knock sounded at the door. Haines barked an annoyed "Enter!" and a trim red-haired Constabulary captain entered, paper flimsy in hand.

The man's permanent weathered tan and crow's-feet around the eyes marked him as old India hand. Tafford knew him, or rather knew of him. Captain Leishman, head of what passed for Haines' intelligence staff. So, Leishman was playing messenger boy himself tonight. Interesting.

"Telegram for Mr. Tafford, sir."

"Well, *give* it to him then," Haines snapped. "Bad enough I have to play your banker, Tafford," he groused. "Now you've got me playing your postmaster."

Tafford took the telegram and read it. He took it as a given Leishman had already read it and would report it to Haines at first chance, so he made no effort at disguising his reaction.

"Bad news?" Haines asked.

"I'm to start back for London tonight."

"Hard cheese for your Tavern, then," Haines said with a snort. "Won't be a steamer sailing for at least a couple days. Labor troubles down at the dock again. And even if you could sail tonight, even P&O's faster steamer takes three weeks to reach London."

Tafford shrugged. He got to his feet and one-handedly place his bush hat back on his head. "Still, I'd better see to making what arrangements I can. Needs must when the devil drives. If you'll excuse me?"

Exiting, he closed the door after him.

∩

"Devil indeed!" Haines growled. "Him and that infernal Tavern of his. For my money, they're as bad as the Rakshasa"

He jabbed his pipe stem at the waiting captain. "Leishman, this time we're going to find out just exactly how our esteemed Mr. Tafford travels back and forth to London. I want you to take a squad of your men and tail that artful dodger, all the way inside his warehouse if you have to." The local Tavern members ran an import-export warehouse as cover for their branch office. Haines knew that much.

Leishman nodded. "Send men to cover the docks as well?"

Haines snorted. "If you want, but it's a waste of time." He signaled for another drink. "I'd be very much surprised if our world traveling Mr. Tafford has ever trod the deck of a steamship in his life."

The Deputy Inspector General polished off his drink in one angry toss of wrist.

∩

Curry and saffron, sewage and jasmine. the sweaty press of seemingly a million unwashed poor all gathered in Bangtala Street; Calcutta with its crowded, fetid, muck-filled alleys was the easiest city in the world to duck away from a pursuer —unless you were a six-foot-four pink-faced Englishman like Tafford, as obvious as a carbon arc searchlight at midnight.

Someone was stalking him, following without trying to be seen. Pink faced and tall as well. Englishman. Plainclothes. Constabulary. One of Leishman's boys, had to be.

Leishman's boys would know the streets of Calcutta, far better than Tafford. But they would see Bangtala as a street. Tafford saw it as a jungle, just as much a jungle as the unknowable hills of the Abujmarh.

Tafford knew how to move through jungles.

The usual pack of small boys followed Tafford down Bangtala, surrounded him, pawing at his arms, grasping at his clothes, begging for loose change. He waited until he was almost abreast of a particularly tall market stall. Then Tafford threw them some, an entire handful of coins.

Copper coins glittered in the sunlight. Even before they struck the filthy cobblestone, the boys—joined by a not inconsiderable number of nearby adults —swarmed at the falling coins like South American piranhas at a chunk of meat.

The shouting crawling scrum turned violent when Tafford threw a second handful of English banknotes.

In the pell-mell confusion of yelling, pushing bodies, Tafford ducked behind the saffron-orange cloth wall of the market stall. He pushed aside a rickety stack of empty wooden crates and crouched down.

He watched as his pursuer, tried first to edge his way around the riot, then violently push his way through when he realized his prey had somehow vanished in the melee. Leishman's stooge wasn't really worried. He'd know where Tafford was heading, after all—a warehouse at the end of dead-end Bang-tala Street, the warehouse the Chapter leased as its operational headquarters in India. The plainclothes copper tore up crowded Bangtala at the best speed manageable in the crowd.

Tafford, on the other hand, doubled back the way he'd come. He was headed to the warehouse, true, but Bangtala wasn't an ordinary dead-end road. It curved back like a fishhook before it dead-ended, the warehouse on the tip of its barbed hook. Leishman's thug had the round bend to traverse.

But back down the shaft a bit lay a disused hidden alley that cut straight across from the shaft from fishhook shaft to hook barb. Tafford would arrive at his warehouse several minutes ahead of his pursuer. He trotted down the alley with a hunter's grin upon his face.

Always a cautious hunter, Tafford paused before emerging from the barb end of the alley. Leishman had a second thug posted outside the alley. He looked bored, sweltering there in the heat of the sun. A fruit stall caught his eye and he sauntered over to avail himself of a policeman's privilege and pinch himself a ripe banana or two. The man turned his back to the street as he did so, and that was all Tafford needed.

Tafford dashed across the street and through the door of the Chapter ware-house before the banana-munching copper could turn back around.

Inside the tin-roofed, tin-sided warehouse, the stifling heat was even worse, if possible. Its stagnant air felt like the inside of an oven.

Tafford wiped sweat out of his eyes. "Haines has Leishman's bullyboys chasing me for some reason," he told the two Irishmen who ran the ersatz ware-house. "They'll be knocking at the door any minute now."

"They might be a'knocking, aye," brogued Kinney, the shorter of the two, "But will they be a'finding?" Kinney, like his partner-in-crime Cassidy, held little love for the English, English coppers in particular. In the world of secrets and subterfuge in which the Chapter operated, hiring Irish rogues and scallywags and born smugglers paid off handsomely.

The two Irishmen were already in motion, enacting what they called Plan A by dragging a twenty-foot stepladder over to a spot under an open window near the roofline. Tafford described with his waving hands an arc of seemingly empty air. The hourglass phylactery on his wrist sparkled.

Tafford, meanwhile, had stepped over to dead center in the near empty warehouse. An innocuous grease stain on the concrete slab floor marked the spot he wanted.

An invisible object wavered into view—a ring of fairy steel, six feet in diameter. The ring hung motionless in the air just an inch or two off the floor, unsupported by any visible means at all. A multicolor shimmer air filled the hollow interior of the ring.

A BOAC ring—British Overseas Alchemic Corridor.

Tafford's kit—a beat-up canvas grip full of clothes, a field pack full of hunting gear, and his cased rifle sat to one side of the warehouse. They might as well be sitting in Australia for all the good they'd do Tafford now.

Fists pounded on the exterior of the warehouse door, accompanied by yelling voices. Leishman's boys were quicker off the mark than he'd guessed. He'd have to leave his kit behind.

"Remember," he told his two grinning Irishmen, "Plan A."

"Aye, Tafford himself t'was," Kinney sing-songed, aping what he'd be telling Leishman's angry agents mere moments from now. "In through the back way and then up and out and over the rooftops like the divvel himself was chasin' and him not saying a word t'the either of us."

Tafford slapped him on the back. "Good man."

And with that, Tafford stepped through the swirling iridescence of the BOAC Ring for London and home.

Moments later
Deptford
London, England

Tafford exited through an identical floating BOAC ring into the darkened subcellar of Chapter headquarters, the Deptford tavern that gave the Chapter its layman's name. Tongues of feeble blue gas flames licked and flickered in brass sconces, the feeble glow barely enough to illuminate the timbered walls. The cellar stank of mold and dead spiders.

He shivered in the sudden chill of England's soggy damp, made worse from his instant transition from India's steam bath. His light cotton drill jacket and khaki shorts, sufficient for the tropics, did nothing to ward off the grave-chill of an English cellar.

His warm clothes were packed away in his kit, abandoned back in Calcutta.

Along with his Pendles rifle.

Tafford fished his 'bulldog'—a well-worn Webley .442 pocket revolver—from his jacket and took aim at the aperture of the BOAC ring in case Leishman's men managed somehow to follow behind him.

No one came through as the glow of the BOAC ring faded, indicating the Calcutta end had gone inactive. Tafford relaxed. Inactive BOAC rings were invisible and intangible to anyone without a phylactery. Leishman's men could search till the end of time and not stumble across it.

The True Name given the rings by the ring's garden fairy originators, the twenty-syllables of trilling word-song that approximated "flittering jump hoop," was far too difficult to pronounce. When the Chapter had up-scaled the spoon-sized originals into a size a man could step through, they'd renamed them with something an Englishman could pronounce: BOACs—British Overseas Alchemic Corridors.

Leave it to us British to reduce fairy magic into Great Western Railway, Tafford thought.

The BOAC ring here in Deptford was the master terminus of the entire BOAC system, linking lesser BOAC rings around the world. One ring in each of the British Empire's overseas colonial possessions.

A potent artifact, indeed.

One that should have been left guarded here at the London end, if only by an old Chapter pensioner sitting with shotgun in his lap to guard the all-important trunkline BOAC.

The bulldog stayed gripped in his hand. Something might be wrong or it might not.

Cautiously, silent as a padding Rakshasa, he then catfooted up the rickety wooden stairs to the main cellar. Empty as well, and there should have been a half-dozen Candles—Chapter support staff members—bustling about.

Easing into a shadowed corner where he could protect his back while pointing his pistol, Tafford whispered, "Kit! *Kit!*"

The ectoplasmic creature that styled itself the Ghost of Christopher Marlowe and haunted this old Deptford tavern materialized. Its blue-white translucent brow furrowed, then arched one eyebrow at Tafford's strange antics of hiding in the Chapter's own cellar with pistol drawn.

The self-appointed ghost laughed.

"*...I think it good/To hide it close; a goodly stratagem,*" the ectoplasm quoted itself from its own play, "*And far from any man that is a fool.*"

"Quit nattering!" Tafford hissed. "Where is everyone? Where's the Albino?"

The ghost pointed a wispy finger upward and outward of the tavern. "*He celebrated her sad funeral/Himself in presence shall unfold at large.*"

Marlowe's *Tamburlaine* again. However sadly deluded the ectoplasm might have been it'd once been human, for two hundred and ninety-six years it had at least been ever-consistent in its delusion, ever-constant in its means of communication. The trick was deciphering it.

A funeral. Tafford frowned. "Whose funeral?" he asked. Surely not the Albino's, surely not Dorian's!

The ectoplasm shrugged. "*Enter five or six Protestants with books,*" it said. "*So, dragge them away/Exeunt.*" And with that, the ectoplasm *exeunt*-ed itself as well, fading from sight.

Tafford relaxed. The five or six were non-Chapter dead then. Not the Albino, not Dorian.

Tafford stood, pocketing his bulldog. A funeral would explain the empty tavern. Dorian and the rest would be in the potter's field in back burying whoever it had been who'd died. Dorian would want every Chapter member present for the cantomancy.

Kit reappeared, holding out a woolen winter cloak for Tafford. "*The townsmen mask in silk and cloth of gold,*" it suggested.

"Right," Tafford said, shrugging on the ankle-length cloak to cover himself and his khaki cotton clothes. "Thanks."

No sense giving any local prying eyes something to talk about—like a suntanned Great White Hunter suddenly appearing still dressed in tropical kit.

Tafford ascended the stairway and slipped out the back entrance of the tavern in search of the funeral party and the man who'd summoned him back to London.

𝕽

A WEED-CHOKED field of fallow ground lay secluded behind the tavern. Tudor townhouses, in all their white-wattled and half-timbered ancient glory, ringed the field completely, blocking it from outside view. Few aside from locals knew of it, and all the locals really knew was that it served as a potter's field of last resort, a dumping ground for burying unfortunates too forgotten for even the simple dignities of casket and cross to mark their graves.

Tafford frowned at the thought as he made his way toward the funeral crowd on the far side of the field. The full truth was far uglier than that.

He slogged through the muddy field, blinking at the incongruity of a morning sun hanging in the sky eight hours behind where he'd left it back in Calcutta. Not that you could really see the sun, hiding as it was behind thickening gray sheet clouds. A freshening breeze promised rain. Rain and damp and cold and misery.

Both weather and the funeral abomination reminded Tafford why years before he'd quit both England and Chapter alike.

Above and to the left, a window sash shifted and a pale face stared down at him. Him and the funeral. Tafford caught the slight movement and his hand started to reach for his pocket pistol.

He relaxed. Forced his jungle instincts into a sullen calm. Everything was alright. The face was friendly. The Chapter owned all the townhouses ringing the field, lodging for its members, the various Bells, Books, and Candles of the organization: Candles, the support staff, the menial drudges like his Calcutta Irishmen; Bells, the Chapter's fighting arm, the field agents like himself; and Books...

Books were what was wrong with the Chapter. At least the one particular Book that ran it.

Tafford reached the edge of the milling crowd. Proceedings couldn't begin until the barrel-shaped steam-man—all pig iron and rivets—finished scooping out the grave.

Coal-fired waste steam chuffed as the clumsy but tireless contraption worked its shovel-hands in metronomic exactitude. Rooster tails of dirt arced up and out of an oversized pit, shortly to serve as the mass grave for the five canvas-wrapped corpses lined up neatly atop the mounded spoil, waited to be callously tossed into the pit, waiting to be callously used by the Chapter as fuel for its operations.

The old angers bubbled up inside Tafford. He pulled his woolen cloak tighter, shivering not just from the sunless dim, but from the very evil of this place. Shadows deepened as the sun fled deeper behind the clouds, as ashamed as he was to witness the coming scene.

Eventually the steam-man clambered out of the pit and waddled off to the side, switching itself to idle. The cacophony of boiler and gearwork faded, leaving only the growing howl of the stiffening wind.

The funeral crowd sorted itself out in a horseshoe-shaped clot of bodies standing around three sides of the pit. At the head of the pit—where a gravestone should have stood had the dead anyone present who cared enough to erect one—the Albino took his position.

The Albino. Dorian Grey, head of the Chapter organization.

Dorian stood there, tall and thin, wisps of his long shoulder-length alabaster hair flaring in the wind. A pale ghost-like figure dressed in vicar's black frock and white Anglican dog collar.

Dorian Grey had been handsome once, almost godlike in appearance, before the Curse had leached all the color from him. Now he stood ethereal in the cloudy gloom, as if only sheer will kept him tethered to this side of the Veil

Some within the Chapter, old-timers mostly, claimed the Curse which had left Dorian ageless and left him handsome still. Claimed that Dorian's face hadn't changed in thirty years.

Tafford wasn't one of them, as he'd known Dorian before the Curse. The Curse had leached not only color from Dorian, but everything else that had made Dorian a human being.

Dorian had changed, alright. The old Dorian would never have allowed a top-hatted human carbuncle like Lord Greatorex to stand next to him in a place of honor. A place of power.

Greatorex, a ginger-haired Anglo-Irish peer with the rangy build of an aristocratic outdoorsman was nothing but a dilettante. A dabbler of the Arts who fancied himself a full-fledged Book. Greatorex had been trying to buy his way into the Chapter for years now. From the looks of things today—his expensive steam-man, his place at Dorian's side—Greatorex must have finally succeeded. The Chapter would be worse for it.

England and the world would be worse for it.

The crowd finally shuffled into their places. Dorian raised a bleached hand to silence them, while with the other hand he extracted a slim leather-bound black book from his breast pocket. He opened the book to a ribbon-marked passage.

To all the world, to any casual observer had there been any, the tableau was that of a Christian burial. But the book the Albino held was no Bible, no Book of Common Prayer, and the words he began to recite no scripture.

Pure eldritch cantomancy tumbled out of his mouth, iambic verse fashioned from the Dark Places, Words of Power growing in a strength at odds with the quiet voice uttering them. A blue glow—noticeable in only the cloudy gloom—emanated not only from the upturned soil of the grave, but from the very bodies of gathered Chapterites, drawing more and more Power from them and flowing through Dorian into the grave itself.

If e're we knew your name it lies forgot
Among the bones today we here inter,
Nor come we now in grief to mark your grave.

'Tis but the magicks of your Death we plant
To bank for selfish use against that day

When hope is lost and needs alone suffice.

Dark forces foul and fell that fell'd thy soul
And twirleth now betwixt each atom space
Of this your corpse shall serve that time of need

In answer, hark!, to beating drum of Drake
And save dear England's shore from haughty foe
In that dread night when naught but Death stands fast.

Upon the last spoken syllable, the pale glow faded as if only a trick of the shifting cloud-shrouded shadows.

Dorian Grey shut his book. The cartomancer trembled, spasmed like a consumptive as if the casting of the magic had drained his very essence even though he'd drawn Power from so many to work the spell.

Services over, the crowd of Candles dispersed, turning their backs on the sight of the inhuman steam-man pitilessly rolling the canvas-covered corpses pell-mell into the pit.

Five more dead in a field filled with naught but the corpses of those slain by magic, magic that even now clung to their decomposing remains, magic that thanks to the spell leached itself into the very grave soil.

Cranking up to full boiler pressure, the hissing, clanking steam-man began methodically spurning the spoil down upon the tumbled corpses, filling the grave in great efficient scoops of his shovel-arms, hurling the dirt in spuming arcs.

The Albino watched the first few shovelfuls, then turned away, only to meet Tafford's eyes instead.

"Hello, Mallory," he said, voice reedy with exhaustion

"Dorian," grudged Tafford.

Neither of the two once-friends made any attempt at a handshake.

"I believe you know Lord Greatorex," Dorian half-said, half-asked.

Rather than answering, Tafford tilted his head in the direction of the rapidly-filling pit. "Who were they?" he challenged.

Dorian made to speak, but Greatorex answered for him. The man's breath stank of pink gin and mutton. "Gutter dregs," he said with a dismissing wave of a lace-wristed hand. "As useless to society as they were useless to themselves."

"Not so useless if you're burying them here." Tafford said. The weight of his pocketed bulldog hung heavy and tempting, but Greatorex wasn't worth the price of a bullet. "If you're burying them here, they died by magic. Your magic?" he asked Dorian. "Or Greatorex's?"

Greatorex bristled, but the Albino held out a bloodless hand to stop him. "They took the Chapter's coin, they died in the Chapter's service," he said. "They were thus entitled to a Chapter burial."

"'Entitled,'" Tafford spat. "Bad enough you spent their lives as like farthing coins, now you're desecrating their corpses for your own twisted purposes."

"I'm doing no more to them than what will be done to my remains when my time comes," Dorian said simply. "Or to yours."

"Waste not, want not." Tafford snapped, the old arguments of twenty years past settled back into their old familiar ruts.

The steam-man pushed the last of the spoil atop the grave and patting it firm. Task completed, he returned to idle mode.

"How'd they die?" Tafford asked.

Dorian's pale colorless eyes flicked across the rind of flanking weather-beaten Tudors. "Not something I'd care to discuss outdoors, unwarded." The Albino nodded in the direction of the half-timbered tavern in all its shabby Tudor glory. "Shall we adjourn?"

The proprietary smugness on Greatorex's face suggested the aristocrat thought the *we* included him as well.

The first hesitant spatters of rain started to fall. "Shouldn't you be putting away your toy before it rusts?" Tafford asked Greatorex, titling his head at the idling steam-man.

Greatorex spun angrily on his heel to begin guiding the machine to safety under a dry shed.

Tafford and Dorian walked side by side toward the tavern as if it were the old days once again. As if ever could be the old days again. "What *do* you see in that man?" Tafford asked.

"At the very least he's here by my side when I need him."

"Only long enough to stick the knife in."

"Would his knife *could* kill me," a life-weary Dorian said, weary smile upon weary face.

The two of them passed through the door just as the spattering droplets turned to downpour.

⋀

DORIAN'S OFFICE lay on the uppermost floor of the tavern, back behind the cluttered workshops and libraries of the Chapter's magic-studying Books. Book-shelves lined the dark-paneled walls, filled with ancient books bound in crumbling leather and various knickknacks and magical curios.

A copper-rimmed military drum, emblazoned with a faded coat of arms, hung from white-clayed straps on a wall hook: Drake's Drum—the actual original artifact, not the counterfeited "original" stored in the nation's vaults or its replicated duplicate on display at Plymouth. This was the authentic Drum Dorian would one day use to draw out that leached magic from the potter's field on the purported Day of Last Resort.

Or animate their desiccated corpses. The legends differed and none could be proven true until the day of need.

Tafford angled his chair slightly before sitting down so he wouldn't have to look at the cursed thing.

Dorian stood by the opened liquor cabinet, staring at the clutch of bottles. "What do you drink these days?"

"Anything but gin. I'm still swimming in the stuff." Tafford frowned. "I swear Haines was trying to get me drunk, loosen up my tongue or something."

"Whereas I'd prefer you sober," Dorian said, handing him plain tonic water.

"Thanks," Tafford said. "I think Haines must suspect the BOAC rings."

"Bad."

"Worse. I think he's bent. I think the ATK's got at him. Maybe even got him." Tafford described the intercepted cable, his tail to the warehouse, and the forced entry.

Dorian poured himself a glass of tonic as well. "Let us hope Haines is merely a curious policeman. If he's ATK and the ATK have gotten wind of..." His voice trailed off. "No matter. This time. They're a day late and a Sextant short."

Tonic water splashed down the front of Tafford's khaki jacket as he jerked upright. "*Sextant?* Don't tell me you—"

"You wanted to know how those five men died," Dorian said. "They died retrieving the Sightless Sextant for us."

🜨

LORD GREATOREX, dripping from the deluge outside, barged in. He made an immediate beeline for the liquor cabinet, helping himself to Dorian's Scotch whisky. He poured himself a double before he sat down next to the roaring fire. "Still fussing about those guttersnipes? They served their purpose."

Tafford turned his head in a slow rachet. "Oh, they did. They most assuredly did," he said in tones as low and threatening as a great cat's growl.

"We needed the Sextant, didn't we?" Greatorex snapped. "There wasn't time to disarm Scowerer's wards."

"Time enough to comb the nearby pubs, though, search the paddocks for five sacrificial lambs."

"Gutter trash, the lot of them," sniffed Greatorex. "Gallows bait, the lot of them. Gallows bait who deserved to die."

Tafford surged out of his chair. Only the disapproving flick of Dorian's gaze stopped him, sat him back down in his chair again.

Pitch-coated logs popped in the fireplace, their burning coals glowing yellow-red.

Tafford unclenched his fists. "Tell me again why you need this fool?" he asked of Dorian. "There must be a dozen Books in the Chapter abler than him."

"Not in use of the Sextant." Dorian said, fingers cradled around his unused glass. "Lord Greatorex is our best cartomancer. We couldn't get anyone else up to speed in time."

Tafford angrily set his empty glass aside. "Ah, yes. Speed. That great excuser. Well, it stands to reason, doesn't it? *Die Toten reisen schnell.*"

The dead travel fast.

Again, the wraithlike gaze of Dorian's colorless eyes pressed hard upon Tafford. "We had no choice—Greatorex had him just that one chance. Scowrer gone up to York, his men nipped off to a pub leaving the storehouse unguarded—"

"Only it wasn't unguarded, was it?" Tafford said, slamming his fist on the arm of his chair. "Scowerer left his usual alchemic ward in place, hadn't he? Ælfweard's Ward. Certain death for the first five men who entered. *The first five!* And Greatorex knew it."

Anger flickered across the albino's face, a face that immediately smoothed itself back into preternatural calm again. "Yes, he knew it. And he also knew his skill wasn't up to the job. Not to disarming it. Not in time."

A snort of derision from Tafford. "He'd have been up to it if he was as good as you say he is. Your precious Greatorex here was just in a hurry, that's all, and never mind the cost. Grabbed the first five men he could find who'd rob the place for a guinea a head—and then deliberately let them step into the ward to deplete it, so he could follow on their heels unscathed."

"And what of it?" Greatorex sneered. "The world's hardly the worse for their passing and very much the better for us having the Sextant and not Scowrer."

"Didn't bother finding out their names, though, did you? We'll never ever know who they were."

"Does it matter?" the Albino asked Tafford, his voice as pale and colorless as his skin. "Not to *them*, surely. Not anymore."

"It matters to *me*, Dorian," Tafford said quietly. "And thirty years ago when we shared digs at Oxford, it would have mattered to you as well. Even twenty years ago you would have still understood death and dying. Now—?" He shrugged.

Dorian stared at his former friend with those pale eyes of his. Irises ice-flecked with the barest of thin, thin blue, the only remnant of his mortal coloring. That pale gaze flicked over every line, every aged crease in Tafford's well-worn, middle-aged face.

If Tafford had hoped for an *I still understand* from his once-friend it never came.

Fire logs crackled in the resultant silence.

⋀

Drinks and accusations finished, they adjourned to the Map Room.

The map-walled room looking more like some Army command center at Sandhurst rather than some sorcerous laboratory. Candle clerks with green eyeshades and sleeve stockings gripped elastic-tight on forearms bustled about as telegraph sounders clicked. Occasionally a Candle would remove color-coded stickpin flags from one of the wall maps or add some, depending on the clacking of the sounder.

A smile crept over the faces of the older timers among the Candles when Tafford nodded at them, only to instantly wilt when Greatorex caught them. The man was a true wonder, all right. Was Dorian blind? Why did he suffer the fool?

Lamplight glittered across the hourglass trinket on Dorian wrist as he spread a large map of Africa out across the main map table that dominated the center of the Map Room.

Greatorex sidled to the center of the table edge, the better to command the discussion. He jabbed his soft, uncalloused finger at the blue ink of paper Lake Victoria. "Here," he pronounced, as utterly certain as only a mand of modicum talents can be. "Here is where a moving Staircase will materialize. One week from now. Walpurgis Night."

"And you know this how?"

Greatorex snapped his fingers and one of the cowed Candles pressed into his hands a slim leatherbound volume fetched up from the cold-iron vault of the Chapter's Recknynge archives.

The title *Tabula Maledicta Cartesiana* in gold-flecked letters ran down the spine. Tafford shuddered. The Cartesian charts were a compilation of Alhazred's insane scribblings. The Cursed Atlas may not be perhaps as cursed as Alhazred's source tome, but Tafford wouldn't want to handle the derivative volume in so cavalier a fashion, knowing as he did what skin had supplied its leather binding.

"The Atlas doesn't lie. The Sextant doesn't lie," Greatorex preened.

"Calculations do," Tafford said. "Interpretations do."

Greatorex's face flushed red.

Before Mt. Vesuvius could erupt, however, Dorian traced ethereal fingers lightly across the lake's outline and in a soothing voice said, "Lord Greatorex ran the computations three times, Mallory. Three different methods. All congruent. We can trust the time and location."

Tafford grunted, as much back-down as he was willing to grudge. Cartomancy wasn't Dorian's field, but he knew enough to spot gross errors. "And the rest of it? Are you certain about this being a Consort's cavern?"

"Not just any Consort, Mallory," Greatorex said, his voice dripping with condescension, "but *the* Consort. The Egg-Layer. The Consort of the Cuttlefish himself."

At the merest sideways mention of Cthulhu—the merest euphemism!—the room's gaslights dimmed and the silver protective ward stones placed round the walls glowed moonlight blue.

Even sleeping, even slumbering, the terrible senses of the Elder Things permeated from afar.

"And you base all this merely on the word of the Mad Arab?" Tafford asked. "Doesn't the 'Mad' suggest anything to you?"

Greatorex hooked both thumbs in his waistcoat pockets. "I don't expect an unlearned ruffian like you to understand. We—Dorian and I—are Books. Because we read them. Because we know them. Because we use them." He snorted. "And do you know why we give you menial Bells that descriptor? Because when we want workmen like you, we ring for you."

"And here I thought you were called Books because you were so hidebound."

A tea kettle screamed in the background.

"Mallory," Dorian said, "believe me; I do understand your objections. I share them. Which is why I combed through the Recknynge for corroboration."

A Candle in the back of the room fiddled with a tea service. They would have all had theirs immediately after returning the graveside, of course. The tea must be meant for the principals. Dorian, Greatorex, and himself.

"I assume you found your corroboration, else we wouldn't still be discussing it," Tafford said.

Dorian nodded. "More people than Alhazred have chanced upon that particular Staircase. Talmage for one, during his African years. And Kalrebach."

"Only if you trust his *Die Finsternis*—which I don't." Tafford said. "I don't trust anything coming out of Vienna."

Tafford smiled at Greatorex's surprise that Tafford not only knew of Kalrebach's opus, but showed familiarity with it.

"Oh, yes," Tafford said to Greatorex, "we Bells *can* read. And occasionally some of us actually do."

Tea things, cups and saucers, clattered in the back of the room.

Dorian smoothed out a folded letter and handed it to Tafford. "Read this. I think you'll find this much harder to dismiss than Kalrebach."

Tafford recognized the signature at once. You needn't have tramped around Africa for a decade to know the name of Dr. David Livingston, the renowned African explorer of "Stanley & Livingston" fame. The letter, written on crumpled scrap paper torn from the flyleaf of some book, was penned in Livingston's distinctive crabbed hand.

The letter should not exist.

"Where did you get this?" Tafford demanded.

Every English schoolboy knew the sad story of Livingston's end, how he'd gone mad from witnessing a brutal slaver's raid-turned-massacre in '71, how he'd then hidden himself away in the interior of darkest Africa, refusing all attempts—even Stanley's—to bring him back to civilization, back home to England. How half-mad and sick with fever, he'd famously attempted to send out forty-four different dispatches from the interior of Africa to the nearest outpost of civilization. Only one had ever made it to Zanzibar on the coast, and that particular scrawled page, addressed to a fellow anti-slavery crusader, proved completely indecipherable save for the phrase "doubtful if I live to see you again."

That one known missive was *not* the letter Tafford now held in his hand.

The one Tafford held contained concise, precise, and utterly unhinged notes about stumbling upon a Staircase on the shores of Lake Victoria, about descending down that Staircase to witness firsthand the Consort's cavern. Much of the third page was taken up with Livingston's scientifically-trained sketches of the cavern and of a very recognizable and very gravid Consort.

"We intercepted it, of course," Dorian said. "Intercepted it as we did its forty-two brothers. We couldn't let Livingston's writings get loose among the British public. A man of Livingston's training both as a scientist and theologian, not to mention his world fame as an explorer, would have been believed."

"And so you left Livingston to rot in the African interior," Tafford said. He paused. "No," he said, putting the pieces together, "you *kept* him in the interior away from the press. Imprisoned him. Immured him behind a wall of jungle."

Dorian gave the faintest of shrugs. "Arab slavers are remarkably cheap to bribe. Particularly when their 'houseguest' is the very man about to eradicate their trade."

"Why didn't you just kill him outright and be done with it?" Tafford spat.

"I wasn't in charge at the time." No remorse, no regret. There really was nothing left of the Dorian he'd known.

Dorian took back the letter, yellowed paper in alabaster hands. "It wasn't the Source of the Nile Livingston was searching for. It was the Staircase. Livingston must have gotten hold of a copy of Alhazred from one of the Arab slavers." He refolded the letter and handed it to a waiting Candle. "Well, he found the Staircase alright, the purblind fool."

"And the Chapter killed him for it."

Dorian's eyes actually flashed with anger. "The old fool thought he could use the Staircase to eradicate the slave trade. Saw it not just as access to power, but power itself. And worse, sold others on that view, including that thrice-damnable freebooter Stanley." His pale eyes bore into Tafford. "Or do you think it coincidence that Europe's mad scramble for Africa started as soon as Stanley returned with news of the moving Staircase? That Stanley himself carved out the Congo Basin for Belgium? That Germany seized the western shore of Lake Victoria? Tell me, Mallory—would you really trust access to the Staircase to power-mad Bismarck?"

A Candle appeared at Tafford's shoulder offering a cup of tea. White steam curled, but the aroma fell flat. Nothing ever tasted right in Chapter offices with all its myriad wards in place. Tafford took the proffered cup and spooned idly. "He's hardly the only one power-mad."

He nodded at spot on the map Greatorex had pointed to—a spot on the German side of Lake Victoria. "You're talking about German sovereign territory here."

"I'm talking about a million Cuttlefish eggs from hatching Walpurgis night," Dorian retorted. "A million Cuttlefish fingerlings squirming up the Staircase into our world.

A million Cuttlefish when only one was enough to destroy all life on the globe.

No wonder Dorian would take any action to prevent it, from killing explorers to risking war with Germany.

And risk it all for nothing anyway, because...

"You'll never destroy a million eggs in time," Tafford said.

"We don't have to destroy them," Dorian said. "Merely stop them from hatching.

"That's why we sent for you," Greatorex said with a smile, the same toothy shark-smile he must have worn when hiring those five unknowns in the pub that day. "We've a little job for you. Simple, really."

Tafford matched him with a predator's smile just as dangerous. "As simple as walking into a warded warehouse?"

"Quite," Greatorex replied.

And it was. A very simple plan. And a desperate and surely fatal one.

꙳

MIDNIGHT TOLLED before the meeting broke up. Despite not having slept for over forty-eight hours, rather than stagger sleepily to the flat the Chapter kept for him in one of those buildings circling the potter's field, Tafford instead stepped outside, stepped into the potter's field itself to clear his head. To remind at least himself of the Chapter's cost of doing business.

Cold for late April. Chill and damp turned Tafford's breath to curl white.

A feeble half-moon peeked down from behind scudding midnight clouds. Save for the barking of a dog, the tumult and clatter of the city had faded into nothingness and shadow. Quiet as the grave, the freshly mounded grave Tafford stood at the foot of.

Five unknowns lay beneath that packed dirt. Five unknowns denied the graveside comforts given even the most wretchedly damned. Dorian had said his Words of power over their cast-off bodies. Very well. Let him. Tafford would say his own words, words of comfort to these unknown wantons.

Golden slumbers kiss your eyes,
Smiles awake you when you rise.

His breath caught, but he continued.

Care is heavy, therefore sleep you;
You are care, and care must keep you;
Sleep, pretty wantons; do not cry,
And I will sing a lullaby...

And if the mounded spoil glimmered silver-blue for the merest of moments, that was surely only an artifact of the shifting moonlight.

"Thomas Dekker? An interesting choice," a thin voice said behind him.

Tafford turned. Dorian stood there ethereal in the moonlight, as if not quite fully a part of this mortal coil.

"You have it within you to be a Book, Mallory, should you ever choose. The needed spark, I mean."

"Any divine spark I ever possessed has long been snuffed out," Tafford said.

Dorian looked at the fresh-turned dirt at his booted feet. "Curious." He toed one clump of dirt still maintaining somehow the faintest of blue glow. The clod fell apart from the prodding, losing its glow. "Dekker was never one of us, and yet you were nearly able to use his Lullaby to—"

"To do what?" Tafford contended. "Undo your foul leeching? Undo your desecration of the dead? Nothing I could say, nothing I could ever do would undo what you've done. What you will continue to do long after I'm dead and gone and buried here, one of *them*."

"That's exhaustion talking, Mallory. You need sleep."

"Do I?" Tafford spat. He gazed down at the dead beneath his feet. "*I hold you ever, ever in my thoughts/Now I must sleep but you must dance.*" He kicked viciously at the loose dirt. "Poor old Theodor Storm had it backward, didn't he? It is they who sleep and I who must dance," he said. "Dance ever to *your* tune, your siren song of saving the living at the expense of the dead."

A breath of wind stirred, blowing wisps of long white hair across Dorian's ageless face.

Standing there before a man who could not age, could not even die, the full weight of Tafford's fifty mortal years pressed down on him, smashed him down almost to the breaking point. "It's the same always everywhere, isn't it? The living do what they can, the dead suffer what they must."

White vapor curled from Dorian's mouth. At last he spoke. "You can't save the dead, Mallory. Only bury therm."

"Salvation," snapped Tafford, "is built by the living upon the bones of the dead." His hands balled into helpless fists. "Salvation. Civilization. The ages' slow bought gain. Everything we have or are was first purchased by our dead. Surely we owe them a place at our council tables. Surely we owe them a vote. Surely when we're saving ourselves, we owe it to them to save *them* as well."

"If the Cuttlefish win, we're all lost," Dorian said, weary resignation in his voice. "The living. The dead. All of us. The Elder Ones would enslave us all."

Tafford stepped past his friend without even a glance. "And that's all that keeping me from putting a well-placed bullet into you, into Kilrea, into the whole lot of us."

Head bowed, Tafford trudged off to bed, to sleep, to dream, and perchance to make amends.

♫

THE HARSH GLARE of the afternoon sun slanted through the bedroom's half-shuttered window, finally waking a dead-to-the-world Tafford. He yawned and stretched, knuckles brushing faded velvet wallpaper. He swung his legs over the mattress edge and stood to face the half-spent day and its sufficient evils thereof.

Twelve hours of uninterrupted sleep had done nothing to change his opinion of the looming plan, but a soft bed with clean sheets and the first civilized bath in a fortnight had at least made Tafford feel somewhat human again.

Though not officially a member, the Chapter still kept rooms for Tafford on the upper floor of one of the Tudor buildings horseshoeing the fallow field. This included a wardrobe of the latest London fashions, all tailored perfectly. Dorian's doing, of course. Usually, Tafford considered such things waste and nonsense, but just this once, having abandoned his kit back in Calcutta, Tafford grudgingly appreciated it.

He donned a pair of checked wool trousers, starched white shirt with black cravat, and a dark frock jacket. The clothes all smelt of mothballs. The naphthalene aroma would dull his ability to "sniff" out the wind, but then again, he'd hardly be needing to track wild beasts through the macadamed streets of Deptford.

Speaking of stepping outside...

"Kit?" Tafford half-called. After a moment's wait, the faint spectre appeared.

The ectoplasmic thing that styled itself a poet's ghost had expanded its hauntings to include all Chapter outbuildings, not just the Deptford tavern proper.

"The Dutchman in yet?" Tafford asked the ghost. That fool plan depended heavily on the Dutchman. Tafford would need a word with the Dutchman then, away from prying eyes and ears.

The ectoplasm counterfeited a nod. *"Thou wouldst do well/To waite at my trencher and tell me lies at dinner-time,"* it recited.

Tafford grunted a thanks. The backrooms for him then.

The Chapter used the bottom floor of its namesake tavern as a working public house for Chapter members. A place members could socialize at and get drunk in and still discuss Chapter secrets without compromising security. It was also the last place Greatorex would deign step foot in, crammed as it was with plebian Candles. And as for Dorian, the albino had ceased partaking in mundane pleasures since first contracting the Curse.

A quick glance out the window showed a dismal cloudy day, one far cooler than the calendar suggested. Tafford shrugged on a sleeveless Inverness cape. Force of habit caused Tafford to pat his pockets, checking contents before setting out from his room. One jacket pocket felt uncomfortably empty. Sheepishly, he dropped his bulldog revolver into it. He wouldn't need it.

Lastly, reluctantly, he fastened the Chapter phylactery around his wrist. Out in the field he could pretend it was just equipment worn for function. Here it was a statement of identity, of loyalty to a cause and a creed Tafford had walked away from. But he'd need it for...

No, he wouldn't need it to talk to the Dutchman. He had no BOACs to step through today.

He undid the clasp and dropped the relic into a pocket. He could be true to himself—and others—at least that much.

Kɪᴛ ꜰᴏʟʟᴏᴡᴇᴅ Tafford down the boarding house's narrow hallway to the top of the landing. Down at the bottom of the stairs a man stood waiting for Tafford.

Turtle Landry.

A short man, as bald and beak-nosed and bandy-legged as his namesake. He stood with hands jammed into the enormous pockets of a shabby workman's overcoat.

Kit sniffed imperiously. *"What, are the Turtles fraide out of their neastes?"* he jibed. The phantasm had never gotten along with Landry and his hooligan team of Bells that guarded the Chapter complex.

"That's enough, Kit," Tafford snapped. "Meet me with the Dutchman later."

The phantasm sniffed again, then faded from sight.

Tafford clomped down the rickety squeaking stairs. He stopped two stairs up from the bottom. "Something I can do for you, Landry?"

The little man looked up at him. "You might tell me why some snooper would be hiding in the alley opposite holding a photograph of you in his hand." he replied. His breath stank of black licorice. The little man usually carried a half-pound of sweets on him.

"ATK?" Tafford asked.

Turtle's eyes narrowed. "And that's the first thing you ask?" He shook his head. "Just some local street artist. Doesn't seem to be carrying the Token, no. " He popped a lump of licorice into his mouth. "But he stank of ATK." A paid informant then. "You in some new tangle with them?"

Tafford relayed the account of himself and Haines' men and his suspicions about BOACs.

Turtle bobbed his head. "I see. So if you suddenly show up here when you should be in Calcutta, they'll have proof. Hence the snooper."

"Hence the snooper." Tafford agreed. "I suppose you're here to tell me there could be more than just the one snooper and to not got out by the front door." Going out the back door would mean crossing the potter's field in daylight, seeing that fresh turned dirt again...

Turtle just stood there chewing his licorice cud. "Like you'd listen to me. Like an army of snoopers could spot you if you didn't want them to."

One last chew and a big swallow. ""No, I'm just here to ask you leave him be. Coshing him over the head would just convince him you were indeed here." The beak-nosed man chawed for a moment. "Besides, Razor Neddie wants to follow him home to his new friends. If ATK really is back in town, I'd like to know."

Turtle reached into the vast expanse of his overcoat pocket and pulled out a *papier-mâché* frowning Melpomene mask. He tossed it at Tafford. "Here. Italian, unfortunately, not one of ours, but it will make things easier on both of us."

Tafford caught the mask. A line of text etched in the rune-like ancient Etruscan alphabet ran around its rim. A Dramatis Masque. He couldn't have used one against an ATK man, or course—the masque reeked of magic which ATK would detect immediately—but it would suffice against a common street tough.

"Picked out a carpenter mask for you," Turtle said. "Nothing a footpad wants to look least at than some honest bloke going about gainfully employed."

Tafford pressed the papier-mâché mask to his face. It instantly bonded. An ethereal warmth ran through his entire body. He began to shimmer with light. The shimmer coalesced into a new and different appearance. To all mortal eyes he now appeared to be a different person, even down to his clothing. It even appeared he held a wooden tool box full of carpenter tools in his left hand.

The illusion would last the few minutes necessary to get past the snooper.

Tafford stepped past the little man toward front door. *"Pupillam excedens magister,"* he grudged.

Turtle doffed his cap as Tafford passed. "Oh, I had a good teacher," he muttered in a whisper meant only for himself. "I just wish he'd come back to the firm."

∩

For the first time in years, Tafford stepped out in broad daylight into the bustling streets of London—and immediately regretted it.

London in the Year of Our Lord 1889 reigned supreme as the greatest and grandest city in all creation. Six-and-a-half million souls stacked on top of each other all higgledy-piggledy.

Even a sleepy corner of Greater London had its streets packed stem-to-stern by horse-drawn conveyances of all shapes and sizes, and Deptford and its docks were no sleepy corner. The cacophony of iron-shod horse hooves clopping on pavement, the clatter of carriage wheels, the shouting and whip cracking of drivers.

And the smell! The stench! No amount of cloying naphthalene could mask the foulness.

Every horse in that stem-to-stern process seemingly kept its fly-blown tail lifted, dropping odious souvenirs each clop along the way. The whole of Bleecker Street—the entire length and breadth of its macadamed surface—lay covered in a half-inch mushy carpet of green manure, squashed and re-squashed flat by those clopping hooves and spinning wheels. An army of dustmen couldn't begin to keep up.

For the first time in his life Tafford found himself somewhat sympathetic to those gadget-mad Americans and their mania for self-pulled steam engine vehicles. While all their engines would have added to the noxious coal-smoke of a million hearths and kitchen stoves, at the least the streets would be clean and free of flies and maggots.

Tafford almost longed for Calcutta and the squalor and filth of honest poverty.

Maybe after his Staircase mission was over, Tafford would swear off cities and people and noise and confusion. Maybe lose himself in the arctic wilds of the Canadian north. The Wendigo could use culling again.

Shrugging, he stepped out of the doorway. Out of the corner of his hunter's eye, he noticed the darkened alley opposite and a malnourished hooligan awkwardly hiding behind a battered dustbin. The snooper didn't give the masked Tafford even a second glance; neither did Tafford give him one in return.

Instead, Tafford strode down Bleeker and around its horseshoe bend out of sight.

The Dramatis Masque's enchantment lasted just long enough for Tafford to reach the front door of a seedy-looking public house before its virtue was spent and the mask fell from his face, crumbling into plaster dust.

THE DILAPIDATED TAVERN on the horseshoe bend of Bleecker Street sported no name, the Chapter not wanting to draw attention to itself. Locals, when they bothered to think about the old tavern at all, called it the Bleaker-On-Bleecker or the Old Stewpot, usually accompanied by a sneer on their faces.

The tavern's ancient rebus sign—the once brightly-painted wooden sign that swing above the door from a wrought-iron arm held no clue to its forgotten name. Only a few peeling flakes of faded paint clung to its grimy surface. Old timers in the Chapter claimed a black cat once used to grace the lefthand side of the sign, so Chapter members—being in the profession they were and black cats having the reputation they had—took to calling the place the Old Familiar.

Tafford pulled open the weather-beaten door and stepped inside, regretting it instantly as he had stepping out into the street.

He blinked against the gloomy darkness. A sickening wave of foul odors all but staggered him—decades of stale beer sploshed about on unmopped floors, sour sweat of unwashed wastrels packed cheek-to-jowl, and from the back kitchen greasy rancid mutton on the boil. The floor under his feet felt tacky with spilt beer. A vocal cacophony of crude billingsgate and murderous oaths assaulted his ears.

The cacophony suddenly stopped and every eye in the place turned toward him. A more perfect murderer's row of cutthroats, thieves, and inbred maniacs could scarce be imagined. They stood up and advanced on him. Snaggled yellow teeth gleamed as their mouths opened into a gleeful rictus.

Every cell of his body screamed at Tafford to back out the way he'd entered, but instead he shakily reached out with his left hand to a shelf of lined-up Toby mugs. He grabbed the one mug shaped in the masked face of highwayman Dick Turpin and spun it clockwise a full three-sixty degrees.

The five-senses illusion popped like a soap bubble.

The Chapter could very well have warded the Old Familiar to keep all outsiders out, but that would have raised more questions that the Chapter wanted asked. Far better to camouflage instead. Let the occasional tourist who wandered in back themselves out immediately, let the locals spread word against that 'orrible place on the bow curve of Bleecker.

Tafford stood in a well-lighted spacious pub, clean wooden floors gleaming with wax and polish.

The homey aroma of broiled savory meats wafted from the back kitchen. The bar's beer-sipping denizens weren't murderous fiends at all but stout-hearted common English-folk. The most menacing crew in the place were a bunch of peach-fuzzed youths in the back corner playing coddem and hooting gleefully at the losers.

The rictus-faced manias approaching him were grinning old friends—old timer Bells and Candles Tafford had served with in years past—making a beeline for him to welcome him with back pats and heartfelt handshakes. Even those who'd never met him seemed happy at his arrival.

That last disquieted Tafford. They were all men and women who believed in the Chapter, believed in Dorian and The Cause. In turning his back on Dorian and the Chapter by leaving hadn't Tafford turned his back on them, too? Why were they so happy to see him? And yet they were.

Tafford shook proffered hands, nodding to those he knew and smiling at the rest. He gently pushed past the crush of well-wishers and made his way to the bar. Aunt Ethel, the proprietress, already had a gin-and-tonic poured for him.

Crab-faced and shovel-nosed, Ethel Maltby had never been what one could call a handsome woman. A decade on the wrong side of fifty, her face wrinkles had deepened into yawning chasms. "I'll suppose you'll be wanting your supper then," she said, her rasping voice that of a corpse-gorged crow. "Lunch crowd near cleaned me out. All I have left is cold Wolvercote Tongue and half a pan of Shepherd's Pie."

The mere mention of food set Tafford's stomach growling. He realized his last meal had been back in Sthanadharaka village, a full forty-eight hours ago. Even so, he'd rather eat a belt-buckle than Wolvercote Tongue, especially cold. "Shepard's Pie, then. In fact, send the entire pan to the backroom," he told Aunt Ethel. "I'm assuming that's where…" Tafford's voice trailed off. *Where the Dutchman is* went unsaid. In the Great Game of secret societies like the Chapter, walls had ears.

Sometimes literally.

He glanced around. "Greatorex hasn't been down here, has he?" he asked her.

Aunt Ethel snorted. "Him? Our high-bred lord-and-master? Rub elbows with us lot?" She snorted again.

"If not him, then, perhaps friends of his?"

"Toffs like him don't have friends," Aunt Ethel spat. "But if you mean paid toadies, there's that Oswald and we know all about *him*."

"This Oswald. He didn't see—" Tafford paused. "He didn't see the *guest* in the backroom did he?".

Aunt Ethel snorted. "The only thing Oswald saw after coming in here was the back of his own eyelids. Put Lullaby Drops in his first beer, I did. Out like a light after just two sips. Had Turtle and his boys toss him out on his unconscious ear." Her beady eyes narrowed in wicked glee. "Hopefully he's lying in some nearby alley drowning in his own vomit."

"By any chance did Oswald leave any—?"

Aunt Ethel reached under the counter and produced a small doll-like object. She set it on the bar. "Like this you mean?"

The doll was a Javanese Tattletale. Its crude, rudimentary body was merely batik cloth, coarse as burlap, stuffed and sewn together. Its grotesque Javanese head, a distorted leering face with oversized ears and eyes had been cunningly carved from Djakarta teak. The doll's eyes, and ears, and tattletale mouth were covered by daubs of mashed potatoes, rendering it useless as a spying device.

"I said we know all about Oswald, didn't I? All his little ways." She returned the Tattletale back under the counter.

Tafford relaxed. Relaxed enough to back the glass of gin that sat waiting for him on the counter. He set the empty down.

"A second-liker?" Aunt Ethel queried, holding up the gin bottle from which the first drink had been poured.

Tafford shook his head. He hadn't really wanted the first one. He wasn't really much of a drinker, but out of politeness he usually drank what was offered. Unfortunately, people had it in their head that Tafford was partial to gin. In truth he despised the nasty stuff, the pink variety in particular.

Drink downed and meal ordered, Tafford was about to push himself away from the bar and head to the backroom Aunt Ethel locked eyes with him.

"It's all very well to play the lad on occasion," she said, glaring at him with studied import, "but you've been off on holiday much too long. When are you going to stop larking about and come back to your job here?"

"I didn't realize I had a job here. I quit the Chapter, remember?"

To that Aunt Ethel only made a rude noise. "Look," she said. "We all know Mr. Dorian—he's a good man, a grand man. A man of learning and vision. We'd follow 'im past the gates of Hell, we would, if he asked us." She picked up her cleaning cloth and started polishing again. "But vision and learning don't do the running the place day-to-day, now does it? They don't see the lads get their pay packets regular like. Don't see the usual argy-bargies on the shop floor get settled peaceable-like. That's *your* job—and you've left it vacant far too long, you have. Long enough for that Lord Greater-Wrecks to come along and think it's his for the taking."

She set down the cloth yet again and this time began to wring her fingers. "That Lord Greatorex, he's a right and proper bad'un, he is. Bad for the lads, bad for the Chapter, bad for England and the World, come to that." She looked at him with pleading eyes. "Unless you slap him down—and there's no one else who can do it—he'll end up pushing Mr. Dorian right out as well. And then Cuttlefish'll have all our guts for garters, they will."

∩

THE BACKROOM WASN'T the cramped, dimly-lit warren Tafford remembered. Unlike the rest of the gas-lit Chapter, the backroom was now lit by new-fangled electric incandescent light bulbs. Two of Swan's Best new filament bulbs dangled from braided electric cords in the ceiling, burning noon-bright above the huge oak-planked table that filled most of the room. A sizable collection of dirty plates and empty beer glasses littered its surface. Stout wooden chairs surrounded the table. One was massive, double the width and stoutness of the other two.

On the far side of the table in one of the regular chairs sat the Dutchman. An ornate women's hat, complete with a thick almost-opaque veil dangling from its brim hung on the wall. Even a life-long bachelor like Tafford could see that neither the color or style of the hat matched the Dutchman's high-collared Continental dress of crushed velvet and lace.

Very blonde and very blue-eyed, Miss Veronike Mertens was neither Dutch or man. She hailed from Belgium. Of Flemish descent, she was one of the best diamond cutters in Antwerp. Like many other gem cutters in the Low Countries, Veronike secretly practiced the art of lapidomancy—the fashioning and use of magic stones. Like Tafford, she occasionally sold her arcane talents to the Chapter.

From the agitated look on her face, Tafford suspected this might be the last time she'd work with the Chapter.

She made to speak as Tafford sat down, but Tafford held a finger to his lips, silencing her. He set the bronze cube of his voice scrambler on the table. He switched it on with an audible click.

"What is going on, Mallory?" Veronike demanded.

Tafford sighed. "I was hoping you could tell me."

Veronike continued as if she had not heard him. "Your horrid little licorice man meets me at the station as agreed. Then without so much as a by-your-leave, he slaps that wretched beekeeper's bonnet—" she jabbed an imperious finger at the hat with the veil—" on my head, then marches me in here practically under lock and key. Under guard, even! Is your precious Chapter that ashamed of having to hire an outsider? *Absurdité!*"

Tafford eyed the cluster of empty beer mugs. From the quantity it was not hard to deduce her keeper. "Speaking of guards, where is our redoubtable Mister Jones?"

Veronike sniffed. "Your redoubtable Deuteronomy Jones has gone where any man who drinks an entire barrel of beer eventually goes."

"Ah," Tafford said. Embarrassed, he cleared his throat and changed the subject. "You weren't taken up to see a Lord Greatorex, were you?"

"I was taken here, I told you! Bodily!" Veronike said, blue eyes flashing. "I know no Lord whatever-you-said. I was cabled by Dorian as usual. Usual fee, usual contract. All by telegram."

Tafford frowned. The answers to his questions only seemed to sprout new questions. Maybe Deuteronomy could answer them.

As if on cue, a great elephantine clomping sound reverberated outside the door. The door pushed open and the great bulk of Deuteronomy Jones followed in its wake. A ruddy-faced chap with triple chins, Jones looked like he weighed in at well over three hundred pounds. Or would have done if he were neatly cut in half vertically. The left side of Deuteronomy was still all too, too solid flesh. His right side, however, was a crude copper-and-brass clockwork half-body, a mockery of human form. Face, eye, torso and limbs all made of cold, insensate metal gleaming under the harsh electric lighting.

Yet, despite his grotesque, horrible fate, Deuteronomy's face held a wide grin. Here was a man who loved his meat and drink, loved company, loved life— even a half-life.

"Mallory!" he boomed happily when he saw Tafford. "Finally awake at last!" He made to shake Tafford's hand, then stopped. "No. First things first," he said, turning away. "Can't let the batteries run flat." He pulled out a spooled electric cord from his brass chest plate and plugged it into a wall socket.

"Ahhh!" he sighed and sank into a chair. "Electrical ambrosia! Fresh from the London Electric Supply Company's own Deptford plant! Much handier than that kerosene engine I used to have to strap to my back."

"I was wondering why they electrified this room," Tafford said.

"My home away from home," Deuteronomy boomed. He pointed to the far wall. "You can't see the door, of course, but there's a bed and a bath beyond. Oh, they wired up my office upstairs, too. But this is closer to refreshments."

"Well maybe you can shed some electric light on what's going on around here," Tafford snapped. "I had a rather interesting conversation with Greatorex last night with Dorian hanging around like Hamlet in the background. They want me to go down a Staircase."

Deuteronomy didn't act too surprised. "One hopes you'll be coming back up."

"A lady Cuttlefish is laying eggs. Greatorex seems to think that if I sneak down the stairs and steal some Makelike the Fishmen priests have made of the eggs and bring it back up for the Dutchman to destroy, the eggs won't hatch."

Deuteronomy nodded. "Sympathetic magic, yes."

"The odd thing is," Tafford continued, "Greatorex made great noises about it all being his plan. Yet he didn't know who the Dutchman was—kept referring to Veronike as *he*—and Greatorex seemed to think the Makelike is a crystal figurine about the size of a salt cellar." He pointed to the shaker on the table.

The half-mechanical man snorted. "Greatorex only knows cartomancy. Doesn't know beggar-all about any other kind of magic, sympathetic or otherwise."

"Neither do I, really," Tafford said. "But I know enough to know a Makelike of a Cuttlefish egg would have to be the same size of a Cuttlefish egg. Roughly the size of rugger ball." He glanced at Veronike. "And I know you don't hire a diamond cutter to smash a crystal, you hire a diamond cutter to cut diamonds."

Veronike bolted upright, eyes widened. "Wait. Are we talking about—?"

"A diamond close to a foot in length. Yes."

Veronike gabbled at the thought. "B-but even the H-Hope Diamond's only an inch across! Something like that would be worth—"

"Millions," Tafford finished. "And Greatorex doesn't know about it."

"Greatorex, Greatorex, Greatorex!" Veronike snapped. "Who is this Greatorex?"

"Lord Greatorex is the man trying to take over the Chapter," Tafford said.

"Is that good? Is that bad?" she asked.

Deuteronomy's half-lip curled upward. "The Greatorex family crest is a mounted nobleman in riding pinks riding down a peasant as if he was a hart or hind. The Greatorex family motto is *Hounds, Blood, and Bayonets*."

Tafford gave the half-man an icy stare. The memories of the potter's field last night were too raw for levity, the mounded dirt over the cold, cold grave too fresh. "Greatorex is the kind of man who, with no remorse at all, killed five men this week to get what he wanted. He isn't the kind of man you give a foot-long diamond too. Or millions of pounds, either."

He ran his fingers over his forehead. "Last night, I thought the plan actually was Greatorex's; not knowing I knew Veronike, he was hoping to use me as an unwitting dupe." He looked at Veronike. "But I know now he's never met the Dutchman, so the plan must be Dorian's after all." He smiled wanly. "He maneuvered Greatorex into it."

The half-metal man chuckled. "With a little help from me slipping Dorian information on the Makelike on the sly. I was there the night those two hashed it out. Greatorex's original idea was to march an army down the Staircase and smash or blast every egg to Kingdom Come."

"The Chapter doesn't have an army."

"He wanted to use Drake's Drum," Deuteronomy said. "Dorian talked him out of it. Said, 'Mallory wouldn't like that.' Then the blue-blooded fool proposed digging up African graves and sending down an army of native zuvembies. 'Mallory wouldn't like that either.' Then Dorian sold Greatorex on the plan of sending you down."

The pieces clicked into place. "Dorian doesn't trust Greatorex with the diamond either."

Deuteronomy swished the scant remains of one of the empty mugs, as if hoping for one last decent-sized swallow. "He trusts us to fix it so Greatorex never even knows about it. He can't. Greatorex has his eye on him. Us, we're beneath the great man's notice."

"Easier said than done," Tafford said. Greatorex would insist on being there at Lake Victoria in order to claim credit for the operation. He meant to use it as a lever to pry his way into Dorian's chair. The Dutchman would have to be there to render the Makelike useless. And how do you hide a rugger-sized diamond? How do you hide destroying it?

The three of them talked it out the rest of the evening, coming up with only a doubtful plan at best. Tafford knew there was only one sure way to solve the problem of Greatorex. Maybe he did have reason for the bulldog in his pocket after all.

THE STALE SMELL of supper hung heavy in the small backroom. To Tafford, used to the outdoors or at the very least a window to let in fresh air, the room's closeness seemed a prison stouter than Newgate, its whitewashed walls oppressive as any steel bars.

Tafford paced the room, irritable as caged tiger.

Deuteronomy looked up from the stack of leather-bound volumes he was working on. A thin wheel-and-cog studded slender brass rod—an electric-powered version of Alhazred's fabled *Etaoin-Shrdulu* quill pen—whined in his hand as he carefully inscribed footnotes on the parchment pages, glosses for new Book recruits. "Oh, do stop pacing, Mallory," the half-man growled. "You're making me as nervous as you are."

Veronike, silver fork in her hand, picked at her nearly-untouched meal. "You English! What you do to perfectly good ingredients with your so-called cooking is a crime! You me serve this—this Wolvercote Tongue!—without a shred of remorse!"

Deuteronomy's mechanical eye rotated toward her lizard-like. "That presumed the cooks had morse in the first place," he chuckled. The eye rotated toward Tafford next. "And do stop pacing, Mallory! We can't do anything until the Candles finish anyway."

"I know that," Tafford snapped, but he sat down as requested. He knew as well as Deuteronomy that a small army of Candles were setting up a temporary BOAC ring on the eastern shores—the British side—of Lake Victoria.

The advent of mechanical steam-men meant the herculean effort to build the East African Railway—a route stretching four thousand miles from Mombasa on the Indian Ocean coast to Lake Victoria—could start ten years earlier than even the most wide-eyed optimist could have dreamed. A battalion of mechanical steam-men had stoically carved a railway through African heat and dust and malarial breeding grounds—taming a region that would have killed crews of mere humans by the hundreds. Yet even these hulking metal monsters were still fifty miles short of the lake.

Even before Tafford had arrived in London, the Candles had disassembled the BOAC ring in Mombasa and shipped it to the railroad's construction terminus. Then began the long, arduous slog to lug the pieces through the East Africa jungle. Until they could reassemble it and start portaging the expedition equipment through, there was nothing for Tafford or Deuteronomy or even Dorian to do.

Deuteronomy continued his inscribing. The high-pitched whirring gears sounded like tiny drills, causing Tafford's teeth to ache. Like chalk upon a blackboard. "Must you do that here?" Tafford asked.

"Glossing texts is what I do around here, when I'm not babysitting diamond cutters and big game hunters," Deuteronomy said absent-mindedly as he concentrated on his scribblings. "About all I'm good for. Glossator." He looked up. "Can't go out on hunts as a Bell anymore, too clumsy and crippled to Candle, lack the innate arcane aptitude to be a full-fledged Book."

Tafford opened his mouth, then shut it. What was there to say to the crippled man?

Scritch, scritch. "You'd be good at this, Mallory. You've the scholarly background and the memory."

"I have a trade." Tafford snapped. "And it doesn't involve sitting behind a desk."

Deuteronomy set down the pen. Its tiny squealing motors idled down to silence. "Be honest with yourself. Even setting death or disfigurement aside, how many more years can you hunt? Three? Five? Hunting's a young man's game."

Tafford bristled. "So, you've joined the rest of the choir in demanding I come back to the Chapter, have you?"

"Who said anything about you coming back here?" the half-man demanded, his jaw rachet clacking. "You can become a tour guide for the British Museum for all I care. All I'm saying is you need to plan for your future. I didn't and look at me."

"Sorry." Tafford said dully.

"I just thought—" Deuteronomy continued. "I just thought that all the Books I've ever met, Dorian included, all go around collecting spells the way a philatelist collects first day issue stamps. Never interested in how those spells came to be. Never interested in the origins of magic at all. You are. I saw how you haunted the archives in our younger days. It's something you're good at. It's something I think the world needs."

He picked up his pen and spun it up to life again. "You can't go through life always shooting things. Bullets don't solve everything, you know."

Deuteronomy suddenly let out a roar in Reconstructed Pictish and flung the book he was working on against the wall.

What the devil? Tafford was on his feet looking for some unseen arcane threat that may have jumped out of the book due to careless handling.

Deuteronomy was doing some looking, too, of a sort. He was pawing through the rest of the stack of books, muttering under his breath.

"Blast, blast, blast!" he roared as he reached the last volume. "All of them!" The half-man smashed metal fist to table. "The fool! That unmitigated fool!"

He calmed himself, then his flesh half grinned wanly at Tafford. "A while back, our precious Lord Greatorex brought in a job lot of books. Regular jumble sale, it was. Some of it was really first rate. Some of it barely primer-level like these. Wanted to show Dorian he had contacts outside the Chapter, I guess. Wouldn't say where he'd got them."

More imprecations in forgotten tongues, this time coldly muttered. "I know where now. All of these—and I shouldn't wonder the rest of his rubbish—are all Viennese adulterations."

Vienna had the well-deserved reputation of being the hub of magical research on the Continent. It also had the equally deserved reputation of being the capital of magical forgery. The Dual Monarchy of Austria-Hungary wasn't a country, it was an unworkable amalgamation of disparate peoples. And those disparate peoples hated each other.

The Germanic Austrians hated the Magyar Hungarians, both hated their captive Balkan Slavic peoples to the south. The Slavs, splintered into a hundred factions and ethnicities, hated each other almost as much as they hated their dual masters to the North.

In such a political cesspit as that, power is everything. Truth is power, knowledge is power—and arcane knowledge the most powerful of all. Of course Vienna would become a hotbed of scholarship with uncounted numbers of ethno-cliques vying for supremacy. The city would naturally become a nexus of arcane forgery and alteration, each group trying to hide truth from each other—and naive outsiders such as Greatorex. Sometimes it was only a word or line altered, sometimes an entire work. But in magic—like in mathematics—a single altered line could render the rest nonsense—or even calamitous.

Tafford didn't try anything that came from Vienna.

The half-man sighed. "I shall have to go through the entire lot, page by page. Sort the wheat from the chaff."

"That will have to wait," a voice said from the doorway. Dorian had slipped into the room during all of Deuteronomy's histrionics. "The Candles have gotten the Lake Victoria BOAC assembled. They're transshipping equipment now. We set out in seven hours, so get some sleep while you can."

ᚾ

Tafford decided to share Deuteronomy's cramped little Chapter backroom flat. He saw no reason to risk slipping past the ATK simply for the dubious privilege of a soft bed. Besides, just like the Dutchman who was similarly sleeping in the scullery maid's quarters next to the kitchen, confining himself to the Old Familiar kept him out of Greatorex's eye. So Tafford had one of the Candles fetch a folding cot down from the office and one of Turtle's boys bring over the clothes and kit from the boarding house.

Deuteronomy snored like a hippo nose-deep in water. His mechanical parts ratcheted and clicked with each somnambulant twitch. Even so, Tafford fell into an exhausted sleep. He dreamed of the past, of the first time he descended a staircase into the Chthonic world.

It was on the shores of the Gulf of Finland. Beneath lurked Iku-Turso—the Finnish Kraken. The Tursa might be only half-breeds—the union of cuttlefish and human servitors—but they wielded enough chthonic power to raze the world. And Iku was stirring, waking from his slumber.

They had little time to plan, the three of them—Dorian, Tafford, and Deuteronomy. And no time at all to call for the rest of the Chapter. The Tursa's main weapon was an eyebeam of solid death incarnate. Death itself as an irresistible force. Their only hope was to place in its path an immovable object as it were—a mortal who could not die. Dorian Grey took the Curse upon himself, donning its unwanted fellborn immortality like a cloak.

He led the way down the Staircase. The two Bells, Tafford and Deuteronomy, followed behind, their hunting rifles slung over their shoulder. For the briefest of moments after firing its beam, the half-moral Tursa would be as vulnerable. Tafford followed on Dorian's right, his companion on Dorian's left.

Down the madding Staircase they descended. The Staircase existed outside, yet within, both the Living and the Chthonic Worlds. Its twisting, shifting non-Euclidean nature was enough to drive even the strongest minds mad, had driven mad the scholar minds of Alhazred and Livingston.

Stairs shifted and swayed, became as giant children's blocks tumbled one upon another at impossible and contradictory angles. Tafford and Deuteronomy had an easier time of it, years of hunting in darkened jungles and caves and blinding snowstorms had honed all their other senses, honed their innate sense of direction and distance. They weren't solely reliant on mere vision as was Dorian. Dorian had only his scholar's mind to cope with the madness.

But it was enough.

After a gibbering eternity, the trio reached the bottom of the Staircase, and reality reasserted itself. Tafford found himself on Dorian's left. Somehow in the descent, he and Deuteronomy had switched places, but no time to think of that now.

The sinuous, snake-twisting tentacled-form of the awakened Tursa crawled and palsied its way toward the Staircase to begin its ascent into the Living World.

As if startled by the sheer audacity of the three mortals, the Tursa raised itself up on squirming tentacles. Its great cyclopean eye irised open, octopus-fashion, and a sickly cerulean beam of instant death flashed toward them.

Dorian spread outstretched arms and stepped into, catching it squarely on his slender frame. The beam writhed and screamed in frustration like a living being, the corona of Death crackling impotently against Dorian's impervious form. Then the beam became inanimate light again and ricocheted, glancing off Dorian and missing Deuteronomy by inches.

Inches were not enough.

The beam of Death may have missed him, but even the mere penumbra of Death's dark shadow was enough to fatally wither the entire right half of Deuteronomy like honeysuckle shriveling before a flame.

No time for Tafford to scream, to turn toward his stricken teammate. No time to wonder if the Curse truly *had* protected his best and only friend. No time to do anything thing but raise his rifle to his shoulder. To feel the release of the trigger and the kick of the gun against his shoulder. To hear the whip-crack of the bullet and see the soggy impact against the gelatinous skin of the monster. To work the bolt again and again until every bullet expended.

Then, and only then, could he turn and see the shattered remains of the half-dead Deuteronomy, see Dorian kneeling down, crooning what magicks he could in a desperate attempt to keep the half-living remains alive.

TAFFORD AWOKE SCREAMING.

"All my fault," Tafford found himself shouting from his camp cot. "All my fault."

A fumbling sound, then the snap of an electric light switch. Instant light showed the pajamaed form of the half-mechanical man rising groggily from a feather bed, duvet tossed to the side.

"It's nobody's fault," Deuteronomy said setting his feet on the wooden floor.

Tafford shuddered. "It should have been me on that right side. It should have been me it struck."

"Nobody blames you. *I* don't blame you."

Deuteronomy shuffled toward him, then squeezed Tafford's shoulder as gently as a mechanical hand could. "Nobody blames you."

Tafford let himself be lowered back down on the camp cot. "Silly, isn't it," he said in a dull voice. "Haven't had that dream in years."

"Not silly at all." Deuteronomy pulled a sweat-sodden blanket back over him then turned out the light. The big man's bed creaked as he settled his ponderous bulk back upon it.

"I suppose it was seeing you again," Tafford said in the darkness, but Deuteronomy's only reply was a snort-start snore.

Tafford lay there, his mind whirling.

It wasn't the thought of going back down a Staircase that gave him the shakes. It was the thought of failing. Again.

Of Greatorex winning.

Aunt Ethel's voice repeating over and over again in his mind: *unless you slap him down, the Cuttlefish will win, the Cuttlefish will win.*

And then a preternatural calm came over Tafford. There in the dark hung his jacket, and in his jacket pocket lay his beautiful bulldog. He could feel its weight in the dark, feel its presence as if its steel was white hot.

It gave him peace of mind, enough to slip fitfully into sleep and better dreams.

After all, he knew better than any man alive, didn't he, just how the splatter of bullets could stop a monster.

The six chambered rounds in his Webley revolver glowed brightly in his dreams.

April 25, 1889
Lake Victoria, Africa

FLICKERING stars wheeled above in the ink-black sky of midnight accompanied by the muffled puffing of the SS *David Livingston's* anemic steam engine. Dressed again in his Calcutta khakis, Tafford stood near the prow of the boat, getting what cool breeze he could from the boat's wallowing passage. The sultry, sodden equatorial air seemed all the worse after his brief stay in chilly London.

They had indeed stepped through London's BOAC to the shores of Lake Victoria at the time appointed by Dorian. What followed after had been a disastrous gymkhana.

The Imperial British East Africa Company, who owned the quasi-colony lock-stock-and-barrel and who ran it as a privately-owned fiefdom, saw little need to bestir itself from its sleepy equatorial somnambulance. The *Livingston* had been hours late pulling into the dock at Kisumu. Loading and replenishing firewood for the boiler had taken several more. It was dusk by the time the *Livingston* cast her lines and set off. At a pitiful seven-to-ten knots (depending on how green each log of firewood was), it'd be after sunrise before she made the western shore of the lake.

Behind him, Greatorex shouted another course correction. He was enjoying himself, standing atop the roof of the pilot house, taking sightings with the Sightless Sextant, bossing around the entire expedition.

Let him. His usefulness would be at an end the moment the *Livingston* dropped anchor and Tafford started down the Staircase.

The weight in Tafford's pocket glowed in his mind. Six bullets. One for each of the five bodies tossed down that mass grave and a sixth for Greatorex himself.

The boat's prow kicked out twin rooster tails of water, faintly phosphorescent in the starlight. Tafford watched their dancing beauty. He started when he realized that Dorian had glided noiselessly up beside him. A trick of the light, perhaps, but Dorian seemed to share the same faint phosphor glow as the bow wake.

Rather than turn to Tafford, Dorian kept his back to the pilot house behind them both. He held a bronze scrambler cube lightly in his hand. What he had to say was for Tafford's ears alone.

Dorian stood for several minutes silent and unmoving, save for the occasional brush of the hand to push away from his face long flowing albino white hair whipping about in the breeze.

"You've a weight in your lower left pocket," he eventually said, "a weight far too heavy for you to bear. I ask of you, as a friend, to hand it to me."

Tafford started again. *What—what witchery—?* Tafford had told no one. Outwardly nothing had changed. The bullpup rested in his pocket the same as it had every day of every year since Tafford could remember. Yet Dorian somehow knew. Dorian was Dorian, after all.

"It isn't heavy at all," Tafford said, turning slightly toward Dorian but not enough for the distant Greatorex—even if he was watching—to see his lips. "I've shot jackals before. Jackals and hyenas and dingo dogs circling the camp. One more won't make a difference."

"There's a fine line between hunter and murderer," Dorian said softly, sadly.

The images of all the female Rakshasa he'd shot, all so that the breed would wither and die. "There's no line at all."

Dorian softly let out a breath, mournful in its susurration. "The Chapter operates under a royal charter. As head of the Chapter, I and I alone hold the Queen's Warrant. The burden in your pocket is mine."

"As if you'd do anything about it! You haven't so far!" Tafford resisted the urge to turn full on and stare Dorian in the face. "You've harbored a viper in your bosom, Dorian," he hissed.

"Better the Chapter where I can keep an eye on him than ATK or with a thug like Scowrer."

"You ever consider he's the one who leaked the BOAC to ATK?"

Dorian said nothing.

Finally he spoke. "How do you erase the stain of that potter's field by adding another body to it? You want the dead to have a voice. Do you really give them that voice by silencing the living?"

After an eternity, I offered up my pistol.

His pale fingers closed around it, the color of death. The color of life.

∩

THE SUN HAD BEEN up an hour before the *Livingston* reached the western shore—the German shore—of Lake Victoria. Greatorex, fussy as an old spinster, checked and rechecked the coordinates with his magic toy.

"The Staircase should be right beyond that canebrake. Maybe a few feet in front of it," he called down from the roof of the pilot house. Tafford wouldn't it be able to actually see it until he was right on top of it.

The *Livingston*'s captain edged her as close to the shore as he could. She was a pig of boat, but shallow bottomed. He got her to within about sixty yards, most of which was shallow enough for Tafford to have waded across if he'd wanted. The captain ordered the ship's lifeboat lowered. He'd be rowed ashore in style.

At least his feet would be dry going down the stairs this time. He remembered how icy the waters of the Gulf of Finland had been the first time down a Staircase.

Tafford slapped idly at mosquitoes as he watched Dorian getting a gaggle of Books aligned on their designated chalk marks on the aft deck. After deck? Back deck? Tafford didn't remember the nautical term and didn't much care. The top deck at the rear of the ship at any rate. Dorian had brought along twenty Books to form a Dekker barrier in the event it was needed.

We don't know what might be coming up the Staircase after you, Dorian had told him back in London. Ten thousand angry fishman or even a wakened Consort. A Dekker barrier wouldn't stop a Cuttlefish, but it would protect the Dutchman from spear-throwing fishmen long enough to chip away the diamond Makelike and render it useless.

Personally, Tafford wasn't worried too much about bringing back unwanted chthonic guests. The Consort was deep asleep, and the fishmen should all be underwater tending to sunken eggs. He was more worried about the Germans. They had a Bismarck-sized chip on their shoulder about colonies and their 'place in the sun'. An intrusion into their side of the lake by a British East India vessel meant trouble. The Germans had a real warship on the lake: the *Einbruch*, an 800-ton vessel boasting a four-inch naval gun and bristling with swivel-mounted Maxims. Tafford doubted a Dekker barrier would stand up to a 4-inch quick-firer—even a twenty-man barrier.

A nineteen-Book barrier, actually. One of the Books was actually the

Dutchman passing herself off as a novice. She was to be placed in the center of the formation, the safest place aboard ship—if any place aboard was safe.

Tafford made his way to the port side of the creaky old *Livingston* where the ship's lifeboat was being lowered.

Deuteronomy clomped over to meet him, mechanical hinges wheezing. The half-man had a clumsy little kerosine two-stroke engine, a little Dugald-Cleark job, strapped to his back to power his metal half.

He handed Tafford a musette shoulder bag which Tafford slipped on. Then he handed him a large bronze mechanical egg to put inside the bag. "Here's your Makelike detector," Deuteronomy said, pitching his voice (but not noticeably so) for Greatorex to overhear. "Try to bring it back. They're difficult to make." Tafford solemnly nodded, wound the fake clockwork gears, and slipped the rugger-sized contraption into the musette back.

How do you conceal bringing back up the Staircase a rugger ball-sized diamond? Haul a rugger ball-sized decoy down the stairs first.

At least in theory.

Just as Tafford was about to descend down the rope ladder into the boat, the Dutchman pulled at his sleeve. She slipped a slim silver bracelet with a shilling-sized gem setting on his left wrist. Three faceted red garnets winked in the early morning sun. "It's sort of a Dekker barrier in gem form," she explained. "Each gem is a single charge." Without warning, Veronike stood on tiptoe and bussed him on the cheek. "Bonne chance," she whispered. Red-faced, she hurried aft.

Tafford swung himself over the combing and climbed awkwardly down into the swaying boat. Just as the oarsman pushed off, Tafford heard a crewman on the *Livingston* shout, "Ship ahoy!"

Black smoke smudged the horizon, the black smoke of a coal-burning steamship. "She's the *Einbruch*, all right," the captain yelled. "Fifteen minutes out, by my reckoning."

As the life boat pulled away, Tafford watched an explosion of crew scampering across the *Livingston's* deck as they manned their singular Maxim to meet the German gunboat.

If facing down a Consort unarmed wasn't enough of a challenge, Tafford had a new constraint: he had less than fifteen minutes to get that giant diamond back to the Dutchman before the flimsy-hulled *Livingston* was blown to flinders.

Λ

TAFFORD HOPPED out of the lifeboat even before it had even finished grinding its bow against the red-soiled shore. He made for the canebrake at a lope.

The early morning sun hung just above the horizon, but even so, heat from that baleful orange orb baked the sweltering air. Sweat trickled down Tafford's back, soaking his bush jacket without cooling him in the least.

Not all his sweat was due to the heat. The very air tingled with chthonic evil. The Staircase was near indeed.

Ten feet past the canebrake, the eldritch form of that Staircase wavered into view. Tafford saw its black basalt lintel, etched in chthonic runes, marking the descent into the abyss. Like a giant cyclopean eye, it seemed to stare at him. Tafford stared back.

Taking one last sweet breath of mortal reality, Tafford plunged into the gaping maw and down the stairs.

The world as he knew it shifted and spun and dissolved into madness. He felt basalt stone under his feet, tilted in crazed angles, but could not see it. True to its non-Euclidean nature, the Staircase—according to Greatorex's cartomancy—was forty-seven steps down but only thirty-nine steps back up.

Before, in Finland, they had gingerly felt their way down each step, feeling with their toes each drop off. He didn't have time for that now, not with the *Einbruch* bearing down on the *Livingston*.

Swallowing hard, Tafford ignored his reeling senses and—eyes closed—trotted down the stairs as if they were equally and regularly and rationally spaced apart. They were. As he'd hoped, their bizarre anglings and size differences were but sensory illusions.

One, two...he counted his way down forty-seven stairs, emerging into reality. Not the reality he'd left topside, but a new reality, the reality of a half-state existence touching both Reality and the invisible Chthonic World.

The world was a hollow ball with a basalt ceiling curving above it as far as the eye could see. No sun shone, but the distant form of the colossal Consort, half submerged in a vast underwater lake, gave off a sickly chartreuse glow that lent feeble light to Tafford's mortal eyes. Green-black tendrils curled aimlessly about the Consort, spinning and swaying in somnambulant sleep. The air hung heavy with the stench of rot and decay, of age and dissolution and pitiless despair.

Tafford shook his head, tossing it almost like a horse, to try to clear his addled senses.

Makelike. Must find the Makelike.

The Staircase had terminated mere yards from the underground lake. A gritty black sand crunched underfoot, reminiscent of volcanic debris, pulverized obsidian pumice.

Then he saw it.

There, inches away from the waterline, a small lump of what appeared to be melted glass protruded from out of the coarse black sand.

A person hears the word diamond and instinctively thinks of brilliant faceted gems. Veronike had warned him that uncut diamonds, diamonds in the raw, looked completely different. They looked like lumps of melted glass, frosted white, with perhaps large clumps of rock—Kimberlite—fused into the lump.

Such was the case of the Makelike.

Oh, the giant gem was roughly egg-shaped alright, but a good quarter of it was lumpy Kimberlite stone, and what wasn't was frosted whiteness. The fishmen, possessing only stone tools and what metals they could steal from black natives in their occasional surface raids, lacked any means of cutting or shaping the gem. How many centuries must they have searched the chthonic equivalent of subterranean diamond pipes to finally find a gargantuan diamond the exact shape and size of a Cuttlefish egg?

And without such a Makelike pseudo-egg, the Cuttlefish eggs would not hatch. Only the Makelike, and the sympathetic magics generations of fishmen priests poured into it, could draw pure Chthonic matter into this half-state world, a world where the eggs could hatch and its fingerling tadpole swarm into Mankind's reality. Destroy the Makelike and the unhatchable eggs would forever be trapped in their chthonic realm.

Knowing seconds were vital, Tafford crouched down next to the exposed tip of the gem. He frantically started scooping away the gritty sand, digging the gem out as fast as he could manage. A few inches down the soil became wet, soaked in seeping lake water, making it easier to dig.

He'd nearly exposed the gem when the lake water in front of him began to bubble. Up arose a spindly fishman in full priestly regalia. The fishman's scaly form was as gaunt as a malnourished ten-year-old child. A huge bulbous mackerel head sat neckless between its narrow shoulders. It worked its fat sea bass lips and blinked asynchronously its beady flounder eyes—both on the same flat side of the head—in surprise at seeing a human pawing at the Sacred stone.

It whooshed clear its gills and burbled some kind of angry shout. In its one hand, it brandished a black obsidian ceremonial dagger. In the other a large sea conch.

Tafford's hand grabbed at his jacket pocket. In his mind's eye, he swung up his revolver and stitched six quick shots across the fishman's torso, the fishman dancing a St. Vitus with each meaty impact.

But his hand clutched only empty air. Dorian had his pistol.

I am a dead man, Tafford thought.

But even as he thought that, his hands scooped up handfuls of wet black muck. He flung it at the fishman's face. The fishman turned his head and the blinding sand struck only the eyeless side of his flounder face.

The fishman dived beneath the waves.

Seconds were now milliseconds. Tafford desperately scooped out the last of the sand holding fast the Makelike in its burial pit. He pulled out the diamond with a wet *splurch*. Dumping the fake detector out of his shoulder bag. Tafford jammed the mud-coated diamond into the bag in its place.

The fishman priest popped back out of the water again, this time knife raised.

Tafford hurled the heavy brass detector. The heavy orb wobbled in flight, striking the priest on his dagger arm. The fishman burbled in pain and dropped the wicked-looking knife. Without a moment's pause, the priest swung the conch up to his blubbery lips and blew like Jericho.

A rising note echoed in the air, sounding the alarm.

A dozen, two dozen, perhaps a hundred fishmen heads broke the surface of the water. All of them carrying wickedly sharp obsidian-tipped spears. Two or three sported spears tipped with surface world *assegai* leaf-blade points of steel.

Tafford was already on his feet. His boots scrabbled in the loose volcanic grit as he sprinted flat out toward the safety of the Staircase, his fifty-year-old knees screaming in protest.

A rain of spears arced through the air toward him. They struck the ground —*shhrttp! shhrttp!*—burying their tips in the gritty sand. Bamboo handles clattered together as the near-misses landed atop one another.

Worse was to come. The constant alarm from the conch had disturbed the Consort's sleep. Inky-black tendrils thick as a woman's arm and flecked with scaly green highlights shot up from underground. The writhing things launched themselves at the human intruder—then recoiled away. No doing on Tafford's part, he knew. Even half-asleep, the tendrils feared jeopardizing the precious Makelike. Tafford was proof against these horrors at least.

Not so fishmen spears.

As they closed the distance their aim improved. Spears started missing by only a hairsbreadth.

One finally struck him, smashing into him squarely on the back. But instead of instantly impaling Tafford, the razor-sharp spear bounced off as if deflected by an invisible glass shield. The Dutchman's bracelet! Tafford risked a quick glance at his wrist. One of the red garnets shattered into slivers. Only two more charges left.

Just as he reached the flat basalt surface of the first stair, a second spear slammed into the base of his spine. A second garnet shattered, but the impact knocked him forward onto the Staircase out of the fishmen's half-state reality. The rain of spears ceased.

The fishmen would follow up the Staircase, of course. Whether the tendrils could snake themselves up the Staircase was a different question, one Tafford had no answer to.

Up the Staircase a winded Tafford fled, counting off the thirty-nine steps not in his mind as before, but in air-starved wheezes.

Then he emerged into sunlit mortal reality.

He emerged so suddenly he lost his footing. He tripped over his own boots and landed sprawling, skidding forward in his momentum across the red-clay African soil, completely knocking the wind out of him in the process. Helplessly he gasped for air his old lungs couldn't seem to draw in, unable to move save to lift his head toward the shoreline.

In the water a tableau from a nautical painting lay before him.

Like the *Merrimac* and the *Monitor*, the *Einbruch* had pulled to within point-blank range of the hapless *Livingston*. Blue cordite smoke wreathed the German vessel as she fired her guns for all she was worth—to seemingly little avail. The shells—and the Maxim bullets—bounced off the invisible globe of the Dekker barrier. In a freak of acoustics, Tafford could hear the bellowed berserker rage of the incredulous German gunners.

Tafford had been wrong. The barrier could withstand the German guns.

While not as strong as a rune ward, the advantage of the Dekker barrier lay in its multiple sources of generation. Destroy the ward stone and the entire rune ward comes crashing down. Bring down one of the twenty chanting Books, and you lose only a fraction of the Dekker barrier's still-functioning strength.

Its disadvantage lay in its susceptibility to multiple blows. Each hit on the barrier by a shell or Maxim bullet resulted in mental pressure upon each chanter. Enough pressure caused a chanter to collapse unconscious. Already two or three Books were down, sprawled insensate upon the wooden deck of the ship. With each fallen Book the barrier grew weaker, the mental pressure of each hit greater.

One last four-inch shell finally got through. It missed the boat proper, but the resultant waterspout from the near-miss rocked the *Livingston* violently, toppling over a dozen chanting Books and breaking their concentration. That was enough to bring down the barrier. Even the fortuitous jamming of the four-inch naval gun with that last critical shot was not enough to save the *Livingston*.

The *Einbruch's* forward swivel Maxim raked the wooden deck over and over. Dorian, in the lead position of the clustered Books, stood unaffected by the stream of steel-jacketed slugs. They might drill through his immortal flesh, but thanks to the Curse, did him no actual harm. The rest of the Books, the ones still standing and the ones groggily getting back on their feet, were shredded by the steel rain, toppled like blood-soaked tenpins.

Only the Dutchman by some miracle survived as yet unscathed. The swinging muzzle of the German Maxim, and the angling stream of red-hot tracers would soon put paid to that.

Then, from seemingly out of nowhere, the huge mechanical bulk of Deuteronomy Jones hurled itself between the Dutchman and the Maxim gun. Steel-jacketed bullets battered against the softer brass metal of Deuteronomy's mechanical half. Pieces of brass plating and shattered gears flung everywhere. The steady stream of bullets gouged and pierced their way through the mechanical half-body, slamming into Deuteronomy's all-too-human flesh and shredding his considerable body to rags.

But his bulk was still enough to shield Veronike from harm.

Deuteronomy's dead flesh slumped, but his metal half-body remained upright as feeble shelter, still enough to shield Veronike from harm. But not for long? The Maxim continued to chew away at Deuteronomy's metal-and-flesh corpse.

Tafford struggled to his feet, his lungs at last gulping in sweet, sweet air.

Before he could take a single step toward the beached lifeboat and the waiting oarsman, a bloodcurdling war cry erupted behind him. The first of the fishmen had emerged from the Staircase. Those still with spears hurled them at him. Only their addled senses, still jumbled from the insanity of the Staircase, saved Tafford. The spears all went wide of the mark, save one lucky cast that glanced off his ribcage, shattering the last garnet.

Then things got worse.

Black-green tendrils, thick as a tree bole, sprouted out of the ground. Waving and curling in bloodlust at the loss of the Makelike, they coiled around everything at hand: the trees lining the shore, that clump of canebrake, even the entire army of its fishmen allies—everything but the Makelike-protected Tafford.

Before Tafford could reach the lifeboat and its putative safety, a tendril sprang from under the boat, coiled around it, and crushed it into splinters. Two separate tendrils grabbed the oarsman and tore him in spurting halves as an afterthought.

A forest of tendrils then erupted from beneath the waters of Lake Victoria itself. Giant tendrils grabbed on to the armored metal hull of the German warship and hurled its entire eight hundred tons into the air. Flailing sailors fell like rain. Lesser tendrils, waiting below, split themselves open, transforming themselves into great gaping hungry maws lined with shark-sharp teeth. They swallowed each falling sailor in turn, gulping them down their tendril-gullets like snakes swallowing still-wriggling mice.

The metal hull of the *Einbruch*, caught fast in the grip of Kraken-sized tendrils, screamed as if in rivet-popping agony as it was crushed into a mangled ball then tossed into the depths of Lake Victoria, sinking out of sight.

Perhaps due to the residue energies of the Dekker barrier, the *Livingston* so far had been spared. Now the curling, twirling tips of the Kraken tendrils turned and quested in its direction.

It was then that Dorian stepped forward, arms raised, gathering magical energy about him in a golden globe of light. Ichorous black dots crackled like nugatory sunspots on the corona of that blazing orb. Then in a voice that shattered the very air about him, Dorian shouted the ancient Maldon: "*Hige sceal þe heardra, heorte þe cenre/Mod sceal þe mare, þe ure mægen lytlað!*"

Minds be thou sharper, hearts be thou harder,
Souls be thou greater—as our strength lessens!

Tafford's senses reeled in a coruscant flash of blinding light as the globe expanded to encompass ship and lake and tendrilled shoreline. A light composed of love and life, of heart and hope, of every singular splendor that makes up the glory that is that fragile creature called Man.

Tafford's mind, his heart, his soul entwined with that of Dorian's, of Veronike's, of all those aboard the *Livingston* to rise up and fuel that expanding globe. So, too, did the virtue emanating from remains of the newly dead, Deuteronomy, and the Books. As if a distilled, palpable force, their sacrifice became part of the Maldon. Tafford felt the warmth of Deuteronomy's lopsided smile brush past his face as the Maldon absorbed and grew.

Through this blinding white Tafford could sense the unadulterated evil that were the chthonic tendrils. He could see their solid blackness stretching back into the Staircase, itself a malevolent blob against the light. Pinioned against the light. the coiling tendrils oozed death and dissolution but to no avail. To the Maldon globe they were but as green twigs upon a blacksmith's furnace. They shriveled and shrank, burned and withered. Not even the Staircase could stand fast against the globe. Like a living thing, the Staircase portal recoiled at the Maldon's touch. It irised itself closed, slicing in twain the extended tendrils.

Like lizard tails shorn from its owner, the tendril remnants continued to spasmed and twitched though dead as doornails.

Triumphant, the Maldon light faded and Tafford stared out at the pyrrhic tableau of a battle won. Blackened husks of tendrils lay scattered about, decaying at impossible speed in the equatorial sun. The water roiled at the distant spot where the crushed *Einbruch* had sunk. Aboard the *Livingston*, bullet-riddled like an abattoir and decks awash with drying blood, the gaunt form of Dorian staggered, his face as desiccated and drawn as a century-old corpse, the price of casting a magick as powerful as the Maldon in defiance of the Curse.

Tafford waded into the water, slogging his way to the drifting ship. He needed to hurry. Nothing, not even a Maldon, could close a Staircase for long. The Makelike, weighing heavy against his hip, still had to be destroyed. He waved to Veronike, then dove into the water proper to swim the remaining distance.

Tafford wasn't the greatest of swimmers but eventually he reached the rope ladder still hanging draped over the ship's side. A smiling Veronike leaned over the combing. She waved down at him.

He started the climb up. Halfway up, he whipped the neck strap from around his head and handed the shoulder bag up to Veronike.

And at that exact moment, the moment Tafford surrendered the protection of the Makelike, the tendril struck.

One last tendril the thickness of a child's arm defied death. Somehow it still had enough life left it, enough purpose, to strike out against the human inter-loper who'd been the cause of its destruction. It spiraled out of the water, releasing from its grasp a fishman warrior it hadn't quite crushed yet. Whipcord fast it wrapped its coils around Tafford's upper right leg and began pulling him down into the water to drown.

Veronike grabbed Tafford's outstretched hand. Not all her desperate tugging could stop the inexorable downward pull of the coiled tendril. But then, just as Tafford's strength began to give way, the pulling stopped.

The tendril—finally admitting death—went limp, relaxing its grip on Tafford's leg. Tafford hung there for a moment, too tired to move, too tired even to pull the slackened coils from his leg,

Veronike screamed again. Tafford turned to face the splashing noise behind him.

The half-crushed fishman lurched out of the water. His one working arm raised his spear, readying it to plunge into Tafford.

Tafford, exhausted, could do nothing to stop it,

A skeletal Dorian suddenly half-toppled over the combing, Tafford's pistol gripped in his hand. The untrained Dorian fired wildly. In his desperation, he managed to hit. Three shots slammed into the fishman, but the warrior—like a dying scorpion—jabbed downward in his death throes, determined to take Tafford with him.

The plunging obsidian spear tip pierced through tendril coils into Tafford's right thigh. The spearpoint carried the tendril's black turgid ichor with it as it penetrated.

Chthonic poisons burned like the fires of Hell as the ichor pumped into his blood stream. Tafford screamed in gibbering madness and pain.

All went black.

June 6, 1889
London, England

I HOLD YOU EVER, *ever in my thoughts,* the words echoed in utter darkness. *Now I must sleep but you must dance.* The echo trailed off into eternity.

Gradually they faded and he—whoever he was—noticed a growing light.

Tafford awoke to find himself in bed in a bright, sunlit room of whitewashed walls and odors of carbolic acid. A hospital?

He blinked his eyes and found he couldn't move. He felt groggy.

Drugged. Morphine or opium or something like that. For the pain, most likely. A muted jangling of fire coursing through some unspecified part of his numbed body confirmed that.

He moaned.

"Finally awake?" he heard Dorian's voice say. "I was beginning to wonder if you ever would."

Tafford found he could turn his head. Dorian—his face once more restored to its immortal elegance—seated in a chair beside him.

A summer robin flittered onto the window sill outside. It twittered at Tafford as it bobbed its head, then flew off again.

"How long?" Tafford managed to croak.

"It's early June," Dorian said softly. Six or seven weeks then.

The muzziness in Tafford's head cleared somewhat. Images cascaded in his head. The Staircase, the battle, the fishman's spear—

He couldn't move enough to look down at his own body. "My leg?"

"We managed to save it." Dorian had managed to save it, he meant, just as he'd manage to save Deuteronomy the first time, at what cost Tafford could only guess at.

"I can't feel it," Tafford said.

"It's the laudanum," Dorian said. "You've a pretty high dose. Now that you're awake, we can taper off."

Tafford tried to move and a jolt of electric fire ran up his right leg. He grunted in pain. "Will I be able to walk?"

"After a fashion," Dorian said, bluntly and truthfully. "Every step will most likely be agony. The spear penetrated the thigh bone. There's ichor in the marrow still—despite my best efforts to draw it out. Your hunting days are over, I'm afraid."

How many more years can you hunt? he heard Deuteronomy's voice echo in his mind.

"Deuteronomy?" Tafford asked. "And the rest of them? All the Books?"

"Potter's field."

Tafford clenched his fist, grabbing the bedsheet between his fingers. Nor come we now in grief to mark your grave.

To be forgotten, willfully forgotten after all they'd sacrificed! Deuteronomy who even as the bullets shredded him, even in death stood fast? *Of this your corpse shall serve that time of need/In that dread night when naught but Death stands fast?*

Dorian continued on. "Eighteen in one grave," he said as that made any difference now. Then he added: "And half a body in its own separate grave." Dorian paused. His voice softened. "The nature of the Drum quite forbids us from laying of any markers. It doesn't require, however, that we dig up an existing willow stump that just happens to lay at the head of that smaller grave."

Tafford let out a breath. He'd be able to find Deuteronomy and say goodbye to his friend then after all. A tear traced its way down one check. Tafford found he could move his arm enough to wipe the tear away.

"And Veronike?" he asked

Dorian chuckled. "The Dutchman? Back in Belgium, safe and sound. But not before she cut up the Makelike for us."

Dorian pulled from his pocket a cloth bag—what Americans would call a poke—plumped up to the size of a tangerine. and he shook it. It rattled as if was full of dry beans. Loosening the drawstring, Dorian extracted a largish size diamond, exquisitely cut and faceted. Brilliant blue-white and sparking in the light from the window. He dropped the diamond back in the bag and placed it on the nightstand.

"According to the bylaws of our Royal Charter, you're due a quarter-share of this as prize money. Most of the Greatorex diamond collection will go to the Crown and the Chapter, but this bag and three more bags like this one go to you."

Yes sir, yes sir, three bags full.

"You're one of the richest men in Britain," Dorian added.

Richest cripple. I'd give it all up to be whole again.

"Wait," Tafford said. "You said the 'Greatorex diamond collection.' I take it he's still with us?"

A curious tone crept into Dorian's voice. "Lord Greatorex did not survive the battle." Again, he reached into a pocket this time to produce Tafford's pistol. " I no longer need to hold this for you." He set it on the nightstand beside the bag of diamonds. Tafford could move his head just enough to see that the six chambers in the revolver cylinders were empty.

Dorian had pumped three bullets into that fishman. If he'd had more, he would have used them. Ergo...

Ergo three of the bullets had already been spent on another target.

"Officially," Dorian said, almost with a sniff, "Lord Greatorex perished in British East Africa hunting diamonds for the Crown. Thus, the collection's name."

"And unofficially? Potter's field as well?"

"As if I'd stain the honor of our dead with that man's corpse!" Dorian replied, an unaccustomed anger in his voice. He calmed himself. "No, Lord Greatorex's remains are resting peacefully in the family crypt, more's the pity."

Minutes passed in silence, broken only by the fluttering return of the robin on the sill. It bobbed once, twice then sped off again. Would that Tafford could fly off with it.

"I need to tell you the worst of it," Dorian said at last. "Greatorex, I mean."

Tafford had enough strength to turn his head. "About him tipping of the ATK? And probably the Germans as well?"

Dorian shook his head. "That wasn't the ATK spying on you. That was Whitehall. Our own government. Seems our own intelligence service thinks a BOAC is just the thing to place assets in Moscow or Berlin."

"Madness."

"As for the Germans," Dorian continued, "that was mere chance their being there. The *Einbruch* sank with all hands. Berlin still has no clue why, nor does she have any idea of our involvement."

Dorian hesitated before speaking again. "No, what you need to know is that when we got back here, I had an immediate check made on all the books Greatorex had brought the Chapter."

"Those ones from Vienna, you mean? The forgeries?"

Dorian nodded. Again that hesitation. "The *Tabula Maledicta Cartesiana*—the Cursed Atlas—was one of them."

Tafford's world reeled. "But it couldn't have been!"

"I should have caught it."

"It couldn't have been. You were there. You saw! The Staircase was there, the Makelike was there, the Consort was there!"

Dorian lowered his head let out a long sigh. "Most of the tables were one-hundred percent genuine. That's why I didn't catch it when I checked. Only the time column was adulterated." He looked up. "The eggs weren't scheduled to hatch for another four hundred years."

It was if the room spun around for Tafford. "All the dead. Deuteronomy, the Books, the Germans—even the poor fishmen—all dead for nothing then. *Nothing!*"

It was Tafford's turn to fall silent. Finally, in a voice as cold and bleak as a Staircase, he said: "It must never happen again. What are you doing to ensure that?"

Dorian shrugged. "What can we do? We've checked Greatorex's books, of course. But as for the rest, do you have any idea just how large our Recknynge archive is alone? That's not counting our day-to-day libraries. We're talking hundreds of thousands—millions!—of volumes."

And any one of them could be a ticking timebomb.

Nevertheless, it needed to be done. No, more than mere checking needed to be done. There needed to be a central clearing house to identify forgeries and disseminated that information. And it needn't be the Chapter doing it.

As these thoughts tumbled out into spoken words, Dorian sadly shook his head. "Mallory, I haven't the manpower. We're down twenty Books or don't you remember? And even if I had the manpower, do you have any idea how much time and money that would take?"

Tafford stared up at him, the pieces in his mind clicking into place. "No, but I've been reliably informed I have plenty of both."

Tafford had been a hunter all his adult life. Now he must start a different kind of hunt after a different kind of quarry. He owed it to Deuteronomy and the rest to show them that the dead weren't the only ones who could stand fast. The living could as well.

Purpose overriding pain, Tafford sat up in his bed. He threw back the bedclothes and swung his legs over the side.

"Help me up," he told Dorian. "I have things to do."

AN IMPERIAL RESCRIPT

INTRODUCTION

Most of my fun in writing stories like "An Imperial Rescript" (a sequel to the previous tale) is getting to blend implausible facts and plausible fictions.

Most of this story takes place in Invergarry and its environs. Invergarry really exists. Invergarry House really exists (although it's now the Glengarry Castle Hotel). You can find hundreds of tourist photos of the manor/hotel and its grounds online. You can even find online videos of drone fly-bys of the lake and walking tours making a complete circuit of the shoreline.

What you won't find online is mention of Edward Balthazar Ellice. He's fictional.

The first two Edward Ellices were real enough, but by the time this story takes place (1900), the Ellice family had run out of Edwards (save a nephew, Edward Charles Ellice, who had no connection to the manor house as far as I've found). I had to make up a third Eddy and move the conversion of manor to hotel up by several decades for story purposes.

The off-again-on-again railroad construction Ellice mentions is quite real as well. So are the inscriptions on the manor's exterior (although I've yet to find photos of them).

You'll also encounter the very real Rose Hartwick Thorpe's 1867 poem "Curfew Must Not Ring Tonight" in this story. "Curfew" was at one time the best-known poem in the English language (and one of Queen Victoria's favorites). Do yourself a favor and watch Katharine Hepburn's send up in the 1957 movie Desk Set. *(And do look online for satirist James Thurber's illustrations of the poem.)*

Not so real—and you don't have to be an English major to suss this out—is the

Emily Dickinson pastiche I concocted. (I'm no Emily Dickinson, news that will come as a great shock to no one.)

I'd intended to use Dickinson's real "Poem 372", but couldn't. Due to the vagaries of the idiotic Sonny Bono copyright extension (spit!), that particular poem is still under copyright. Yes, a poem written in the mid-19th-Century but not published until 1929 is, as of this writing, still under copyright, despite the current year (2022) being 136 years after Emily's death. "Poem 372" won't lapse into public domain until three years hence (2025).

Missed it by that much, as Maxwell Smart used to say.

Speaking of public domain, The Little Princess, *the 1939 Shirley Temple movie, is in the public domain. Not that "Rescript" bears any similarity to it or anything, particularly not the film's final eight minutes (one of my favorite movie moments).*

As to the story itself, "An Imperial Rescript" is another Deseret Clockwork novella written for this collection. You'll find Tafford and the Domesday Chapter making another appearance, although Tafford (now an Oxford don) is old, lame, and fat. Time marches on for all of us (even certain authors). Several of the minor problems the Chapter faced in "Naught" have bubbled up into full-fledged crises in "Rescript".

One last note:

During my first rotation in the Iraq War (the first of three), I was an occasionally "casually" helping Air Force EOD (the bomb disposal guys) destroy captured Iraqi ammunition and explosives.

This involved digging a big pit with a backhoe then stacking up captured artillery shells and sundry, placing land mines face down for mutual destruction, and finally shaping and stringing C4 plastic explosive around to initiate the actual detonation. The EOD pretty much let us do all the work, everything but inserting the detonators into the C4 and triggering the radio control that ignited them. The stacked ammo made quite a boom even from a couple miles away.

The Latvian troops who lived in the tent next to ours were there as experts on Soviet-made ammunition, which is how our non-EOD Engineering & Installations team got involved. (Have backhoe, will travel.) Later, I found out from the Latvians just how past-their-expiration-date and unstable some of that Soviet made export junk was. Now they tell me.

Some of the research I did for this piece brought back these old memories: research comprising the watching of a fascinating real-life documentary detailing the process of how to fish with dynamite. No, not Paul Hogan's Crocodile Dundee II.

Anyway, that Dundee opening scene is sadly inaccurate. Cigarettes don't burn hot enough to ignite dynamite fuses. Cigars do.

And apparently so do steampunk magic spells.

January 4th, 1900
Invergarry, Scotland

S even-year-old Sarah Crewes scrambled across the snow, wreathed in the white fog of panting breaths. Each step, borrowed boots—several sizes too big—crunched in the chill night air. Her thin nightshift caught and tore on wild ferns and straggly bare-branched saplings. She stumbled on a moss-slick rock buried and hidden in a drift. She went sprawling, the long tail of her loose unbuttoned sweater flapping behind her.

Sarah rose to her feet and resumed her frantic dash up the hill to the House. Cheeks red with the beginning of frostbite, fingertips beginning to blue—she ignored it all in her desperate need to get back to Invergarry House.

Sarah's friend was in trouble. The bad men were trying to hurt her. Sarah had to get help. She had to save her friend.

Sarah knew her parents wouldn't believe her. They never did. And even if they did, what could they do?

Only one person in the House could help—the lady lodger Sarah's parents had told her never to speak to—but would that person believe?

Three days earlier
New Year's Day
London, England

THE MIDNIGHT BLAST had ripped away almost the entire east side of Windsor Castle. Most of the apartments—private and state—were little more than a heap of tumbled stones. A dozen palace functionaries, all dead of course, had been dragged from the rubble with dozens more thought to still be buried.

Only by a miracle and a last-minute affair of state had Queen Victoria escaped being another casualty.

As a feeble winter sun had risen on a snowy New Year's morning, a veritable army of law enforcements—from lowly bobbies to Scotland Yard inspectors—milled about uselessly. Uniformed military and household guards swelled their ranks, as did a more or less equal number of bowler-hatted Whitehall civil servants. Despite all that, only two men in the crowd really mattered.

The first man was a ministry official of no set portfolio, not even set ministry. The name of Percival Moxton appeared on no official document. Average in height, a bit on the slim side, light complected, Moxton had fine sandy hair, almost baby-fine. So fine were his eyebrows that it almost looked like he had none, just bony angular ridges above his deep eye sockets.

Otherwise, he was a rather nondescript chap, save one personal affectation: Moxton wore one of those rakish new trilby hats fashionable among a certain set in London. A tilted trilby in a sea of Whitehall bowlers.

The second man who mattered was the person Moxton hated most in the world.

Hatless, Dorian Grey needed no trilby to stand out. Grey was an albino. Flowing silver hair, shoulder-length, and frosted grey irises. He wore a sin-black vicar's outfit complete with clerical collar. His face was that of a death-pallor Adonis, beautiful and just as dead in emotion as a Greek statue. Grey had worn that unchanging beauty for thirty years and would for another three thousand.

Only Moxton noticed that, as Dorian Grey moved through the crowd, each man in turn was seemingly compelled to look away. As striking a black-clad albino with cleric's collar should have been, he moved unseen. Moxton noticed as well that the albino's footsteps left almost no dint on the freshly falling snow.

Reaching Moxton, Grey nodded almost imperceptibly. "Moxton." The voice held no emotion in it.

Neither much did Moxton's. "Grey."

"Moxton." Grey eyed Moxton the way he would a mouse the cat dragged in. "I half-hoped General Ardagh would meet me."

"Sir John is busy holding the panicked hands of Parliament."

The corner of Grey's mouth ticked. "Where he can't do any harm, you mean. Harm to you," he added.

Moxton shrugged. "Directors of Military Intelligence come and go with the frequency of mayflies. Superannuated mediocre generals given one last post before being put to pasture. It falls on us mere underlings to carry out the actual work."

Snow had already started to collect upon Grey's shoulders. He reached up an ungloved hand to brush it off. "Rare for you to beg for Chapter help. Unprecedented, even."

Grey titled his head in the direction of the carnage. "Why is any of this our affair? Anything we'd be interested in the wards should have stopped." No building on earth was more mystically warded than the royal Residences, save perhaps Westminster and Parliament.

Moxton allowed himself a thin smile. "I hope to make you choke on those words." He gestured. "This way." Moxton led the albino through the rubble.

The snow was really coming down now. Large feathery flakes drifted and struck Moxton's face as he walked, tickling his eyelashes. Moxton's ankle-length boots *scrunched* in the snow, syncopated by the barest of whisks from Grey's footsteps. "Mixed blessing, this snow. Serves quite nicely to cover up the extent of damage. Also covers up the cause, alas."

At a particular spot in the rubble a young portage of Moxton's waited. Sharp-eyed and alert, the young man's elongated facial profile had the unfortunate cast of a rodent to it. Not some homey field mouse, but that of a weasel. A snaggle of front teeth did nothing to dispel that impression.

"This is Griggs," Moxton said. The pinched-face Griggs seemed even less inclined to greet Grey than Grigg's master had been.

"Griggs was here on the scene when it happened, luckily far enough away to survive."

Griggs gave a curt nod. "A male intruder got past the gate, the guards, the wards, and everything else before he was spotted here at the southeast corner. The guards caught up with him as he was trying to force open a window and gain access inside. I heard the guards challenge the intruder. The next thing I knew, half the building had exploded."

"Go on," Moxton ordered.

"As far as I could see, the intruder had no satchel or anything of bulk strapped to him. Nothing but whatever he carried in his pockets. He was a thin man. Nearly as thin as you."

"So, tell me, Grey. What kind of explosive could do all this?" Moxton demanded. "Had to be something in your line." He nodded at Griggs. "Show him what you showed me."

With a look of contempt on his rodent face for the albino, Griggs lifted up the corner of a snow-covered tarp to expose a pile of shattered stone junks of the outer wall's facade dry from snow. "This is more or less the center of the blast. You can see scorch marks from the explosion. Residue of the explosive."

Griggs took a curious jade carving from his pocket. The piece of jade was roughly the shape and size of his thumb. A simple *hsin* stone, carried by the tongs of Hong Kong. A *hsin* was possibly the most rudimentary of arcane objects. Easy enough for even untrained Westerners like Moxton's men to use.

That's all Grey and his precious chapter allowed Moxton. Table scraps, hog trough leavings. How Grey must be laughing at Moxton.

"Now watch," Griggs said—a finger-painting child explaining to a Dutch Master. Griggs held the *hsin* loosely in the center between thumb and forefinger. He slowly waved it a half-inch above the scorched stone. The *hsin* spun and pivoted like a lodestone needle. "That isn't chemical residue, that's—"

"That's why you called me in," Grey finished. The cheeky devil already had a liquid vial and an eyedropper out. He'd come already prepared. He knew. Even before he'd arrived, Grey knew.

He squirted a couple drops of the vial's liquid onto the scorch spot the *hsin* had reacted to. The liquid hissed and bubbled and then turned lavender. "I was afraid of that," Grey said, half-muttering.

Grey replaced the vial in his pocket. "Moolman's Clay," he said. "Your culprit was a Boer."

Moxton's guts clenched. Of course it would be what he feared most. "You're sure? Couldn't it have been an Irish Fenian or a Russian anarchist? I'd even take a German over a Boer."

Grey shook his head. "Moolman's is an admixture made from a pinch of mud from the River Orange, the plucked beard hairs from a Boer, and the prickled blood from the slender finger of a young *huisvrou*—all ground into powder and consecrated in a Dopper Church on sacred Dingaan's Day. Be a funny kind of Irishman to do all of that."

Boers.

And Grey just happened to have the exact vial needed to identify a Boer compound on him when he arrived. He knew—he ruddy well knew before he came it had been the Boers. "So why didn't your precious rune wards protect against it?"

The layers of runic wards secretly carved into the castle grounds should have stopped the bomber in his tracks, preventing his physical approach so long as he carried on his person any sort of arcane weapon. They hadn't.

Grey sighed, as if having to explain to a child. "Moolman's Clay is a binary agent. By itself, it's harmless. Almost totally inert as arcane substances go. Of course the wards wouldn't react to it. It's only when it's combined with some fulminator, some mundane chemical explosive, that it's dangerous." He faced Moxton full-on. "And normal explosives, may I remind you, are *your* remit not that of our wardings."

The albino took a deep breath, deep that is for a man who barely seemed to breathe at all. "The assailant probably poured a pinch of Moolman's into a whiskey flask, then tied a wad of gun cotton around the flask. Smash the glass flask against stone or steel and the whole thing explodes. That's probably what the Boers are using against your armored trains down in Cape Colony."

"And you knew," Moxton hissed, choking with anger. "You knew and didn't even tell us."

"You know the proscriptions of our Charter," Grey retorted. "It's not our brief. Not our concern."

"*Not your concern!*" Bile rose in Moxton's throat. "By all that's holy, man! We're losing the war. Isn't *that* your concern?"

"Do soldiers trapped in Mafeking worry about two schoolboys back in Manchester shooting at each other with toy pistols?" Grey asked. "My Chapter contends with entities you cannot even image, entities that could peel away all life upon this planet as easily as you or I might peel an orange. And with as much malice aforethought or reflection afterword."

"That's always your answer, isn't it?" Moxton spat. "Your unseen crawlies."

"And your answer is always to demand ransacking our Chapter, demanding to carry away anything you might use as a weapon. To dragoon my members into becoming assassins and spies and soldiers for you."

"Not for me. Never for me"

"For Queen and country, then." sneered Grey. "And once the British government has our secrets, the Germans will have them, too, and the Russians and the Austrians and the French and Americans and on and on. That's how your world of espionage works, isn't it?"

Grey's anger grew. "And then those secrets powerful enough to fight ancient entities will be used for fighting wars, nation against nation, until the planet itself is destroyed. No, Moxton. Our Chapter will continue to keep our secrets, and you shall not have them."

Moxton jerked his head aside in frustration, flinging the snow accumulated on his hat brim in a powdery cloud.

How to explain to an imbecile? "Can't you see, Grey? By your own admission, the cat's already out of the bag. The Boers are already using magic for war, nation against nation, just as you said. And if the Boers win this war—and they will unless you give us the means to counter them—their German patrons will soon have this clay stuff. And the French and so on. Can you imagine French artillery batteries at Calais with Moolman's wrapped around their shell casings? Can you imagine German zeppelins dropping five-hundred-pound Moolman whiskey flasks on London?"

The two men fell silent.

What more was there to say in an argument that had gone round and round and round for over a decade?

Talking a deep breath, Moxton said at last. "Let's talk about, then, what you *can* do to help. Can you at least refit the palace wards to stop future Moolman attacks?"

Grey nodded glumly. "Difficult, but it could be done. It will take weeks, though. Do you know how many individual wards even a single royal residence has?"

"Weeks," Moxton repeated morosely, "And in the meantime—"

"Sir," young Griggs hissed urgently. "The Prime Minister. He's coming this way."

Young Griggs must have phenomenal eyesight. In this flurry of snow, Moxton could hardly make out a dark shape of a man approaching, let alone identify that shape as Lord Salisbury.

But then, the wheezy old septuagenarian was rather distinctive.

The old man shuffled gingerly in the slippery snow toward them, aided by the dubious help of a silver-tipped walking stick. Salisbury's shoulders were white with accumulated snow, white as the brim of his silk top hat. The effort taxed his notoriously bad lungs. He panted white streams of breath vapor as he walked.

"Gentlemen," he wheezed, "let's make this brief. I shouldn't really be seen talking to you—although who could see anything in this muck!—shouldn't even know either of you exist. You especially, Grey." He paused to suck air into his lungs. "So out with it. I see from your faces you've bad news."

"It was the Boers, sir" Moxton said. Salisbury grunted.

Moxton continued, nodding at the albino, "Grey says it's some form of Boer ju-ju, something his wards can't stop. He can make them proof against it, but it will take weeks."

"Weeks," Salisbury gloomed. "In the meantime, the Residences aren't safe, are they? And there are probably more of these ju-ju bombers about."

Moxton nodded. "We've men in the field passing themselves off as Boers. They surely have men here passing themselves off as English."

British intelligence even knew the pipeline. The Boer Republics overland to German East Africa. Zeppelins from Africa to Hamburg. Norddeutscher Lloyd liners from Hamburg to Southampton or London docks. And nothing Moxton could do to stop it, not without risking a row with Imperial Germany.

"So," Lord Salisbury sighed, grasping the nettle. "What do we do about the Queen? The Crown Prince is easy. Hand him a sailor suit, and he's happy. I've already bundled him off, in fact, for a visit to the Med Fleet at Gibraltar. But Her Majesty? I can't very well squirrel her away in your Deptford tavern, Grey. Not that she'd go. She'd see defiantly staying put as her duty."

Griggs cleared his throat and spoke up. It was a measure of Lord Salisbury's concern that he didn't even raise an eyebrow at the affrontery of a junior-nobody interrupting a conference of his betters.

"What about Scotland?" Griggs asked.

The Prime Minister pursed his lips. "That's the one place I could probably convince her nibs to go, her beloved Scotland. But Balmoral's an ice box even in summer. I wouldn't kennel a dog in it in winter. Besides, the residences aren't safe. You said so yourself."

Griggs persisted, ignoring Moxton's frowning glare. "That's just it, sir. The palace wards might as well not exist at this moment, so why not someplace else? Someplace the Boers aren't expecting?"

Lord Salisbury brushed snow off his face. "Go on."

"What about a small country place, a place where the locals all know everybody and would recognize strangers. These Boers might can pass themselves off as English. I doubt they can pass themselves off as Scots."

Moxton snorted. Nobody north of Hadrian's Wall could speak the Queen's English. But then again, the same could be said of Yorkies or Geordies or those idiot Liverpudlians. And then there were those double-elled sesquipedalian Welsh.

"I'm assuming you have a place in mind, Griggs?" Moxton asked.

"Yes, sir. Small village called Invergarry. Southeast of Inverness. There's a big manor house converted into a modern salmon fishing resort. Invergarry House. Empty in winter. Off the beaten track."

Lord Salisbury brushed snow out of his beard. He wheezed white vapor while he thought. "How do we get the Queen there?" he asked.

Griggs had that all thought out as well. "Those three brothers at Mafeking? The ones being put up for a Victoria Cross. They hail—hailed—from Invergarry or near enough."

Salisbury nodded. "And the Queen could be talked into presenting posthumous awards to the family. She'd see it as her duty. Well done, lad."

Salisbury started considering all the ifs and buts. He'd not thrice helmed the British Government for nothing.

After only a couple minutes, Salisbury spoke to Moxton and Grey. "It'll take at least a day to set this up. We'll have to risk the Queen in Buckingham Palace for one night."

The Queen wouldn't like that. Buck House had been her husband's home. After Albert's death, she'd refused setting foot in the place.

Salisbury chuckled sourly, "After a night's stay in that drafty old pile, I could probably convince her to lodge at the North Pole. It'd be warmer." He let out a white breath. "We'll set the award ceremony for Sunday next on the pretext of holding it when all the locals are off work. That's about as long as she'll agree to stay put there." He set his gaze at Grey. "That gives you until Monday next to refit as many wards on Osborne House as you can. Just Osborne House for now and just the living quarters. The rest will have to wait."

Moxton gave a grudging nod. Osborn House, Queen Victoria's favorite, was fairly isolated on the Isle of Wright. The best long-term security they could probably manage for now. Once Grey got it warded.

"I'll want both of you up at Invergarry, of course. Pick a couple of your good men, but no more. Need to keep this circus as small as possible."

Moxton groaned inwardly. The need for a small a footprint as possible seemed at loggerheads with the need for a public medal ceremony, but politicians often thought in oxymorons.

Salisbury pursed his lips. "No, better send up some Army as well. Be questions in the House if I don't."

Politicians! "No more than a squad," Moxton said, "or there'll be questions among the locals. I'll handle it." Moxton would need to oversee who the Army sent up. Pick some men who'll just pitch their tent and crawl in them. The object was to go as unnoticed as possible. Last thing they needed was some bright-eyed subaltern with drive and ambition, or some hidebound, drill-happy sergeant major.

"I trust that's everything?" the prime minister asked. "Then let's get going, Grey, get those pet wizards of yours working on those wards." He turned to Moxton. "And you, think up some excuse for this explosion. One that doesn't involve Boers. The Press are baying like basset hounds."

Like Moxton needed to be told. He'd put it in place hours ago. Gas main leak. His men were even now doctoring engineering drawings.

Salisbury took his leave and shuffled off the way he'd come. Grey gave a curt nod and strolled in the opposite direction toward his waiting carriage.

Moxton felt like spitting at them both.

"Let's get out of the cold, boy," Moxton told his assistant. The snow was really coming down now. Luckily, he'd planned ahead.

Moxton had had the Yard set up a command tent for him. Heaven knows where they'd scrounged it from. Some forgotten army barracks, most likely. The wretched thing dated back to the Crimean War and stunk of mildew and cosmoline. Lacking a tent stove, it felt almost as freezing inside as out.

For some reason, the idiots at the Yard had oh-so-thoughtfully put up a wooden easel with a situation map and a brace of colored pushpins. Moxton left that sort of thing to underlings.

Underlings like that idiot Griggs.

He waited for Griggs to finally stop making a big show of stomping snow from his boots and enter.

As soon as the younger man had fastened down the tent flap, Moxton lit into him: "What the devil are you on about, Griggs?" he demanded. "This Inverness and Scotland nonsense?"

Griggs took one last swipe at the snow on his left shoulder. "Invergarry, sir," he soothed.

"Whatever. Nobody cares except the Scots." Moxton unclenched his teeth. "You *know* the department has bolt holes arranged for the Royals for just this sort of contingency. And here you go and ask to pack the Queen off to some salmon lodge."

Outside somewhere, a faint clanking of metal and grinding of gears could be heard. A metal man from the sounds of it. The police were using a mechanical man to lift rubble away in an attempt to find more survivors. Moxton doubted there'd be any.

Moxton suddenly remembered something. "You take your holiday every year salmon fishing, don't you, Griggs? At Invergarry."

Griggs flashed a snaggle-toothed grin. It only made him look all the more weaselly. "I've had this plan in my mind for a while now, sir. Invergarry has one outstanding attraction that isn't in any guide book, and I think it's the solution to all our problems. Getting the Queen there will guarantee it."

"Guarantee what?" Moxton's voice rasped with irritation. He liked initiative in his young men; he just hated them getting bright ideas.

Griggs started playing with one of the colored stickpins, pushing it in and out of the map. "You've said it yourself often enough, sir. We'll never get official approval for our special section while King Log's his parliamentary throne."

Salisbury was indeed a reactionary old Tory who preferred doing nothing, that was true. The old wheezer's personal credo was nothing ever good came of things happening, so it's in Parliament's best interest to see that as little as possible happens.

British intelligence had gone into the Boer War with a grand total of thirteen officers. Not even enough to start a cricket match, let alone enough to safeguard Britain's secrets. Yet Salisbury steadfastly refused to expand the department. And as for Moxton's special section...

Moxton had had to cook the books, divert secret funds, recruit adepts like Griggs on the sly even to assemble what he had. He was risking prison or worse for even that widow's mite.

Yet it had to be done.

Other governments had already set up arcane agencies. The American Yankees their Bureau of Alchemy, Science, and Firearms. The French their Société de la Rue Morgue. Mormon Deseret their Correlation Department. Now, even the Boers had theirs—their bomb throwing *Dopper Kirkkoor*. The Dopper Church Choir.

Britain couldn't afford to keep relying on Grey's volunteer amateurs. It was the Twentieth Century now. The days of the gentleman adventurer or the amateur-expert was over. Just as Henry Fielding's ragtag Bow Street Runners hooligans had given way to Bobby Peel's Metropolitan Police professionals, so too must Grey's Domesday Chapter give way to a professionally run and orga-nized ministerial department for arcane intelligence.

Griggs gave one last push of the pin. "So let's not go through Salisbury, let's—"

"Let's go direct to the Queen?" Moxton finished for him. "And who will bell the cat?" he said sourly.

The single biggest obstacle to standing up his special section—bigger than Salisbury, bigger than the obdurate Grey and his Chapter—was an imperial rescript was needed to authorize its establishment. That meant telling the Queen, and the Queen was a genuinely pious, God-fearing woman. Nobody—not her ministers, not her advisers, not Moxton—wanted to tell her magic existed. Certainly not Salisbury. He wouldn't even discuss discussing the matter.

"That's what Invergarry does for us," Griggs oozed, confident as only a young man can be.

Alarm bells kicked off in Moxton's mind. Griggs was not only ambitious, he had a ruthless streak in him—without the judgement to temper that ruthlessness.

Still, the Gordian knot needed cut. If Griggs succeeded, good. If he failed...

Well, Moxton had other ambitious bright young men.

"What you do," he told Griggs, "you do on your own initiative—without my approval or authority. I don't want to know anything about it. And remember: the Queen is not to be threatened or harmed in any way."

The young man looked up from his map pins. He flashed another weasel grin. "No one will be harmed. Except maybe a salmon or two."

Moxton didn't like the way he said *salmon*.

Griggs exited. Moxton watched the tent flap swing behind him.

It was several minutes before Moxton noticed that Griggs had rearranged the map pins to spell out the word "boom".

Moxton's blood ran cold.

Just how ambitious *was* Griggs? Did Moxton dare find out?

ᘉ

DORIAN GREY'S steam carriage sat idling its engine as it waited for Grey's return, chuffing the occasional plume of waste steam. The poor driver looked like a polar bear, buried in white snow.

The steam carriage was a Dugald-Cleark rig. Old Cleark pig-headedly stuck to designs that were increasingly old-fashioned. The rig was built on the same lines as a traditional handsome cab, the only change being Cleark had tacked the engine and drivetrain on the back. The driver sat up on his cabbie shelve, a tiller in his hand instead of reins, exposed up there to all the elements. Newer steam carriage designs put the driver in an enclosed, same as passengers.

"We're done here, Henry." Grey called up to the driver. "Back to the Tavern.

Henry leaned down, piled snow sloughing off him with the movement. "'Ere! What about Mr. Tafford's train?"

"Mr. Tafford won't be taking his train. He's coming back to the Tavern with me. We're going on a little trip."

Henry chuckled. "'E's not going to like that, he won't."

No indeed he wouldn't, Grey thought as he opened the door to the cab and crawled in.

Grey seated himself opposite the waiting passenger, one Mallory Millrace Tafford. A tall, fat man in his sixties, lame in one leg and fat around his middle, twenty stones worth of fat.

The fat showed particularly now in Tafford's face—its lower half was a cascade of chins and jowl pouches. Bald as well, his hairline had receded over the top of his head and down the back of his skull to the level of his ears. Worst of all, he'd inherited the Tafford nose, a thin wedge-like beak of a proboscis. Between the beak and the jowls and round eyes blinking beneath busy eyebrows, Tafford resembled an owl.

Years ago, Tafford and Grey had been best friends. A falling out resulted in Tafford breaking away from the Chapter. In the performance of one last mission for them, Tafford had been left crippled, his right leg shattered after a battle with an ancient chthonic entity. The once active big game hunter had had to settle for a sedentary scholarly life at Oxford, delving into the hidden secrets of the arcane world. On rare occasion, Tafford's and the Chapter's interests still ran together.

This was one of those times, whether Tafford wanted them to or not.

"I say," Tafford said, closing his book at Grey's arrival, "rather high-handed of you, dragging me off to Scotland without so much as asking first." He spoke in the affected plummy tones of an Oxford don. He'd adopted the accent years ago as protective coloration. Now it seemed it was his natural speaking voice.

Grey ignored Tafford's protests, instead unpinning a small ear-shaped silver ornament from the inside of his jacket lapel. A Jenkins Ear.

He placed it in its velvet-lined soundproof box. Tafford removed its twin and deposited it beside the first. Sitting here in the cab, he'd heard every word spoken out at the rubble pile.

The steam-carriage spun its wooden wheels a bit before its rubber rims gained purchase in the snow. The sudden traction caused the rear-facing Grey to lurch forward in his seat. Regaining his balance, he leaned back into the red velvet seats. Whatever Cleark self-propelled carriages might lack in exterior aesthetics, their interior comforts made up for it.

Tafford's black Malacca cane had shifted during the lurch. Grey put it back, leaning it against the cab wall where Tafford could reach it.

"You were right," Grey told him. "It was the Boers."

Tafford shrugged. "Regrettable, but not surprising. The Boers built their entirely new culture out of their supremacy of black powder rifles. Quite natural, then, they'd fashion a magic discipline based on explosives. Nitromancy for lack of a better term, I suppose. Strange how a nation's character is reflected in—"

Grey cut off the lecture. "Who's the best man I've got for ju-ju magicks?"

"Young Hallawell, I should imagine," Tafford answered. "He's the one who ran up that purple test reagent at any rate." The fat man then harrumphed, clearing his throat for another go. "As I was saying about national character: you have the factory-mad Yankees specializing in alchemical chemicals and formulae, the gem-cutters of Antwerp dabbling in the lapidary arts, and we British—"

"Hallawell's the one I'll put on the palace runes then."

"—whereas we English," Tafford continued, undeterred, "with our legacy of great poets prefer utilizing the resonance and cadence of the spoken—"

"What can you tell me about this Invergarry place?"

Tafford shrugged. "Nothing other than it's north of Hadrian's Wall. Not being fond of haggis or caber tossing, I've very little interest in Scottish geography."

Grey sighed. How much of Tafford's pedantic patter was an act and how much was from the shock of his crippling, Grey could never tell.

"They mentioned salmon fishing and about it being near Inverness," Grey said.

Tafford pursed his lips. "Likely in the Great Glen, then, on the shore of a Scottish lake. The Great Glen's a connected string of lakes that run northwest up to Inverness and the sea."

"Lakes." Grey frowned. "Don't like that. Nothing good ever happens under a lake."

Grey spoke from experience. The chthonic Elder Beings that Grey and his Chapter opposed—Cthulhu and the rest the Cuttlefish—were ancient beyond reckoning and exhibited corresponding torpor. Each fashioned their own "Halls of R'lyeh"—an underground chthonic den invariably created underneath a fresh water lake or the salty brine of a harbor inlet. Grey and Tafford both were two of the very few humans ever to descend into these chthonic dens and return alive.

Much of the Chapter's effort a century ago was preventing the relatively young Yog-Hastur and his consorts from awakening and rising up out of their watery dens in England's Lake District. Decades of constant vigil by the Lake Poets was to prevent this and to induce the stirring Cuttlefish to return to their slumbers under Lake Windemere.

But Tafford had been correct. Poets and playwrights had always been part of the shadow world of arcane espionage. Chaucer had been a spy for the Crown,

Kit Marlowe one of Walsingham's Men. But it was the advent of the Elizabethan playwrights and the founding of the Chapter that had seen the true flowering of English magical scholarship. Theories and discoveries were embedded and encrypted in the texts of their works. Ben Johnson's famous feuds, the codes in Shakespeare decrying the heresies of Francis Bacon and his Rosicrucians, Alexander Pope's "Dunciad", the heated *poetomachia* between Thomas Dekker and his contemporaries. Not all had been Chapter members. Many had been like Tafford, frequently traveling alongside the Chapter.

"I wouldn't worry. The lakes have been quiescent of late," Tafford said.

The chuff of the steam engine, the monotonous crunch of snow under the tires, the rattle of chassis springs all filled the short silence.

"Curious," Tafford mused aloud, "now that I think of it, there's never been any report of a Cuttlefish in a Scottish lake."

Grey raised one eyebrow. "No report? I'd thought there were nothing but reports of strange sightings in those lakes." Long-necked reptiles, just the sort of thing that sounded like Cuttlefish servitors.

Tafford pooh-pooh him. "Lake monster stories. Ha! There isn't a lake in the world that somebody hasn't claimed to have seen a sea monster in. Stronsay in Norway, Chesapeake Bay in America. Even the Mormons in their parched desert claim a couple. Legends are all they are. Nobody in the Chapter or any other arcane societies have ever made a confirmed sighting."

Bored, the fat man reopened his book. "I know. I tried looking for a couple of them back in my younger days." He peered over the top of his book at Grey. "Tell you what. We find a sea monster in Invergarry, I'll shoot it and cook it for you."

The fat man's cane continued rattling against the cab as the carriage trundled its way down snowy streets toward Deptford.

January 3rd
Windsor Station
London, England

Moxton's breath curled upward. The snow may have stopped last night, but the weather had turned all the colder for it, even under the arched roof of the busy station platforms. The cold and the roof seemed to amplify the cacophony. Idling locomotives venting steam. Trains chugging out of the station. Whistle toots and blasts of conductor whistles. The murmuring babble of passengers. Everything smelt of smoke and coal dust.

Moxton hated railway stations.

Bad enough to have to stand here, but to have to watch this charade...

"Idiots," Moxton spat.

Did Scotland Yard really think nobody would notice the absurd number of station porters—all of whom were unusually fit and trim—loitering around in the area. That nobody would notice the pistol-sized bulges under their jackets. *Save us from imbeciles!*

At least he'd managed to talk the Yard out of the worst of their follies. Closing down the entire station or hanging tarps around a platform to block it from view. The list went on for pages.

Easier to hide a field mouse than an elephant, he'd told them.

Just bring up a normal train to the platform. A busy station with passengers worried only about catching the train they've tickets for, they aren't going to pay any attention to a train they don't have tickets for unless you create a big spectacle that causes them *to* notice it.

Nor are they going to notice one old lady in a wheelchair get on the train unless she's surrounded by a royal retinue.

One lady, one nurse, and a couple maids. The train takes off. The fact that the rest of the train was empty, nobody would notice that, either.

Idiots.

"You say something," Grey asked diffidently. He stood a couple feet from Moxton, flanked by his fat flunky, Tafford.

Moxton didn't have nearly the file on Tafford he'd like. What he did have was damning. He wondered how much the supposed estrangement between the Tafford and Grey was genuine.

"Your brusque young assistant is absent," Grey noted. "You all by yourself today?"

"Griggs took the night train up last night," Moxton said. "Thought that somebody should be keeping an eye on the local community, not just the fishing lodge."

"How very commendable," Grey said archly. White breath streamed from the albino's mouth, too. Only the barest trickle as if Grey hardly breathed at all.

Rumor had it Grey had a curse on him, a Curse of Immortality. Chapter gossip, perhaps, but the albino didn't seem entirely tethered to this world.

"You've no one else to back you up at the lodge?" Grey asked.

"The nurse traveling with our principal is an asset of mine," Moxton replied, "just as those two—" Moxton gestured at two conductors looking ill at ease in their uniform that didn't quite fit "—are two of yours."

One conductor was a hulking giant with droopy eyes and a nasty razor scar down his face, the other was a bald little runt of man who smelled of licorice drops. Two of what Grey liked to call his Chapter's security forces, but they were little better than street hooligans and hired killers.

"Let us say they'll be taking special pains to make sure everybody on board has a proper ticket," Grey said, smiling coldly. "Unfortunately, they'll be with us only for the journey. Other duties call."

Moxton shrugged. "Well," he said, nodding in the direction of the 300-pound cripple standing next to Grey, "If we do run into trouble at the lodge, your companion can always sit on it."

A truck cart piled high with Grey's and Tafford's luggage sat nearby. Moxton pointed to one particular item of Tafford's baggage, a well-worn leather case just long enough and flat enough to contain a rifle—specifically a Pendles game rifle Moxton knew Tafford favored. The boys of Scotland Yard would have kittens if they noticed it. "What's in that one?" Moxton asked archly. "A gross of billiard cues?"

"Fishing rod," Tafford said.

"Salmon are out of season."

"The pleasure in fishing isn't the catching of the fish," Tafford replied pedantically in plummy Oxford tones, "but in the casting of the line. I find fishing is ever so much more pleasant without all the guts and mess."

The imitation porters lazing about suddenly became alert.

"It appears our principal has arrived," Moxton said.

A small party approached: a lady invalid, her face covered in a black veil, pushed along in her wheelchair by a young trim nurse and trailed by two plump maids. The entirety of Queen Victoria's retinue for this trip.

Getting her to agree to that must have taxed even Salisbury's famous persuasion.

The wheelchair stopped short of Moxton's feet. "Our keepers, we presume?" the Queen asked from beneath her veil, her voice sharp and penetrating.

Moxton wasn't certain whether she was aggrieved at being shorn of the pomp and dignity of high office or of being shorn of the favorites in her retinue. It went without saying she must be ill-pleased at being coerced into running away from her attackers.

"Percival Moxton, your Majesty," Moxton said forsaking any bow so as not to call undue attention.

"*Hmmpff*," the Queen sniffed under her veil. "You're one of those grubby little men in gabardine who skulk about on foreign shores."

Moxton felt the heat rise up the back of his neck. "I'm allergic to gabardine, mum, and the furthest shore I've ever been to is Folkstone."

"You've spirit at any rate," the Queen said. "We don't approve of what you do, but my ministers insist we need you to do them. Even Elizabeth had her Walsingham, I suppose."

Ignoring Grey entirely, the Queen made a jabbing motion with her hand and the nurse pushed the wheelchair to a waiting railway coach. She was helped aboard, and after a decent interval, Moxton, Grey, and Tafford boarded as well.

The three men waited until their luggage had been loaded and the train had pulled out of the station to make their way to the private railway car used by the Queen. It wasn't her usual royal rail coach but a cut-rate one borrowed from a London merchant Moxton had his thumb on. The velvet-papered interior was genteel, but a bit shabby. The curtains, of course, were drawn.

The Queen, her veil pushed back, frowned when she saw Grey approach.

"We're told you are the man behind that mysterious Royal Charter," she said, distain creeping into her voice. "On the day of our coronation we were shown a sealed parchment along with a handwritten note from James the First admonishing his successors to leave the seal unbroken and acquiesce to its continuance, sight unseen." She shook her head. "'For the sake of England and All Christendom and for our hope in the Resurrection,'" she quoted.

She sniffed. "We like this less than we like gabardine men."

The Queen fell silent for a moment as she stared him. "You're a strange one. We don't recall seeing an albino before. How do you come to be dressed a man of the cloth?"

Grey bowed, the long strands of his silver hair obscuring his face as effectively as a widow's veil. "The Royal Charter requires I hold a deanship."

"*Faugh!*" The Queen's scowl showed what she thought of that.

"My duties are best described as administrative and not ecclesiastic," Grey explained. If the albino had hoped to mollify the Queen with that, he failed.

She glared upward at him. "One of these modern theologians, no doubt, who believe in the pay and position due that collar, but not in the doctrine."

Grey's colorless eyes of frosted lead held steady, Moxton gave him that much.

"I can't deny I have questions or doubts. But they are private doubts. I make no preachments on them." His pale hands fluttered, undoubtedly in consternation at the need to describe his Charter post without describing magic. "I have seen Evil, in my work. Evil supposes Good. I dearly wish to believe in that existence." He sighed. "I've yet to see it so."

"Then you're a fool," the Queen snapped, her quivering voice verging on anger. "You're as blind as you are pale." Her own hands gripped the chair wheels and spun viciously, turning it away from Grey.

Her voice caught. "Evil is great, evil is strong. Stronger than we ever suppose. Why it does not swallow us all in a trice, that's the question of the age."

She turned the chair around to face Grey again. "I imagine you suppose it is held back by strength alone. Yours and your Charter."

She bowed her head. "*I say that Evil is held at bay the power of the ordinary heart. By the absolute faith of a child. Above all by innocence. Innocence, Mr. Grey, by which we would all fail and Evil rend us asunder. I never cease believing in that innocence, that ordinary goodness. I dare not.*"

The Queen sagged in her chair. "I am tired now. Leave me."

Moxton and the other two men turned to go, but as they did, the Queen's frail voice followed.

"Lord Salisbury trusts you to protect me from harm during this journey," she breathed. "His trust is misplaced. The only evil I face on this fool's errand is in the hearts of my protectors."

January 4th
Invergarry, Scotland

GRIGGS SMIRKED. If you look hard enough, there's always one in any community no matter how small. Some dissolute reprobate who'll do anything for money and keep his gob shut for a pound note more. Inverness had its Angus MacKean, an itinerate fishing guide and poacher. The derelict shanty Griggs sat in belonged to MacKean, not that there was much to belong. Its wooden slats had visible gaps between them. Some of them were tar-papered over, some weren't. Bitter cold didn't just seep in, it poured in, opposed only by the feeblest of stove fires—two coal lumps salvaged from train tracks and a wad of paper wrapping Griggs had brought.

MacKean, a crab apple of a man sporting a fringe of dirty white hair, watched Griggs with interest, tippling every few moments from Griggs's own silver whiskey flask. The Scot was dressed in every stitch he owned against the cold, with a few burlap bags stuffed down his jacket for extra insulation.

Griggs had been cultivating the old reprobate for years. The old man must live off the ten pounds Griggs handed MacKean every summer, and it undoubtedly was mostly spent on booze.

The twenty Griggs had slipped him tonight should finish off the old man's liver. Twenty pounds might have been a bit much, but what did Griggs care? Wasn't his. It came from the departmental purse.

A hissing camp lantern burned bright on the table, the only light on this side of the lake. It was getting on ten o'clock and most of the village had quenched their candles, banked their fireplaces, and gone to bed.

MacKean, fingering the leather pouch containing his newfound wealth, stared with owl-eyed fascination as Griggs cut up several strips of fancy Chinese silk—gold and embroidered with wriggling dragons—then tied each strip around a stick of dynamite.

He watched owl-eyed as Griggs cut several lengths of detonator cord. "Och aye, I'm not so blootered as nae wonder how ye think you won't wake up the neebs w'yer dynamite."

Griggs smiled. "No danger there, old son," he said. Not with this silencing cloth Chinese tongs used to muffle explosions when cracking safes. If the Boers could tie magicks around their explosives, so could Griggs.

Not that Griggs had much in the way of magicks.

Chinese trinkets. That's all he and Moxton's crew had managed to scrouge up thanks to that high-and-mighty Grey and his Chapter. Dribs and drabs. Magical table scraps, purchased mostly from the criminal tongs of China.

But not always. The Laplander carved bone in his pocket glowed warmly against the keening wind outside, keeping him nice and toasty. He hoped it lived up to its reputation in keeping him dry out on the lake.

It took a while to tie cloth around all the sticks—Griggs had brought three cases of dynamite—but eventually he finished his task. He carefully put the dynamite sticks back in their packing cases. They'd be safe enough leaving them there tonight—it was far too windy tonight to go out on the lake. He'd left the spool of time fuse cord uncut for now, so the only danger would be from fire. *No chance of that*, Griggs thought, glancing at the iron stove with its surely guttering flame inside.

Unless of course that fool of a MacKean took it in his head to break up the wooden packing cases for kindling.

Griggs thought about warning him, then decided that not putting the idea in MacKean's head was the better course. Besides, with the load of single malt MacKean was carrying, the only idea he'd have in a minute would be passing out on the floor.

Griggs picked up the single dynamite stick he'd left out and fitted a length of fuse cord. He stood up from the rickety table. "Come on, old man. Let's see how this works, shall we?" He made for the door and a blinking MacKean wobbled behind him.

The wind smashed into him like a brick wall. The chill was nearly as bad. MacKean gave a drunken gasp, but Griggs was kept blanket-snuggle warm by the bone scrimshaw in his pocket.

The two trudged through drifting snow, Griggs blazing a trail like Good King Wenceslas and MacKean, wrapping his coat all the tighter, stepping into his prints and following in his wake.

They reached the shore of the lake. "See anyone around?" Griggs asked the old poacher.

"Goan take a keek yerself," MacKean sneered through chattering teeth. "Ach, there's nae about in this muck."

"Good," MacKean said. "By the way, that water cold?"

"Dook yer haun in't ye'self and see if it's cauld, ye sleekit Sassenach!" MacKean spat.

"Better stand back then," he warned, "or you'll get dunked."

Dynamite in his throwing hand, he pulled off the glove of his other with his teeth. Griggs quickly ran his left pointer finger down the seam of his trousers as if striking a lucifer.

Flame enveloped his finger, his one trick of true magic he'd picked up from the tongs.

The yellow flame flickered and danced in the wind, but did not blow out. It burnt at a temperature easily over 700° F—Griggs had measured—and yet left the skin unburnt and unharmed.

Griggs touched his fiery finger to the fuse and then hurled the dynamite out into the lake for all he was worth. Fuse still sputtering, it plunked into the water.

An instant later, a shockwave dimpled a ring on the lake surface, followed by a massive waterspout erupting upward into the air.

The huge explosion had been totally silent. Only the splash of falling water as the spout collapsed made any noise.

Water spray splashed down as far as the shoreline, drenching a sputtering MacKean but leaving Griggs perfectly dry. The scrimshaw trinket protected against wet as well.

Trinket.

Soon Griggs wouldn't have to depend on mere trinkets. He'll have real magicks and real items at his command after they finally stood up the section.

And it wouldn't be Moxton running the section, it'd be Griggs. Because it will have been Griggs who convinced the Queen and pushed the Imperial Rescript through.

Griggs flicked his finger, extinguishing the magic flame. He stood content in the sudden darkness.

☙

A HALF MILE away on the opposite side of Loch Oich, little Sarah and her friend played along the shoreline. It wasn't their usual play spot. That was too visible from the grounds of the House where all those soldiers were. They were being awfully fussy about anyone approaching the House so Sarah just knew they'd be sure to yell at Sarah's friend if they saw her. Sarah had therefore slipped past them and ducked through a hole in the hedge that only she knew about and met her friend at this new spot on the shore, a spot hidden from the house and the grounds by a thick stand of pines.

Those silly old soldiers couldn't see them here

Of course, this new spot wasn't so nice as the usual spot. The shore here was nothing but boulders and big rocks—rocks covered in slick moss at that. Sarah and her friend had tried to clear away some of the rocks but they were awfully big for Sarah. Sarah's friend instead pushed some snow over the rocks and packed it down so they could play as best they could.

It was cold here, though, and windy. Their old spot had a nice big holly shrub with red berries that sheltered them from the wind. The bush sat under a huge oak tree with lots of acorns. Sometimes when she was certain Daddy wouldn't catch her, Sarah would build a little fire and roast them.

Sarah's friend didn't care for acorns too much, but Sarah loved eating roast acorns better than all most anything.

There weren't any acorns here. That was what they were playing now, looking for acorns. Both of them were bent down, looking at the ground.

Suddenly Sarah's friend lifted her head.

Her friend said she'd heard a noise—a bad noise—but Sarah hadn't heard anything. She'd heard nothing at all, save maybe a distant splash of water and even that might have been just a trick of the wind.

Sarah looked out across the lake but saw nothing in the dark. Nothing but swirling snow.

That same evening
Invergarry House

THE GRANDFATHER CLOCK in the hall chimed eleven, caroling its tinny rendition of Westminster Quarters. The Queen and her entourage had long since retired for the evening. Lights still burned in the manor's downstairs, however.

Fire crackled in the library's gothic-arched marble fireplace, paraffin lanterns hissed. Invergarry House was a sanctuary of light and warmth against the howling swirl of snow outside, but not against the frayed tempers of the four men seated inside.

Mallory Millrace Tafford sighed.

Moxton and Grey glared at each other from opposite stuffed ottomans as was to be expected.

He'd hoped more from Edward Balthazar Ellice, the owner of Invergarry House. Ellice was an overgroomed man sporting a flaring moustache which only accentuated his overbite. He stood dithering next to the fireplace, dithering about the Queen all but snubbing him on her arrival, dithering about Grey and Moxton feuding, dithering about the price of mustache wax, Tafford shouldn't wonder.

Ellice wasn't Tafford's only disappointment. He didn't think much of the manor's library as a library. David Bryce, who'd built Invergarry House, was partial to tall narrow gothic windows, a battery of them lining each outer wall of the rambling gothic mansion, leaving little wall space for bookshelves.

What shelves there were had been filled with books chosen for the colors of their outward-facing spines, not their contents. Good enough for trout fishermen, perhaps, but not for an avid reader like Tafford. Had he not brought his own books, he'd have found little to read, despite the all those prettily-spined books about.

Tafford had next to him, stacked on a side table, a selection of poetry volumes—mostly Wordsworth, Coleridge, and the other Lake Poets. The volume he had in his hands now was that of a recently deceased American poetess whose oddities in punctuation and capitalization and line breakage were matched by the oddities of her subject matter. The volume he held was not available to the public but a folio containing poems filched from Dickinson's unsuspecting heirs by Chapter agents at Tafford's bequest.

A fascinating volume, but Tafford found it hard to concentrate with all of Ellice's mournful fidgeting.

Sighing, Tafford took off his reading spectacles and set aside his book. "You mustn't mind those two, Edward," he said. "They're just missing the comforts of London. Electric lighting, gas heating."

Ellice blinked at him rabbit-like, grateful that somebody at last was speaking. "That's why we close in winter, why I warned them in London that—" He gulped, his prominent Adam's apple pistoning up and down. "It simply takes *days* to heat up this old ruin." Another gulp. "And we *will* have electricity soon," he said, changing subjects. "That is if they ever finished the railroad spur across the lake. They're bringing the powerlines down its right of way, you know."

Ellice's hands fidgeted with his pocket watch, winding it again for the third time that night. "Though when that will be—oh! I do try to do what I can as a backbencher for the constituency, but..." His voice trailed off. Ellice was the third in a family line of Edward Ellices to have been English transplants representing the environs of Invergarry in Parliament. But whereas his grandfather Edward had been a brilliant politician and his father Edward had been an adequate politician, poor Edward Balthazar Ellice, MP, had been a dismal failure. A failure as a financier and a landowner as well. He'd had to turn the family manor into a trout hotel to try to make ends meet.

"The small local concern that holds the right-of-way easements hasn't the capital, and the large Inverness concerns that have the capital haven't the rights-of-way, and they're all screaming at me and dragging the mess onto the floor of the House and they've gotten a ten-year truce declared so that nothing's getting finished and—"

"Interesting inscriptions you have carved on the manor's exterior," Tafford said, interrupting the poor man's babbling. Interesting because they acted in effect as protective wards, though of layman quality.

"Oh, those," Ellice said, still agitated. "That was David Bryce's idea. He designed the place for my father. There's Bible quotes and Scottish mottos in Gaelic and I don't know all what."

"I particularly liked the one that read 'A merciful man will be merciful to his beast,'" Tafford said.

"See? No rhyme or reason to them. Father loved his horses, doted on them."

"Speaking of beasts," Tafford slipped in, "any truth to those rumors about those creatures in the lake?"

For the first time that evening, Ellice asserted himself. "Those!" he snorted. "Some fool of an Englishman," he said, forgetting that he himself was as English as Punch and Judy and kidney pudding, "comes up here on holiday and sees a tree branch in the water and thinks it's a sea serpent! One of those long-necked lizards of Darwin! Plea-o-something or other."

"Plesiosaurus," Tafford supplied. Longnecked, blimp-bodied, and sporting four long paddle-flippers for legs according to fossil remains.

"Whatever," Ellice snapped. "Bad for business, it what it is. Scaring off paying customers."

"I would think it would bring in more. Gawkers who want to see the beast."

"And anyway," Ellice sniffed, continued as if he'd not heard Tafford. "That fuss was all north of here. Loch Ness." He nodded in the direction of the lake outside. "*This* is Loch Oich. And there's been no sightings here. If there had, I'd —" He made a strangling gesture.

Tafford smiled at the vehemence in Ellice's voice. Merciful to his beast, indeed.

"Aren't all the lakes interconnected?" The narrow valley of the Great Glen had been formed by an ancient glacier scouring its way northeastward to the sea. A line of ribbon-like lakes connected by short river segments all flowed to Inverness harbor.

Ellice fluffed his moustache. "It's all canal locks now. I should think a giant sea monster queuing up for the lock to fill would attract notice."

Pitch-coated pine logs crackled in the hearth.

"Well," grunted Tafford, grabbing his Malacca cane and heavy his crippled body up out of the stuffed chair. "I think I'll go out for some fresh air."

"Tonight?!" Ellice bleated, suddenly a hotel host again worrying about liabilities. "It's a blizzard outside."

"Sounds as if it's tapering off," Tafford said as he stumped his way across the room, wincing at every step his right leg took. "Besides, unlike those two," he titled his head in the vague direction of Moxton and Grey, "who enjoy living behind a desk, I'm a former outdoorsman. Cooped inside up too long, I go a bit crazy."

He donned the heavy bearskin coat and hat he'd left in the entrance hall, and ventured into the night.

∩

THE SNOW MAY HAVE TAPERED off some, but wind still gusted in fits and starts. The night was dark, very dark. A mere day or two had passed since the new moon. Not that even the light of a full moon could have punched through the thick cloud cover of a Scottish storm.

Snow-laden boughs of surrounding pine trees drooped, creaking and cracking under threat of breaking in two completely. The snow on the ground was nearly a foot deep where it hadn't drifted deeper. A walkway around the mansion had been shoveled, though, and Tafford limped his way to a certain spot both out of the wind and out of sight from prying eyes, both inside the house and out.

Invergarry House wasn't so much a single building but a sprawling series of interconnected building chained together, echoing the lakes of the Great Glen itself. The exteriors were thin-windowed and gothic-arched, as well as flanked by the occasional cone-nosed Victorian tower,

Bryce's design left lots of convenient nooks and crannies. Convenient for hiding spots. Not so convenient if you were one of those poor freezing soldiers posted about the grounds trying to watch for possible intruders. Between the dark and the storm and the architectural blind spots, even a lame crippled old man like Tafford could stump around unseen.

Tafford wedged his fat body into the cranny he'd chosen earlier that day, back when he'd reconnoitered the building exterior in daylight. Here he could hear himself over the wind, and here the temporary wards Grey had chalked upon the walls were at their weakest.

Tafford had not been reading that Emily Dickinson book by accident.

Moxton, visibly disappointed that Tafford hadn't lugged along stacks of arcane tomes to study had no idea that Tafford actually had. He'd been reading a magic tract in plain sight.

Tafford had—at least he hoped he had—decoded Emily Dickinson's embedded cyphers hidden within her strange executions of the written word. In one of those unpublished poems, he'd found the Formula of Power he'd need this night.

The cost would be heavy—the poem itself warned of that—but the need was great.

Dipping into memory, Tafford recited from the very page he'd left the book open on. Stripping out Dickinson's superfluous lines of padding, he recited:

Long since Spoilage, a lancing numbness Comes
Nerves lay brooding, in the Marrow-bone of Tombs
Legs, clockwork, Ratchet in their trace
Until this the Hour of leaden grace

White sparks raced across Tafford's retinas. Decade-old agonies lanced down his leg, igniting ichor-poisoned nerves.

Then nothing.

He felt nothing.

A blessed absence of pain. The sweet release of normalcy in nerve and limb. Tafford's leg was its old self. He could walk again, he could run.

For an hour.

And then the leaden hour would return. Pain delayed paid triple-fold.

But until then, Tafford could act.

Tafford set out, gliding across the grounds in a powerful, panther-like prowl —moving like the jungle-honed hunter he'd been, his trained senses still undimmed from a decade of disuse.

The sprawling Invergarry House lay on a hillside that jutted arrowhead-fashion into Loch Oich, north side bounded by the rock-and-rapids flow of the River Garry tributary, still pristine in its natural state, unlike the between-lake rivers man-built into canal locks. Loch Oich lapped the arrowhead's south edge.

A path southward down the hill from the House led to the rock-strewn shoreline.

The mansion itself lay in a tangle of old pine and winter-bare oak, but the grounds—a square of manicured lawn—formed a clearing between lake and manor. Soldiers huddled and shivered on the grounds, posted about as sentries at the mansion's main entrance or shivering in canvas army tents set up that afternoon.

The soldiers might as well have been on the moon for all the good they were doing guarding Invergarry House. Tafford flitted past them unseen, a dark fleeting shadow in a blackened night.

He circled the manor's exterior walls to a spot beneath the Queen's top floor window. The chalked-up wards were strong here. Tafford shouldn't have been able to even approach, but he knew the precise ward Grey would use here and knew the means to counter it.

Tafford needed to approach here to confirm no one else had been there before. The snow beneath the Queen's window remained virgin-smooth.

Tafford breathed a sigh of relief.

He continued to circle the manor. There may have not been any footprints under the Queen's window, but around to the side of the manor a trail of prints in the snow led from a ground floor window to a hedgerow.

If Tafford remembered the manor's layout correctly, the window belonged to the rooms used by the caretaker and his family. A man named Crewes served as head groundskeeper in the summer, and he and his wife as the manor's caretakers during its winter season closure.

The prints in the snow were too small for an adult, however. Child-sized. The Creweses had a small daughter. A shy little thing, as Tafford recalled, but apparently one with a predilection for climbing out windows in the middle of snowstorms.

A slim patch of ground right up next to the exterior wall was bare of snow, protected by the gothic eaves above. The dirt under the window looked well tramped down. The little scamp must climb out the window on a regular basis.

Tafford examined the tracks in the snow more closely. The tracks were a double trail of footsteps, coming and going from window to hedge. The girl must be back in her bed. Those return prints were perhaps an hour old. Hard to tell in the storm and wind.

Tafford followed the trail to the hedge. The tracks disappeared into a child-size gap in the hedge. He skirted around until he found them on the other side again. He followed them down to the lake.

The shoreline had its share of snow-capped rocks and boulders strewn around. The spot the track led to had far fewer, as if the rocks had been pushed aside by a plow or something. Several of them were freshly turned up in the snow. Tafford could see moss on bare rocks. The snow here had been tamped down by something heavy as well.

Perhaps Ellice meant to build a dock here. Strange time of the year to be building anything, though.

Tafford cast about, looking for more prints. He found more of the girl's tracks. They wandered around—she must have wandered about for quite a time here—but they eventually led back to the smoothed over area.

Frowning, Tafford took two small objects from his pocket. The first was a duplicate of the jade carving Moxton's man had used at Windsor. He knew the Chinese trinket to be almost worthless, but he also knew it to be the equipment Moxton's people used. He wanted to see things as Moxton's men would see them.

Nothing.

The jade stone showed no reaction to the smoothed spot at all. That man of Moxton's supposedly running around—Griggs was it?—would have detected nothing also.

The second object he used was a Chapter divination rod. It swung faintly, but noticeably, over the smoothed spot. Something arcane had pressed that snow.

Brambles and thick growth and rocky moss-slick boulders made passage tricky, but he followed the shoreline around until he arrived at the cobblestone path

The spot was observable by the sentries if they'd been paying attention instead of shivering against the cold.

The snow was undisturbed here. There was a good-sized holly bush under a giant oak that would serve as a natural windbreak. Just the spot for a child to play. Tafford would try divining here.

The rod swung, but barely at all.

This is where he'd expected the girl's prints to lead. Perhaps she had in times past before the soldiers' arrival. Perhaps the whatever had smoothed the shore in the first spot had smoothed it here back then as well.

Tafford looked out across Loch Oich. According to the map, the manor sat at the center point of the long narrow lake. A half-mile at its widest, the lake narrowed considerably here, tucking in like a woman's corseted waist.

The lake's only appreciable island —Long Island—lay dead center of that narrow waist. Long Island was a pumpernickel-shaped mounded knoll laying in the center of the lake channel's narrowest width.

Tafford squinted against the dark of the moonless night and the swirl of falling snow. He could just barely make out the outline of the mound-like island.

Yet he sensed something else...something about the way...

He realized what this feeling was, this tingle of upright hairs on the back of his neck, the clenching of his gut.

He'd felt it before: the tingle of a Staircase.

Twice in his life, he'd descended down a Staircase into the Chthonic Realm. Down and back again.

This feeling was the same but different. Perhaps the Staircase was underwater? He hadn't the means to test that now, but that was his best guess.

He stared at that island again. He got the oddest impression the mound was hallow. Another unprovable, but he was convinced just the same.

He stood there in the snow, his breath pluming while he thought.

Whatever this mystery was, that might-be Staircase had no connection to a Boer assailant, thanks heavens.

One thing at a time, Tafford told himself. Besides, the leaden hour was fast approaching.

He ghosted up the cobblestone path, past the oblivious soldiers, returning to the putative warmth and shelter of Invergarry House. He was almost in his bed when the pain in his re-crippled leg returned, its agony all the more for the brief respite and the fresh remembrance of being hale, being whole.

Of being once more a man.

Next morning
January 5th
Invergarry, Scotland

MID-MORNING AND OVERCAST, grey light filtered through the windows of Invergarry House. Tafford hobbled his way down the staircase from his room to the library, but just as he feared, breakfast had long since been served and cleared away. He'd slept like the dead after his exertions last night. Smell of past bacons was sheer torture, but maybe more could be found in the kitchen. Where ever that was.

He stumped down the hall, glancing out the tall gothic windows as he did so. The snow had stopped for the moment, but from the look of the gray clouds above—a complete overcast of snow-laden fluff—it might resume again any minute.

He saw a man who must be Crewes clearing the snow off with an angle-bladed horse plow.

Bacon would have to wait.

Retrieving hat and coat from the entrance closet, he shrugged them on and gingerly plodded down the snow-slick path. The soldiers must all be in their tents having tea, as none were out and about. Tafford didn't blame them. Too cold for a mad bomber, anyway.

Crewes saw Tafford approach and *whoa*-ed his horse. He flashed a wide grin and yelled, "The trick is pulling the plow back up the steps." Tafford hadn't noticed it last night in his haste to get back before the spell wore off and Cinderella lost her leg, but the hill was less of a natural slope and more of a series of terraced flats. Where the edge of a terrace ended, three or four stone steps led down to the next.

"How *do* you get it back up?" Tafford asked.

"Strong back, stout heart, and lots of grunting and cursing while I lift," Crewes said, chuckling.

Tafford pointed at the plowed path. "You do this often?"

"Only when we've winter guests which isn't often." Crewes slapped his gloved hands for warmth. His gloves were only knitted wool, not fur-lined leather like Tafford's. Crewes's hands must be freezing. Ellice must be a Scrooge of an employer.

"His nibs had the bright idea one year of opening for a Scottish Christmas." Crewes laughed bitterly. "Seems trout fishermen aren't very interest in Scottish Christmases. Not with trout out of season."

A mass of pines mostly hid it, but if Tafford looked at just the right angle he could just see the mounded lump of Long Island. He turned back to Crewes and his plow, slowly grinding its way down the hill.

"I hope you're not plowing this for my sake," Tafford said. "Doubt I could make it down and back all the way with this gammy leg of mine."

Crewes blushed and looked away. "Actually, I thought I'd clear it in case our lady lodger might care to look at the lake."

Tafford hadn't the heart to tell him that the infirm and elderly Widow of Windsor was even less likely to stroll down the path than Tafford was.

Quickly changing the subject, Tafford asked, "You're the one with a daughter, aren't you?"

Crewes beamed. "Our Sarah. Seven years old. Knows these grounds better than I do." His smile faded. "It hasn't been easy on our Sarah. The only English girl in a Scottish village. Children can be far crueler than adults sometimes."

"No friends I take it."

Crewes shook his head. "Coventry treatment. The few times they speak to her it's 'dirty Sassenach.'" He pulled his gloves tight. "She's had to make up her own friend. Calls her Bess. Takes my newspaper down to the lake and pretends to read it to her."

"Surprised she doesn't freeze out here."

Crewes laughed. "She's a hardy one, our Sarah. Never seems to get cold. If her mother doesn't catch her first, she's out the door with no coat, just that raggedy old sweater of hers she loves to wear."

Changing the subject again, Tafford looked over the Grey waters of the lake. "Don't suppose there's any truth to all those rumors about that lake creature? Fellow in my club was telling me all about it."

"That nonsense?" Crewes just shook his head. "I can only wish there were.

His Nibs could advertise as a 'Monster Viewing Hotel' and open all year round. Plenty of Londoners crazy enough to believe in monsters. More of them than fishermen crazy enough to come up here in winter." He hocked and spat on the snow. "No, all that nonsense is just that. Nonsense. Besides, that's all up at Loch Ness to the north. The only thing happens around here is weather."

"Loch Ness. That's the next lake up the chain, isn't it?" Tafford asked. Crewes nodded.

Tafford sighed. "Well, I'd better get back to the house and let you get back to your plowing," he said, taking his leave. He paused. "But if there were a monster..." he said, trailing off. "I don't suppose you've ever seen a seal wriggle across a beach? Or an otter across snow? Utter demons they are. Quick as a whip."

Tafford shrugged. "I don't imagine a plesiosaurus would be much different." Up and over the banks next to the loch and back in the water as fast as Jack Robinson.

He started his trudge up the path. After a few agonizing steps, Tafford stopped and turned. "I'll tell our lady lodger about your nice clean path. Maybe she and I will hobble down and look for monsters on the lake together."

∩

TAFFORD SHRUGGED out of his coat, hung it in the hall closet again, and plodded his way to the kitchen, following the smell of baking rolls. He pushed the swinging door to the kitchen open just a crack. Crewe's wife was bustling about the kitchen, preparing lunch enough for both the lodgers and the poor freezing soldiers outside. Her daughter was dutifully helping her. Pulled out of school most likely. Probably a relief to the girl, knowing her classmates.

Mrs. Crewe looked quite stressed. Not a pleasant task, Tafford supposed, having to suddenly cook for the Queen.

Now that he'd confirmed all three Crewses were otherwise occupied. Tafford hurried to their suite of rooms. Locked, of course, but not against the arcane tools at Tafford's disposal. He was in quicker than if he'd had the door key.

He stumped straight to the girl's room, the one the footprints had led from. He raggedy red sweater was hanging on a hook. He searched its pockets, finding a small river-rounded stone. Black granite, same as the rocks that lined the Loch Oich shore. He wrapped his fat paw around it, and pulling open the window, stuck his fist out into the frigid air.

The stone began radiating a feeble heat, that heat spreading through his body. Enough to keep warm in just a sweater, he supposed.

He closed the window, put back the stone, and made his way out.

Curiouser and curiouser, he mused. Little Sarah couldn't have fashioned a Fornax stone. He wondered who had.

He had his suspicions.

In the meantime, back to the kitchen to wheedle what breakfast he could from the harried Mrs. Crewe.

IT HAPPENED that afternoon while Tafford was cleaning his rifle in the library. Their host, the hapless Edward Ellice number three, annoyed the Queen once too often. From what Tafford could hear, it involved Ellice doing a little politicking for his precious railroad and the Queen's royal temper snapping.

The Queen had declared in no uncertain terms that she would not remain in this house one second longer if *that man* remained in it as well. Needless to say, Ellice was sent packing. Off to Inverness or London or anywhere else out of sight of Her Majesty he could best scurry off to. His last act before scarpering out the door was that of a penurious landlord: he locked the library liquor cabinet.

Tafford wasn't much of a drinker, but Moxton was. Moxton was also as adept with locks as Tafford was, though the spymaster's tool of choice was a hank of wire. Ellice wasn't even down the front steps before Moxton had poured himself a double of ten-year-old Laphroaig whisky. "I suppose the ice is all outdoors," he sniffed.

Ellice's hurricane departure ushered in a new era of peace and quiet. Sunlight poured through the library's windows, bright despite the leaden grey clouds masking the winter sun. The smell of mutton wafted in from the kitchen. Mrs. Crewe had no sooner served lunch than she was back in the kitchen engaged in the Sisyphean task of preparing the evening meal.

Moxton wandered over to where Tafford was busy cleaning his rifle. An old square of canvas Tafford kept in the gun case served as a drop cloth to protect the Hepplewhite dropleaf table. "Cleaning our fishing rod, are we? Providing tonight's tucker? Poached salmon, perhaps?" He smiled, shark-like. "Or perhaps roast grouse. Freshly shot out of season."

"I was thinking of something larger," Tafford replied affably, snapping the rifle's receiver back in place. "Civil Servant a l'Orange."

Moxton hissed snake-like with amusement. His fingers traced the rifle's wooden stock. "Krag-Jorgensen?"

"Pendles," Tafford said, knowing full well a spymaster like Moxton knew what make the rifle was. "I've modified it a bit. Cut out a new magazine well and fitted it with a custom Doering clamp for a detachable semi-automatic cartridge and drop release."

To demonstrate he slapped an empty magazine in place then thumbed its release. He dry fired the bolt action a few times to make sure he'd reassembled things right, then set the rifle down on the drop cloth and picked up the empty magazine to begin thumbing in bullets.

The cartridge box lay opened, a couple or so loose rounds scattered on the table. The casings themselves were common enough, simple brass, but the bullets themselves glinted silver in the window light. Silver and finely etched with intricate designs.

As if idly curious Moxton made to reach for one. Tafford slammed his meaty paw down upon Moxton's hand, pinning it to the table.

"Baby mustn't touch," Grey said archly from across the room.

"Special reload," Tafford said. He released Moxton's hand. Moxton pulled it pointedly away, rubbing away the pain with his other hand. "They have a tendency to go off if you don't know what you're doing," Tafford added.

"Alas, I have a one-handed armorer who knows that danger all too well," Moxton mused.

Somewhere in the process Moxton had dropped his whisky to the floor. He sauntered over to pour a fresh one. "That particular shell has a two-step fabrication process." He swirled the amber liquid in his glass. "The bottleneck for us has always been engraving the Boudicca's War Glyph, second variant. So difficult to get right and so explosive when you don't."

Moxton sipped at his Laphroaig. "I imagine *your* organization's bottleneck is convincing the Archbishop of Canterbury to bless and dip them in holy water." He titled the glass up to his mouth, then stopped. "Ah. Of course. The deanship and the dog collar. You sanctify them yourself, don't you, Grey?"

Grey said nothing. The look he gave Moxton, however, was colder than the frost outside.

Moxton drained his glass and set it down. "Archibald Gowers would still have two hands if he'd only had ten minutes to peruse the books in your Recknynge vault and copy down the correct glyph, rather than try to rely on a Viennese forged text."

The corner of Moxton's mouth quirked at Grey started at the mention of the Recknynge. Moxton knew things he shouldn't.

"But then again," Moxton continued, "What does a hand matter in the grand scheme of things? A hand. Or—" he glanced at Tafford "—a leg. Just as long as you and you alone can continue your holy crusade, what does the cost matter? The evils done by two-legged threats are beneath you."

The grandfather clock chimed quarter past.

Tafford stirred. He wished that Moxton hadn't mentioned his leg. That made what had to be said all the harder. "Dorian, he's right, you know."

Grey whipsawed around, giving Tafford the same look Julius Caesar must have given his friend Brutus.

"Why isn't our security crew—Turtle and Razor Eddie and his men—here helping protect the Queen?" Tafford asked. "Because you want them in Cornwall. Why aren't they looking for the nest of Boer bombers? Cornwall again."

"That's not fair. You know what's in Cornwall."

"And why isn't Moxton looking for the Boers?" Tafford continued. "Because he can't scrape up even four or five good men to look for them. Without official standing—and you block him from gaining it—all he can dredge up for recruits are dregs even Scowerer wouldn't hire."

A pine log popped in the hearth.

"Both your organizations are needed," Tafford said. "Arcane agents against arcane threats. Arcane agents against other arcane agents. There can be a clear demarcation between your two areas of operations. You're just too stubborn to admit it, Dorian."

Grey sat chin resting on fist for several long moments. "Even if what you say is true, I *can't* allow it. Our royal charter doesn't allow me to allow it."

"Royal charters can be amended by other royals," Tafford said softly. "I believe we have one upstairs."

ᴧ

GRIGGS WAS WHISTLING as he clambered into the weathered dinghy.

The faintest remains of daylight had faded to black as Griggs and MacKean set out on the lake. MacKean pulled the oars with practiced ease, circling a bit to point the bow in the desired course. Griggs had one of Misell's new-fangled electric torches that ran off dry-cell batteries. He clicked it on to glance at a map of Loch Oich, as if he hadn't spent most of the day going over it with MacKean.

"We'll go around the lake counter-clockwise," Griggs said, clicking off the torch. "Down to the south locks first then up to the North." He dug a dynamite stick out of the first opened crate. "Remember to give the manor a wide berth. Don't want them seeing what we're doing until we have something to show."

"Och, aye," muttered MacKean under his breath, "an' whin we kitch ta wee cow'rin beastie, ah'm sure ye'll be remimberin' this 'we' part."

The old man backed the oars. "Here be a deep spoot."

Griggs squinted against the dark. "Where? I can't see."

MacKean unstoppered his flask. "Take a keek t' yer raight. Plain as dey." He downed a swig. "Eejit."

Griggs stared all the harder. Then he saw what MacKean was yammering about. Rippling water—the slow flow of the lake current to the north—reflected what little light there was to be had under the overcast night sky. A dark spot where there were no ripples must be a deep spot.

He swiped his finger against the wooden seat of the dinghy to strike its flame. Holding the dynamite in his throwing hand, he lit the fuse and tossed it over hand into the deep spot.

A soundless geyser of water leaped into the air, splashing around them.

MacKean sputtered against the expected wet and the cold. "Och, mon! M'clothes are drookit fae y'r dynamite!" The old rumpot blinked again. He was still dry!

Griggs hadn't been quite sure his attempt at duplicating a Laplander scrimshaw carved from a soup bone would actually work, but it had. Enough at least to keep the old souse warm and dry.

Griggs risked the torch again, clicking it on and quickly skimming its beam over the spot he'd just dynamited. No monster carcass.

Well, the night was young, and he had a whole lake to search and three cases of dynamite to flush the creature out with.

Still marveling over being dry and warm, the old Scot flashed the first grin Griggs had ever seen him make. MacKean restoppered his flask and grabbed his oars. "Aye, on t'next deep spoot."

ᑎ

THEY FOUND nothing on the south lobe of the lake. They oared quietly past the manor house. Not until they were a hundred feet around the bend and screened by oaks and ink-black pines, did Griggs start the search again.

It had been lightly snowing off and on all night. Light flakes started tumbling down again.

There. thought Griggs. There near the bolder strewn shore on the manor side oof the lake "Another deeps spot," Griggs hissed. MacKean shipped oars.

Finger aflame, Griggs lit the fuse and tossed another stick. Another sound-less tower of water splashed down.

Griggs made a quick sweep of the electric torch "I think I hear something," he snapped. "Quiet!"

MacKean nodded. He was rather blootered by now, to use his own phrase.

Griggs made another sweep of the torch, this time closer to the shore where he thought he'd heard that sound. The light skittered over the boulder-strewn shoreline. For a second, he thought he saw movement. He swung the light back.

Just an old newspaper, fluttering on the breeze.

"Nothing," he grumbled, flicking off the torch. "Well, on to the next spot. If we run out of dynamite tonight, I'll head up to Inverness in the morrow and get some more."

MacKean leaned into the oars. "Sleekit, timo'rous beastie!" he slurred. "Dinnae think ye kin run!"

They paddled northward up the shoreline, not realizing a small pair of eyes followed their progress, staring at them from behind one of the very boulders the electric light had played over.

SARAH HAD HAD to wait until all the guests and all the soldiers had been served supper and then the dishes and kitchen cleaned before she could slip away to meet her friend Bess. Bess had probably given up waiting for her. Still, Sarah had to try.

Newspaper in hand, Sarah slipped out her window. Those silly old soldiers were still poking about the grounds, so instead of heading down the main path to the lake, Sarah retraced last night's steps and cut through the hedge and nipped down to her new spot on the shore.

Reaching it, she slapped the water a few times and waited.

No Bess.

Sarah was about to try again when she saw a flicker of flame a few yards offshore. She could make out a dinghy in that feeble flicker. A dinghy and two men aboard it. The flicker of flame turned into a sputtering sizzle of sparks. The sparks soared skyward in an arc and *splooshed* into the water.

Suddenly a geyser of water exploded upward. A soundless explosion!

Water splashed down around her, but the black rock in her sweater pocket that Bess had made for her kept her mostly dry. Her clothes and hair were only a little damp. In the freshening breeze, the dampness caked into ice. The damp and the ice and the breeze were all more than Bess's rock could handle. Sarah shivered, her teeth chattered.

A beam of light coming from the dinghy swept over the water where the sizzle had fallen. Sarah took a step back in surprise, slipping on a rock and tumbling behind a big boulder onto her backside. She lost her hold on the newspaper she'd brought Bess and it danced away in the breeze, plastering its waggling pages against the side of the big boulder.

A voice from the dinghy hissed "Quiet!" The beam of light swept again, this time over the shoreline. Frightened, Sarah flattened as low as she could out of sight. The light pinned itself to the fluttering newspaper before clicking off.

It was hard to hear over the wind, but she heard a man's voice quite clearly say "dynamite" and "more" and the other man in the boat, a Scotsman, say something about a "beastie" and about how they'd eventually catch it.

Dynamite!

Sarah didn't know why it hadn't made any noise, but that was what they'd been thrown in the water. That's what caused the waterspout.

They were rowing up and down the lake throwing dynamite in the water, trying to kill her friend, trying to kill Bess!

Sarah picked up a stick to slap the water, to call Bess so she could warn her. But then Sarah realized she shouldn't do that. The bad men in the boat would hear Bess, see Bess. And when they saw her, they'd—

Sarah had to get help. She had to get that help from the House. The soldiers, they wouldn't believe her. Her parents, they wouldn't believe her either. Even if they did what could they do?

But the House had one person who would believe her. One person who could help her and Bess. Sarah wasn't supposed to know who the lady lodger was, but of course she did. Everybody in Britain knew the lady lodger.

All her books at school said Queen Victoria was kind and wise and an unceasing defender of Truth. And if the Queen defended Truth, of course she'd recognize Truth when she heard it, when Sarah told it. And she then could tell all the soldiers—

Sarah scrabbled up the rock-strewn hill. She dived through the hole in the hedge and scrambled out the other side.

Golden light shining through the windows beckoned.

HUNTING big game had taught Tafford the art of waiting patiently. Game tends to spook if one paces nervously around a watering hole.

Moxton wasn't exactly pacing around his watering hole—poor Ellice's severely depleted liquor cabinet—but he wasn't exactly waiting patiently, either. For the fifth time in as many minutes, he stubbed out a barely touched cigarette then lit up a new one. Greasy blue smoke wreathed his head as he puffed.

Sitting opposite Moxton, Grey also waited with ill grace. Outwardly he sat preternaturally still as usual, but his pale face told another story. He wore the scowl of a declawed pet cat forcibly held under a bathtub spigot.

They both were waiting for the Queen to come downstairs, Moxton to present his case and gain his long-sought establishment, Grey to acquiesce to it. Both should just learn to relax.

Tafford shrugged and returned to his newest book, a slim notebook, the kind sold to schoolchildren.

He'd found it the day of the arrival sitting with some other odds and ends in the far corner of the library. One small shelf that wasn't just a display of beautiful book spines. The books on this shelf weren't all that interesting, but they seemed to have been a collection of books owned and personally annotated by the first Edward Ellice, presumably kept around for sentimental reasons by the family.

Tafford remembered idly thumbing through this notebook that day, but putting it back on the shelf and returning to his poetry. The notebook was scarcely his field of interest.

Its first few rule-lined pages were just handwritten notes on the construction of beaver mounds. Not too surprising; first Ellice had, after all, made his first fortune in the Canadian beaver fur trade. The notes went on at pedantic length about beavers' penchant to build their mounds in the center of beaver ponds, preferably atop small islets when possible, but building them out of sticks when they must.

Ellice had even sketched out a cut-away view of a beaver mound with its attendant tunnels and den chambers.

Possibly it had been vague memories of flipping past that sketch that had caused Tafford to suppose mound-shaped Long Island was hollow.

Following the handwritten notes, Ellice had pasted in pages cut out of some naturalist magazine: engraved illustrations of how a common mole appeared.

The book also contained some pages cut out from a naturalist magazine—engraved illustrations on how a common mole dug its tunnels with its flipper-like forefeet.

Hardly riveting reading material.

But it hadn't been until this evening that he'd finally realized what had been tickling the back of his mind: the shape of Ellice's cut-away sketch matched exactly the profile of Long Island.

And Ellice had scrawled under his sketch the legend *drawn to scale*.

Which was why Tafford was now slowly going over the notebook page by page. And why he'd checked the other books on the shelf as well, including an Edinburgh-printed monogram of nonsense words entitled *Lexico Aquaticum*.

Tafford wasn't quite sure what it all meant but was beginning to guess why 'a merciful man will be merciful to his beast' had been carved on the Ellice manor's exterior.

ᴧ

Tafford set the notebook down when he heard the noise of a slow procession down the hall stairs. There was little doubt as to who was making that descent.

In his fiduciary need, the third Ellice had converted the whole of Invergarry House except the library and the kitchen to rentable bedrooms. Other than one's room, there was no place for a guest to go but the library. One can only stay in one's bedroom just so long, even a Queen. The muffled sound of the slow progress of heavy, halting footsteps sounded a descant to the murmured sounds of the nurse's encouragement. The Queen, though not totally infirm, walked with even more difficulty than Tafford.

At last, she entered the library, the Widow of Windsor, her black velvet widow's dress trailing the floor, her veil pushed back to frame her round and weary face.

Tafford heaved himself to his feet. Grey and Moxton followed suit. "Your Majesty," the three intoned, heads bowed.

The Queen gave them a desultory wave. Her nurse helped her lower herself awkwardly into the softest chair in the room. Her imperial face glowered with a scowl that seemed to say *we are not amused*.

Tafford shouldn't wonder. Trundled off to Scotland, stripped of her pomp and dignity, not to mention her advisers and retinue, shorn even of her favorite attendants, only to find her host a mewling idiot and her only company two noxious spymasters and a fat fool.

The Queen lifted her chin. "We are of a mind for poetry," she commanded. *We are not amused. Amuse us.*

The Queen's love for poetry was well known. Tafford glanced at the poetry books stacked next to him. The Queen would hate the modern poet Dickinson as much as she hated modern theologians. Nor were the Lake Poets safe choices. Byron and Keats and Shelley and even Wordsworth—libertines, iconoclasts, and curmudgeons all. Who knew which particular literary badger trap might set the Queen off and snap Tafford's metaphoric leg in two?

Better to play it safe. Better to recite the Queen's favorite poem, even though he must do it from memory.

"*Slowly England's sun was setting,*" he began, "*o'er the hilltops far away—*"

The Queen's face softened and her eyes closed, the better to imagine every vivid detail in Rose Hartwick Thorpe's "Curfew Must Not Ring Tonight."

The poem spoke of a young girl Bessie whose lover was scheduled to be executed upon the sounding of curfew bell. Bessie's vain attempts to win his release culminate in her desperate attempt to physically prevent the bell's clapper from striking by holding on to it for dear life as the bell swings wildly in the tower. Even the stern and implacable Cromwell is moved by Bessie's devotion and at the end he pardons her lover.

On and on Tafford recited, the poem's droning *DA-dum-DA-dum* trochaic octameter meter lulling the non-royal portion of his captive audience half-asleep.

Tafford had only gotten as far as the stanza *She has reached the topmost ladder; o'er her hangs the great, dark bell* when the double doors of the library crashed open and a frantic sobbing Sarah Crewes tumbled pell-mell into the room.

"Curfew shall not ring tonight!" mumbled Tafford, suddenly bereft of audience.

SARAH THREW herself at the feet of the Queen. "Please, your majesty!" she sobbed. "My friend, you've got to save my friend Bess! Bad men are trying to kill her!"

"Calm yourself, child," the Queen with solemn dignity said to her. *Queen Victoria actually speaking to her, Sarah Crewes!* The Queen did not reach out herself for Sarah, but gestured at her nurse who gently lifted Sarah from the floor.

Sarah sniffled and wiped her eyes. Only now did Sarah realize what a sight she must be. All scratched by branches, her boots spattered with mud and snow, her sweater caked with ice.

Sarah's eyes were on the Queen, but out of the corner of her eyes she saw the three other guests, those three men. The fat one still was seated, but the other two were on their feet: the albino looking horrible stern and that other man, the fair-complected one with no eyebrows. He had his hand under his jacket lapel for some reason. He looked awfully mean.

All of them looked at Sarah like they didn't understand what she was trying to say, so she took a deep sobbing breath, and tried to explain again. "There's men on the lake in a boat throwing dynamite. They're doing it to try to kill Bess with it. You've got to stop them, Your Majesty, you've just *got* to." Not until she blurted it out so baldly did Sarah realize how ridiculous it might sound.

"Dynamite?" the Queen asked. "Our ears aren't what they used to be, but surely we would have heard dynamite on the lake." Her tone implied she hated lies and the little girls who speak them.

To make things worse, her parents had entered the room. Bowing and scraping, embarrassing and fearing for their positions, her parents made a hash of things. "Your Majesty," her father stammered, his voice equal parts shame and desperation, "there isn't any friend. Our daughter's a very lonely girl. H-her f-friend's all in our Sarah's imagination. The rest of her story must be as well."

The Queen looked up sharply. "An imaginary friend?" she asked softly as if recalling a personal memory. She opened her mouth to speak, but whatever next the Queen was about to say never passed her lips, for the fat man grabbed at his cane and pushed himself to his feet.

"Your Majesty, if I may," the fat man said as if asking for her leave but he was already next to Sarah looking down on her. "Sarah, look at me," he ordered, gentle but firm. His eyes seemed to glitter in the lantern light.

"_Ællyaa'ai'ae_," he said and Sarah felt her own eyes grow wide as saucers. The fat man knew it! He knew Bess's language!

The fat man made a peculiar gesture, like he was playing shadow puppets against a screen. His cupped hand bent over at the wrist and his forearm waggled like a long-necked goose. "Bess?" he asked.

Sarah threw her arms around his neck. He believed her, he believed her!

Wincing, the fat man stood. "Mr. and Mrs. Crewes, I'm afraid you're very much mistaken. Sarah's friend Bess is very, very real. And she's no ordinary personage, this Bess of hers."

"Explain!" the Queen ordered.

The fat man got a funny look on his face, almost as if he were sad for the Queen. "Your Majesty, there are some things once spoken that cannot be unheard. If I tell you, your world, your Christian faith may never be the same."

That made the Queen mad. The Queen banged her hand on her chair arm. _Thump-thump-thump!_ "Do not presume to tell a queen what she can and cannot be told."

Her eyes narrowed and she looked at the other two guests. "Are we to assume, then, that this touches on what you two wish to discuss with us? Something that we assume by your presence, Moxton, impinges on the safety of the Realm?"

The two men nodded. Sarah didn't understand. They were just standing and talking. "Bess!" she said. "You're forgetting about Bess!"

"The safety of the Realm _and_ this child's friend," the Queen amended. "It is our duty, then, to listen to your unpleasantries, Mr. Tafford."

The Queen lifted her imperial chin at the fat man. "And Mr. Tafford? If the death of my beloved husband could not shake our faith in God Eternal, nothing you could ever say will."

THE FAT MAN started talking about all kinds of things Sarah didn't understand, about other worlds outside the Bible and outside science, of broken barriers and evils seeping into our world. About how men like him and the albino fought those evils with what he called "powers" but how bad men used those same "powers" to do evil things and that the eyebrow-less man needed to fight bad men if the Queen would let him.

Bad men like the men on the boat hunting Bess.

"This Bess," the fat men said, trying to explain her friend to the Queen. "Bess is not a little girl but one of those beings I spoke of outside our ken. I believe her to be a lake monster, similar in form at least to a Plesiosaurus."

Monster, indeed! Sarah didn't know what a plea-something was, but the Queen seemed to understand. She cut off the fat man's attempt to explain. "We are the royal patron of the British Museum, Mr. Tafford. Credit us with a little knowledge of Mr. Darwin's pets."

The Queen pursed her lips then, to think this all this over—as if Bess could wait!

Eventually the Queen finished thinking. "And this is all, Mr. Tafford?" she asked, royal irritation in her voice. "This trifle is what our advisors have been so hesitant to breach for sixty years now?" She sniffed. "You do not question our faith in God and Bible, sir! You question our faith in our advisors!"

The Queen made to touch Sarah's cheeks, as if to brush the mud from it, then stopped. The Queen's hand returned to her lap. "You've more, Mr. Tafford?"

The fat man kind of shuffled his good foot, hesitating to speak further. "Your Majesty, there's something I must say," he said, glancing sadly at Sarah of all people. "Bess might come from that other plane I spoke of, that place of evil. She may *be* evil, no friend to the girl or us or our world."

Sarah wanted to shout no, Sarah's my friend, she isn't bad but before she could, the Queen held up her hand to Sarah, ordering Sarah to silence. The look on the Queen's face was as hard as it was righteous in its wrath.

"I believe I told you three gentlemen earlier," the Queen said, "that evil is held at bay not by the strength of arms—" she looked at the fat man "—not by 'powers'—" she looked at the albino "—and not by clever stratagems—" she looked at No Eyebrows "—but by goodness and the everyday and the human heart. By innocence."

The Queen gently placed her aged hand on Sarah's shoulder. "I will continue to believe in innocence. I dare not do otherwise."

SARAH THOUGHT THE FAT MAN, Mr. Tafford, was just some silly old duffer like those old summer guests and their trout. Instead, Mr. Tafford started barking orders left and right, bossing all the others—her parents and the nurse, even the Queen, even those other two, Eyebrows and the albino. Those two sure didn't like it. Sarah just knew those two were men bossy men used to doing the bossing, not being bossed.

Mr. Tafford said all of them—the three guests, Sarah and her family, the Queen and her nurse—they were all going outside to find Bess and keep her safe.

They hauled down the Queen's wheelchair and bundled her up in shawls and a coat and big thick blankets. Sarah's parents forced her into a heavy coat, too, even though she had Bess's stone to keep her warm. The rest of them put on coats, too, except the albino who said he couldn't get cold when I asked. Maybe he had a stone, too. The fat man looked funny like a roly-poly bear himself in his fur coat and hat. He made Sarah want to laugh.

But then Sarah wasn't laughing anymore.

Mr. Tafford picked up a rifle and held in his hands. Was he going to shoot Bess?

Sarah's father knelt down. "The Queen is going with us and the she must be protected no matter what. We want to believe in Bess, Sarah, we all do, but if...if something happens...Mr. Tafford must do what needs done to protect the Queen. You must be a brave little soldier yourself, Sarah. Can you do that for us?"

Sarah nodded, tears welling. Of course they must all protect the Queen. And the bad men were out there, too.

They set off. Out of the library and down the manor's big front hall.

"Speaking of soldiers," the albino sniffed, as the party reached the front door. "I suppose I'd best do something about them." His face looked sad when he said that. "A lot of young men with guns and no brains running around. They may interpret things badly."

Mr. Grey, the albino, opened the door, some strange object in his hand. The crooked stick-thing sort of sparkled, only the reverse of sparkling. Black shadow instead of light. He waved it at the front lawn—the grounds as Mr. Ellice always called it—and at the soldiers all posted there or in their tents.

They all sort of froze. Not like frozen like covered in ice, but frozen like statues.

Sarah watched the albino's face as he did this. He seemed to bite his lip in pain and despite the freezing cold outside a sheen of sweat covered his brow.

In Sarah's picture books, magic was a wonderful thing, like princes and castles. But here in real life, magic seemed to hurt to use, and the even the mention of it made the albino and those other men and even the Queen sad to hear of it.

Would Bess and her magic make them hurt and feel sad, too?

The group slowly proceeded down the hill to the lake. The fat man slow and limping, carefully placing each step like the old man he was. The nurse struggling to push the Queen's chair down the icy path, wheels sticking sometimes in the snow, sliding sometimes on packed ice.

Sarah's mother held Sarah's hand. Her father carried a paraffin lantern, but the man with no eyebrows wouldn't let him light it just yet. So that they could keep their night vision, he said. He was a funny man, Mr. Moxton—not jolly-funny like the fat man—but strange-funny. He wore only one glove and it didn't have any fingers to it at all, just a metal plate in the palm. In Mr. Moxton's other hand he carried a long metal tube. An electric torch he called it. Sarah had seen one in a store in Inverness. He must be awfully clever and rich to own one.

The walk down the hill seemed to take forever, but at last they reached the lakeshore.

Light snow was falling, but the air was calm. Calm but bitter cold.

"Call your friend, child," the Queen commanded. Sarah heard the fat man cock his rifle in the dark.

Sarah looked around for a stick, found one, and slapped the water with it.

Nothing.

Again, she slapped.

Again nothing.

"Bess must be hiding from the bad men and afraid to come out," Sarah said, apologizing for her friend. "Bess probably thinks it's the bad men trying to trick her. She's ever so smart."

"The creature talks to you?" the albino asked. Sarah didn't like him calling Bess a creature and didn't like the tone he said it in. *As if Bess couldn't talk!* But the poor man looked like he was really hurting after that magic, so Sarah decided maybe Mr. Grey didn't mean to be mean. "Does it speak, child? In its language or ours?" he pressed.

"In ours, of course," she said, answering his silly question. "I only know a few words in hers, it's really hard, so I taught her English"

"You taught her?"

"At first I did," Sarah said, "but she learned mostly on her own. Really, all I did was just talk to her. The more I talked, the more she learned. Just as fast as I could speak a word, she seemed to learn it. She's terribly bright," Sarah repeated.

Sarah added: "She wanted to learn hard grownup words, but I didn't know the ones she wanted, so I started reading the newspaper to her."

"You read the newspaper to her," Eyebrows said in a tone that made it seem the most ridiculous thing ever said, like he didn't believe her.

"Oh, not anymore," Sarah said. "I was too slow. Bess reads it herself now. I just hold it for her and turn the pages because she can't turn them herself. She'd get them wet."

"A newspaper-reading plesiosaur," Eyebrows said, shaking his head. He wasn't a very nice man.

Sarah looked out on the lake again. It was so dark down with all the clouds and no moon. Sarah squinted, but she still couldn't see her friend.

"I'll try again," she said, but the fat man told her to wait.

He cupped a free hand to his lips and yelled "Ællyaa'ai'ae!" and then some other stuff in Bess's language that Sarah didn't understand.

Sarah came close to stamping her foot. "That's not going to do any good. Bess doesn't know you. She'll just think you're one of the bad men."

Then you try, the fat man suggested, so Sarah did. She called, "Ællyaa'ai'ae!" —I greet you!—and slapped the water again. "It's me, Sarah," she called. "It's safe over here. My friends will protect you!"

There came a burbling sound out in the water.

"Light that lantern, you fool," Eyebrows hissed at Sarah's father even as he clicked on his electric torch and swept a beam of yellow light across the water in the direction of the sound. He homed the light on a patch of frothing water.

The bubbles and burbles grew and grew until Sarah's friend Bess arose swanlike out of the water.

∩

"MAGNIFICENT."

Tafford realized the awed voice was his own.

The creature—no, the intelligent being, for it took only one look at Bess to know she was intelligent and sentient—was nothing if not magnificent.

Long neck, flipper-paddle legs, and bulbous streamlined body—a bald listing of her component parts made her a plesiosaurus the way arms, legs, and clothing made a scarecrow a man. Instead of reptilian scales, serpentine undulating neck, and vicious needle teeth Tafford had expected, Bess was—was—

"A Dolphin to a shark," he finally murmured.

That had been the word he'd been looking for: dolphin. Bess's wet, glossy grey skin was the smooth skin of a dolphin, the teeth in her rounded gentle jaws utilitarianly carnivorous but hardly frightening. You immediately grasped that Bess—though nothing like dolphins or whales—was a Cetacean, just as you knew that tarsiers and lemurs—though nothing like men—were primates.

Bess's long, supple neck moved not in snakelike coilings but with swanlike grace, her large eyes gentle, the flecks of her irises reflecting glittering gold in the lantern light. One push of her fore paddles glided her to shore where she wriggled otter-like onto the stone-covered bank. She was still partially submerged, but Tafford estimated her body ten feet in length with her neck being another ten.

She emitted a slight musk that hinted of, of all things, sandalwood. Her breath plumed white against the cold; whatever she was, she was warm-blooded mammal.

Bess gently lowered her head and Sarah hugged her neck in sobbing relief.

"You're alright," the little girl sniffled over and over before letting go and composing herself.

"These are my friends," Sarah said, wiping her face, "they're here to help you from the bad men." Then turning to point to the Queen, she said, "And this is—"

Bess pressed herself to the ground Japanese-style, head, neck and body. "Your Majesty," Bess said, her English perfect and unaccented. Her voice held that same almost-painful pellucid clarity found in the voices of young English girls, though Bess's voice was a throaty contralto.

"You know of us?" the Queen asked, wonderingly.

Bess's head rose slightly to look up at her. "What British subject doesn't know the face of their monarch?"

ᐱ

"British subject!" Moxton all but snorted. He couldn't have sounded more affronted than if a Hottentot in grass skirts had walked through the doors of his Pall Mall club claiming membership.

"Moxton is still upset we let Scotland into the Union." Grey said.

"Gentleman!" Queen Victoria snapped, in a voice Tafford had no doubt had quailed many a prime minster in her time. "Can't you see this poor thing's hurt? That she's weak?"

Tafford knelt down in the snow, letting his rifle take the strain as a makeshift cane. He ran his fingers over Bess's dolphin-slick skin. Ancient battle scars marred its surface. So, too did more recent gashes. Very recent—the still bled.

But that's not drew Tafford's eye.

"It's not so much that she's hurt, Your Majesty, but that she's starving."

Tafford had never seen one of Bess's kind before, didn't know its physiology, but he'd seen a lot of animals in his younger days as big game hunter and could recognize the signs of malnourishment.

Bess swanned her head upward, curving her neck up and over to face Tafford. "The egg beds are played out," she modulated. "Depleted and the we can find no more. The Egg Layers have fled their clutches."

Moxton exploded, focusing on the word we. Grey heard only eggs. "Tafford, you don't suppose—?" he whispered. To the creature he said: "This island lair of yours, it contains a Staircase."

Golden-flecked eyes blinked. "Staircase?"

"A—a—" Grey struggled. He looked to Tafford.

"*K'my't*," Tafford supplied, hoping he was correctly remembering a half-read entry from the *Lexico Aquaticum*. "A fish ladder."

Bess only blinked again. Then she nodded as she puzzled out Tafford's human accent.

"Ah, the Pantry Door," she said, reaching for the English words. "The door to the larder."

"You eat Cuttlefish eggs?" Grey said, as astounded as Tafford had ever heard him. Cuttlefish Consorts—the chthonic mates of Cthulhu and his ilk—laid vast beds of eggs numbering in the millions on the muddy bottoms of their under-lake chthonic caverns.

A hint of a sardonic smile curved on Bess's face. "Surely you don't think my clan could subsist solely on the fish in your lakes. They wouldn't last us a day."

Tafford levered himself up, using his rifle as fulcrum. He grunted at the white-hot pain that lanced from knee to hip. "Well, Dorian," he said to Grey. "We were wondering why Scotland was free of Cuttlefish. Now we know."

"We were too efficient," Bess smiled wanly. "The Egg Layers fled."

Like Dolphins chasing away schools of sharks.

"Eggs, pantries—what the devil are you talking about?" demanded poor Moxton, who knew only the evils men do, not the ways of the Cuttlefish.

"We're talking about the Chapter being free to release assets to you," Grey said. "If we can work things out with Bess here and her clan." He looked at Tafford. "Lake Victoria?" he asked.

Tafford's old wound twinged. Most definitely Lake Victoria. And dozens of other lakes Tafford could name just for starters.

"Your Majesty," Tafford said, patting the cetacean's head. "You must help them. Bess and her kind have done you, done the nation and the world, greater services that you can ever know."

The Queen reached out her own hand and brushed Bess's brow. "We must help them, Mr. Tafford, because that is the Christian thing to do, and because they are our loyal subjects."

If the Queen had more to say on the subject, she never said it.

Nurse Brown, who'd been silent through all of this pointed at the lake and shouted, "Dynamite!"

As the dinghy returned through the narrow channel between Long Island and the lake's east shore, Griggs swore disgustedly. The north lobe of Loch Oich had been as big a bust as the south end, and Griggs was down to his last case of dynamite. He thought he might have winged the beast a couple times, but it must have been only branches floating in the drink.

Speaking of drink, old MacKean was almost completely soused. He'd fallen into a state of sullen silence. He was barely able to keep rowing the oars. The dinghy weaved an erratic course, too close to shore and occasionally scraping bottom.

Griggs hated to quit while he had this window of comparatively good weather—no wind and scant snow—but there wasn't much more he could accomplish tonight, not with MacKean three Scottish sheets to the wind.

He patted his vest pocket. In an emergency, of course, Griggs could propel the boat himself, but with the night half-over and no quarry sighted, this didn't constitute that.

He sighed. "Head for home," he told the old Scotsman. "But steer wide of the manor."

MacKean mumbled something unintelligible and Gaelic. He increased his oar strokes.

They splashed along the east shore—too near for Grigg's liking—in the dark still night. Over on the left he could see the manor on the hills, windows lighted and bright, round into view.

Suddenly a lantern flared into life on the west shoreline. Griggs squinted A group of people stood around it, one with a rifle in his hand.

Then some dark enormous shape rose out of the water, silhouetted in the lantern light.

The beast! That was the beast!

And that was Moxton on shore, he was sure of it.

Moxton on shore and about to take the credit for Grigg's plan!

He grabbed the front of MacKean's jacket. "The monster!" he pointed. "Make for the monster!" They had to reach it first. They had to kill it first.

MacKean turned his head in the direction of the silhouetted monster. His bloodshot eyes nearly popped from his head. His mouth worked like a goldfish but no words came. He scrambled to his feet, nearly swamping the boat, and jumped over the side into knee-deep water. He splashed his way to shore and fled into the darkness.

This constituted an emergency.

Griggs pulled another Chinese trinket from his pocket, a little jade stone used to speed smuggler's sampans out of the reach of the harbor patrol.

Holding it in his hand, he pointed the direction he wanted the boat to go—directly for the monster—and set it on the splintery rear seat, still warm from MacKean's bottom. The little dinghy shot forward, lifting its nose in thrust as the keel pushed foreward at a wave slapping speed.

Griggs reached down and grabbed a stick of dynamite, his magic finger already aflame. He'd claim he seen they were in danger from the beast, that he was trying to protect them. And if the blast took out Moxton as well, so much the better. He'd blame that on the beast as well. More proof for the Queen that magic existed and that Griggs should head up the new section. After all, poor old Moxton—rest his soul—would have wanted it that way.

A shark's smile spread across his face as Griggs pulled back his arm, readying to throw.

Λ

TAFFORD WHIRLED at the nurse's shout, cursing himself for forgetting all about the danger on the lake.

Across the lake, weakly limned by the feeble light of Crewe's oil lantern, a dinghy sped directly toward them. The tiny boat leaped across the water as if propelled by steam turbines, just how Tafford couldn't say. The boat's sole occupant was too busy throwing a stick of dynamite to work any oars.

The man threw something and Tafford saw the fluttering spark of a fuse describe an upward arc.

Without conscious thought, Tafford swung the barrel of his Pendles rifle to intersect that arc. He'd done this a million times. his movements all automatic. One eye squinted as he sighted. A gentle pull on the trigger. The snap of the sear release. The crack of the bullet.

The silver bullet, scribed with runes and consecrated with holy water, slammed into the silk cloth wrapped around the outer paper of the explosive and reacted violently to the magic in the cloth.

A soundless explosion lit up the night, followed by a noiseless concussion that nearly knocked Tafford off his feet.

The boat continued to draw closer, though and Tafford could see the dynamiter reaching for another stick.

Tafford swung his rifle down to aim at their attacker.

"Don't!" Grey yelled, grabbing the barrel and yanking it off target. "That boat's stacked with dynamite! Half the lake could go up!"

"I'll handle this," Moxton shouted, stepping in front of them both.

Grey whirled. "With what? More of your Chinese trinkets?"

For once Moxton ignored Grey's jibe. He raised his odd-gloved hand palm out, fingers splayed.

Concentric blue rings of force emanated from the metal palm plate in a tight beam. The force beam smashed full-on into the chest of the half-standing Griggs, knocking him halfway across the lake. The ignited stick of dynamite still clutched in his hand exploded in a hail of gibbets of flesh and a spray of fluids.

As Griggs had flown out of the boat, his boot heel had struck the sampan stone, sending it flying as well. The dinghy, caught in the magic of the stone, attempted to follow wherever the stone pointed. The boat leapt skyward in pursuit, spinning and twirling end over end in imitation, spilling the case of dynamite harmlessly into the lake water. The rickety boat smashed itself into flinders when it eventually hit the surface of the lake

"What was *that?*" Grey said, staring in astonishment.

Moxton lowered his hand. He turned to face them. "Just something I picked up in Peking from the rebels of the Society of Righteous and Harmonious Fists," he said. He had the actual audacity to smile. "A Boxer Glove."

Many days later
Somewhere in Whitehall
London, England

MOXTON SAT BACK in his new chair at his new desk at his new office. The cover of the Illustrated London News boasted an engraving depicting an imagined first meeting between Queen Victoria and that loathsome lake beast. She was depicted petting its muzzle as it looked up at her with oversized adoring eyes. Above the illustration screamed a banner headline: "Nessie is Bessie!" underscored with "Loch Ness Monster Real" underneath.

Idiot press. Couldn't even name the right lake.

No mention of the beast's supposed sentience or that it talked. Or that the beast and its clan was hard at work for the British Government, eating evil eggs or whatever nonsense that Grey had them doing.

No matter. The mere public depiction of the Queen with the creature had served notice in the corridors of Europe that England now not only admitted magic existed but fielded an agency to deal with it. There'd be no more clandestine Dopper-style attacks by Boers or anybody else. Foreign governments wouldn't dare. England would strike back.

Moxton flipped through the rest of the paper. He paused briefly at a small article headlined "Nest of Boer Bombers Captured". Now that Grey had some free assets, it hadn't taken that licorice man of his long at all to find the remaining *Dopper Kirkkoor* agents in England. Too bad Moxton couldn't recruit him.

The paper drew no connection between the Boer spies and the unfortunate gas main explosion at Windsor. Good.

The Dopper bombing had eventually worked out quite nicely for Moxton. He'd gotten his section. He'd even manage to sluff off that fool Griggs as one of the Boer bombers. Tafford suspected the truth, and maybe Grey did as well, but without the corroboration of the late Angus MacKean, dead of exposure after collapsing drunk that night, they couldn't be totally sure. Moxton could live with that.

Almost on the last page of news a tiny squib of an article announced in the blandest prose possible an unspecified reorganization of British military intelligence in line with wartime needs.

Salisbury had gotten his wartime expansion of the Directorate of Military Intelligence—including Moxton's section—through Parliament, and once expanded government agencies never shrink.

Moxton's nominal boss, the pedantic Sir John Ardagh was even now busy beavering away at his beloved paperwork. Ardagh had already created a dozen-and-a-half separate sections and was happily busy numbering them MI1 through MI18, sections 5 and 6 being the main workhorses handling home and foreign operations.

In a fit of either whimsy or gratitude, Ardagh had allowed Moxton to number his own special section.

Moxton should have refused the offer and taken whatever number Sir John assigned. But one is afforded so few harmless little pleasures in this job. Moxton just couldn't resist.

He folded his newspaper, laying aside. He placed his sheet of official stationery atop his desk blotter in preparation of writing his first official memo.

The sheet of stationery was emblazed at its top with the new name and logo of his new section: MI666.

SARAH STOOD at the shoreline of Loch Oich, wrapped in the woolen scarf the Queen had given her. She'd also given Sarah something else in a big palace ceremony with a sword and everything: a damehood. Sarah guess that made her a lady knight. The scarf had a little embroidery of a fancy blue cross with the words Most Excellent Order of the British Empire. It matched the blue cross medal the Queen had draped around her neck. Sarah wondered if the Queen had embroidered the scarf herself. Did queens embroider?

She felt a little silly being Dame Sarah except Bess was Dame Bess, too, so that made it alright except the Queen had given Bess only the medal. A scarf on Bess would just get wet.

Sarah watched her breath puff white. It matched the white puffs from the locomotive across the lake. They were working on the railroad again. Mr. Ellice kept bragging about doing something in Parliament to get it going, but Sarah thinks it was more due to Mr. Grey and the Queen.

Mr. Grey had already begun loading up Bess's clanmates in big water tanks on railroad cars and taking them to lakes with more food, even one in Africa. Mr. Grey had tried to explain why Bess's people couldn't just leave Scotland on their own to get to English lakes. Something about Hadrian's Wall and Roman enchantments, but Sarah didn't really understand him.

All Sarah knew was that, with only Bess left, the remaining eggs in Scotland were more than enough. That was nice, it meant that Bess didn't have to leave, too. That made Mr. Ellis happy, too. He'd finally done what her father had told him to and change the hotel to a Nessie-watching hotel. Nessie is what people called Bess and her kind. People were silly. Loch Ness was the next lake over, the one just north of Invergarry, but it was too late to change their minds. The name had stuck.

Mr. Tafford had gotten Bess some stick-things with fingers so Bess could turn pages herself. Mr. Tafford was nice that way. The Queen was nice, too. Sarah hadn't ever known before, but queens could feel sad as well.

Sarah had heard Mr. Tafford and the Queen talking before they left for London. They didn't know Sarah was in the manor library, too, lying on the floor behind the couch and reading that book all about Bess's language Mr. Tafford had given her.

Mr. Tafford and the Queen began talking about some old poem. Sarah had only paid attention to their conversation because she thought at first they were talking about Bess, but they only spoke about some girl in the poem named Bessie.

"I suppose you think it appeals to the romantic young girl in me, Right and Wrong and True Love conquering all," the Queen said, her voice somehow very sad and very far away. "You wouldn't be the first.

"Or perhaps you think it is the thrill of young Bessie swinging wildly above the landscape, clinging to that bell." she added.

Mr. Tafford didn't say anything. Sarah liked talking to him because he listened a lot.

"It might surprise you to know, that a queen is more a prisoner of her duties than any wretch in Newgate. She must close her heart to what she wants to do, doing only what she needs must. She must acquiesce to bad laws, bad treaties, bad elections. She must send soldiers off to die in needless wars. She must harden her heart, becoming as stern and unyielding and implacable as Cromwell in the performance of her duties.

There came a sniffling noise. Surely not the Queen!

"I love that poem because it *isn't* about Bessie or the saving of Basil Underwood, Mr. Tafford" the Queen said, her voice growing stronger. "It's about the saving of Cromwell."

A pause.

"For once in his life, he could listen to his heart, do what his heart told him to do. For one brief moment, he could be free and save himself and his soul. *Go! Your lover lives, said Cromwell, Curfew shall not ring to-night.*"

Again, the Queen paused.

"I'm an old woman, Mr. Tafford. I've ruled for more than sixty years and my days are dwindling," she said at last. "Never once in all that time have I allowed myself a Cromwell moment."

Her voice grew stronger, grew into the firm voice Sarah knew so well. "So when young Sarah knelt before me *'hands all bruised and torn'* and *'face so sweet and pleading,'* how could I not act as I did? For once I could follow my Cromwell heart. I had, at last, my own imperial rescript. It wasn't Sarah or her friend Bess I was saving, Mr. Moxton. I was saving myself."

Even now, after all this time, standing here on the lake shore, the words made Sarah cry and she didn't even know why.

Wiping her eyes, Sarah slapped the water again. Bess was very busy these days.

Water rippled, then burbled and Bess emerged with the royal grace of a swan.

Sarah threw herself around Bess's neck, hugging her with all her might, the tears flowing not for herself or for Bess or the remembrance of the loneliness Sarah felt before she'd found her friend, but for that same aching loneliness she'd heard in the Queen's voice.

"It's not easy being a queen," Sarah sobbed.

Bess, her voice just as regal as her sister monarch, Victoria, and just as sad, replied, "No it isn't."

ABOUT THE AUTHOR

LEE ALLRED's fiction has appeared in *Asimov's Science Fiction* and *Pulphouse* magazines, as well as in dozens of science fiction anthologies such as the acclaimed *Fiction River* series and Baen's *Alternate Generals III* and *Drakas!* volumes.

He has scripted fan-favorite stories for Marvel (*Fantastic Four*), DC Comics (*Batman '66, Batman Black and White*), and IDW (*Dick Tracy*). He wrote *Bug! The Adventures of Forager* for Gerard Way's (of *My Chemical Romance / Umbrella Academy* fame) quirky Young Animal comic book imprint line.

His novella, "For the Strength of the Hills", was named a Sidewise Award for Alternate History finalist. A great love of history and historical detail infuses all of his work, whether he's writing steampunk, vampire tales, alternate history, or military SF.

After serving three tours in Iraq for the United States Air Force, Lee retired as a Master Sergeant. You can find out more at leeallred.com.

 twitter.com/lee_allred

ADDITIONAL COPYRIGHT INFORMATION

ABOUT THE COVER ARTIST

FREDERIC EDWIN CHURCH (May 4, 1826 – April 7, 1900) was an American landscape painter born in Hartford, Connecticut. He was a central figure in the Hudson River School of American landscape painters, best known for painting large landscapes, often depicting mountains, waterfalls, and sunsets. Church's paintings put an emphasis on realistic detail, dramatic light, and panoramic views. He debuted some of his major works in single-painting exhibitions to a paying and often enthralled audience in New York City. In his prime, he was one of the most famous painters in the United States.

In 1844, Church became the pupil of landscape artist Thomas Cole in Catskill, New York after a family neighbor introduced the two. Church studied with him for two years. Cole wrote that Church had "the finest eye for drawing in the world". During his time with Cole, he travelled around New England and New York to make sketches, visiting East Hampton, Long Island, the Catskill Mountain House, the Berkshires, New Haven, and Vermont. His first recorded sale of a painting was in 1846 to Hartford's Wadsworth Athenaeum for $130. In 1848, he was elected as the youngest Associate of the National Academy of Design and was promoted to full member the following year. He took on his own students, including Walter Launt Palmer, William James Stillman, and Jervis McEntee.

Church was the product of the second generation of the Hudson River School, a movement in American landscape art founded by Cole and characterized by a focus on traditional pastoral settings and their Romantic qualities, especially the Catskill Mountains. The movement attempted to capture the wild realism of an unsettled America that was quickly disappearing, and the appreciation of natural beauty. During his career, Church created over 80 finished paintings and thousands of sketches.

His wife, Isabel, died on May 12, 1899, at the home of their late friend and patron, William H. Osborn, on Park Avenue in New York. Less than a year later, at the age of 73, Church also died at the home of Osborn's widow. Frederic and

Isabel were buried in the family plot at Spring Grove Cemetery, Hartford, Connecticut.

BOOKS IN THE
LEGACY OF THE CORRIDOR
SERIES

The Florilegium of Madness
D. J. Butler (July 2021)

Dragon Soup for the Soul
Emily Martha Sorensen (December 2021)

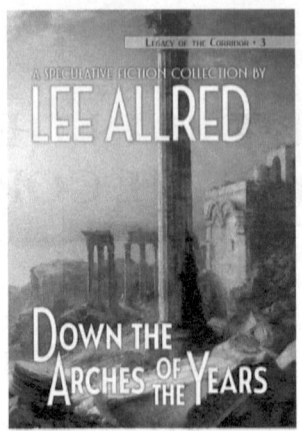

Down the Arches of the Years
Lee Allred (April 2022)

Sharks in an Inland Sea
Lehua Parker (June 2022)

The Bacillus of Beauty
Harriet Stark (July 2022)

LTUE BENEFIT ANTHOLOGIES

Trace the Stars (February 2019)

A Dragon and Her Girl (February 2020)

Twilight Tales (February 2021)

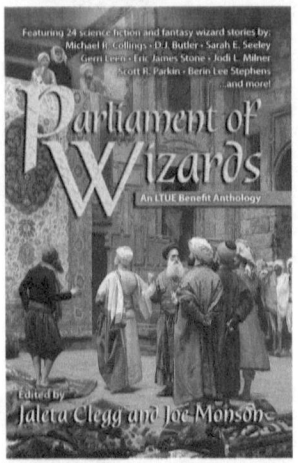

Parliament of Wizards (February 2022)

OTHER BOOKS FROM HEMELEIN

A Universe of Stories (June 2021)

Killing London (October 2021)

www.ingramcontent.com/pod-product-compliance
Lightning Source LLC
Chambersburg PA
CBHW021457110726
47899CB00001BA/184